THE GLASS MAN

ALSO BY ANDERS DE LA MOTTE

Game

Buzz

Bubble

MemoRandom

Ultimatum

The Asker Series

The Mountain King

THE GLASS MAN

A NOVEL

THE ASKER SERIES · PART II

Anders de la Motte

Translated by Alex Fleming

EMILY BESTLER BOOKS

ATRIA

NEW YORK   AMSTERDAM/ANTWERP   LONDON
TORONTO   SYDNEY/MELBOURNE   NEW DELHI

EMILY BESTLER BOOKS

ATRIA

An Imprint of Simon & Schuster, LLC
1230 Avenue of the Americas
New York, NY 10020

Copyright © 2023 by Anders de la Motte
English language translation copyright © 2025 by Alex Fleming
Originally published in Sweden in 2023 by Bokförlaget Forum as *Glasmannen*
Published by agreement with Salomonsson Agency

First Emily Bestler Books/Atria Books hardcover edition August 2025

EMILY BESTLER BOOKS/ATRIA BOOKS and colophon are trademarks of Simon & Schuster, LLC

Interior design by Esther Paradelo

Manufactured in the United States of America

1   3   5   7   9   10   8   6   4   2

Library of Congress Control Number: 2025939949

ISBN 978-1-6680-3086-8
ISBN 978-1-6680-3088-2 (ebook)

THE GLASS MAN

WINTER 2019

"What the hell was that?"

Something scrapes ominously against the bottom of the rowboat, and Elis starts to splash with the oars.

He and Nick have been rowing for almost half an hour, in more or less pitch darkness, and the sudden noise scares him.

"Shit! Did it make a hole?" he gasps, once he has managed to back up the rowboat a few feet in the black waters of the lake. His breaths rise like plumes of steam from his mouth before being consumed by the cold night air.

"No," says Nick, who is sitting at the bow. "It takes a lot to sink a plastic tub like this."

He raises his binoculars again and peers into the darkness before them.

Elis isn't satisfied with that answer.

"I told you we should have brought life jackets," he hisses. "It's the middle of winter; the water's ice-cold. There's no way we can swim back."

He points toward the stern of the boat. Far off in the darkness by the water's edge, the lights of the Boy Scouts' cabin where they stole the rowboat are still visible. It is one of few sources of light in the wooded hills around the lake.

"Shall we go back? Try in daylight instead?"

Just as Elis says the words the cloud cover breaks. The full moon peers out, transforming the lake's black waters into liquid glass.

"Look," Nick says excitedly. "We're nearly there. I can see the headframe and observatory."

He points at the island that looms beyond the bow. A bank of mist hovers at its shore, but the faint moonlight picks out a tall tower with a domed top just above the treetops.

Elis gives a shudder. It is probably caused by the chill in the damp air, but he can't be completely sure. A bad feeling has stalked him ever since they pushed off from the jetty at the Boy Scouts' cabin.

He casts a glance toward the mainland.

It's far away, all too far.

He pulls his hat up a little, wipes his forehead with his jacket sleeve. Both of them are dressed in black, with gloves, boots, and tightly rolled-up balaclavas.

Their *urbex uniforms*, as they call them.

Nick lowers the binoculars and checks his watch.

"It's almost midnight. Veer left and row along the shore, and I'll keep an eye out for more rocks," he instructs Elis. "The dock should be on the southern side."

Elis reluctantly starts to row again. The creak of the oarlocks melts into the lapping of the water.

As they round the island, more details emerge from the mist. The creeping spruces along the shoreline are perched upon a spiky carpet of sharp stones that extends out into the lake, the largest crags of which rise up like the menacing teeth of beasts of prey, just yards from the boat's plastic hull.

Elis rows cautiously, only lets the stone teeth out of his sight to cast the odd glance back at the light of the Boy Scouts' cabin.

Nick seems to realize that he needs to lighten the mood.

"Do you think those two UFO nuts who gave us the map watch alien porn at home?" he asks over his shoulder. "Dress up as Martians for a bit of role-play?"

Elis can't help but smirk.

"Definitely," he says. "I still don't know how you persuaded them to help us."

"Oh, that was a piece of cake," Nick laughs. "I just convinced them I believe in the whole story, too—old 'Space-Case' Gunnar Irving and the flying saucer, the spaceman. Then I gave them Martin Hill's book and wrote *the truth is out there* in it. They practically peed themselves they were so excited."

Elis chuckles, and the tension lifts slightly.

"There's the dock," Nick says and points.

From out of the mists a cracked concrete jetty emerges. At its very end a dented sign hangs askew, only just legible in the moonlight.

"Risk of collapse. No trespassing," reads Nick. "Then we've come to the right place."

They moor the boat next to a rusty ladder, pull on their backpacks, and climb out. Elis turns back to the mainland.

The southern shores of the lake are mostly swathed in forest and darkness, just like the north. But on a headland directly across the water stands a large, palatial building with subdued lighting along its façade.

"How far do you think it is to Astroholm?" Elis asks.

"A third of a mile, maybe," Nick replies. "Much closer than the Scouts' cabin. But there's no need to worry, the Irving family aren't looking this way. They'll be too busy scouring the skies for flying saucers."

He makes an overblown gesture up at the night sky, then turns and makes for dry land.

Elis hangs back for a few seconds. He shivers again, or shudders, he can't tell. The uneasy feeling doesn't seem to want to settle.

Where the jetty meets land there stands a ramshackle hut without a door. Nick stops, unfolds a hand-drawn map, and tries to orient himself in the mist and murky light.

"This way!" he says, then walks another thirty feet along the edge of the forest. "Here it is! The old mining road!"

Two almost completely overgrown wheel tracks carve a path between the spruce trees, hardly visible for all the undergrowth. Elis and Nick wait to turn on their headlamps until they are out of sight of the water.

The fog is thicker here in the forest, making the lamplight milky.

The forest floor is blanketed with moss and fern thickets, interrupted here and there by windfalls or subsidence holes. Crooked stone teeth jut up all around, just like in the water.

"Creepy," Elis mumbles to himself, without quite knowing why. He isn't usually afraid of the dark, but something about both the island and the forest makes his skin crawl.

Nick, on the other hand, seems completely unperturbed. He stops and shines his headlamp on a large boulder by the road. The rock is pale and grainy, with a faint sheen.

"Rhyolite," he says with satisfaction, patting the rock. "Boulder

Isle is one of the few places in all of Scandinavia where this type of rock can be found. And look at that!"

Nick points at an engraving on the rock.

"*GUS 2009*," Elis reads.

"Göinge UFO Society," Nick sneers. "Even the name is corny. But at least now we know they were telling the truth."

Nick pulls out his multi-tool and unfolds a sharp screwdriver.

URBEX 2019, he carves.

"There, now we've proved that we got at least as far as them."

They go on, following the wheel tracks. The forest sprawl extends so far over the road that on several occasions they must part the branches to pass.

In one place the road has collapsed into a three-foot hollow.

"A cave-in," Nick says. "The whole island's like Swiss cheese. The tunnels are filled with water; they can buckle at any time. Drown us like those poor guys in 1965."

He laughs, but Elis doesn't find it quite as funny. The thought of those black waters beneath his feet makes his blood run cold.

After a few hundred yards a large shape appears on the edge of their lights. A tall, rust-flecked steel gate with pendulous lichen that dangles like giant cobwebs from its mesh.

Above the gate runs a metal arch with rusted lettering.

ASTROFIELD MINE.

Beneath it, on either side of the thick chain that secures the gate, hang two signs. The first is identical to the one down on the jetty.

RISK OF COLLAPSE. NO TRESPASSING!

The other sign contains a single word.

DANGER!

Nick is already at the gate, testing the chain.

"It won't budge," he says. "And I'm not so keen on climbing this tetanus pile—are you?"

He sweeps his headlamp upward. The gate and fencing on either side must be almost fifteen feet tall. At the top is a Y-shaped bracket laden with rusty barbed wire.

"But thanks to our UFO buddies we have a back door."

Nick takes another look at the map and starts walking along the fence to their left.

Elis hesitates, his eyes still locked on the gate. He has seen his fair share of warning signs in the past, and has never given them a second thought. But something about this one puts him on edge.

The rust, the font, the faded yellow color. Or maybe it's just the short message.

Danger!

He gulps instinctively.

"What the hell are you waiting for?" Nick whispers over his shoulder. "Come on!"

Elis reluctantly tears his gaze from the sign and follows him.

Soon Nick stops by a large bush that has grown through the fence. He takes one last look at the map, crouches down, and crawls under it.

"Here it is!" He pulls a few branches aside to reveal a small sluice that runs under the fence.

The sluice is shallow and dry, and they must first shove their backpacks under the fence before they can follow.

"Shit," Nick puffs once they are out of the bush on the other side, brushing the soil and dead leaves from their pants. "I'm surprised those UFO chubsters managed to get through that. Though I guess it was ten years ago, so maybe they were more mobile then."

Elis isn't listening. He is too busy sweeping his headlamp around anxiously. Despite his excitement, his anxiety won't let up.

The area within the fence is populated by a different kind of vegetation. Instead of dense spruce trees, the land is scattered with self-seeded birches whose trunks have a ghostly white shimmer. In the mist beyond the birches, the mine buildings loom like big, oppressive shadows.

"Finally," Nick says excitedly. "Are you ready to travel back to 1965?"

Elis doesn't respond.

As they approach the buildings, the grass underfoot increasingly gives way to bare patches of concrete and crushed stone. Eventually a yard opens up before them, flanked by two forbidding buildings.

The building on the right is twice as large as its counterpart, its gabled roof and walls made of rusty corrugated sheet metal. Beneath its eaves runs a row of squat, horizontal factory windows.

Nick points his headlamp toward them.

"See, the windows are intact. And no graffiti either."

Elis knows that this is good news: it means that few—if any—others have set foot here in a very long time. Even so, he struggles to muster the right level of enthusiasm. They are currently exploring a deserted island, in the middle of a dark and icy lake, and no one knows they are here. Not to mention the fact that the whole island is mined by waterlogged tunnels that could collapse at any second.

He checks his cellphone. Its lonely, flickering signal bar does nothing to improve his mood.

"Lousy signal, right?" says Nick. "Those UFO nuts had a theory that it might be something to do with alien interference on the radio waves. Their eyes got all twinkly just talking about it. But I asked a friend who works at one of the phone companies, and he said it's just that the lake's at the bottom of a deep crater, so it's difficult for phone signals to reach all the way down here. So much for the fucking *X-Files*."

He starts walking along the factory wall. Elis stuffs his phone away and follows suit.

The moon peeps out again, and from out of the mist and darkness at the far end of the yard he sees a tall and gloomy concrete tower soar up toward the sky.

The tower must be at least fifty feet tall. Its sides are open, allowing them to see straight through its three-story concrete frame.

"The headframe," says Nick, sweeping his flashlight over the gloomy construction. "It's where they used to hoist the carts up from the mine. And up there on the roof . . ."

On the flat roof of the tower, next to the hoist wheel, the dark dome they glimpsed from the water is visible once again.

"Bernhard Irving's observatory," Elis says softly. Finally the right sense of excitement sets in, dispelling all the unease.

"Exactly," Nick agrees with a smile. "The spot where the giant, red-eyed creature landed."

Their footsteps crunch as they draw closer, and when Elis shines his headlamp down at the ground he discovers that the crushed stone is mixed with shards of black glass.

Nick steps in under the headframe and takes a closer look.

"Solid stuff," he says, illuminating the six concrete columns on which the tower rests. "This'll still be standing in another hundred years."

He stops beside a moss-topped slab on the ground.

"And below that's the mine shaft. The trapdoor to the underworld."

Elis simply hums in reply, too busy searching for a way up the tower. The next story must be around twenty-five feet off the ground. A steel staircase zigzags down the left-hand side of the tower, but it ends abruptly at the second floor.

"The stairs have been cut," he says. "Just like the UFO flunkeys said."

"Good thing a cut staircase won't stop us," says Nick, giving Elis's backpack a pat. "But before we get out the rope, I have another idea. Look!"

He points his headlamp upward. A sloping footbridge links the third story of the tower to the factory building, where it meets a dormer with a wooden hatch.

"That must be where they rolled the mine carts once they'd been hoisted up. The stone crusher must be inside there, and maybe even some stairs that haven't been demolished. Much easier than hanging from a fucking rope, wouldn't you say?"

Elis can only agree. He is a good thirty pounds heavier than Nick, so is happy to avoid climbing where he can.

The door to the factory building is shut and locked. But when Elis gives the handle a tug, the doorframe creaks alarmingly. They look at each other.

Nick takes off his backpack and pulls out a crowbar. It's against the rules, they both know that. Urban explorers must never force entry. But this is a special case. A once-in-a-lifetime event.

The door gives way almost immediately, flying open with a short, sharp clap as soon as Nick puts a little weight behind the crowbar.

Inside they find a vast, dark industrial hall that stinks of stone dust, oil, and bird shit.

In the middle of the hall stands a large crusher that reaches almost all the way to the ceiling. A narrow staircase right beside it leads down to a closed door. Under normal circumstances that is where they would begin: go as far down into the building's underbelly as possible, to then methodically work their way up.

But tonight the normal rules don't apply.

They turn their headlamps up toward the ceiling. Up there,

supported by wooden posts, runs the footbridge they saw from the outside.

"Bingo!" Nick shines his lamp at a wooden staircase just below the wooden hatch.

A sudden noise makes them jump. Something takes flight from the top of the stairs, casts itself into the hall on flapping wings before disappearing into the darkness.

"Pigeons." Elis sighs in relief. "They get us every fucking time."

"Speak for yourself," Nick sneers. "You seem jumpier than usual tonight. Are you scared of aliens with glowing eyes?"

"Get lost," Elis mutters.

Nick climbs the creaking staircase with Elis at his heels.

The wooden hatch up in the dormer proves easy to open. The footbridge to the tower turns out to be no footbridge at all, but a fifteen-foot-long section of narrow-gauge rail track that inclines quite steeply in the direction of the tower. Between the two tracks run metal crossbars that give the whole construction the appearance of a crude ladder.

Nick places a tentative foot on the first crossbar, then bends forward, takes one rail in each hand, and starts to climb. Elis watches his lithe movements with envy.

"Easy peasy!" says Nick once he has reached the tower. "Your turn!"

Elis copies Nick's climbing technique, trying not to look down. Not that he's afraid of heights, but the feeling of clambering across a sixty-year-old metal construction is unsettling enough without knowing exactly how far he risks falling. Especially when the ground beneath him is a mix of rock and shattered glass. Just as he reaches the tower, the metal emits a crack that echoes between the buildings like a whip, making his heart pound a few frenzied double beats.

Elis wipes away the sweat that has beaded on his forehead in spite of the cold. They are now on the tower's third and upper story. As expected, the rails continue to a large hole in the middle of the floor, where the cage would have been hoisted up, loaded with the full mine carts.

Nick has already rounded the hole and made his way to the steel staircase outside. Elis follows him. They are fairly high up now, thirty-five feet at least.

Above them the staircase zigzags up toward the roof. Nick's excited footsteps make the steel grating tremble. Elis hurries to keep up with him.

Upon reaching the top, they walk to the middle of the roof. To their right hangs the rusty old hoist wheel, while to their left the dark dome looms large.

"Bernhard's observatory." Nick's tone of voice is almost reverent.

"No wonder he had it built up here," says Elis, pointing over the treetops. "You can see the whole lake."

They are now above the bank of mist that has spread across the black waters. Beyond the lake the forest-lined hills rise up, equally high and steep in every direction.

"It's like standing in the middle of a funnel. And just look up! Wow!"

Through the gaps in the clouds they glimpse flashes of the full moon and the star-filled sky. From this vantage point the celestial bodies look brighter, more luminous.

"All the light pollution is blocked by the edges of the crater," says Nick. "Even the lights at Astroholm Manor are dimmed."

Elis turns to follow his gaze. The estate across the water is clearly visible, but its outdoor lighting is unusually sparing for a building of its size. He looks back at the observatory.

"Fucking hell, what a place."

"I told you it'd be worth it." Nick gives him a clap on the back. "Come on, let's see what it's like inside."

The lower section of the observatory is made of concrete, while the dome itself is topped with flaking, rust-flecked sheet metal. Before them stands a normal door.

Nick slips the crowbar into the gap in the door, as close to the lock as possible. The door creaks but doesn't give way. He puts his foot up against the wall and tries a second time, but the result is the same.

"Wait, let me try," says Elis. He puts his foot against the wall, just as Nick did, and leans back, pulling against the crowbar with all his weight. The door flies open with a muffled crack, and he falls backward.

By the time he has scrambled to his feet, Nick is already in the observatory.

"Fucking hell!" he cries. "Get a load of this!"

The inside of the dome is made of wood painted black. A platform on the floor reveals where the telescope once stood.

But that isn't what has attracted Nick's attention. Around almost the entire circumference of the dome runs a shelf brimming with strange objects: books, yellowing magazines, random coffee mugs; dark glass jars with some sort of cloudy liquid inside.

In a much creepier section of the shelf, a number of plastic heads of varying sizes are lined up on display: dolls, action figures, even the head of a mannequin. Their eye sockets gape emptily as they stare blindly out into the dark room. The back of Elis's neck starts to tingle.

"Check this out!"

Nick shines his headlamp at the ceiling.

Only now does Elis see that there are objects affixed to the inside of the dome.

Blue, brown, big, small.

Paper, plastic, glass. Cut from newspapers and magazines, scooped from toys and dolls' heads.

The tingle turns to a shudder.

The ceiling is full of eyes.

Hundreds of eyes.

"What the fuck is this . . . ?" Nick asks.

Elis doesn't reply. Another feeling has started to take root within him. It grows with every breath he takes, intensified by the eyes observing them from up above.

"Look at this."

Nick lights up a green toy alien with plumose antennae on its head. He flicks it with his finger, and the antennae start to sway.

"Shall we take it back to the UFO nuts as a thanks for the help?"

"Don't touch it," says Elis.

Nick laughs.

"Why the hell not?"

Elis has no good reply. But the feeling he has is only getting stronger.

Nick takes his camera out of his backpack and starts snapping off shots in quick succession.

The light of his bright flash bounces around the dome, reflecting off the glass, metal, and plastic in the room. The eyes in the ceiling.

Flash.

Darkness.

Flash.

Darkness.

As though the eyes up in the ceiling were blinking.

Moving.

Watching them.

Elis's blood runs cold.

All of a sudden his feeling turns to a conviction.

This is no forgotten place. No derelict ruin.

Someone owns this place. Someone who has collected important objects and carefully arranged them. Who has built themselves a small shrine inside the dome, one whose meaning Elis doesn't grasp. But he is certain of one thing.

Right now, in this place, he and Nick aren't urban explorers.

They are intruders.

He thinks back to the sign on the gate.

DANGER!

Then of the tall fence topped with barbed wire that angled both outward and in.

To all appearances intended to keep intruders out. But perhaps just as much to keep someone else inside.

"We have to go," he mumbles.

"Not until I've taken my pictures."

Nick goes on setting off flashes. He moves with such excitement that he knocks the shelf, sending one of the dark glass jars tumbling to the ground. It shatters with a loud crash.

Its contents, a liquid with a sharp alcoholic scent, spills out over the floor, carrying on it what appear to be small white balls.

Elis recoils in horror.

Eyeballs of different sizes scatter across the floor.

And they aren't from dolls or toys; these come from creatures that once lived.

Elis and Nick stand there for a few seconds, their headlamps bowed at the floor.

"What the fuuck . . ." says Nick. "Do you think those are animals' eyes?"

The excitement in his voice has disappeared, replaced by something wholly different. Uncertainty, fear.

"We have to get out of here," Elis says. "Right now."

This time Nick heeds his words.

The night sky outside is now almost entirely shrouded in cloud, the moonlight growing all the fainter. They run toward the staircase.

After a few steps a familiar sound rings out in the darkness.

The flap of wings echoing down in the factory building.

"The pigeons," says Nick. "Something must have frightened them."

They hurry to the edge of the tower, from where they can make out the open railway hatch.

The factory building is bathed in a red glow. The light moves quickly in their direction, then disappears out of sight, only to be replaced by the creak of the wooden staircase.

"Someone's coming," Nick hisses.

They turn out their headlamps and dash to the steel staircase.

"The rope," Elis says. "We can lower ourselves down from where the steps have been cut."

He races down the steps without waiting for a reply, pulling off his backpack to get out their rope and grappling hook.

The moonlight disappears completely, flooding the staircase in darkness. Elis almost misses the last step, but he grabs the railing just in time to stop himself from running straight into thin air.

He catches Nick, who is close on his heels, and gestures at him to be quiet.

The sound of groaning metal is clearly audible over their breaths. Whiplike cracks that echo between the buildings. Someone is climbing the railway track. Someone much bigger and heavier than them.

"Hurry," Nick hisses.

Together they attach the grappling hook to the railing and sling their backpacks down. Elis grips the rope with both hands and rappels himself backward from the last step, down into the darkness. Above him he sees Nick's feet through the grating on the bottom step.

"Come on!" he whispers, but Nick doesn't move. "Come on, Nick," he repeats while lowering himself further. He feels a tug in the rope, a vibration that grows all the stronger. Heavy footsteps on the staircase.

"Nick!" he cries, but his friend appears to be frozen. He stands gazing up the staircase, as the steps come all the closer.

Elis inches his way down.

"Nick!"

He is silenced by the sight of a gigantic silhouette through the grating. It approaches slowly, a red glow hovering around its head.

Elis's heart stops. The creature is huge and black and its eyes are red, just like in the legend. He gasps for breath.

The steps get closer.

Thud

Thud

Thud

The scream comes so unexpectedly that Elis almost wets himself, but it speeds his heart up again.

It is Nick who is screaming, howling in sheer terror.

He goes on screaming long after his lungs should be out of air.

Then suddenly the scream stops, replaced by a nasty crack.

Elis can see Nick's feet leave the step. His toes hover a few inches in the air, as though the creature has raised him up.

Something wet and warm splashes down through the metal grating. It lands on Elis's face, forcing him to blink.

It's blood.

Nick's blood.

When Elis opens his eyes he sees Nick's body fly down through the air, less than a foot away. A second later he hits the ground with a dull thud.

Elis looks up again.

The creature is staring down at him through the staircase. Its face is cloaked by darkness, and where its eyes should be he sees only two big, red orbs.

Elis is as though petrified.

The creature unfastens the grappling hook and lifts up the rope, apparently effortlessly. Holds Elis in the air for a few seconds, its red eyes fixed on him.

Then it drops the rope.

Lets him fall.

Elis lands heavily. His upper back hits a rock. The wind is knocked out of him, and he thinks he hears one of his ribs snap. But at least he hasn't landed on the shattered glass.

Nick is lying a few feet away. Elis crawls over to him and turns on his headlamp. Knows even before he has touched the soft body that his friend is dead.

Nick's face is white as chalk, his eyes bulging, and his half-severed tongue is dangling through his clenched jaws, covering his chin in blood.

Elis's stomach contracts, but he doesn't have time to puke.

Not if he wants to survive.

He can already hear footsteps up there, hear the creature lumbering up to the railway track to get back down to the factory. To find him and finish the job.

Elis scrambles to his feet, forces his legs to move. His ankles hurt, but to his surprise they carry him anyway.

His ribs feel worse. Every breath is like a knife through his lungs. But his heart is pumping wildly, pressing the adrenaline through his body, and with that he can move in spite of the pain.

The light of his headlamp whips through the darkness as he races toward the fence. He hears the bang of the factory door being hurled open. Then footsteps over the crushed stone.

He doesn't look back, just sprints as fast as he can toward the bush. Leaps under it and crawls on all fours toward the sluice. Sharp thorns scratch at his face, tear at his knees and elbows.

His lamp finds the sluice. He presses his belly to the ground and starts wriggling under the fence.

Behind him he hears the sound of twigs snapping, and above that a faint growl, as though from an animal. Elis worms his way forward as fast as he can.

The sluice is way too narrow for the creature; he can make it.

He is almost out on the other side when a wire from the fence catches on his pants.

He rolls over onto his back and tries to prize himself free while tugging and pulling with his leg. The sharp wire digs through the fabric and into his skin.

The growl approaches, embodied in the form of a giant-like silhouette with glowing red eyes on the other side of the fence.

Elis's heart is bolting. He gives his leg one last jerk. The wire takes a clump of flesh and skin as it releases him, but Elis hardly feels it. He is through, the creature stuck on the other side.

He twists back onto his stomach and tries to scramble to his feet.

One foot finds purchase.

Just as he starts running, something grabs hold of his ankle.

Pulls him to the ground with such brute force that his headlamp flies off and lands out of reach.

Desperately he digs his fingers into the soft soil to hold on, tries to kick with his free foot.

Lets loose an agonized scream.

But it's hopeless.

The creature drags him back under the fence.

Away from the light.

And into the darkness.

THE GLASS MAN

He awakens unwillingly. Fights to the very last to remain in the abyss.

In the deep, nocturnal darkness where he belongs.

But, as always, his resistance is in vain.

He has sensed this awakening for a while now. Detected the small signals as they started to find their way down. Faint voices, the sounds of various devices. Felt the weightlessness abating as he was summoned back to the surface.

Forced back into his body.

He despises this feeling, more than anything else.

Knows what it means.

Discomfort, suffering, pain.

Slowly he opens his eyes. The room is cool and dark, the only source of light the small diodes on the machines around his bed.

Yet that is all that his eyes can cope with.

The price he pays to travel between worlds.

At least that's what the Servants whisper when they think he doesn't hear.

Soon they will be here. One or more of the machines must have already betrayed his return.

The imminent resumption of their efforts.

And with that, his torments, too.

He shuts his eyes and shudders. His body is weak, and the cold within him will linger for some time. But once it finally passes— once his strength has returned—he will find her. She who is always in his thoughts.

He will watch her from afar as he usually does, cloaked in shadow.

Someday he will tell her what he has seen deep down in the abyss.

Tell her of death and rot, of insects and worms, and of the nameless, blind creatures that creep, crawl, and slither.

Of how it feels to travel into the eternal, ice-cold darkness from which no one ever returns.

No one—except him.

MONDAY

ASKER

"Hello Leo, it's your father."

Detective Inspector Leonore Asker clasps the handset tightly to her ear. The scar on her arm is itching furiously, her pulse thundering against her eardrums. Her small office on level minus one, her off-kilter colleagues at the Department of Lost Souls, Jonas Hell man who stole her investigation, Martin Hill, Smilla Holst, Julia, the Mountain King and his horrific lair—all of it shrinks to a mere murmur on the outskirts of her conscience.

The only thing that her brain receives clearly is the deep, rasping voice on the other end of the line. Fifteen years have passed since she last heard this voice, yet it still makes her blood turn to ice.

"So, Leo," says her father. "I hear you've become quite the police officer. One of the force's loyal lackeys. A lowly public servant. Your mother must be almost as disappointed as I am."

Asker clenches her teeth.

"W-what do you want?" she says with some effort.

Her stutter bothers her, her tone, too. She sounds like a spooked teen.

Per picks up on this, of course. Savors her uncertainty. Her fear.

"You ask me that, after everything I've done for you . . ." He jeers. "And after everything you did to me. Got me locked up with the cuckoos, pumped full of drugs like a lame, slobbering dope. I've never thanked you properly for that experience."

His tone of voice makes her brain fog clear. Per is steering this conversation, toying with her, thinking he knows who she is.

She corrects herself: fills her lungs with air, clamps her eyes shut, and exhales slowly through her nose. Her pulse slows, and teenage Leo retreats back to her subconscious.

"What do you want, Per?" she asks with her adult voice.

A brief silence arises.

"I'm going to be suspected of murder," he says. "A body's been found on a plot next to the Farm. Within days the police will be here to arrest me."

Asker gives a start. This conversation already felt unreal, to say the least, but now it has well and truly lost contact with the ground.

"But why?" Her voice sounds surprisingly collected.

"Because someone's trying to frame me," says Per. "And the State's just been waiting for its chance to lock me up for good."

He pauses again, but this time Asker chooses to hold her tongue.

Per Asker, the father she hasn't had contact with in fifteen years—not since he tried to blow both of them to shreds—suddenly calls her out of the blue to say he will soon be suspected of murder. Why?

"As I'm sure you realize, I've already analyzed the situation," he goes on. "Weighed up my options."

His tone turns caustic again, and as it does so Asker realizes the answer to her question.

"Turns out you're my best option, Leo. You're the only one with enough skills to get to the bottom of it."

Asker shuts her eyes and does her breathing exercise again.

"And why would I do that?" she asks, as calmly as she can.

"You mean to say fatherly love isn't reason enough?"

She bites her lip, waits for him to go on.

"OK, Leo, I'll cut to the chase," he says coldly. "If you don't agree to help me, I'm not going down without a fight. You, if anyone, should know what I'm capable of, how well I've prepared myself over the years. They'll rue the day they ever came to the Farm to try to take me by force."

There follows an exaggerated pause, to give the words enough time to sink in.

"You might not care about your dad," he then goes on. "But can you really live with your colleagues' blood on your hands? The knowledge that you could have prevented it all? Besides, what kind of career can you expect on the force after an incident like that, do you think?"

There comes another pause, and for a second Asker wonders if he has hung up. But no, she can still feel his presence through the line.

"Hurry up and make your decision before it's too late, dear daughter," he says quietly.

She hears a clatter, and the call ends.

HILL

The taxi stops just outside a glass building in the middle of the tech district that has sprung up in the east of Lund, and with some effort Martin Hill clambers out. He stops on the sidewalk, supporting himself with the crutch he was given by the hospital.

Of course he should have stayed in for a few more days' observation. Let the doctors assure themselves—and him—that the bullet wound in his thigh is healing well. That there have been no complications.

But he has spent far too many days of his life in hospitals. He loathes their smells, loathes their sounds—perhaps even the thought of his own mortality.

At least that's what Sofie claimed.

She has gone home to her husband in Brussels. He may have started to suspect that her trips to Sweden aren't only work-related. May have started to sense that she is seeing someone else.

Not long ago Hill wouldn't have been all that unhappy with that turn of events. He likes Sofie, and he could definitely have envisioned a future with her.

But that was before Leo Asker came back into his life.

Before she saved him from the Mountain King's lair. Before she revealed her secret to him while he hovered between life and death. The secret of how her father tried to end both of their lives, and of how she outwitted him and broke free.

He has thought about Leo's story a lot in the week he has been in hospital. Has thought about Leo a lot.

Maybe even too much.

But this highly unexpected invitation has given him a chance to clear his head.

Hill stands up a little straighter. The air is damp, a light rainy mist typical of Skåne's late falls and winters, but it doesn't bother him in the slightest.

ALPHACENT INDUSTRIES, CORPORATE HEADQUARTERS reads the large, illuminated sign by the entrance. Hill lets his eyes drift farther upward, along the façade. The building really is something else: story upon story of matte-black glass, every one of its surfaces angling up toward the sky. The structure is much wider at the base than at the top, which, combined with its futuristic architecture, gives the whole thing the air of a spaceship. Not exactly surprising if you know a thing or two about the company's history or owners, the Irving family. And Hill does, better than most.

There is a ramp to one side of the door, but Hill decides to take the stairs. A stupid idea, he realizes, as soon as the pain from his bullet wound makes itself known.

He stops, grimaces.

The door opens and a man steps out. He appears to be in his late forties, dressed in a black, well-fitted suit and turtleneck that accentuate his broad shoulders and muscular upper body. His hair, like his beard, is flecked with gray, his gaze steely.

"Welcome, Associate Professor Hill," he says. "Allow me to assist you."

In a matter of seconds the man has helped him up the steps and into the lobby, without the slightest sign of exertion.

"My name's Samuel," he goes on. "I'm chief security officer here at AlphaCent. You'll find the reception straight ahead."

Hill nods by way of a thank-you, then looks around in curiosity. The lobby is at least equally impressive as the outside of the building: pale stone floors, white walls, a thirty-foot-high ceiling.

In the middle of the lobby stands a sculpture of a man approximately twice life-size. The man in the sculpture appears to be shading his eyes with one hand, while with the other he is pointing up at the sky. Or perhaps, more accurately, at the ceiling, where the lamps twinkle like distant stars. Hill hobbles closer.

The statue is pitch-black, and although the facial features are only just perceptible, the man appears to be gazing up longingly at the would-be stars.

Hill has seen this sculpture in photos before, but it is only when he is right beside it that he realizes it isn't made of stone or ceramic, but of black glass.

"Gunnar Irving in his youth." Samuel has stolen up silently beside him. "AlphaCent's founder."

"Mm-hm," Hill says.

Hill waits for some sort of continuation, a look or a gesture to imply that the reverence in the man's voice is intentionally overblown. But Samuel simply nods at Hill, as though to usher him in toward the lobby.

With the support of his crutch Hill limps over to reception. The woman behind the desk is wearing identical black clothes to Samuel, and she looks more like a model than a receptionist.

"Associate Professor, welcome," she says, with a smile just a touch too wide. "I'm afraid Nova Irving is running a few minutes late—please accept our sincere apologies for the delay. If you wouldn't mind taking a seat, I'll fetch you as soon as she's ready. Might I offer you some refreshments in the meantime? An espresso, cappuccino, or mineral water, perhaps?"

"Thanks, I'm fine."

It feels somewhat old-fashioned to Hill—perhaps more in line with American social mores than Swedish—to be attended upon with such overt politeness and addressed by his official academic title.

Hill slowly makes his way over to the chrome-and-leather waiting suite, sinks down into an armchair, and pulls out his cellphone.

Instead of scrolling aimlessly, he finds that his gaze is drawn to the large sculpture once again. The way the light catches on the glass alters its ambiguous facial expression, which is constantly shifting from fascination, to longing, to determination.

And then something else, something more alarming.

He takes a photo of the statue with his phone but is interrupted by a message from Leo.

Have time to talk? she asks. Hill glances over at the receptionist. The woman has left her seat and is walking toward him with another one of those overbaked smiles.

Not right now, he replies reluctantly.

OK, call me later. Something's come up that I need to talk about.

"Do excuse us for the wait, Associate Professor Hill," the receptionist says upon reaching him. "Nova Irving will see you now."

She guides him through the glass barriers and over to an elevator, swipes a pass against a reader, and presses the top button before giving him a parting smile.

The elevator accelerates smoothly and so quickly that it makes his ears pop.

This whole situation is mildly surreal, but it's also exciting.

Just two hours ago, Hill received a call from a woman who claimed to be Nova Irving's assistant. She asked straight-out if he had time to come in for a meeting, ideally that very day, but remained tight-lipped as to what the matter concerned. Since Hill had been trying to make contact with AlphaCent and the Irving family for several years, he had hardly any choice but to agree.

The elevator glides to a halt and the doors sail open almost soundlessly.

Outside awaits a woman of Hill's age. She, too, is dressed in black, but unlike the staff in the lobby she wears a shirt rather than a turtleneck beneath her blazer. A silver pendant hangs around her neck.

"Associate Professor Hill, welcome. I'm Nova Irving, CEO of AlphaCent Industries. Thank you for coming in at such short notice."

Nova Irving's voice is surprisingly deep, and her handshake is firm. Her strawberry-blond hair is tied back in a ponytail, and she has tanned skin, scarlet lips, and eyes that are so bright blue they look almost unreal.

"Call me Martin," says Hill. "I must admit, I was curious what this could be about. Your assistant was very cryptic on the phone."

She gestures toward a conference room with glass walls.

"All will be revealed. Let's take a seat in here."

Hill follows her, still using his crutch.

The table in the conference room is oval in shape, with five chairs along each side. The windows offer a view over the entire northern side of Lund.

At one end of the room, near the door, a bust is displayed, also made of black glass. More detailed than the sculpture in the lobby, it depicts an elderly man with angular cheekbones, a high hairline, and a fixed gaze that Hill immediately recognizes.

"Gunnar Irving. My father," Nova says with the same tone of voice that Hill detected in Samuel's down in the lobby.

Respect, even awe.

Nova gestures at Hill to take a seat, then sits down opposite him and places a tablet on the table.

Hill flops down heavily on his chair and props his crutch up against the tabletop.

He is expecting an explanation as to why he is there, but a question is posed instead.

"You reached out to us a few years ago, didn't you, Martin? To both AlphaCent Industries and the family?"

"That's right." Hill nods. "I was writing a chapter on Gunnar Irving and the Astroholm estate for my book *Forgotten Places and Their Stories*. But sadly no one was willing to be interviewed, or to let me visit Boulder Isle."

"No, back then my sister Maud was CEO. She took a rather different approach. More conservative, one might say. My leadership is more transparent."

Nova's smile is both attractive and infectious.

"So, how much do you know about AlphaCent, Martin?"

Hill clears his throat.

"Uh, well, I know that you're dynamic players in the medical technology sector: surgical instruments, robot-assisted surgery systems, and the like. Among other things you were one of the pioneers of DNA profiling technologies."

"Quite right," says Nova. "But we also develop technologies that go inside people. Pacemakers, implants, replacement heart valves . . ."

One of her eyebrows rises a quarter of an inch, as though waiting for him to react. Hill is confused. Does she know about his titanium heart valve? And if so, what does that have to do with this meeting?

"It was Eric Holst who mentioned your name," she goes on. "Eric's the chairman of our board. He told us that you risked your life to rescue his granddaughter Smilla from her kidnapper. And that you didn't run off to the media to brag about what you'd done. Eric is a hard man to impress, so my interest was piqued, and I had a little research done on you."

She flicks on her tablet without waiting for Hill's response.

"Martin Hill," she reads. "Thirty-one years of age, raised in a number of regions around Sweden but currently lecturer at Lund University, where you teach a course entitled 'the Architecture of

Decay.' Very popular with your students, you also authored a best-selling book that is something of a bible for those with an interest in urban exploration, that's to say the study of abandoned buildings and sites."

She raises her eyebrow again. Hill is still lost for words. This situation is bizarre, yet at the same time—exciting. All the secrecy, the futuristic office building, the far-too-congenial staff. And then of course Nova Irving herself: beautiful, intelligent, charismatic; the kind of person who can command an entire room in seconds. The contrast with the hospital bed he left just an hour ago, and his chilling flashbacks to the Mountain King's lair, could hardly be greater.

"And you also happen to have a titanium heart valve," she goes on. "One of ours, in fact, which makes you one of the AlphaCent family, so to speak."

"I see," Hill eventually utters, for want of anything better.

He should, of course, be asking how she can have access to that kind of confidential medical information, but Hill's mind is too busy trying to figure out where this conversation is going.

"What else do you know about the company, Martin?"

Something about Nova's eyes, and the little hint of a smile lurking at the side of her mouth, suggests that she is testing him; that she won't put her cards on the table until he has won her approval.

"AlphaCent was founded by your grandfather Bernhard Irving," he begins. "Back then the company was called All Preserves, and it operated in the food industry. Bernhard made a fortune during and after the war, but by the end of the fifties the company was beginning to flounder."

He clears his throat, skips over the reasons as to why that came to pass.

"In the sixties your father, Gunnar, took the helm. He changed the company's name to AlphaCent Industries, redirected its operations toward medical technologies, and presented some ground-breaking discoveries that had the company back on its feet in record time."

He stops there, as a matter of courtesy. But Nova isn't satisfied with that.

"And . . ." Her eyes twinkle, as though the next point is crucial.

Hill weighs his words. But if Nova's researcher has dug up his mechanical heart valve, it's reasonable to assume she already knows exactly what he wrote about the Irving family in his book.

"Gunnar, your father . . ." he goes on, with a nod at the glass bust, ". . . claimed that the ideas for his inventions stemmed from a UFO encounter that he had as a child, at Bernhard's observatory out on Boulder Isle. The alien was supposedly from the Alpha Centauri star system, which is also why, with his father's blessing, Gunnar renamed the company AlphaCent. The tale has given rise to a whole slew of conspiracy theories about your family estate, Astroholm Manor. One such theory is that Bernhard is interred in an underground burial chamber on the estate, while another claims there's a secret network of mining tunnels from the manor house all the way under Miresjön Lake and out to Boulder Isle."

Nova Irving studies him carefully for several seconds, but says nothing.

Then, without the slightest warning, that elusive smile blooms out in full. Her teeth are straight and white, in contrast to her blood-red lipstick.

"Well summarized, Martin!" She swipes the tablet aside. "Especially all that about the myths. A lot of garbage has been said about the company and my family over the years. Which is actually the reason why I've brought you here."

Hill sits up a little straighter.

"AlphaCent will soon be celebrating its centenary, and Gunnar his eightieth birthday," Nova goes on. "In light of these celebrations, the board and I thought it would be fitting to bring out a book about our . . ." she pauses, apparently searching for the right word, ". . . *colorful* history. Air out all the drivel and focus on our contribution to humanity. And who better to do that than a best-selling author with one of AlphaCent's very own heart valves in his chest? Someone who is already well informed about the company and the family, and who has credibility and discretion to boot."

She dials up the warmth in her smile another few degrees.

"In short, we'd like to commission you, Martin."

"OK . . ." Hill's brain freezes for a few seconds.

"Naturally we'll offer generous compensation," Nova goes on. "And you'll have full access to the company and family archives at

Astroholm Manor. We'll even provide you with accommodation on the estate, so that you can write in peace and quiet."

"Wait, hold on." Hill's common sense has now caught up. "I mean, I have a job, for starters."

Nova pulls an amused expression.

"As I understand it, you've been granted medical leave. Until the New Year, at least. We've spoken to your head of department, and he has no problem with you doing some writing in the meantime."

"OK, but . . ." Hill's mind skips over the fact that she has already spoken to his manager and instead fast-forwards to his next objection. ". . . As you can see, I'm on leave for a reason. My mobility is limited, and I need regular checkups."

He raises his crutch to underline his argument.

"Astroholm has its own state-of-the-art medical facility," Nova says. "We can offer constant medical supervision and cutting-edge treatments for your rehabilitation."

"Uh . . ." Hill clasps at his neck.

The offer *is* flattering. And besides, there's one other factor in the equation, one that Nova Irving isn't fully aware of. One that makes it extremely difficult for him to heed the objections coming from his superego.

Nova leans forward. Her pendant grazes the tabletop. It's a frog, Hill now sees. Upon catching a glimpse of her cleavage, he quickly looks away.

"It goes without saying that you'll get to meet Gunnar in person," she says, more quietly. "And visit the old observatory on Boulder Isle, just like you've always dreamed of. Hardly a soul has been there since the sixties. All of it's still there, untouched. I'd imagine it's a dream come true for an urban explorer like you. You lived not too far from the estate in your teenage years, didn't you?"

Her bright blue eyes twinkle again.

Hill takes a deep breath while waiting for the next objection from his superego, but it seems that his common sense has finally admitted defeat.

In its place is another voice entirely, one that whispers softly and enticingly in his head.

. . . visit the old observatory on Boulder Isle.

Just like you've always dreamed of.

SEVENTEEN YEARS EARLIER

He is fourteen years old. Just a few months ago his family moved again, this time to the forests on the borderlands between the southern provinces of Småland and Skåne. He doesn't know anyone here, but as always he tries his best to fit in. Tries to be sociable and funny, make new friends, and turn a blind eye to the fact that some of the kids call him Darky Marty.

Some days are better than others.

Soon he'll find someone just as fun and smart as he is. At least that's what his mom says. And since he doesn't want to make her sad he doesn't disagree.

He has noticed a girl whose locker is next to his. She's tall and broad-shouldered, and most of the other pupils seem a little scared of her.

Something about Leo Asker appeals to him, and he has started to cook up ways that he might dare to approach her.

But tonight his mind isn't on any of that.

He is standing down by the shore. Before him lies the almost perfect circle of Miresjön Lake, and off in the distance he sees the jagged outline of Boulder Isle.

It has taken him all of three long bus rides to get here. After that, a fairly taxing walk down to the Boy Scouts' cabin, the only place along the lakeshore—besides Astroholm Manor—where the slope is gentle enough that you can access the water.

He first read about the place in a chat room for urban explorers, where he became fascinated by Bernhard Irving and his son, "Space-Case" Gunnar Irving. Ever since he first chanced upon the story of their family, he has spent many an hour at the library reading up on everything he could find about Astroholm Manor, Boulder Isle, Astrofield Mine, and the observatory.

Several people in the chat room have made the same journey as him, have trekked down to the cabin at the shore only to realize they won't get any closer. There are no boats on the lake, and Boulder Isle is over half a mile from the shore. On top of that, the lake is almost a hundred feet deep, *which means that the water is ice-cold even in summer, and very difficult to swim.*

And even if you did manage to swim across, the island's shoreline is full of sharp rocks and crags, making it impossible to wade ashore without tearing up your feet and knees.

He knows all of this, knows he won't be able to make it to the island.

But to be able to stand on this shore, look into his binoculars, and pick out the dome of Bernhard's observatory just above the treetops, makes the whole journey worthwhile. To get to see the very spot where Gunnar Irving claimed a UFO came floating down to land.

Where the black creature with glowing red eyes then stepped out to speak to him.

For two hours he has stood here on the shore, stopping only to eat his picnic and every now and then give his arms a rest from holding the binoculars. He has been loath to miss a single second, even though the only movements to speak of have been the trees swaying in the wind, the odd bird.

Dusk has just started to fall. Darkness sneaks across the lake, making the stars pop up in the sky.

One last look, then he has to leave if he is going to make it to his bus on time.

He raises his binoculars, twists the observatory's dark silhouette into focus.

Slowly he sweeps his binoculars along the island and across the water to Astroholm Manor. According to the chat forum there is a secret tunnel that links the island to the mainland, but no one has ever found it. There may even be a whole complex of tunnels to explore, and an underground burial chamber. Even after two hours of watching and waiting, the thought still gives his heart a little flutter.

In the distance a tawny owl calls. The eerie sound sails across the lake before all falls silent again. He sweeps his binoculars back to the island and lands on the observatory once more. Hovers there for a minute or two, as a farewell of sorts.

Then, just as he is about to leave, he thinks he sees something.

Something that makes him stop in his tracks, makes him freeze so long he misses his bus.

In the years that follow he will lean toward it being his imagination that was playing tricks on him. That he saw something he wanted to see, because there and then it was all he had.

And maybe that was all it was. It is the best explanation, logically speaking. But a small part of him still stands by what he glimpsed for a few seconds on Boulder Isle that night, high up in the sky directly above the observatory.

A bright white light, which glinted and then disappeared.

ASKER

The air in her boxy office feels stagnant. On the desk in front of her lies her cellphone, with Martin's reply still visible. Her brain is working in overdrive, but all it can tell her is that she wants to talk to Martin Hill. He knows her upbringing, was the one who gave her father his nickname.

Prepper Per.

Her father, the madman who builds bunkers, who stockpiles weapons, explosives, and supplies in preparation for doomsday. The man who, until a few minutes ago, she thought she would never hear from again. And now all of a sudden he's trying to force his way back into her life.

Slowly she rolls up her shirtsleeve. Her scar is still itching, and she runs her fingertips along it. Traces the tattooed lettering that runs through it.

Ten letters.

Resilience

After a while this ritual makes the itching stop and her stress levels fall. She rolls down her shirtsleeve again.

Is what Per claimed even true?

She wakes up her computer. What people usually refer to as the "police database" in fact consists of a number of different systems, some of which are ancient, others more middle-aged. What they all have in common is a general refusal to cooperate—be that with the user, or with one another.

After a little typing, Asker manages to at least pull a list of recent police reports. She quickly scrolls through them. Nothing about a body in the vicinity of the Farm.

She exhales, tries to gather her thoughts.

Was the phone call just a way for Per to mess with her, an attempt to manipulate her? She puts her hypothesis to the usual test.

Hypothesis: Per lied to her.

Question: But why?

Answer: To mess with her.

Question: But why?

Answer: Because he thinks he has something to gain from it.

Question: But what?

What would Per stand to gain from contacting her after fifteen years of silence, just to toy with her? Why would he make a claim that she could so easily check? And why now?

She picks up her phone again and dials the number to the police control center.

"Asker here, from Serious Crime," she says when one of the operators picks up. "Has a car been sent out on a case up in the Göinge forests? Deceased human body?"

She crosses her fingers that her colleague on the other end of the line will be unaware that she no longer works on the sixth floor and instead heads up the Department of Lost Souls down in the basement.

"Just a moment . . ."

She hears the tap of keys.

"Yes, that's right," the operator goes on. "It's just come in, less than an hour ago. The patrol's still on-site. I can patch you straight through if you want."

"That would be great, thank you."

Asker frowns. So Per *was* telling the truth about the body. But how could he already know that it had been found? Or that its discovery would make him a suspect?

The officer on the scene answers so quickly he must have been holding the phone in his hand.

"Asker here, Serious Crime," she says by way of introduction. "I hear you've found a body."

"Yes, that's right." The man's voice sounds puzzled. "But I've already spoken to your colleague. He said you were on your way."

"We must have gotten our wires crossed. Could you fill me in, please? Where are you now?"

"Just north of the border with Småland province. A place called Hultet. It was a couple of guys from the municipality who called it in. They were clearing an old compost dump when they stumbled across a body."

Asker can see the very place before her. She has cycled past it hundreds of times. It lies at a turnoff less than six hundred yards from the Farm's gates.

"Like I just said to your colleague, the victim's an adult male," the officer on the line continues. "I'd guess somewhere around fifty. The body is lying facedown on the ground. We can't see any more than that just now, and we didn't want to touch the body needlessly. Forensics are on their way."

"How long do you think he's been there?" she asks.

"Hard to say. According to the guys from the municipality, they stopped dumping waste here almost fifteen years ago, because the space was at capacity. After the last dump they closed off the access road with a barrier. But since they're now laying power lines in the area, they decided to clear up some of the waste. The victim was under the very first pile the digger cleared. The one nearest the barrier."

"So you're saying the last pile had been dumped on top of the body?"

"Yeah, exactly. I'm struggling to see how else it could have happened. It's a big pile of trash we're talking about, easily a couple of pickups' worth, and the body was pretty much right under it."

"So the body has been lying there for fifteen years or more?"

"Probably," the officer replies. "Though it looks really well preserved. His hair's still there, his clothing's intact."

"Can you send me some pictures?"

"Is that really necessary? The guy I just spoke to said you'd have someone on the scene soon—"

"It would be great if you could send me some photos straightaway," she says, cutting him off.

He takes her phone number, and she stares at the phone while she waits.

Fifteen years ago she was still living at the Farm with Prepper Per. She remembers both the barrier and the huge piles of waste beyond it, would pass them on her way to and from school. So the dead man was probably already lying there then.

After a minute or two her phone starts to buzz.

The first photo is of a digger standing beside a two-foot-deep hole in the ground. Around the hole and digger rise huge piles of partly decomposed yard waste: branches and twigs interspersed with soil, gravel, and stones. In the background she can just make out an open road barrier.

The next photo is taken at closer range. In it the dead man is fully dressed. He is lying on his front with his arms at his sides, still half-buried in the boggy ground.

His broad back is clothed in a sturdy blue beaver-nylon jacket. The collar of a checkered flannel shirt juts out above it, and above that a head with sticky tufts of hair.

She zooms in and out a few times. Focuses on the more visible of his palms. The skin is filthy, but it shows no real signs of decomposition.

The police officer is right; at first glance the body looks far too well preserved to have lain in the ground for fifteen years or more. Though that might not be so strange, given where the body was found. The low-lying terrain east of the Farm consists mainly of waterlogged swampland. And swamps are low in oxygen, which halts the breakdown of tissues and textiles. So the body could very well be as old as the police officer suggests.

But something about the images bothers her, something she can't quite put her finger on.

She stands up impatiently and walks into the kitchen to get herself a cup of coffee. Virgilsson, Rosen, and Zafer are sitting at one of the tables, engrossed in what appears to be a lively conversation. They fall silent when she steps into the room.

"I was just sharing the exciting news," Virgilsson says with one of his toady smiles. The sweater-vest that he has donned on top of his shirt is multicolored with small checks, giving him the look of a TV test card. "That you are henceforth to be the Resources Unit's permanent chief."

"It's so great," Rosen exclaims, with a gasp that makes her sound more terrified than pleased.

Zafer is speaking five decibels too loud, as usual.

"Congratulations," he says, adjusting his glasses, which have hearing aids fixed to the back of each temple.

"Thanks," she says. "No Attila?"

"No . . ." Virgilsson and the others exchanges glances. "Kent's off sick. As he tends to be at this time of year."

"Doesn't he just," Rosen agrees with a sigh. She puts on a sorrowful little smile.

Asker pours her coffee. She ought to ask some kind of follow-up question about Attila, but right now she is struggling to keep her mind on staff welfare.

"Well, what do you both say? Time to get back to the salt mines?"

Virgilsson gets up, taking the other two with him. It's almost as though they are afraid that Asker will sit down with them—not that she had any intention of doing so.

"Oh, Rosen," Asker says, just as the diminutive woman is leaving the room. "I need your help with something."

Rosen, whose real name is Gunilla Rosén, fiddles nervously with her cardigan sleeve while following Asker to her office.

Asker sees Virgilsson stop at the pigeonholes and pretend to leaf through some papers, while casting furtive glances in their direction. As soon as Rosen has entered her office, Asker makes sure to shut the door behind them.

"I need a few database searches."

"I see." Rosen exhales.

"A man aged between forty and sixty, missing for the last fifteen years. Of relatively strong build, with dark, longish hair, wearing workmen's clothing at the time of his disappearance. He may have some connection to the borderlands between Skåne and Småland."

"I see," Rosen says again. "That's not much to go on."

"No, I know," says Asker. "But I also know that you're a ninja when it comes to our IT systems. Fact is, I've never met anyone who even comes close."

"Oh, not really." Rosen self-consciously picks at one of the burls on her cardigan. Clearly she isn't used to receiving praise.

"And we'll keep this between us, please. No one—not in this building or outside it—has anything to do with it. Not even Virgilsson. Are we agreed?"

Asker holds Rosen's gaze.

"Of course," the tiny woman says.

"Thank you. With any luck there'll be a little treat in it for your journalist friend at *Sydsvenskan*."

Asker doesn't like leaking things to the press, but Rosen's infatuation with an obviously gay reporter at *Sydsvenskan* is one of the few trump cards she has in her possession.

Rosen lights up. "I'll get straight on it."

As soon as Rosen has left the room, Asker pulls up the images again. She zooms in, one section at a time, and plays around with the contrast and color settings to try to find more leads on the body's identity, or what it is that makes her think she has missed something.

In the wet ground between the man's knees she spots something angular sticking out. She zooms in as much as she can and switches the image to black-and-white. When she strains her eyes, she thinks she can make out the corner of something that appears to be made of leather.

She calls the police officer at the scene again.

"It's Asker again, at Serious Crime," she says when he picks up. "In the image it looks like there's something buried in the ground between the victim's knees. It could be a wallet. Could one of you check?"

"Hold on."

His voice sounds more sheepish than last time. She hears the mumble of voices, a scraping, and a few beeps. Only once it's too late does she realize that he has transferred her call.

"Hi, Leo," Jonas Hellman says down the line. She stifles a curse word. "As far as I recall, you were transferred from Serious Crime a few weeks ago."

There is an amused tone to his voice, as though he is enjoying this situation, which is almost certainly true.

"And just today you turned down the chance to return to the department," he goes on. "So I'm sure you'll understand my surprise to hear that you've been calling around, claiming you still work with us."

Asker takes a deep breath. Considers simply hanging up.

"Here's what we're going to do," Hellman goes on. "I'll choose to view this little slip as a workplace accident. You're a good detective, Leo, I've always thought so. And you did great work on the Smilla Holst case."

Now his tone changes, sharpens.

"But you were also stupid enough to throw away my very generous offer. You chose to stay with the rejects and the joke cases down in the Resources Unit, rather than work for me. It's hard not to take that kind of rejection personally, especially given . . ."

He trails off, leaving the rest of the sentence hanging in the air, but Asker still hears it loud and clear.

. . . *especially given our history.*

"So, going forward, Leo," Hellman says with an exaggerated calm. "Going forward, you're going to stay the fuck away from my department and our investigations. Is that understood?"

Asker opens her mouth to say something—anything to stop him from getting the last word. But the line is already dead.

THE GLASS MAN

The first weeks after the awakening are excruciating.

His body is drained of certain fluids, replenished with others.

Fed, weighed, pricked—trained to regain its strength.

Nourishment, medication, exercise, samples, tests.

An endless, painful cycle that he must endure before he is granted his freedom.

Until the Father is satisfied.

So he holds it in. Obeys, bides his time.

He longs to return to the darkness and the underground.

To the damp and the cold. The secret chamber never penetrated by light.

As his strength grows, something else begins to take root in him, too. A familiar feeling of restlessness.

And of hunger.

HILL

The first thing Hill does when he gets back to his apartment is dig up a copy of *Forgotten Places and Their Stories*.

For years he was very interested in the Irving family, and he had planned to write a book on them alone. Perhaps even find an explanation for the flash of light he thought he saw as a teenager.

It has since occurred to him that it could well have been a meteorite or weather balloon, even the lights of an airplane that his teenage imagination transformed into something more. Whatever the case may be, he was obsessed with the thought of visiting Boulder Isle and the observatory, of trying to find out whether there was a grain of truth to the many rumors.

But when he was denied access to both the site and family members for interviews, the whole project ran out of steam. Despite having a whole computer full of research and various unconfirmed rumors, he was forced to boil it all down to one measly chapter in *Forgotten Places*, which, for sheer frustration, he hasn't been able to read since.

With today's turn of events, he needs to remind himself of what he actually wrote. Laboriously he lowers himself onto the couch and flicks through to the chapter entitled "Astrofield Mine and the Observatory at Boulder Isle."

Miresjön Lake is one of a kind, he reads. *Situated in the borderlands between the historic provinces of Skåne, Blekinge, and Småland, the lake is almost perfectly round and remarkably deep. In the middle of the lake lies Boulder Isle, which in turn is unique: its ground mostly consists of rhyolite, an unusual rock formed only at extremely high temperatures. Geologists therefore tend to agree that the lake is in fact the crater of an enormous volcanic eruption that took place some fifty million years ago.*

The text is interrupted by a drone photo of a round, dark lake surrounded by spruce-topped hills. In the middle of the lake, like a green dot, lies a flat island also covered by forest.

But there is another, more local, theory. Namely that the crater, lake, and island are the result of a meteorite landing. Grocery magnate Bernhard Irving would come to be obsessed by this theory, and it would prove his downfall.

Another image, this time a black-and-white photo of a man aged around fifty with thinning hair, dark glasses, and a pointed beard. He is looking to the right of the camera, which lends him a somewhat dreamy expression.

Bernhard Irving had been raised with the meteorite legend. He was fascinated by the idea that a piece of rock that had been traveling through the cold darkness of space for millions of years could have ended its journey in these very forests. With the help of the fortune he had amassed in the foodstuffs industry, Bernhard devoted ever more time to trying to prove the legend true.

He purchased Boulder Isle and large parts of the land around the lake, founding a mine on the island that he would name Astrofield Mine.

On the roof of the mine's headframe he also installed an observatory. The area boasts very few other buildings, and the shape of the crater means there is little interference from artificial light sources, which makes it an ideal spot for stargazing.

Bernhard Irving used the rhyolite extracted from the mine to build the family estate, Astroholm Manor, on the other side of the lake. But the mine's real purpose was to find traces of the meteorite that Bernhard was convinced lay buried somewhere deep beneath the lake. A discovery like that would have made him immortal.

The next photo is also black-and-white. A group photo of a dozen men, most of whom are wearing overalls and mining helmets, standing in front of a metal façade.

In the middle of the frame stands Bernhard Irving. He has a big smile on his face, and his arm is draped over the shoulders of the mine's manager, a shorter man with round spectacles, who wears a shirt and tie beneath his overalls and holds a clipboard in one hand. In the background stand the pillars of the concrete tower that forms the headframe for the mine's hoist.

Staff of Astrofield Mine, 1956, the caption reads.

Hill turns the page and goes on reading.

Geologists and astronomers alike rejected Irving's theory outright. Rumors also started to spread that obsidian had been found in the mine.

Obsidian, also known as volcanic glass, is formed during volcanic erup-
tions, so its purported discovery was a clear sign that Irving's meteorite
theory was flawed, and that he had squandered his fortune on a project
doomed to failure.

Bernhard Irving didn't heed the warnings. His space fixation developed
into a full-blown mania that would come to have tragic consequences.

After a collapse in 1965 that cost three men their lives, Astrofield Mine
was forced to close. By then, both the company and the Irving family were
on the brink of ruin. In an unexpected move, Bernhard's son, Gunnar,
convinced his father to depart as CEO, and, aged just twenty-two, he took to
the helm of the family business.

Another photo, this time in color, depicting a young Gunnar
Irving. Sharp features, an intense gaze. The text continues with a
brief section on how Gunnar transformed the company, redirecting
its operations toward medical technologies.

Gunnar's very first patent was obtained for a scalpel made from shards
of obsidian glass. As fate would have it, the very same glass that had all but
ruined Bernhard later came to save family and company alike.

Gunnar claimed that this and other groundbreaking ideas had been
inspired by an encounter he supposedly had with an extraterrestrial at the
observatory on Boulder Isle. An enormous black creature with glowing red
eyes.

Hill would have loved to interview Gunnar about that encounter,
but even there he was foiled. Gunnar Irving hasn't given a single
interview in years.

The last part of the chapter is devoted to the Astroholm estate
and features an image of a forbidding building in an unusual architectural style, situated within vast gardens.

The Astroholm estate has remained in the family's possession. The sin-
gular architecture of its manor house is described as an example of gothic
futurism.

Bernhard Irving, who passed away in 1996, lies buried within the
grounds. Rumors abound that he rests in a burial chamber that he per-
sonally designed, but these have been impossible to verify. As has the claim
that a system of would-be tunnels links Boulder Isle to Astroholm Manor
itself.

Gunnar's account of his very own close encounter has occasionally fueled
waves of tourism to the area, particularly among UFO enthusiasts.

The latest wave came in 2001, the year that Bernhard would have turned one hundred. In that year there were reports of a bright light in the sky, followed by a loud bang, which created quite the stir locally. The phenomenon turned out to be a bolide, an unusually bright meteorite, which entered the atmosphere just above the lake.

The chapter ends with another aerial photo, this time zoomed in on Boulder Isle itself. In the middle of the island, in a break in the otherwise dense woodland, appear two rusty corrugated sheet-metal roofs, and beside them a tall, concrete tower with open sides. It is vaguely reminiscent of a medieval watchtower. At the top of the structure a dark dome rises.

On the nearby Boulder Isle, the mining buildings and Bernhard's observatory still remain. The natural conditions make the island very difficult to access, and landings are forbidden due to the risk of ground collapse and subsidence caused by the old mining tunnels that run beneath the island.

Hill struggles to tear his eyes from the image. Nova Irving was completely right: Boulder Isle has been skulking at the back of his mind ever since he was a teen. The promise of getting to visit the island, stay on the Astroholm estate, and even interview the secretive Gunnar Irving in the flesh was more than enough to make his response an immediate yes during their meeting.

Another reason for his immediate acceptance was his need for something new to focus on. Something to draw his mind away from the Mountain King's house of horrors, or how close to death he came.

The chance to explore the Irving family's secrets is just the medicine he needs.

He closes the book and puts it down on the coffee table. Only now does he remember that he promised to call Leo. He takes out his phone.

She picks up straightaway.

"Can I come by for a coffee?" she asks, without so much as a hello. "Something's come up."

ASKER

"So Prepper Per calls you out of the blue and expects you to help him escape murder charges?"

"Yep."

She is sitting with Martin in his kitchen, at an austere designer table that doesn't remotely fit the rest of the furniture in his apartment. She has made them coffee and brought some rolls, despite his protests that he isn't nearly as incapacitated as he looks, which is a clear lie. Still, it's nice to see him on his feet and not in a hospital bed. And he did seem to be in good spirits—at least until she told him about the phone call from her father.

"Damn, Leo," he sighs. "And here I was thinking *my* day was unexpectedly exciting. Congratulations, you win by a country mile."

"Thanks!"

Despite the gravity of the situation, she can't help but smile. This is the first time that she has been to his place. A new, tentative step in their adult relationship. As teenagers they were best friends. But that was followed by years of separation, with no contact. Had it not been for the Holst case, their paths might never have crossed. But she is very glad that they did.

It was thanks to Martin that she dared to break free from Prepper Per. He saved her life, and maybe someday she will tell him that. But not tonight. Tonight she's just happy to have taken this small step of visiting his home.

Swanky designer table aside, Martin's apartment is pleasantly cozy: jam-packed bookshelves, well-worn IKEA couches, an eighties record player. On the walls hang framed antique movie posters that appear to be originals. Asker has been scouring the place for signs of his girlfriend Sofie, but so far she hasn't found any. On the other hand, she hasn't checked his bedroom or bathroom. And nor should she, she tells herself.

"So what are you going to do?" he asks.

"I really don't know. Per knows who the body is, but he doesn't want to say. And he called from a private number so I can't reach him—not unless I want to head out to the Farm."

"Hell no! You're not considering that, are you?" Martin exclaims.

"Oh no, there's no risk of that."

Asker quickly hides her face behind her coffee mug. Martin is worried about her, which feels pretty nice.

"Obviously I'm not setting foot on the Farm," she goes on. "Per's testing me, just like he used to do when I was a kid. But if I want to prevent a bloodbath, then I have to play along. The problem is I'm fumbling in the dark, and Hellman's bound to have ordered everyone at police HQ to keep me at arm's length."

"And that weird little guy in your department who helped you last time, the one who smuggled you into Forensics? Can't he do that again?"

"Virgilsson? He sold me out to Hellman at the first chance he got. It's thanks to him that Hellman was in the right place at the right time to steal the glory of catching the Mountain King and make himself everyone's hero."

"And a good thing he was," Martin objects. "If Hellman hadn't turned up when he did, then Smilla Holst wouldn't be alive."

Asker shakes her head. She knows Martin has a point, but she would rather not admit it.

"Hellman's the commissioner's golden boy," she goes on. "Which in Virgilsson's eyes makes him a much better business partner than me. He can't be trusted. Much less asked for any favors."

"I get it . . ."

For a few seconds they drink their coffee in silence.

"So what happens now?" Martin asks. "With the case, I mean?"

"Forensics are finishing their work on the crime scene up in the forest. The body will be taken to the nearest forensic medicine division for autopsy tonight. They'll compare fingerprints, dental records, or DNA to find out who the dead man was. Try to establish a cause of death, if that's possible after all these years."

"You mean the forensic medicine division here in Lund?"

"That's the one."

Martin appears to be thinking. "So, here's the thing. I have an old urban explorer friend who used to be a night worker there; maybe he still is. Would it help if you could take a look at the corpse?"

Asker gives a start.

"That would be amazing."

"Good. I'll call him right now and see if he still works there."

He starts looking around for his cellphone.

"Wait," she says. "Ever since I got here, we've only talked about me. But you mentioned something about an unexpectedly exciting day?"

"Yes, actually," Martin says eagerly. "I've been asked to write a book. About Gunnar Irving."

"'Space-Case' Gunnar Irving? The one up at Astroholm?"

"You know who he is?"

"Of course I do. Everyone up in those forests does. I mean, the place is only about thirty miles from the Farm. I remember there used to be a seedy UFO café nearby that had a flying saucer on the roof."

"It's Gunnar's daughter Nova who hired me," says Martin. "She's CEO of the family's company, AlphaCent. They've promised me an exclusive interview with Gunnar, and accommodation on the estate while I'm writing."

"Wow. So you'll get to the bottom of the UFO story?"

Martin nods eagerly.

"That might not be my exact job description, but I've been more or less obsessed with Astroholm, Boulder Isle, and Gunnar the Space Case ever since I first got into urban exploration in my early teens. Rumor has it there are tunnels between Boulder Isle and the mainland, maybe even a secret burial chamber under the estate. For a while I'd planned to write a book about it all, but that project came to a grinding halt. I had to condense it to a chapter in *Forgotten Places*."

His eyes twinkle. She likes it when they do that.

"Oh, I get it," she says. "So now you're going to write this commission for AlphaCent, all while secretly gathering the material you need for your own book."

"Man, you should be a detective!" Martin smirks. "But yeah, I guess I was thinking something along those lines. Of course, I've had to sign a confidentiality agreement, but as far as I can tell that only prevents me from revealing anything that hasn't already been approved for publication in this book or isn't already public knowledge. So the broader I go with the AlphaCent story now, the more freedom I'll give myself for a future book. The company's history is deeply intertwined with the Irving family's past, and it's a pretty fascinating story, too. They've had their fair share of tragedy. Bernhard Irving, Gunnar's father, went insane and all but ruined them. His mine out on Boulder Isle collapsed, killing three people. And Gunnar's eldest son, Viggo, drove his car off the road and straight into Miresjön Lake. His future brother-in-law was in the car with him and died."

"Ah," Asker nods. "UFO legends, tunnels, family sagas. I can see why it interests you so much."

She likes seeing him so passionate: it reminds her of the Martin she once knew. The Martin she has missed.

"So when do you start?"

"They're sending a car for me tomorrow," he replies. "I can't go back to the university till the New Year anyway, and after three, four days, max, I'll be climbing the walls here at home. A change of scene is just what I need, and it really is a dream project." Martin pauses, gives her a long look. "By the way, you haven't lectured me for discharging myself from hospital early, like everyone else."

Asker is about to ask if by *like everyone else* he means Sofie, but she checks herself.

"I thought you must have your reasons," she says instead. "Besides, you're a grown man; you can take responsibility for your own stupid decisions."

"Yes!" Martin laughs. "I'm an expert at facing up to the consequences of my own stupidity."

He gives himself a gentle pat on his thigh, right next to his bullet wound.

"Speaking of stupidity, I haven't thanked you for what you did down there in the mountain. And in the helicopter. You kept me alive . . ."

Asker tries to meet his gaze, but it's harder than she anticipated.

"Don't mention it," she mutters down into her mug. "I'm sure you'd have done the same for me."

The words slip out of her, and she already regrets them. Martin observes her for a few seconds, then gives a slow nod.

"More coffee?" he eventually asks, as if noticing that the atmosphere has become all too charged.

With some effort he gets to his feet, waving away her attempts to help him.

"I have to get back in shape," he goes on. "Especially if I'm going to visit Boulder Isle in the near future."

He pours coffee for them both.

"Though first things first, let's try to smuggle you into forensics so that you can get a sneak peek at your bog body. Say what you will, Leo, but being friends with you certainly isn't boring."

On her way back to her car Asker notices an uptick in her mood.

She isn't used to having someone to talk to. And on top of that Martin has offered to help her, even though he has his hands full with his own dream project.

It's almost as though their friendship has picked up exactly where it left off. As though the break of sixteen years has hardly made any difference. He's still her ally, her counterweight to Prepper Per.

She likes that thought.

But alongside it another thought is circling at the back of her mind. A much more concerning prospect.

Jonas Hellman knows she's interested in the bog body, and he isn't so stupid that he won't find out why. She never told him about her father, not even during that intense period long ago when their affair was at its most forbidden and exciting.

For fifteen years she has kept Prepper Per locked up in her head. Her specter; her ghost. Occasionally her savior, however strange that might sound.

And at the same time: her Achilles' heel.

All it will take is for someone to pull the names of the landowners in the area around where the body was found, and Hellman will know why she was prying into the case.

Jonas lives with the knowledge that, for all his golden-boy reputation and the vast resources he has at his disposal up in Serious Crime, he was the one who led the Holst investigation astray. He lives with the shame that it was in fact Asker who—with the help of Martin Hill and a few oddballs from the Department of Lost Souls—freed

Smilla Holst and put a stop to the Mountain King. And, to top it all off, the shame that she has *let* him steal the glory.

For an alpha male like Jonas Hellman it would be hard to imagine a greater affront. But having Asker's father put away for murder would certainly help him to regain some shred of his honor.

And for that reason she now has no choice but to help Prepper Per, the man who once tried to kill her, avoid suspicion of murder—all while Hellman and the entirety of her former department will be breathing down her neck.

She pinches the bridge of her nose.

Martin's right.

Her fucking day beats his by a country mile.

And this is probably only the beginning.

THE GLASS MAN

He has always known that he was special, ever since the day he was born.

Even before.

His mother was expecting twins. Castor and Pollux, just like the constellation. But his brother came out malformed, a deaf and blind little creature that didn't survive birth.

He, however, was the antithesis: strong, healthy, and living. All the healthy strands of DNA, gathered in one body. Prince Pollux, that's what his father called him. The stronger twin. The immortal.

How true would that prediction prove to be?

His mother worshipped him, indulged his every whim. She followed him wherever he went, praising his every minor piece of progress. Saw to it that the world he lived in was flush and free of hindrances.

Free of hardship and disappointment.

He was the prince, the heir, the chosen one.

But it wasn't the suffocating love of his mother that he sought.

His father worked a great deal. He had VERY IMPORTANT tasks that they were hardly allowed to discuss at home. Much less disturb.

The Father was a brilliant man. A great man.

An all-seeing eye that never blinked.

Everyone knew it. Him, his mother, their staff.

And still, almost every night, the Father would take the time to come by his bedroom. He would sit down on the edge of the bed and pat him on his head.

"Prince Pollux," the Father would say. "You and I shall change the world."

These words would make his chest swell, make him feel as though everything were possible. That no misfortune could ever befall him.

One day, after one of his long business trips, the Father came home bearing a gift: a sealed glass container filled with a clear liquid. Inside, floating almost weightlessly, was an amphibian.

"It's a glass frog," said the Father. "They call it that because its abdomen is transparent. Here, look!"

When he leaned in toward the container, he saw that the Father was right. Through the skin of the frog's belly he could see straight into its body. Make out its eggs, its stomach, its static heart.

"Is it alive?" he asked in awe.

The Father chuckled at his stupid question.

"Not this one. But there's a different species of frog that can indeed come back from the dead."

"But how?"

"Frogs hibernate through winter, just like bears and hedgehogs. But that particular species of frog, *Rana sylvatica*, goes much further than that. It can withstand being frozen completely, until its very heart stops and all life ceases. For two hundred days it can lie like that, the whole winter through. Just as dead as this little fellow."

The Father gave the glass container a gentle tap.

"But then, when the warmth of spring arrives, *Rana sylvatica* thaws out. Its heart starts beating and the frog lives again. Like some kind of miracle. In actual fact it's science: an advanced chemical process that no other creature has managed to replicate. Isn't that fantastic?"

He kept the glass container on his bookshelf. For many years, just before he went to bed, he would walk over to it, stand so close that his breath would fog on the glass, and tap the container, half-expecting to see its little frog heart start to beat, its body jerk back to life.

But the frog remained still, its eyes closed.

As though it were only sleeping.

As though it were waiting for the warmth of spring.

He always wondered what it was dreaming, down there in the eternal darkness.

Now he knows.

ASKER

The forensic medicine division's premises lie on the outskirts of central Lund, in a sixties brick building that skulks in the shadows of the enormous hospital complex beside it. The darkness of night and the streetlights' shadows make it shrink even further.

Asker drives past the address a few times, then parks a little way away. She sits for a while and studies her surroundings, to make sure that Hellman hasn't posted anyone to watch the building.

Finding no sign to suggest that Jonas has had quite so much foresight, she steps out of the car. As she does, her hand instinctively drops to her hip, to adjust her firearm holster. But the gun is still with Forensics after the Holst case. They will hold it there for at least another week, according to her latest update. Though standard procedure when live ammunition is fired in service, it's irritating nonetheless. Without her firearm at her side, she feels naked.

The time is three minutes to two a.m., and the streetlights are gently swaying. The temperature is in the low thirties, but with the November wind and mizzle it feels colder.

Asker walks calmly toward the building. Tries to make it seem like she's just out on a nighttime stroll as she approaches the doors.

She knocks on one of the two garage-door entrances, as instructed. Looks over her shoulder once more while waiting for a response.

The door slowly rattles open. Inside it stands a man in a white coat, somewhere between thirty-five and forty. He is short, pale, and thin as a rake. On his forehead a thin patch of fringe hovers forlornly, a brave little island of follicles in a sea of baldness. His white coat bears a stain that she hopes is mustard. An iPad sticks out of one pocket.

"Martin Hill's friend?" he asks while chewing on a Snickers.

The risk of a randomer knocking on the allotted door at exactly the appointed time in the middle of the night is probably slim to none, but instead of pointing that out, Asker just nods.

"Sven," he says by way of an introduction. "Follow me!"

He waves her inside and shuts the door behind them, then leads her through the garage intake, using a pass to open a set of metal doors.

Asker can smell it as soon as the doors glide open. A rancid, soapy scent that all morgues share. Even so, it's one of death's more palatable smells.

The room within is big and cool, and only half of the fluorescent strip lights in the ceiling are lit. The walls and floor are lined with white tiles. Two examination tables stand in the middle of the room, and between them a table trolley with various surgical tools. The floor is still wet, as though it has recently been mopped.

Asker has been here several times before, while working in Serious Crime. Those visits would take place during the day, with the lights on. Tonight is something quite different.

The deathly smell doesn't appear to bother Sven, who takes the last few bites of his Snickers before scrunching the wrapper away into his empty coat pocket. He licks a few flakes of chocolate from the corners of his mouth while making for the cold-chamber doors on the far wall.

He stops by the door on the right and grabs the handle.

"The body came in around seven," he says. "I'm the one who receives and registers any bodies that come in outside working hours. I called Martin as soon as the transportation had gone."

"So he said." Asker waits for Sven to open the door, but apparently he has more to say.

"Are you close friends, you and Martin?" he asks.

Asker has no wish to be interrogated, but she gets the sense that Sven won't open the door until she has replied.

"We're childhood friends."

"Oh really?" Sven clicks his tongue. "He's never mentioned you."

"Oh well."

"Martin and I have been out on a few UE things together," he goes on, though she never asked. "But it's been a while since . . ."

A hint of regret has entered his voice. He still shows no sign of opening the door.

"Martin has a lot going on," she says. "I think he's had to cut down on his outings."

Sven's tone switches to curiosity.

"Is he working on a new book?"

Asker thinks of Martin's double book project with Space-Case Gunnar Irving and the rest of his family.

"He might be," she says. Throws in a conspiratorial wink.

Sven lights up and gives her such an exaggerated wink in return that it looks like some kind of tic.

"I get it, I get it. My lips are sealed." To ram the message home he signs an air zip across his mouth. "Well, let's have a look, shall we?"

Finally he opens the large cold-chamber door and presses a button that makes the strip lights inside flicker to life.

This room is much colder than the first. The air feels thick and greasy. Holds so many nuances of rot that Asker automatically switches to breathing through her mouth.

"Here he is."

Sven walks over to one of the cold lockers along the wall, opens a stainless-steel hatch, and pulls a lever. With a faint whine the tray inside glides out into the room.

The body lies in a white body bag that has been zipped shut.

"Do we have an ID?"

Sven pulls out his iPad and taps the screen to life.

"Yes! A Walter Konrad Kurtz."

Asker snorts. She was worried that Hellman's gang might have already identified the dead man from the items in his wallet. That they would already be one step ahead.

But that fake name is a dead end they can happily waste their time on.

"Any personal belongings?"

Sven shakes his head.

"No, only the clothes he's wearing."

Nor did she expect anything else. The wallet containing the man's fake ID card and any other belongings must be at police forensics, where she can't reach them. Still, she has done well to get this far as it is.

"Shall we take a look?" Sven pulls down the zipper.

In contrast to the photos, the dead man is now lying on his back. As previously noted, his body is surprisingly well preserved.

The man is somewhere around middle age, with a relatively stocky build. The flannel shirt, jacket, and work pants that Asker already saw in the photos are intact, albeit dirty and discolored after so many years underground. One flap of his shirt hangs outside his pants.

His face is bearded, the mouth black and half-open. His eyes are closed, and his nose and cheeks are slightly misshapen from having lain compressed in the soil.

Asker pulls on a pair of plastic gloves, leans in closer, and checks the man's pockets. All empty, as expected. His clothes lack name tags or other leads. His hands are coarse and callused, and he wears no wedding ring.

The pinky finger on his right hand is missing its tip, an injury that to all appearances took place long before his death.

Asker's eyes linger on the finger stump for a few seconds. Something about the injury seems familiar, builds on the nagging feeling that she felt when viewing the photographs.

Ideally she would like to undress the man and examine his body more closely. But that can't be done on this narrow tray.

"Can we move him?"

Sven gives her an apologetic look.

"Too risky. I'm already breaking enough rules as it is."

"OK, I understand."

Asker examines the upper body again, as much as she can while he's clothed. There are no marks on his neck to suggest strangulation, and none of his arms or legs appear to be broken. His lips are gashed, and when she forces the mouth open she finds it full of clotted blood. His front teeth are also shattered.

"Looks like someone beat the shit out of him," Sven remarks.

Asker isn't so sure. She tugs at the dead man's lower lip.

The broken tooth stumps are angled outward, as though smashed from the inside.

"Help me get him on his side," she says.

Sven looks skeptical.

"Come on, pull him toward you. I want to check the back of his head."

Sven reluctantly obeys, and after a little huffing and puffing he manages to get the body up on its side.

The dead man's longish hair is caked with wet dirt. Asker searches for a point just between the neck and the base of the skull, at roughly the same height as the mouth. There is something there, just as she suspected. The skin has partly swollen back over, but when she stretches it back the wound is clear. A circular hole the width of a pinky finger.

"What is that?" Sven asks curiously.

"A bullet hole." Asker straightens up. "He was shot through the back of the head. The bullet's gone straight through the mouth, taking the front teeth with it. You can put him down now."

Sven does as she says, and Asker tugs off the plastic gloves.

An unmarried laborer with a fake ID, executed with a shot to the back of the head. That's what she knows. Plus that he's missing the tip of one finger.

She takes a step back and looks at the dead man again, and as she does so it is as though something clicks in her head. That nagging feeling finally relents.

"Shit," she mumbles to herself. "Uncle Tord."

SIXTEEN YEARS EARLIER

The summer heat has come in early, making the corrugated metal roofs of the Farm's barracks look like they are vibrating. Around the obstacle course and on the shooting range the weeds are already knee-high.

"Leo, this is Uncle Tord. He'll be staying with us every now and then."

The man her father is introducing is a few years older than him. He is also of a stockier build and has a salt-and-pepper beard.

"Hi!" she says, forcing a polite smile, and since Per throws her a stern glare, she even holds out her hand.

Per will give her a grilling once their guest has gone. Tell me five things about . . . is one of his favorite games, and if she makes the grade, it usually puts him in a good mood. If she really impresses him, he might even let her go camping with Martin at the weekend.

Per doesn't like her friendship with Martin Hill, doesn't like that she has her own life. But to forbid them from seeing each other would also be to admit that Martin poses some kind of threat. That a spindly little kid is so dangerous that Per Asker can only handle him by dishing out bans.

This gives Leo some wiggle room.

So, five things about Uncle Tord.

She looks him up and down. His hands are rough and callused, which means he uses them in his work. The pinky finger on his right hand is missing its tip, so on one occasion he was either unlucky or too hasty in his work.

No wedding ring—nor any indentation where one once was, or a ring on a necklace—so Uncle Tord is either single or long since divorced.

He is wearing a jacket, sturdy workman's pants, a flannel shirt, and boots. Looks like your average laborer. But Per wouldn't have invited him here if that was all he was.

"Nice to meet you, Leo."

Tord's accent is from the north. Far north, even. His gaze is keen, pleasant. He has noticed that her eyes have different colors.

She lets go of his hand.

An unmarried laborer, from the north, missing part of his finger.

That's not enough for any camping trip.

"Follow me, Tord, I'll show you around."

Per and the new guest head off toward one of the barracks. Leo watches their backs. Uncle Tord's movements are smooth and supple. He looks around attentively, though not out of curiosity; there's something more methodical to it. As though he were checking off one thing at a time, mapping out the whole place in his head.

Just before they disappear around the corner, he looks back over his shoulder and meets her gaze. Raises his chin a little, as if to say that he knows she's watching him.

What laborer does something like that?

As soon as the men are out of sight, she walks over to the cars.

Uncle Tord's pickup is positioned next to her father's. They are parked exactly the same way, backed in with the front facing out. Ready to go, as Prepper Per would say. He snorts at all the jackasses who don't realize that in an emergency the last thing you want is to have to reverse.

Tord's pickup has four doors and a covered cargo bed at the back instead of an open box. It's old, at least ten or fifteen years, and one of the passenger doors is in another color to the rest of the paintwork. The cover is locked with a hefty padlock, its small peephole reinforced with a metal grille.

She cups her hands to the tinted pane and tries to peer inside the cargo bed.

Closest to the peephole lie a few folded-up tripods, which doesn't give her much to go on. Beyond them she sees reels of cables, construction lights, and a few hefty toolboxes. All of them look a little rough around the edges and well used.

She walks around the car and peers into the cab. It hasn't been cleaned, the dashboard is dusty, and the front and back seats are badly worn. On the floor lie empty soda cans and fast-food packaging.

So Uncle Tord is a workman who likes junk food. That's hardly going to impress Per either.

Still, she gets the feeling that Tord's car, just like his workman's getup, is something of a front. Camouflage to hide what he's really up to.

A lazily folded tarpaulin on the floor of the back seat catches her eye. Why is it in the cab, and not in the cargo bed with all the other equipment?

She moves to get a better view.

It looks like there's something underneath it.

She checks the doors. They are locked, which might perhaps seem obvious. But who locks their car out here, in the middle of nowhere, inside a double-barbed-wire fence with surveillance cameras at every turn?

There are several possible answers to that question:

A) Someone who is used to always locking his car, no matter where it's parked.

B) Someone of a cautious disposition.

C) Someone who has something in his car that's of particular value to him.

Or, which she's already started to suspect:

D) All of the above.

She peers over the car roofs. Tord and her father are nowhere to be seen. But if she's going to find anything else, something that will satisfy Prepper Per, she's going to have to act fast.

She sneaks around the corner and into her trailer. Fetches the steel ruler that Per notched at one end.

She stands by the back door of the pickup that's closest to the tarpaulin, looks around once more, and then slips the ruler into the gap along the bottom of the window. Moves the ruler sideways along the inside of the door until it reaches the cable that runs between the inside handle and lock.

Per has made her practice this maneuver on every old, scrap-metal car at the Farm. Timed her. Even drove her to a superstore parking lot one night, so that she could practice in what he termed "real-life-adjacent circumstances."

With her practiced hand she catches the cable in the ruler's notch and pulls it up.

The cable is stretched, making the car door open with a faint click.

She slips the door open, crouches in the opening, and lifts the tarp.

The object beneath it is a black duffel bag.

The bag is full of money rolls; tight wads of hundred-kronor bills, each secured by a rubber band. She reaches her hand in farther and is about to pull one of them out when her fingers brush against something else. Something cold and familiar. Metal with a greasy oil film.

A revolver.

She wrenches it out of the bag. It's a snub-nosed thirty-eight with six cartridges in the chambers. She weighs the gun in her hand. Its serial number is missing, but Uncle Tord hasn't tried to sand it off like an amateur: he has used acid, which is guaranteed to make the figures illegible. Prepper Per would have given him an A+ for that method.

So engrossed is she with the gun that at first she doesn't notice the sounds. The approaching voices, the scrape of feet on gravel. Her father and Uncle Tord are coming back.

She quickly puts the revolver away, closes the duffel bag, and shoves it under the tarpaulin. Then shuts the car door as quietly as she can and prepares to slip away. But it's too late.

Per and Tord are already by the cars. She hears her father saying good-bye and something about going to open the gate. The sound of steps as they part ways.

Leo presses her back up against the door. Behind her and to her right and left lies only empty yard. She is on the driver's side of the car, and any second now Tord will round the corner and find her. There is only one way for her to avoid being caught.

She lies down flat on the ground and rolls under the pickup. It's tight— her arm brushes against the chassis—but she manages to get under just as Tord's feet and the rest of his body round the corner of the car.

She lies on her back, the steel ruler pressed to her chest. His feet are only a foot and a half from her face. Black army boots, just like Prepper Per's, a detail she should have picked up on before.

She holds her breath, waits for Tord to hop into the driver's seat so that she can roll on under Per's car.

Instead he stands by the door. Has he noticed that something is wrong? Did she forget to lock the car door?

Her pulse is pounding against her eardrums, and her entire body is screaming at her to get under Per's car and out the other side. But right now the yard is so quiet you could hear a pin drop. The slightest movement and Uncle Tord will hear her.

Something clatters to the gravel just a few feet from her face. A car key.

She sees Tord's knees bend, his upper body lean forward. Tries to press herself as far back into the car's shadows as possible. She sees his head, his face.

All he has to do is shift his gaze a matter of inches and he will see her squeezed under there like a frightened rabbit.

A cellphone starts to ring. Tord rummages around in his jacket pocket, sweeps up the car key, and stands up again.

"I'm on my way," she hears him say. "I'll be there in around an hour. Just calm down."

Leo inhales. Her heart is throbbing so hard that she fears he will hear it.

The car door opens, and the suspension rocks when he sits down in the driver's seat. Then the engine starts. Leo forces herself to stay put. If she's too hasty to roll out, she risks him seeing the movement in his right wing mirror. But if she lies there too long and the car pulls off, she will be fully visible in every rearview mirror.

She tenses up her body, readies herself.

The very second she hears the squeak of him declutching she pushes off with her feet and elbows.

She does two quick turns. Feels, rather than sees, the wheels of the pickup pass right by her head.

Then she's in under Per's car. Lies there waiting for the squeak of brakes. For Uncle Tord to come rushing out to confirm what he glimpsed on the ground in the rearview mirror.

But all she hears is the sound of a car disappearing into the distance.

"How many rolls were in the bag?" her father asks when she tells him about her discovery just minutes later.

His eyes twinkle with interest.

"At least twenty-five," she says. "And a snub-nosed thirty-eight. Loaded."

"Twenty-five rolls of hundreds." He strokes his chin as though trying to calculate a sum. "And you got no idea of who he was talking to on the phone?"

"No," said Leo. "Though he said he'd be with that person in an hour. With his beat-up car and these narrow roads, that gives a radius of fifty miles, max. Probably less."

Per nods slowly.

"Excellent," he says with a pleased nod that makes her heart thrum a few jubilant double beats. "Good work, Leo!"

HILL

He has had trouble sleeping ever since those first nights at the hospital. Has been plagued by nightmares—by flashbacks to darkness, blood, and grave danger.

But tonight his sleeplessness has another, much more positive, cause.

The prospect of getting to explore Boulder Isle and Astrofield Mine is so exciting that his brain just can't switch off. Not to mention the fact that he will be staying on the Astroholm estate, where he will get to meet Space-Case Gunnar Irving in the flesh.

At around two a.m. he gives up, drags himself out of bed, makes himself a cup of chamomile tea, and sits down on the couch. He resists the impulse to binge-watch some mindless TV series and instead checks his phone, but Leo still hasn't messaged to say how things went at the forensic medicine division.

The whole situation with her father concerns him. Prepper Per's narcissism is so great that he has the nerve to ask Leo for help, even though he once tried to kill her.

And she has no other choice but to go along with it.

Hill feels bad that he can't be more involved, but Astroholm, AlphaCent, and the Irving family have come to occupy most of his thoughts. He takes comfort in the fact that at least he was able to help Leo get a look at the corpse. And he plans to keep in touch with her while he's away.

They are coming to collect him that very morning. It was his suggestion; it's hardly like he has anything better to do. Nova Irving seemed delighted by his eagerness to get started, and she promised to send a car by ten a.m. Since then he has been busy: his bag is packed, his plants watered, his fridge emptied.

He takes a sip of tea. Normally he doesn't like chamomile—it's Sofie who wants to have it in the pantry. But if it helps him sleep, then he's prepared to down a whole tub of it. He needs to be fresh and alert tomorrow.

Ready to take on the assignment with zeal.

While waiting for the tea to take effect, he googles AlphaCent. Five years have passed since he wrote his book, and his research isn't completely up to date, so this feels like a good use of his time. He finds a few interviews with Nova Irving about the company's latest ventures, including a collaboration with NASA, which one droll finance journalist likened to being *summoned to the mothership*.

After that Hill does searches on Miresjön Lake and Boulder Isle, which bring up an unexpectedly dramatic result. "Man Found Dead in Miresjön." The article is over three years old, and it comes from one of the bigger morning papers.

> The body of a 77 year old Malmö resident reported missing last winter was found yesterday on the shore of Miresjön Lake.
>
> In February this year police discovered a car parked behind a Boy Scouts' cabin on the eastern side of the lake that was linked to two men from Malmö who had been reported missing some weeks before. It was also noted that the red boat belonging to the Scout cabin was missing.
>
> Since the men had a documented interest in urban exploration, that's to say the exploration of abandoned buildings and sites, the police concluded that they had likely stolen the boat in an attempt to reach Boulder Isle and explore the abandoned mine located beneath it.
>
> A search of Boulder Isle found no traces of either man or the missing boat, leading to fears that they had come into trouble on the lake and lost their lives, a hypothesis borne out by yesterday's tragic discovery.
>
> The police and rescue services have resumed dragging the lake for the other missing man, but it is a complex undertaking given the depth of the lake and the difficulty of the conditions at its bed.

Hill does more searches into the incident but finds only variants of the same information.

Two urban explorers drowned while trying to reach Boulder Isle. Why didn't he know about this before?

Of course, it could have something to do with the fact that he has stopped frequenting the usual chat forums. Besides his excursions with Sofie in search of her missing brother, it has been a long time since Hill went on an outing with anyone from the UE world.

He navigates to one of the forums he used to visit when he was at his most active, but finds that it has been shut down. He tries another. It takes a while for him to remember his username and password.

Does anyone know anything about the guys who drowned in Miresjön Lake three years ago? he writes, then sends the question out into cyberspace.

A faint sound makes him look up from his phone screen.

The mail slot in his door clicks, then falls silent. It's not even three a.m., so the paperboy must be out very early.

With some effort he gets to his feet and walks over to fetch the newspaper, only to find a long white envelope lying on his hallway mat instead.

For Martin Hill, it reads.

He opens the envelope. It contains a single sheet of paper, folded neatly in three. The paper is thick and expensive, and the handwriting rounded, written in marker pen.

Astroholm Manor is a haunted place. A treacherous place.
   He who goes there in search of Irving secrets must tread very carefully.

                             Regards
                             A friend

TUESDAY

HELLMAN

As always he is the first into work, a habit he picked up early on in his police career. That the chief is the first one on the job sends a message, sets a benchmark of professionalism.

He makes sure that all lights on the sixth floor are lit, and that the vertical blinds on the glass partition wall to his office are drawn open. After that he turns on his computer, works through his emails and checks the news so that he is completely up to date.

At seven thirty on the dot he makes himself a double espresso from the expensive coffee machine in the kitchen, after which he does his rounds of the office.

He greets his colleagues, while meticulously noting who is there and already hard at work, and who has elected not to show up until just before the morning briefing at eight a.m.

Just days ago, when he formally took over as department chief, the latter group was considerably larger. But that ratio is swiftly changing, thanks to his morning routine. Their department needs to up its productivity, and significantly, at that. The gang shootings are draining far too many resources, and there are plenty of other cases that need investigating before the leads run cold.

Within three months he expects to have full control—to have stripped away the dead meat and replenished the team with new, hungrier colleagues. Made the department more professional, more efficient, fast.

After his rounds he returns to his desk.

In three minutes Eskil will knock on his door for a quick update before the morning briefing. Hellman has promoted Eskil to head of section and given him Asker's old job and office. Informally he has also made him his second-in-command.

Since Eskil had his ear blown off in the search for Smilla Holst's kidnappers, no one can say the promotion is undeserved.

Still, Hellman can't help but find him irritating.

His vanity, his men's-mag fashion sense, and his Tinder swiping; the way he persists in detailing the story of his gunshot wound for anyone who cares to listen, parading the dressings on his injured ear like an accessory.

Though of course it isn't really Eskil who annoys him. The Holst case may have been a triumph that landed him the job of department chief, but something about the whole thing leaves a bitter taste in his mouth.

He would rather not be reminded of what happened.

What *actually* happened.

Which leads his thoughts to Leo Asker.

He has been wondering what she is up to ever since her little telephone charade. Why was she trying to bluff her way to information about a cold case out in the sticks?

Perhaps she's just out to mess with him. Wants to hijack the case and solve it under his and her former department's nose, just like she did with the Holst case.

But if it was merely a case of her wanting to show off her skills, she would have no shortage of current cases to choose from. Instead she has chosen an ice-cold case that would normally sail under the radar. Which means that something about the case must be important, at least to her.

Something that he hasn't understood. It is just one of the many things that annoy him about Leo Asker: that she always seems to be one step ahead. She sees details and connections that he must exert himself to catch.

He dreams about her sometimes. About them together.

The attraction, the tension.

Their bodies intertwining, her movements following his in a slow progression toward the climax that his dreams always cheat him of.

Instead he wakes up in the dead of night, rock-hard, while his wife lies asleep beside him. Sometimes he has to sneak to the bathroom and take matters into his own hands. Force Leo Asker out of his system, at least temporarily.

Maybe that's what riles him the most: that she still has power over him. That no matter how hard he tries, he can never quite rid himself of her.

Eskil knocks on the glass door and Hellman waves him in.

He is carrying a file under his right arm, and as usual he is dressed as though he's about to shoot an ad campaign for Hugo Boss, reeking of aftershave and expensive moisturizer. The dressing over his ear is a size smaller now, which is something, at least.

"The day's cases . . ." Eskil begins as soon as he's sat down, but Hellman holds up his hand.

"The body found up in the borderlands, where are we on that?" he asks.

Eskil looks thrown, but quickly finds his feet.

"Well, the body's at the forensic medicine division in Lund. You could say it's not exactly going anywhere fast . . ."

He looks as though he's about to drop a punchline.

"What do we know about him?" Hellman cuts him off.

Eskil sits up straighter, now more serious.

"We found a driver's license in his wallet, so we have a preliminary identity. I'm assuming the autopsy will take a week or so; the same for the dental records and DNA tests. I was going to suggest we transfer the whole investigation to another department. I mean, we have more important things to be working on than cold cases."

He pauses, as though expecting agreement.

"What's the dead man's name?" Hellman asks.

"Uh . . ." Eskil leafs through the file. "Kurtz. Walter Konrad Kurtz."

Hellman raises his eyebrows.

"Did you say Walter *Konrad* Kurtz?"

Eskil nods. "That's the name on his license, anyway. I can ask someone to check him out, if you want. We haven't given it any time; I thought that that would be a task for whichever department takes over the investigation . . ."

Hellman shakes his head.

"There's no point. The license is a fake."

"How do you know that?"

Hellman sighs. He should have chosen a different right-hand man. One of the sharper tools in the box.

"Because Walter Kurtz is Marlon Brando's character in *Apocalypse Now*," he says.

Eskil shrugs.

"So what? Can't someone have the same name?"

Hellman shakes his head.

"The film happens to be based on a book written by Joseph Conrad. Walter *Konrad* Kurtz."

"Ah."

Eskil finally seems to have cottoned on.

Hellman thinks for a while. A murdered man with a fake ID who has piqued Leo Asker's interest.

He simply can't ignore it.

"OK, here's what we're going to do," he says. "We're keeping the case. Tell the forensic medicine division to prioritize that autopsy. Dental profile, DNA, everything. I want the corpse identified and the cause of death established today. And send out patrols to knock on doors at nearby properties."

Eskil appears to want to protest, but Hellman interrupts him before he can open his mouth.

"What the fuck are you waiting for? Hop to it!"

ASKER

She is at work long before dawn. Through her grimy window at the bottom of the internal atrium she sees the lights go on up in Serious Crime.

Jonas Hellman is up there, in the office that should be hers. Presumably by now he has figured out that the dead man's ID is a fake, and, having pieced that together with her own interest in the investigation, has made the case a priority.

That means that her narrow head start has already shrunk.

She slept restlessly, got up in the middle of the night and took her backpack out of the wardrobe.

The same backpack that Prepper Per taught her to fill with everything she might need should a quick getaway be required. She still has it at the ready after all these years, easy to reach, all set for an escape.

Unpacking and repacking it usually gives her some kind of solace. But not tonight.

After she confided in Martin about what really happened to her as a teenager, the night her father tried to kill them both with his own homemade explosives, she experienced a few wonderful days of total freedom. As though an enormous burden had lifted.

But now Prepper Per is back, after fifteen years of complete silence, almost as if he knew she was about to cast off those last remnants of his influence.

She steps into the corridor to see if Rosen is in yet, but of course it's still too early.

Instead she calls her former local municipality and reaches an early-bird staffer whom she persuades to go down into the archives and locate the work order for the road barrier.

As soon as she has those details, she puts pen to paper and starts outlining what she knows. Uncle Tord's body was buried under the spot where the last trash heap was dumped before the facility was closed with a road barrier. Thanks to the lady at the municipality she now knows that the barrier was installed on September 9, 2006, that's to say just over sixteen years ago, just weeks after she last saw Uncle Tord at the Farm. This gives her some kind of time frame for the murder.

And one clear conclusion: Her father is absolutely a possible suspect.

Money was always scarce on the Farm, and Uncle Tord's duffel bag and money rolls certainly interested Per. He also had the skills, weapons, and cold-blooded ruthlessness to perform the execution. It is only too easy for her to imagine him pulling the trigger.

But if Per murdered Uncle Tord, why would he dump the body on his own doorstep? He's far too smart for that.

Besides, Tord was buried only a few feet deep, right at the entrance to the dump. In normal cases one would assume the body would have been found pretty quickly. Scavengers would have dug it up, birds attracted the attention of a passing mushroom forager. But instead municipality workers came along and dumped a giant pile of branches and soil right on top of the corpse. Threw up a barrier and shut off the facility, making the body almost impossible to find. Had the assassin really been able to count on that?

It feels unlikely. Had they wanted to prevent the body from being found, why not bury it deeper, or somewhere much less frequented than a public dump?

Her father knows many such places.

No, her inkling is that whoever dumped the body actually wanted it to be found, but a twist of fate foiled their plans.

She tries to summon more memories of Uncle Tord, but that's easier said than done, especially when she has spent the last fifteen years actively trying to forget as much as she can about both her father and the Farm. Bury whatever there was left, as deeply as her consciousness would allow. She shuts her eyes, pinches the bridge of her nose.

Uncle Tord visited the Farm sporadically that summer. Stayed the night a few times, she seems to recall.

But, much to her frustration, despite her best attempts she can find no other memory of him that she can use to get any further, not even so much as a surname.

And up on the sixth floor Hellman is getting closer.

When the clock is nearing nine, she gets up and steps into the corridor on the hunt for Rosen for what must be the tenth time that morning, but the diminutive woman is still yet to be seen.

Virgilsson, however, appears to have taken note of her interest.

"Might I be of assistance with anything?" he asks through his open office door.

Asker shakes her head.

"Are you sure, Chief? You do seem rather restless."

He peers at her over the rims of his reading glasses.

"Impatient, more like," she says. "Do you know where Rosen is?"

"No, sadly." He slides his glasses up his nose while studying her carefully. "It's only you, Zafer, and I here. Attila's off sick for at least the rest of the week. Typical that it should happen to be the same week he was scheduled to visit Madame Rind."

Virgilsson raises his eyebrows. It takes Asker a few seconds to grasp what he's getting at. Madame Rind is the medium whom the department staff take turns to visit, to prevent her from swamping the police switchboard with well-intended tips and predictions. Asker has neither the time nor the inclination to humor that kind of nonsense, and she is about to say as much to Virgilsson when the elevator doors open and Rosen steps out. Though it's only November, the woman is wrapped up in a thick winter coat, a scarf looped around her neck three times, and a knitted hat pulled so far down her forehead that you can barely see her eyes.

"Where have you been?" Asker hisses.

"At the dentist . . ."

Rosen hurries past her and into her office. Asker follows her, shuts the door behind them, and waits for Rosen to take off her outdoor clothes.

"The searches I asked you for . . ." she begins, without high hopes. But Rosen surprises her.

"Oh yes, they're ready. I stayed in for a while last night since I knew I'd be late this morning. Unfortunately there were rather a lot of names, so I created a database."

She sits down at her desk and turns on the computer.

"Do you have anyone there with the first name Tord?" Asker asks. "From Norrland, missing for sixteen years?"

Rosen taps her keyboard in keen concentration.

"I have a Tord Olof Korpi, forty-nine years old, from Kiruna," she says. "Reported missing in 2006. Could that be him?"

Asker tries to contain her excitement.

"Possibly. Is there any data about a car?" she asks, remembering Uncle Tord's dark pickup.

Rosen types again. Her fingers dash across the keys at lightning speed.

"Nothing registered in his name. He's strangely clean in almost every database, except that of the National Enforcement Agency, for debts. No cars, no valid passport, no criminal record. No employment, property, or fixed address—just a PO box."

"But he had a driver's license?"

"Oh yes, I'll try to pull up a photo." She starts typing again.

Asker rounds the desk and stands over Rosen's shoulder to take in her double screens. The woman works breathtakingly fast, with at least ten different databases open on her screens at any given time. The police database, of course, but also directories belonging to several other authorities, and the records of a few private actors, as well.

Rosen bounces information from screen to screen, almost like she's playing table tennis. She takes one piece of information from one place, cross-checks it in another, then pulls up new information that she bounces somewhere else. All while copying everything she finds to her own Excel database.

It's impossible to be anything but impressed.

"You mentioned debts with the National Enforcement Agency?" Asker asks.

"Yes." Rosen's eyes don't leave the screens. "One massive tax debt, and a company that went bust. He doesn't appear to have had any assets left, and he hadn't had any income for several years before his disappearance."

Rosen's fingers continue to fly across the keys. Her usual nervous energy is as though vanished, replaced by self-confidence.

"There," she says with one final keyboard crescendo. "I've found the original missing person's report and Korpi's driving license photo."

She points at the right-hand screen. The man in the image is clean-shaven and younger than Asker remembers him, but there's still no doubt about it. It's Uncle Tord.

"That's him!" she says. "What else do we know about him?"

Rosen reads off the screen. "His ex-wife Gertrud Korpi reported him missing in December 2006. She said she hadn't heard from him in a few months, and that he'd stopped paying rent. The case was closed after a week since there was no sign of any crime."

"Was the ex-wife interviewed?"

"I'm sure she was, but back then the whole process wasn't digitized, so I'd imagine the original's lying at the bottom of some police archive up in Kiruna."

Rosen seems to sense Asker's disappointment, because she immediately opens a new window and taps on the keys.

"But you can call his ex-wife directly," she says, pointing at the result. "Gertrud Korpi still lives at the same address. I'll print out her phone number for you, along with the other documents. You can collect them from the printer."

Asker heads toward the door. As she does so, it is as though Rosen shrinks a few inches. She becomes her usual self again, starts anxiously picking at the sleeve of her cardigan.

Asker stops with one hand on the door handle.

"Good work, Rosen," she says. "You really are an asset to this department."

The diminutive woman blushes and looks away, but her back straightens up a touch.

When Asker is approaching the print room, she sees the back of Virgilsson's sweater vest. The nosy little toad is flicking through her printouts.

"Those are mine," she says sharply.

He turns around, and for a second he looks genuinely surprised. But he quickly finds his feet.

"Of course. I had a few printouts, too; they seem to have gotten mixed up. Here you are!"

He hands over a few sheets of paper. Asker skims them. The missing person's report, Tord Korpi's driving license details, the address and phone number of his ex-wife; all of it is there.

"It must be an important case," says Virgilsson, conjuring up one of his slippery little smiles. "I mean, since you asked Rosen for help?"

"Not exactly," she says.

She takes the papers and heads for her office while his eyes burn holes in the back of her head. She makes sure the door is shut securely before sitting down in her creaky desk chair.

Now she knows who the dead man was. And it's probably only a matter of time before Hellman knows, too.

Still, Hellman couldn't possibly know that Korpi was a guest at the Farm.

Besides the fact that his body was found just outside the property's gates, there is nothing to definitively link Korpi to Prepper Per.

No immediate danger.

At least not yet.

THE GLASS MAN

The worst of the awakening is behind him now. The pain has faded; the cold that had pierced his very marrow has finally relented.

His muscles have grown a great deal, his fine motor skills are almost restored, and his eyes are sensitive to light. His daily exercises are going all the better.

Soon he will be ready for release, will be allowed to move freely once again.

He spends much of his time in front of the mirror. Studies his face in the dim light. Lingers on his eyes.

They are so different from how he remembers them.

Sometimes this worries him.

He has always been fascinated by eyes. *With the eyes one can travel between worlds, Prince Pollux,* as his father used to say.

Waking and sleep.

Light and dark.

Life and death.

The eyes are the windows to the soul. So powerful, and yet so incredibly slight. All the parts so flimsy you can all but hear it in their names.

Cornea, lens, pupil.

And then his favorite.

The vitreous body; the glassy body.

These fragile spheres float weightlessly in the eye sockets, just like the frog he was once given by his father.

He thinks of that glass frog sometimes. Wonders where it went; if it is still waiting for the warmth of spring, for the life that will never return. This thought saddens him.

He carefully touches his face. It has changed so much he hardly recognizes it. Has grown wider and more angular, as though it were no longer his.

His eyes have also grown. Become darker with each new awakening.

The Father says that is a side effect of the treatment, that it poses no danger. Most of the time he contents himself with that. The thought that his father's all-seeing eye is watching over him.

But sometimes, like now, a quiet voice will slip into his head.

Whisper that he is losing what little of him still remains.

And that there is no way back.

ASKER

Gertrud Korpi picks up the phone after two rings. Asker introduces herself, keeping her story fairly close to the truth.

"And you're sure it's him?"

Uncle Tord's ex-wife sounds more tired than sad as she poses the question.

"I'm afraid so," Asker replies. "I'm sorry for your loss."

Gertrud sighs.

"Well, I suppose I've suspected this day would come. Sixteen years is a long time. But sorry, where did you say you found him?"

"In the borderlands between the provinces of Skåne and Småland."

A lighter clicks, followed by a deep drag, the faint crackle of burning cigarette paper.

"Do you know if Tord knew anyone in the area?"

Asker tries to maintain a neutral tone of voice. The woman on the end of the line exhales the smoke in what sounds like one long sigh.

"No idea. We'd been divorced five years when he disappeared."

"But you were still in contact?" Asker asks. "Since you're the one who reported him missing, I mean."

"Tord rented a cottage from my brother, so he'd come by now and then to pay the rent. Have a cup of coffee, a little chat. We weren't enemies. When he stopped coming by, I started to wonder. My brother checked the cottage, and the few possessions Tord had were still there. That's when I called the police."

"Tord paid the rent in cash, didn't he?"

"Well, uh . . ."

"I only ask because Tord doesn't appear to have had any fixed employment—he declared no income, took no benefits. But since he still kept up with the rent, I presume he must have been working off the books. Would that be a reasonable conclusion to draw?"

Another smoke-sigh.

"That's probably the case. But I didn't involve myself in any of that. And, like I said, it was sixteen years ago."

"So you wouldn't know who he worked for, or with?"

"No, no idea."

This answer comes as a relief to Asker. She can't ask about Prepper Per outright—especially not if Hellman's gang are hot on her heels—but this is close enough. Still, she needs to probe a little further, try to find out if there is anything else that could link Tord to the Farm.

"How did you meet?" she asks.

"At a pub in town. Tord had just moved back up north to work as some kind of overman at the mine. He was from round here, but he'd lived abroad for many years."

"Do you know where?"

"No, not really. Here and there, I think. Tord kept pretty tight-lipped about his past. I'm sure he had his fair share of shady dealings behind him, but I found him exciting. Back then he had money, and he'd whisk me away for dinners and trips."

"And how long did he work at the mine?"

"Not so long. He started his own company just after we got married. Went on working for the mine, but as a consultant. And it all went well for a few years. We bought a house, did some traveling."

"And then what?"

"Tord ran into problems. The Tax Agency found out he'd sold an overseas company without declaring the profits. Tord appealed and kept working, but it made no difference. By then he was already broke."

"So he was declared bankrupt."

"Eventually. But we'd divorced long before that. Things had been difficult for a while. I mean, Tord was ten years older than me, and living with him was no bed of roses. But he was very generous in the divorce; he let me keep the house and cars."

Gertrud pauses to take another drag. She is surprisingly talkative, Asker notes. Perhaps she is relieved to finally get answers to what happened to her ex-husband and so wants to be as helpful as possible. That or she's just glad that someone is taking an interest in what she has to say.

"Tord took the bankruptcy hard," Gertrud goes on. "He felt like the authorities were out to get him. Claimed they were tracking his bank accounts, credit card statements, even his cell. So he did his best to fly under the radar. But I don't actually know what he was doing."

"But if you were to guess?" Asker pushes.

The woman gives a few dry coughs.

"Well, I'd assume it was some kind of construction work. The few times I did see him he'd be wearing workman's clothes, and he drove around in this rickety old pickup packed full of tools, which of course wasn't registered in his name."

"What color was it, do you remember?"

"Only that it was dark, and that one of the doors was a different color from the rest."

Asker nods to herself. It must be the same truck she broke into at the Farm.

Her mind jumps back to something the woman said right at the start of the call.

"Your brother owned the cottage that Tord rented. And you mentioned that he'd checked the place and found his belongings still there?"

"Yes, that's right."

"Did you find a computer, or a cellphone?"

The woman laughs.

"No, Tord was terrified of being tracked. He didn't own a computer, and only used prepaid phones that he was changing all the time. All we found in the cottage were some clothes and a few other odds and ends."

"Did you keep them, by any chance?"

"Not the clothes—I donated them to charity long ago—but I do still have one box of small things out in my garage. I suppose I should have gotten rid of them, but for a long time I held out hope that Tord would get in touch. Say that he'd moved abroad or something. So the box just stayed there. You can have it if you want."

Tempted as Asker is, there is no way that she can ask Gertrud to send her the belongings. If Hellman were to find out, he could charge her with withholding evidence.

On the other hand, looking isn't a crime.

"If you could take some photos of the items, that would be plenty," she says. "At least for the time being. Ideally right now, if you have time?"

"Of course." Silence, which means the woman has just realized something. "So . . . do you think he was murdered?"

"We're awaiting the results of the autopsy, but I'm afraid everything points that way," Asker replies.

The woman lets out a sigh, which could equally be a sob.

Asker gives her a few seconds.

"It would be really good if you could send me the photos of his belongings as soon as possible," she says, as gently as she can.

Gertrude takes a shaky breath. Seems to be composing herself.

"OK," she says. "Give me a few minutes."

While waiting at her desk for Tord's ex-wife to send the photos, Asker notes that she still hasn't come across any traceable link between Tord and Per.

Perhaps the old tinfoil-hatters were paranoid enough not to leave any trace of how their paths crossed. If so, she can rest easy. Step back and let the investigation die out on its own on a cold-case shelf in Hellman's office.

Her phone beeps.

She glances through the images. In an open cardboard box on a garage floor lie a couple of paperback thrillers, a stress ball bearing a company logo, an old framed photograph, a thick textbook on underground construction, and then, finally, a prize plaque of some kind.

She transfers the images to her computer and enlarges them, starting with the old photograph. The colors are faded with age. Five men in overalls and hard hats, taken in a location much closer to the equator. What is presumably the eighties version of Tord Korpi stands in the middle. She zooms in and carefully inspects the men's faces, one at a time. Fortunately none of them look remotely familiar.

In the background a truck tarpaulin is visible. Something is written in spray paint on one side. She zooms in even more, until she can make out the text. THE BUNKER RATS.

So Tord Korpi built bunkers for a living.

That would explain why Prepper Per invited him to the Farm. But it's no definitive proof that the two men knew each other.

She flicks through the rest of the images. The books are uninteresting, and the logo on the stress ball turns out to belong to Korpi's now-defunct company, which according to Google offered "consulting services within the mining industry."

Which leaves the prize plaque. Something about it looks familiar. Asker zooms in and stiffens.

It's no prize plaque; it's a coat of arms. A yellow parachute against a red background, with three words engraved beneath it.

She knows what they say, even though the text in the image is blurred.

And she knows who has an identical plaque.

TWENTY-FOUR YEARS EARLIER

It is the middle of the night, she is six years old, and they all live together in the big, luxurious apartment in the very center of Malmö. No one in the world does she admire more than her father.

But recently she has noticed that something is troubling him, and he is staying up later and later at night. He clatters angrily on his keyboard, speaks loudly on the phone, has heated conversations with her mother.

Her little sister Camille is only four, so she is too young to see it, but Leo can tell that something is up. Something she doesn't like. Maybe that's why she is sleeping so restlessly?

She climbs out of bed, peers into the hall, and sees that the light is still on in her father's study.

She sneaks over to it, spies through the crack in the door.

He is sitting in his favorite armchair, with his head tipped back against the backrest. His eyes are shut, and he might be asleep, but she doubts it. She has never seen her father sleeping—not really, at least.

But she sneaks inside anyway.

Before him on the desk lie stacks of paper. Drawings, maps. Some of them with angry notes in red ink.

She knows she isn't allowed to be here without permission. This is his sacred place, and no kids may enter.

But tonight her father looks so lonely there in that armchair. So tired.

She sneaks up onto the chair opposite him.

Sits there, quiet as a mouse, studying his face.

His brow is furrowed and his jaws gently clench, as though he is having an unpleasant dream.

Only now does she notice that he is holding something in his hands.

The coat of arms that usually hangs on the wall behind his desk.

In the years to come she will understand why he took it down; that he was dreaming his way back to simpler times. Trying to quell the seed of Prepper Per that had started to sprout in his brain.

But Leo has no idea what is yet to come. What that poisonous seed will turn into.

Tonight she is just a six-year-old girl keeping her father company in the middle of the night, since she thinks he looks so lonely.

"What are you doing up so late, Leo?" her father asks without warning, and Leo gives a start in fright.

He hasn't moved an inch, has just half-opened his eyes.

Exactly as she suspected. Her father never sleeps. He is always present, ever watchful, always ready.

She gets up hastily, expecting to be told off, to be sent straight back to bed.

Instead something unexpected happens.

"Sit with me awhile," he says softly.

He shifts position, setting the coat of arms down on the desk.

Her eyes follow it.

A yellow parachute against a red background.

Three engraved words that she knows are very important to him. That she has learned by heart for that very reason.

Courage, endurance, resolve.

HILL

Hill steps out of his front door in good time before the car is scheduled to arrive. The November air is piercing, and a blanket of mist hangs over the roof ridges and treetops. He shudders, buttons his jacket tighter around him, and leans onto his crutch.

A big, black Mercedes pulls up to the curb. At the wheel sits Samuel, the athletic, slightly grizzled man who met him on the steps the day before and introduced himself as the chief security officer. Samuel loads Hill's bag into the trunk, then holds the door for him while he bundles himself and his crutch onto the spacious back seat. Hill notices that his wound feels tighter than the previous day.

"So, off to Astroholm," Samuel says as he pulls off. "Feel free to rest if you want; the journey will take a little while."

But Hill is far too excited to sleep. His assignment has just begun, and finally he has the chance not only to ask questions, but also to get answers—real answers that aren't rumor or legend.

"How long have you worked for the Irving family?" he asks.

"Almost twenty years."

"You must like your job."

Samuel nods. "It's an honor to work for Gunnar Irving."

Hill once again finds himself searching for something to offset this somewhat overblown statement, but he comes up empty.

"And what did you do before?" he tries.

"Private security. The army before that."

Samuel speaks perfect Swedish, but Hill nevertheless picks up a hint of an accent.

"American?" he asks.

"Israeli, actually, but I've spent some time in the USA."

Samuel deigns to throw him a curt smile.

"Oh, you're a long way from home."

"Astroholm is my home."

Yet another surprising response. Hill loses his train of thought.

"Your injury," Samuel says, just when Hill has resigned himself to the fact that the rest of the journey will be made in silence. "I heard you got shot? By a serial killer?"

Hill nods.

"You are lucky to have survived."

"Mm-hm."

Hill would rather not be reminded of the Mountain King, but the topic appears to interest Samuel.

"And if I understood correctly, the murderer's dead? Shot by a female police officer?"

"That's right." Hill notes that their roles have reversed; now Samuel is the one asking the questions.

"Detective Inspector Leo Asker, wasn't that her name?" Samuel looks at him in the rearview mirror.

"Mm-hm."

"How well do you know each other?"

"You could say we're old friends."

This line of questioning is putting Hill on edge, and he turns away demonstratively. Samuel takes the hint.

"Astroholm has an excellent doctor," he offers, as though to smooth things over. "Dr. Schiller has worked for Gunnar for even longer than I have. He has access to the absolute latest treatment methods. You'll be feeling better in no time."

A faint phone signal rings out. Samuel places a Bluetooth ear-piece in one ear.

"We're on our way," he says to the person on the line. "It's foggy, so we'll be a little late. ETA of eleven fifty."

He says something else, but Hill has stopped listening, relieved at the interruption. Samuel certainly seems well informed; perhaps he is the one who did all the research into him on Nova Irving's behalf. Either way, Hill has no interest in talking about Leo with him.

He sits back in his seat. This is the most luxurious car he has ever traveled in. The back seats are plush and adjustable, the legroom enormous.

At around the same time that they join the freeway, Hill's eyelids start to feel heavy. The mysterious letter that he received occupied his brain for most of the night, but his thoughts haven't gotten him all that far.

Who could have already known that he had been commissioned to write AlphaCent's book? And why was the anonymous letter-writer so keen to warn him that they felt compelled to personally deliver a handwritten message in the dead of the night—as opposed to an anonymous email or text message, say?

And what kind of warning is the letter anyway?

On first reading, the easiest conclusion to draw was that the letter was intended to make him steer clear of Astroholm. However, after a few more readings, he now believes the secret letter-writer had another purpose in mind: they didn't want to prevent him from going, but simply to *warn* him.

He who goes there in search of Irving secrets must tread very carefully.

His mind turns to the tragedy involving the two urban explorers. They set out in search of Irving family secrets, only to drown in the icy waters of Miresjön Lake.

And now he, too, is embarking on a similar quest. Should he turn down the job? A stupid question—no warning letter in the world could convince him to pass up this opportunity.

Besides, he has the Irving family's full backing, and he won't need to go out onto the lake in the middle of the night. His thoughts can get no further before his eyelids fall shut.

Hill wakes up when the car jolts over a speedbump next to some roadwork. He stretches, trying to figure out if he might have drooled, snored, or slumped into some less flattering position during his nap.

He quickly adjusts his blazer and shirt, as if to restore his dignity. It is almost quarter to twelve, so they must be close. Rifts in the dense forest reveal patches of farmland, pastures, and dry-stone walls.

Fog skulks at the edges of the forest, egged on by the low cloud.

They travel through a village that Hill remembers from his research for the chapter in his book. Unassuming houses with corrugated fiber-cement roofs, wooden façades, and algae-green aboveground swimming pools. A few older buildings from more prosperous times. The center is clustered around a square, which boasts a florist, a small grocery store, a hairdresser, a small community library, and the obligatory all-purpose fast-food restaurant, with a sign out on the sidewalk bearing a pizza, a salad, and a kebab.

A little way out of the center they pass a low building that has seen better days. On its roof stands a large, red, fiberglass flying saucer that looks very homemade, alongside a plastic sign that reads UFO CAFÉ.

The place was closed the last time he was here, but now a car is parked in the parking lot and the lights are on inside. Perhaps he should make another attempt to visit the café one of these days? Find out how much of the UFO hysteria has survived.

They have reached the end of the village, and once again the fields start to give way to forest, this time consisting more of broad-leaved trees than conifers. Bare crowns extend their splayed branches up toward the low sky.

The car drives down a long avenue of trees before Samuel comes to a stop in front of a beautiful, stately wrought-iron gate. On either side of the gate, a solid brick wall at least fifteen feet high extends so far in both directions that it is swallowed up by the fog. Up on the gateposts sit two surveillance cameras. Beneath them, identical signs clearly announce that this is private property.

"The Irvings prefer a certain level of seclusion," Samuel explains as the gate opens. "The grounds cover almost a thousand acres."

"How many people live on the estate?" Hill asks.

Samuel hesitates for a second, as if considering what to say.

"About a dozen," he eventually decides.

"Mostly family members?"

"Yes, that's right."

They drive through the gates. Just inside them and to the right stands a concrete box with mirrored glass windows. Behind it a small parking lot with a few parked cars.

"The guard station," Samuel says. "It's manned at all times."

The road is slightly hilly, and it winds through a deciduous forest with bare crowns. The fog hangs over the ground like gray smoke.

After a few hundred yards they reach a peak. The forest retreats, and before them appear gardens with large flowerbeds and lawns. Turnoffs along either side of the road lead to houses nestled along the forest's edge.

"Those are the guest villas," says Samuel. "You'll be staying in one of them, but we'll head down to the manor house first, to give you an overview of the grounds."

The road leads to a low bridge over a large pond full of water lilies. On the far side of the pond, a large, manor-like building in an extraordinary architectural style towers up out of the mist. Hill's heart beats a little faster.

"So this is Astroholm Manor," Samuel says as they slowly circle a large fountain.

Hill presses his face to the window. He has seen photos of Astroholm before, but never taken at such close range. The building is two stories tall and must be over two hundred feet wide and perhaps half as deep. Its design is bizarre to say the least, with gloomy arched windows that stand in sharp contrast to the brutalist columns lining its façade. The roof is topped with all manner of pinnacles, ledges, and sharp angles, creating the same upward-striving impression as AlphaCent's headquarters did. It is built in a kind of light stone that Hill hasn't seen in person before.

"Rhyolite," he says to himself. "From Astrofield Mine on Boulder Isle."

Astroholm Manor is fascinating enough from the outside; Hill can only imagine what the inside holds in store. When he was younger he used to have a sixth sense for sniffing out buildings' hidden secrets.

He would like nothing more than to get started right away, but Samuel has already circled the fountain and started to drive back the same way they came.

Only now does Hill notice that in the middle of the fountain stands an identical sculpture to the one he saw in the lobby at Alpha-Cent's headquarters.

The young Gunnar Irving in black glass, gazing up at the stars.

They cross the bridge and once again pass the turnoffs to the guesthouses. At the farthest one Samuel turns off. He follows the drive up to the forest's edge, where he stops before a residence built in the same rhyolite material and incongruous style as the manor house.

The house is two stories tall, topped with a green copper roof. Stone gargoyles perch beneath the eaves.

"Villa Arcturus," says Samuel. "This is where you'll be staying."

THE GLASS MAN

For many years the Father's light shone down on him, raised him up, bathed him in gold. Made him brilliant.

He was the son, the heir.

Prince Pollux, for whom nothing and no one was good enough.

His school years were one single, uninterrupted victory march.

He was tall, blond, and muscular, came top in every class, and was team captain in both the soccer and handball teams.

Friends flocked to him, all vying to be the closest.

As though hoping that his unique gifts would rub off on them.

Everyone wanted to be like him; even the teachers and the school staff admired him. He was the star around which everything revolved.

His future lay staked out before him. The world was his.

Until it was suddenly snatched from him.

He remembers it clearly. It happened one Saturday in May. He was fifteen years old, and his team was playing a soccer match in a neighboring town. An older kid, Bure, who vaguely reminded him of a gorilla, tackled him heavily just inside the penalty area.

He jumped to his feet, brushed the grass off his clothes and knees, and was preparing to take the penalty when Bure stood right in front of him. Said something degrading about his family—about his father—in a contemptuous tone.

He said it loudly enough for everyone to hear, opponents and teammates alike.

He barely remembers the words: they weren't what mattered, and they paled in comparison to the deed itself. That someone should dare say such a thing to him.

Nothing like that had ever happened before.

A line had been crossed, and he could feel his teammates' eyes on him. As though expecting him to do something. But Bure was bigger than him, and the malicious look in his eyes told him that a fight in the middle of the pitch would not end well.

So he set the ball down on the penalty spot. Tried to ignore Bure and his friends as they smirked at him.

His face flushed as he took the run-up.

Normally his execution would have been stone-cold. He would have hit the back of the net without blinking. Turned around confidently to receive his teammates' adoration.

But not on that day.

Instead he sent the ball flying over the bar, and they lost the match.

He should have realized it was a sign.

An omen.

When he arrived home that night, everything had changed. Without warning their belongings had been moved out of the manor house and into Villa Canopus. The house that had always been their home was suddenly forbidden territory.

"Father needs to be left in peace," as his mother explained it to him. "He needs peace and quiet for his VERY IMPORTANT work."

But he knew that she was lying. He could see it in the way her bottom lip trembled, in her red, blotchy eyes.

He put on a brave face all the same. Did his best to be helpful. Hoped that the banishment wasn't about him. Or that—for him, at least—it would only be temporary.

After all, he was Prince Pollux, the son, the heir. The one on whom the sun always shone.

It would be weeks before he saw his father again.

A stiff family dinner in the great dining chamber, at which the Father looked none of them in the eye. Just explained tersely that his work had become so vital that it would now take up all his time, and that under no circumstances was he to be disturbed.

He tried to catch the Father's attention. Find the slightest hint that he was the exception to the rule. But the Father simply rose from the table and left them, while his mother tried to suppress her sobs.

Somewhere he sensed that all of it was his fault, that he had failed the Father somehow and had thus caused their banishment.

For the first time in his life he felt weak.

Powerless.

But furious, too.

ASKER

Now that she knows where to look, it takes her only an hour or two to flesh out the link between Prepper Per and Tord Korpi. A few phone calls and some hits in a members' directory is all it takes.

She needs air. But just as she is getting up to step outside, her phone rings.

A private number, which can only mean one person.

"Hello," she says.

The scar on her left forearm has already started to itch.

"How are we getting along?" Prepper Per asks brusquely.

Asker doesn't know what annoys her more—his assumption that they are somehow in this together, or the fact that, all these years later, he is still forcing her to play *Tell me five things about* . . .

She takes a deep breath.

"The deceased is Tord Korpi. He was an expert in building tunnels and bunkers, which was why he visited the Farm. You met through the paratroopers' regimental association, of which you were both members. Korpi hated the authorities and tried to stay under the radar. A paranoid loner, just like you. And if I can dig up that link between you, sooner or later my colleagues will, too."

A short silence on the line.

"Not bad," he eventually says. "So you're not completely hopeless."

She doesn't take the bait. Besides, behind his wry tone she hears something that could be a hint of reluctant admiration. He is testing her, just like before. And she has exceeded his expectations, which bothers him. Just like it bothers her how important it is to her to win this game, be a good girl. Subconsciously her fingers drift toward her forearm.

"So, how did you know it was Korpi?" she asks. "If it wasn't you who dumped him there, that is."

The question needles him, just as she hoped it would.

"I have my contacts," he snorts. "People who call me if anything unusual turns up around the Farm."

"Like a municipal worker who accidentally digs up a corpse? Maybe even takes a few photos on their phone?"

He doesn't reply, which presumably means her guess was right.

"Now that you know of our links, Leo, it's high time you found out who killed Tord Korpi," he says instead. "You don't have much time."

"What do you mean?" she asks.

"Because as we speak, two uniformed police officers are ringing the bell outside my gate. I'm not going to open it, and soon they'll be off on their merry little way. But something tells me your colleagues will be back soon, and that next time they won't bother ringing. We both know how that's going to end."

"That wasn't our deal!" she protests. "You were going to cooperate if I helped you. And as you can see, I'm already making progress."

He snorts. "Do you really think I have that kind of confidence in your abilities? That your word is enough?"

Asker rolls up her shirtsleeve, tries to trace the letters of her tattoo. But his voice is too distracting.

"I'm not going anywhere till you've found a better prime suspect, Leo."

Asker forces herself to clench her right fist to stop herself from scratching the scar.

"Why don't you just leave?" she asks. "You have your backpack packed and ready, cash and a fake passport. In fifteen minutes you could be gone without a trace."

"Because I'm not going to let anyone drive me from my own home," he hisses. "Accuse me of things I haven't done, force their way onto my property, and take what's mine."

He stops himself just as his tone turns caustic.

"Besides, it's less easy to hide when you're missing a hand and an eye," he goes on, somewhat more calmly. "Two not insignificant handicaps that I have you to thank for, dear daughter. So run along now and solve this case quickly, before anyone else comes to harm."

The call ends.

Asker puts down her phone. She must repress an almost overwhelming urge to dig her nails into her scar and tear deep wounds in her flesh.

HILL

When Hill shuts the car door behind him, a clamor of rooks takes flight from the surrounding trees. They circle the bare tree crowns while cawing. When he lowers his gaze again, he sees a woman standing in the doorway of Villa Arcturus. Aged around seventy, she is tall and elegant, dressed in the same kind of black clothes as everyone else on AlphaCent's payroll.

"Associate Professor Hill, welcome. I am Mrs. Schiller," the woman says softly when they shake hands.

Something about her bearing and appearance calls to mind a retired stewardess.

"Call me Martin," he says, putting on his most charming smile. "It's great to be here."

"Mrs. Schiller is Astroholm's housekeeper," Samuel says.

"And we are most pleased to have you here, Associate Professor Hill," the woman adds, seemingly ignoring his request to address him by his first name. "If you need anything, then I am the one you should contact. Any time, day or night. Please don't hesitate."

She signals toward the door.

"Shall we go inside?"

She opens the heavy front door. In the middle of it hangs a heavy door knocker in the shape of a bear's head. Hill half expects the hinge to creak ominously, but the door glides open without a peep. Mrs. Schiller steps inside, and Hill shuffles behind her with Samuel at his heels.

She shows Hill through the hallway and into the living room. The furnishings are old-fashioned: chest-high wainscoting in dark wood, thick rugs, heavy curtains. On the walls hang drawings and small paintings of strange figures, some of which have human heads atop animal bodies. Two winged armchairs are angled before a large fireplace. One of the chairs bears many more signs of use than the other.

On the mantelpiece stands a framed graphite portrait of an aged man with a pointed beard and dark spectacles. He must be thirty years older than in the photographs in Hill's book, but he can still tell who he is.

"Bernhard Irving," he notes.

Mrs. Schiller nods. "The very same. Bernhard retired to Villa Arcturus when Gunnar and his family moved into the manor house. As you may perhaps know, Bernhard was a distinguished artist. In fact, all of the drawings and paintings in this house were done by his own hand. And there you have his desk."

She nods almost reverently at a large desk in a heavy, dark wood that stands in front of the windows on the far side of the living room.

"Like so many other pieces on the estate, it was designed by Bernhard himself. The desk was formerly in the manor house, but Gunnar had it moved here so that his father could continue his important work."

She pauses, gives Hill another smile.

"You are of course welcome to make use of the desk should you need to, Professor," she goes on. "We have also arranged a work-space for you in the library, but more on that later."

They walk on past a kitchen, bathroom, and a guest room. After that, a basement door.

"You'll find a laundry down there," says Mrs. Schiller. "But if you need to have anything laundered, all you need do is call and we'll see to it on your behalf. Naturally you should be able to focus on your work."

The master bedroom lies at the back of the house, its tall windows looking out onto the forest behind. In the middle of the room stands a large bed with immense carved bedposts. The vaulted ceiling is a midnight blue, and it is bedecked with hand-painted stars.

"Did Bernhard paint them, too?" Hill asks.

"Quite right," says Mrs. Schiller with a nod. "It is the view from the observatory on Boulder Isle."

Hill gazes up at the mural. It is beautiful, and very ambitiously done. The stars aren't simply white dots against a dark background; each individual star has its own color and brightness.

Every constellation is accompanied by its Latin name, painted in swirly, old-fashioned lettering.

Ursa Major.
Cassiopeia.
Leo.

Hill feels a pang of guilt. He should call Leo, see how her investigation is progressing. Make sure she isn't getting drawn back into Prepper Per's insane world.

But the thought is quickly pushed aside by his fascination for this place. He has fantasized about it ever since he was a teen, and so far Astroholm has surpassed his expectations and then some.

They walk back into the hallway, where they stop by a steep staircase leading upstairs.

"There isn't much to see up there," says Mrs. Schiller, who must have noticed his hesitation. "Simply a large loft space that served as Bernhard's studio. Drawing boards, easels, a few unfinished projects. Best to wait until you are a little more mobile before you go up there." She nods at Hill's crutch.

"Speaking of which," Samuel cuts in, having been silent for a while. "Dr. Schiller would like to take a look at your injury as soon as possible. Would two p.m. this afternoon be convenient?"

"Certainly," Hill replies.

"Good. Mrs. Schiller will arrange for someone to come and collect you."

He nods at the woman, who immediately confirms as much.

"So then," Mrs. Schiller says in summary as they return to the kitchen. "The house keys are hanging on the hook by the door. There is extra bedding and towels in the linen closet. The fridge and pantry are filled, and I have set out a lunch platter of cold cuts in case you're hungry. Should you need anything else then all you need do is contact me, Associate Professor Hill."

"Speaking of communication," Samuel adds. "At Astroholm we use an app. You'll find the information on how to download it here."

He points at a laminated QR code that is lying on the kitchen table.

"You'll see that the phone signal out here is rather bad. But through the app you can access a wireless network that should cover most of the grounds. In the app you'll also find a tab with practical information on the estate, which I very much recommend that you read. Above all the section on security and rules of conduct."

Samuel holds his gaze for another few seconds.

"Of course," says Hill. "By the way, when do you think I'll get to meet Gunnar?"

Samuel and Mrs. Schiller exchange glances.

"I'm afraid we couldn't possibly say," Mrs. Schiller replies.

"But he's here? On the estate, I mean?"

"Naturally," Samuel says. "But he's very busy. You'll get to meet Gunnar when he feels the time is ripe."

"Most of what you need to know is in the app," Mrs. Schiller adds. "Now, make yourself at home, and you'll be collected at two p.m."

Once the two of them have driven off in Samuel's Mercedes, Hill checks his cellphone. True enough, he has just one measly bar of signal, so he scans the QR code on the kitchen table. While the app downloads, he hobbles back into the living room and takes a seat in Bernhard's well-indented winged armchair.

It all feels unreal, but at the same time very exciting.

After a minute or so the app has finished downloading. He types in his name and selects a password before it logs him in. The Wi-Fi symbol flickers to life, and all of a sudden he has full coverage.

Welcome to Astroholm, the app greets him, after which three tabs appear:

Contact.

Security and Rules of Conduct.

Map.

The first tab contains contact information for Mrs. Schiller, her husband, and Samuel, as well as that of the medical center and guard station. In addition to phone numbers, there is the option to communicate directly through the app.

His thoughts once again turn to Leo, and he fires off a quick message to her. *Just got to Astroholm. An interesting place, to say the least. How are you doing?*

For a brief moment he thinks of ending the message with *hugs*, but he ditches the idea almost immediately. Instead he goes for a mildly personal */M.*

He waits a few seconds for a reply, but nothing happens. Leo

must be busy. He goes back to the Astroholm app and opens the tab
Security and Rules of Conduct.

> Astroholm Manor and the surrounding grounds were created by
> Bernhard Irving as a place for meditation and quiet reflection. A
> tranquil place where one can think freely and without interruption,
> while opening one's mind to insights beyond what is customary. For
> this reason it is important that guests respect the special spirit of
> seclusion and contemplation that prevails here.
>
> Guests and residents of the estate are not to be contacted un-
> invited.
>
> The manor house is only to be visited upon prior arrangement.
>
> Please note: The rear side of the manor house, including the se-
> cluded grounds between the manor and the lake, are completely pri-
> vate and must under no circumstances be visited without express
> permission. The same applies to Boulder Isle.

A sound makes Hill look up from his phone. A metallic rap that must
be coming from the heavy knocker on his door. He gets to his feet
and limps over to the front door.

Outside stands a girl in her early teens with a black dog on a harness.

"Hello," she says. "My name's Elsa, and this is Orion."

The girl is wearing a hat and dark sunglasses that cover all of her
eyes, which is strange given the wintery-gray fog and murky light
outside. Only when Hill notices the white cane in the girl's hand
does he realize that she is blind.

"You must be the new Bear Guardian," she says.

ASKER

Asker takes a brisk walk along the canal towpath while trying to get her thoughts in order. The biting wind from the Öresund Strait blows straight through her clothes, but she hardly notices.

At some point in 2006, Tord Korpi is shot in the back of the head and dumped just a few hundred yards from the Farm's main gate. His car disappears, but in the absence of any license number, she can't try to trace it to any scrapyard. And, as far as she knows, no gun or bag of money has been found at the shallow grave. Nor any other clues.

And then there's Korpi's revolver. She has had time to give that some thought. It was a snub-nosed thirty-eight: hopeless from a distance of over twenty-six feet, but easy to draw, and effective at close range. A typical defensive weapon.

Was the revolver just a general precaution, given all the cash Korpi was carrying? Because he was as paranoid as Prepper Per? Or was he carrying the gun because of a specific threat?

She phones Rosen.

"I need some help with more database searches," she says as soon as she hears the click of the line. "I want every police report or record from 2006 that relates to the area where Tord Korpi's body was found. Everything that came in, no matter how minor. Even parking fines and speeding tickets."

Asker knows it's a long shot, but right now she is clutching at straws.

"O-OK," Rosen replies. "I'm assuming it's urgent."

"It is. It'd be good if you could prioritize this. And not a word to anyone."

"Of course. I'll be in touch as soon as that's ready."

Asker ends the call. She sees a message from Martin and is just wondering whether to give him a call when her phone starts to ring.

"Hello," she says, thinking it's Rosen calling her back.

Instead another familiar voice comes reaching down the line. British monarch with a hint of great white.

"Leonore?" her mother asks.

"Yes."

"Good. Would you mind coming down to the office? There's something I'd like to speak to you about. Urgently."

She hangs up before Asker can even reply.

Her mother's tone was clipped and cold, as usual. But Asker thinks she noticed an additional hue to her voice.

An ominous gravity that she has never before heard from her mother; one that puts her on edge.

HILL

"In case you're wondering, I'm not actually blind," Elsa says between gulps of the soda that Hill offers her from the fridge.

She has taken off her jacket and plopped herself down at his kitchen table as though it were the most natural thing in the world. The black dog lies at her feet, glaring suspiciously up at Hill. Hill doesn't know much about dogs, but he thinks it could be a Labrador.

"I can make out changes in light," Elsa goes on. "So it's more correct to call me visually impaired rather than blind."

Hill still has hardly any idea who this girl is and what she is doing in his kitchen. But he is curious to find out more—about both her and Astroholm.

"You said something about a Bear Guardian?" he asks.

"Sure did. The house you're staying in is called Arcturus. It's a star in the Boötes constellation, and its name means 'Bear Guardian.'"

"Ah," Hill says with a nod. "That explains why the door knocker is a bear's head."

"Exactly," the girl says with a nod, as if she has all the answers. "All the villas are named after stars. Mom, Grandma, and I live over in Canopus." She points over her shoulder. "Canopus is part of a constellation that means 'keel,' so our knocker's shaped like a . . ."

She pauses, nods encouragingly in Hill's direction.

"Boat?" he fills in.

"Exactly. You're not so stupid for a Bear Guardian."

She takes another swig of soda.

"It was Bernhard Irving who named all the villas. He designed almost everything on the entire estate, from the manor house right down to the door knockers. Did you know he lived here in Arcturus in his later years?"

"Oh yes," Hill replies. "I was just given the grand tour."

"By Mrs. Schiller, no doubt. She loves to talk about Bernhard. Or

Burrnerrd, as she calls him, did you notice? She talks about him like he was some kind of saint. And Gunnar's basically a god."

Hill chuckles. "Yes, Mrs. Schiller did give me the tour. I'm Martin Hill, by the way."

"Elsa," she says again, holding out her hand for Hill to take. "Elsa Irving."

The girl seems to notice that Hill gives a start—that or she simply assumes he does.

"My mom's Maud Irving, daughter of Karin Irving, Gunnar's first wife. Gunnar's my grandfather, and Bernhard was my great-grandfather."

"Oh, wow."

"Yeah, that's what people usually say."

"And do you and your mother live here?"

"Temporarily. Orion and I are at boarding school, and Mom has an apartment in Malmö. But she's been staying with Grandma over in Canopus for a while now."

Elsa pauses to take another swig.

"Does anyone else live in the guest villas?" Hill asks.

"Oh yeah. Nova, my half-aunt, lives in Sirius when she's here. But that's not all that often. We should live there, really, given Orion and all."

The dog tilts his head at the sound of his name.

"Sirius is the Dog Star," Elsa explains. "But Mom said it fits Nova really well, since she's the *big dog* of the family."

She gives a big smile.

"It was Nova who hired me," Hill says. "I'm going to be writing a book about AlphaCent."

"I know. Will there be a Braille edition?"

"Uh . . ." Hill stutters.

"I'm just messing with you," the girl laughs. "By the way, I'm not really supposed to drink soda on weekdays. A stupid rule, if you ask me. But Astroholm's full of stupid rules. In theory I wasn't even allowed to come here and knock on your door. But I can get away with it since I'm only thirteen. And besides, everyone pities me because I can't see. The Irving curse and all."

Elsa drains the last of her soda can and gives a loud belch.

"I'd better go, before Mom starts to wonder where I am. But

you'll come by and say hi to her sometime, won't you? I think Mom would appreciate some adult company. Grandma can be a little . . ."

She makes a circling motion with her index finger to her temple, then gets to her feet. The dog stands up and guides her out of the kitchen, while Elsa deftly sweeps her cane across the floor.

"Are there any other Astroholmers I should know about?" Hill asks while following her to the hallway.

"Dr. and Mrs. Schiller live in Villa Procyon, which is the one closest to the manor. Then there's some other staff who come and go. Chefs, cleaners, security guards. Next to Villa Procyon there's an annex with small apartments where staff stay the night sometimes. People like Samuel."

Hill tries to commit this information to memory.

"Oh yeah, I almost forgot Groundskeeper Willy!" Elsa says with a smile.

"Who?"

"Willy, the caretaker. I call him Groundskeeper Willy after the character in *The Simpsons*. Willy lives in the annex permanently. He's pretty snippy, just so you know."

"OK," says Hill. "And Gunnar, your grandfather, where does he live?"

Elsa shrugs.

"He lives in the manor house, in the west wing. But I hardly see him. Gunnar works a lot, and he doesn't like being around people. Besides, I don't think he and Mom really speak to each other."

Hill opens the front door for her.

"One last thing—what did you mean by 'the Irving curse'?" he asks, just as she crosses the threshold.

"Don't you know?" Elsa lowers her voice. "We're cursed, you see: the Astrofield Mine collapse, Great-Grandpa Bernhard who basically ruined us, my uncle's car crash, Grandma being cuckoo, and then me. The only grandchild, and I was born with a visual impairment."

She taps her dark sunglasses.

"I hope you're not afraid of the dark, Martin," she says with mock gravity. "There's plenty of people who'll tell you Astroholm is a haunted place, with aliens and ghosts at every turn."

She laughs again and starts walking down the drive, the dog's harness in one hand and her cane in the other. Despite this she moves much more freely than Hill does with his crutch.

Only once she is some way down the road does Hill realize what she said.

Astroholm is a haunted place.

The exact same words as in his mysterious warning letter.

ASKER

The law firm Lissander and Partners' central-Malmö headquarters are just as spotlessly perfect and well appointed as ever, Asker notes as she steps out of the elevator.

"Welcome," says the receptionist, a short-haired woman in her forties whom Asker doesn't remember from before.

Normally the firm's receptionists are young, immaculately dressed individuals with wireless headsets and an ambivalent attitude to the local dialect. This woman is a welcome bucking of that trend.

"You must be Leo," she says. "You can head straight in. Isabel's expecting you."

Asker nods in thanks and takes the corridor to her mother's office. Her little sister Camille's office door is ajar, and she considers poking her head in to say hello. Not that she's in any mood for chitchat, but she does always like to hear how her nieces are getting along. However, when she hears Fredric's voice inside she decides to keep on walking.

Her brother-in-law is such a personality vacuum that the automatic doors at the supermarket barely register his presence. That Asker dated him briefly in her twenties, before she dumped him and he eventually moved on with Camille, is a mistake she has had to pay for dearly at every awkward family shindig ever since. To make matters worse, somehow she has been landed with the role of villain in this big, embarrassing comedy of errors.

ISABEL LISSANDER, LAWYER AND SENIOR PARTNER, reads the brass plate on the door to her mother's office. Asker gives it a gentle knock.

"Come in!"

Her mother is sitting at her desk, which despite its size never makes her look small. A pair of reading glasses is perched on the tip of her nose, and her clothes, hair, nails, and makeup are perfect, as usual.

"Hi, Mom."

"Take a seat, Leonore. I'll be with you in a moment."

Her mother gestures at one of the chairs opposite, before returning her attention to her computer.

Asker sits down, crosses her legs. It feels like she has been summoned by the principal for a serious talking-to.

Her mother clatters away at her keyboard.

A power play, of course, to show she has more important things to do.

Asker takes out her cellphone in the meantime. No new messages from Martin since he confirmed he had arrived at the estate. She gets that he's excited, that he's busy exploring the manor. Still, she can't help but feel a tad irritated that he would just take off like that—even though she has no right to ask anything of him.

"Right then," her mother says eventually. "So good of you to come in. How are you?"

Her tone is surprisingly soft, which reinforces Asker's wariness.

"Good, thanks," she replies. "And I hope the same goes for you and Junot. But since I'm here on work time, how about we get straight to the point? What is it you want to talk about that you couldn't discuss over the phone?"

Isabel sits in silence for a few seconds. Draws it out into one of those loaded attack silences that she's so expert in. Her face is an icy mask—one that doesn't betray the slightest hint of the nature of this meeting.

"Not long ago I received a call from Detective Superintendent Jonas Hellman," she eventually says. "He asked me a number of questions about you and your father."

"I see . . ."

Asker tries to make it seem like this doesn't concern her in the slightest, though of course the opposite is true. She should have predicted this move from Hellman.

"So what did you tell him?"

"Naturally I told him the truth," her mother replies. "I'm not in the habit of lying to the police."

Her ice mask again, this time combined with a reproachful look.

Asker takes a deep breath. "You told Jonas Hellman about Dad. About the accident . . ."

"I did. I told him your father's so unreliable that he almost killed you both out of sheer carelessness."

Asker is finding it all the harder to keep her cool.

"Hellman is a good detective," Isabel goes on. "He saved Smilla Holst, for which both I and her family are eternally grateful. Besides, he's wise enough to call me before he takes action, which means he wants to go on building future alliances."

Asker bites her lip. Hearing her own mother singing Jonas Hellman's praises for a case that she and Martin Hill solved is approaching the limit of what she can stomach.

"Hellman told me your father has been implicated in a sixteen-year-old murder case," Isabel says. "A corpse has been found just outside the Farm. A certain Tord Korpi, shot in the back of the head. It's only a matter of time before the police link the victim to your father, as I'm sure you realize."

She raises her eyebrows, as though waiting for Asker to say something.

She doesn't.

So Hellman and his gang have already identified Korpi and established the cause of death. Which means Hellman must have put pressure on the pathologist and allocated new resources to the case. The only conceivable reason why he would do that is to get back at Asker through her father—in other words, exactly what she feared.

"It doesn't really surprise me that Per should be guilty of something like this," her mother goes on. "Far more concerning is the fact that apparently you have been snooping around the case."

Her mother leans in, no more than an inch. And yet that simple movement, combined with a slight change of tone, makes the atmosphere between them change, transforms the conversation into an interrogation.

"Leonore, was it your father who dragged you into all of this?"

Asker still doesn't reply. Once again Hellman has used Isabel as a pawn against her, and once again her mother has taken his side just like that.

Isabel tilts her head to one side.

"As you know, Per can be extremely manipulative. You can't trust a thing he says. For years he's been living on borrowed time, and now his past has finally caught up with him. So why would you, of all people, want to help him? It truly is beyond me."

Asker tries to keep her cool. "Because Per's dangerous," she says collectedly. "If the police go to the Farm to try to arrest him, there'll be a bloodbath."

"I've explained to Jonas Hellman that Per may pose a certain risk," says Isabel. "The best thing you can do now is contact Hellman directly and tell him everything you know about your father and the Farm, all the memories you have of Korpi, and how they can best bring him in without any unnecessary risks."

"You mean let Hellman and his gang pursue Dad, whether he's guilty or not? That's a strange attitude for a lawyer to take."

Isabel leans in another inch, which somehow, oddly, makes the room start to incline toward Asker. Her voice becomes even softer.

"Right now I'm not here as a lawyer, Leonore, but first and foremost as your mother."

It's impossible not to admire her. Her rejoinder is so perfect, so clinical, that there is no possible defense against it.

Asker knows that, and her mother does, too.

The best she can do now is simply get up and leave. Clench her fist in her pocket and swallow her rage that Hellman has convinced her own mother to encourage—no—*order* her not only to collaborate with him, but to stay out of his way while he sends her father to jail.

But then Asker realizes that something jars; one detail in this whole charade doesn't quite fit. It takes her a few seconds to figure out what it is.

"All the memories you have of Korpi . . ." she says slowly.

"What?"

"You said *all the memories you have of Korpi.*"

Her mother waves her hand irritably.

"What are you trying to get at, Leonore?"

"Hellman still hasn't linked Tord Korpi to Per," Asker says. "You said that yourself just a minute ago. So he can't know that I've met him."

Her mother raises her eyebrows in puzzlement, as though she has no idea where this discussion is going.

Asker maintains eye contact.

She catches a slight tremor in Isabel's gaze. A microscopic crack in the ice mask, one that tells her all she needs to know.

She inhales and leans in just an inch, in the same way that her mother just did.

Slowly the room comes back to equilibrium, before starting to tip the other way.

"Only one other person knows I've met Tord Korpi," she says. "So how long ago was it that you spoke to him? To Dad?"

THE GLASS MAN

One night, a few weeks after the banishment, he waited outside the other team's clubhouse. He had cut some holes in a woolen hat and taken with him a heavy axe handle that he had found down in the workshop. Cycled there with both hidden in his backpack.

He couldn't say why he did it, was simply following some kind of instinct.

A need to sate the feelings of humiliation and powerlessness that were consuming him from within.

When Bure stepped out with his sports bag slung over his shoulder, he stayed hidden behind some trees. Waited, heart pounding, while the gorilla-like youth sloped over to his bicycle in a dark corner of the parking lot.

Had Bure been with anyone, it's unlikely he would have left that spot. But instead he was alone. Perhaps it was a sign?

He sneaked over with the axe handle in his hands, his pulse thundering through his eardrums. Somewhere he felt as though the Father were watching him through his all-seeing eye. Judging him, to see if he was still worthy.

The thought made his arms fail him.

The first blow landed across Bure's back, neither decisively nor exactly enough to settle the score. Bure spun around with a howl, then leapt at him in full force.

Until then he had only imagined that he would give Bure a good beating. Restore his and his family's glory.

But what would become of him if the reverse were to happen? If his father were to find out that he had been humbled yet again by an outsider? That he was weak? Irredeemable? Unworthy?

The fear overwhelmed him. It filled his arms with brute force, transforming his axe handle to a bludgeon.

His second blow met Bure's temple with a sound not unlike that of a snapping branch. Without a word the tall lad slumped to the ground.

Lay there while the asphalt turned red beneath his head.

His first impulse was to get out of there. Run in panic, as far as possible.

But instead he stood there with the dying boy, as though rooted to the spot.

A strange impulse took hold of his body, and at its bidding he kneeled down beside Bure, took the boy's hand and looked him in the eye.

Studied him in the same way he once studied the glass frog.

Watched his faltering gaze slowly fade; watched his journey between worlds begin.

Watched everything slowly still.

In that moment it was as though he was changed.

As though he grew.

Became someone else—someone bigger, stronger, better.

No longer an uncertain young man, but a mighty creature, one with power.

Real power.

The only thing that really mattered.

The power over life and death.

HILL

At five minutes to two Hill steps out of the front door to Villa Arcturus, ready for his appointment with Dr. Schiller. As he does, he sees something resembling a golf cart approaching from the road. In the driving seat is a man in his forties wearing workman's clothes.

He brakes suddenly in front of Hill and uses one of the roof supports to swing himself out of the vehicle. This movement, combined with the man's long arms and slightly stooping posture, makes Hill think of a chimpanzee. This impression is further reinforced by the man's sideburns, which stretch all the way down to his jaw.

"Hill?" the man grunts.

"That's right. And you must be Willy?"

The man's eyes narrow.

"My name's Ville. Ville Knudsen."

"Sorry, Ville."

Hill clears his throat in embarrassment. He is certain he didn't mishear Elsa when she mentioned the caretaker's name. It must have been a prank.

"Need a hand?" Ville nods at Hill's crutch.

"No thanks, I'm fine."

Hill climbs into the passenger seat, and Willy-whose-name-is-actually-Ville swings back in behind the wheel. He hits the gas and swerves the cart around so fast that Hill has to grab one of the supports to stop himself from falling out the side.

"So, what do you do here at Astroholm?" Hill asks tentatively.

"This and that. Whatever needs doing," Ville replies.

"How long have you been here?"

The man gives him a quick sideways glance.

"All my life," he mutters. "I took over from my dad."

"Do you enjoy it?"

"Uh-huh."

Hill pauses. Elsa wasn't kidding when she said Ville's snippy, at least.

The air streaming through the moving cart is cold and damp, and Hill must put his hands in his pockets to stop himself from getting cold in the open vehicle.

The fog is still thick, but Ville doesn't let up on the gas. Even so, he manages to avoid every pothole and frost patch on the ground with a race-car driver's precision.

They drive across the pond and on toward the fountain.

Hill notices that his driver's eyes linger on the glass sculpture of the young Gunnar Irving a few seconds longer than necessary.

"Was it Bernhard who designed it?" he asks, in one last attempt to spark something resembling a conversation. "The sculpture, I mean."

"Uh-huh," Ville mumbles.

"It really is special," Hill goes on. "Do you know if it has a name?"

No response.

They drive around the manor house, but instead of heading toward the imposing front steps Ville turns off to the right and follows a road that runs parallel to the façade. He rounds the right-hand corner of the building, drives for another ten yards, then stops before a smaller entrance at ground level.

From the wall above the door, a dark camera dome stares mutely down at Hill.

"Here we are," says Ville.

Hill clambers out of the cart.

"Thanks for the lift," he says. "You drive like a pro."

Ville nods, and one corner of his mouth rises to form an expression that suggests he isn't used to being thanked, much less to receiving praise.

"The sculpture you asked about," he says, just as Hill is about to turn away. "Its name is *The Diviner of Stars*. But here on the estate it's known as *The Glass Man*."

ASKER

Asker chooses to walk from Lissander and Partners' offices back to police HQ, mainly because she needs to cool down. Her head is roiling, and she can't tell what annoys her most: that Hellman is using her mother to manipulate her, that Prepper Per also rang Isabel for help, or that they both tried to hide it from her. Or might there be a fourth option? One that she would rather not acknowledge, because it's completely insane.

That what gets to her most is that Isabel was Per's first choice, and not her.

The two times Per called her he did so from a hidden number, leaving no contact details. *I can reach you, but you can't reach me*—a classic Per mind game.

Isabel, on the other hand, has apparently been given a number. And not to the burner cell Per otherwise uses, but to a satellite telephone. An expensive resource that he especially treasures. Clearly he feels Isabel is worth it.

Yet Isabel would rather throw Per under the bus. Let Hellman storm in with SWAT teams and guns drawn, causing a bloodbath.

Asker knows exactly what the gang up in Serious Crime are doing: slowly and methodically they are tightening the net around Prepper Per. Mapping out his life, thinking they know who he is. How they can tackle him.

When in fact they have no idea. Per is no average roughneck.

His spell in the psych ward aside, he has been preparing for an attack of this very nature for some twenty-five years. He has drilled for every conceivable scenario, amassed weapons and equipment, built bunkers, tunnels, and defenses. Has transformed the Farm into a deathtrap for anyone who tries to breach it by force.

And on top of that he knows that they are coming. He isn't going to let himself be caught unawares in a superstore parking lot in flip-flops and lazy-day sweatpants.

He will lie low at the Farm. Wait them out.

A crafty old wolf in his den.

Meanwhile, she has gotten nowhere in her investigation into who else might have murdered Korpi.

She stops and realizes that she has been walking way too fast, and that, even with the cold, damp, and piercing wind, she is already dripping with sweat.

Asker opens her jacket to release the heat from her body, then takes a few deep breaths. She has to calm down, get her thoughts in order.

Find a way forward.

A movement makes her turn her head.

She has stopped by the window of a gym. Inside it, poor so-and-sos are torturing themselves on treadmills. Near them a young woman is trying her hand at the bench press, while her boyfriend stands by her head and helps her to lift the bar those last few inches.

The whole scene—the young woman, the bench, the barbell, the man spotting her—opens up a little door in her head.

And suddenly she remembers something else about Tord Korpi.

One tiny detail, but it may prove crucial.

SIXTEEN YEARS EARLIER

She is in the gym at the Farm, a barracks built from Leca blocks and corrugated sheet metal. Prepper Per picked up some of the equipment from bankruptcy auctions, but most of it they made themselves: they ran cables through blocks and tackles; welded brackets, handles, and weights out of scrap metal; hung up sandbags and mirrors; and laid rubber floors.

"It may not be beautiful," as her father often says. "But it works."

She has almost finished her session when Uncle Tord steps in. He nods politely while heading to the deadlift station in the corner.

They have hardly exchanged a word since he turned up again, and even though he is staying in one of the guest trailers, she hasn't been able to find out anything more about him, beyond his fondness for beer and cigarettes.

But her father is interested in him, and for that reason she is keen to gather more intel. To be ready the next time he decides to play Tell me five things about . . .

She studies Uncle Tord in the mirrors on the sly.

He is wearing a weight-lifting belt that is buckled on the outermost hole, over shorts and a gym top. He is huffing and puffing, but he fiddles with his lifting straps and slams down the weights in a way that suggests he knows what he is doing.

She has just been doing pull-ups, and her arms and back are burning. In theory she should have just one set left.

But she has just had an idea.

The bench press is right next to the deadlift station. She walks over to it, hangs a pair of heavy disc weights onto the bar, and lies back on the bench.

She adjusts her grip and takes a few deep breaths, as though preparing for a particularly tough lift. Then she raises the bar out of the holder and lowers it smoothly toward her chest while breathing in.

Her arms wobble on the way up, but she manages to straighten them out. She sneaks a glance at Uncle Tord, to make sure he is looking her way. Slowly lowers the bar again.

When it reaches her chest, she pushes back up, but her strength suddenly ebbs. The bar falters halfway up, then starts to sink back down toward her chest. She groans loudly with exertion.

"Just bear down!"

Uncle Tord has moved to the head of the bench. He takes the bar between her hands and, inch by inch, helps her to send it back up to its place on the holder.

"Thanks!" she sighs while sitting up. "That weight sneaked up on me."

"No problem."

"Do you work out a lot?" she asks, before he can go back to his weights.

He shrugs. "When I get the time. But I'm a little out of shape. Eat too much junk food, travel too much."

"Oh, where?"

She can see from his reaction that she has jumped the gun. That she should have held off on the questions until he was more relaxed.

"Here and there," he replies. Then he turns away and starts fiddling with his weights.

She thinks the conversation is over, and curses inwardly for getting ahead of herself. But then he turns back around.

"Your dad. He's pretty hard on you, isn't he?"

She doesn't reply, simply does a hand gesture that means neither yes nor no.

"I saw you doing close-combat training yesterday, and the shooting range has seen a lot of use. Do you drive, too?"

"Sometimes."

"And you're what, fifteen? And you live out here all alone with your dad?"

"Uh-huh . . ."

"What does your mom have to say about all this? Or your friends?"

Suddenly she is the one being interrogated, which Per wouldn't have liked. He doesn't like anyone asking questions about him or the Farm.

"I'd better get going." She gets up off the bench.

For a brief moment they stand opposite each other. It feels as though Uncle Tord wants to ask something else, but before he can say anything she makes for the door.

Just before leaving the gym, she turns around and steals another glance at him in the mirrors on the wall. He has just taken hold of the barbell and tenses his chest before pushing away with his legs.

Even though it's inverted in the mirror, she can clearly read the text on his top.

"Freedom Gym, Hörby."

HILL

When Hill steps through the side entrance to the manor house, a nurse is waiting to guide him through. Nova Irving wasn't exaggerating when she described their medical suite.

It is hypermodern, with white walls and good lighting, and metal signs suggest it houses both an X-ray department and its own in-house laboratory. The air is cool, with a scent more reminiscent of a boutique hotel than a hospital.

The nurse shows him through to a windowless consulting room. On one wall hangs a large display screen, while the others are decorated with various framed drawings. In one corner stands a machine bearing AlphaCent's logo.

"Please take a seat while you wait."

The nurse points at the examination table, which resembles a daybed and is topped with white sheets instead of coarse protective paper.

After less than a minute, a thickset man wearing a doctor's coat and round spectacles steps in. He is in his seventies, with a horseshoe of gray hair that separates the rolls of fat on his neck from his shiny scalp. In his hands he is holding an iPad.

"Dr. Schiller," he introduces himself. "Welcome to Astroholm. You met my wife a little while ago."

His voice is clipped and his handshake aloof, just like his gaze. The contrast to his warm and friendly wife is sharp.

"Let's see." The doctor scrolls on the iPad's screen. "A bullet wound in your thigh, if I'm not mistaken? Barely a week old."

"That's right."

Although Hill did tick off a number of digital documents the previous evening after accepting the job, he is still surprised that the doctor should already have access to his personal medical records.

"First and foremost I should like to take a look at the wound," Dr. Schiller says. "Then we'll do some tests to rule out any infections."

He scrolls down on his tablet.

"And then I'd suggest we try one of our most recently developed treatments. It involves a combination of cryotherapy and laser treatment, to accelerate the healing process. Are you still taking blood thinners because of your mechanical heart valve?"

"No," Hill replies. "The doctor told me to take a break from them while I'm on antibiotics for my bullet wound."

"Sound advice," Dr. Schiller says with a nod. "So, if you'd be so kind as to take down your trousers."

Hill obliges. As he noticed earlier that morning, his wound feels tighter than usual, so he tries to restrict his movements as much as possible.

Dr. Schiller takes a seat on a tall wheelie stool. From a drawer he extracts a headlamp and pair of rubber gloves, then he beckons Hill to shift closer. With deft movements he removes the protective dressing from his thigh.

"Aha," he says, mostly to himself. He lights his headlamp, leans in closer, and carefully runs his fingers over the surface of the wound.

Hill doesn't know where to look, but after some wandering his eyes eventually land on one of the graphite sketches on the wall. It depicts a round lake with an island almost exactly in its center. In the middle of the island a few dark buildings are visible, alongside something that resembles a tower, a dome at its very top.

"That's Boulder Isle, isn't it?" he asks without looking down.

Dr. Schiller appears to be too wrapped up in his consultation to respond.

"With Astrofield Mine in the middle," Hill goes on. "And Bernhard's observatory."

The doctor hums in response, his eyes still on the wound.

"When do you think I'll be able to go there?"

Dr. Schiller rolls his stool back a few feet and turns off his headlamp.

"I'm not informed on such matters. But in any case I should wait until your wound has had time to heal a little better. Your wound is hot to the touch and red at the edges, so I'd suspect the antibiotics you were given at the hospital aren't working entirely optimally."

He gets to his feet and fetches new dressings, which he applies over the wound.

"Now we'll just take a few blood tests and then we'll be done. You can get yourself dressed in the meantime."

While Hill puts his pants back on, Dr. Schiller prepares a metal tray with test tubes, a hypodermic needle, and other paraphernalia.

"Take a seat on the bed and roll up your sleeve."

Hill does as he is instructed. He is used to having blood taken; must have had it done hundreds of times over the years. But that doesn't mean he likes it.

Dr. Schiller is quick and effective. It takes him just a minute to fill four tubes with blood, after which he removes the needle and covers the puncture with a Band-Aid.

"There now, we're done for today. But you ought to have something to eat and drink before you stand up."

The doctor points at a bottle of mineral water and a small dish of oatmeal cookies that have been placed on a slender bedside table.

"We'll have the test results tomorrow, so I suggest you come back at the same time, and we'll take it from there."

"OK." Hill nods.

He puts a cookie in his mouth, chews, and washes it down with mineral water. The water is ice-cold, so it must have been set out just before he arrived. And the cookie tastes freshly baked. It's a whole other level of healthcare than the kind he is used to.

"Sit tight and relax for a minute or two," Dr. Schiller goes on. "My wife will be here any minute to take you on a tour of the library. Goodbye for now, and I'll see you tomorrow. And should anything come up before then, you have my number in the app. You can call me at any time."

When the doctor has gone, Hill sits back and munches on his cookie. Despite his somewhat cold bedside manner, there is no denying that Dr. Schiller radiates competence and experience. Hill is clearly in very capable hands, just as Nova Irving promised.

His eyes are once again drawn to the drawings of Boulder Isle; another one of Nova's promises that he would so dearly like to see fulfilled.

He takes his phone out and checks the chat forum, but no one has responded to his question about the two urban explorers who drowned in the lake.

After a few minutes there comes a knock on the door, and Mrs. Schiller pokes her head inside.

"Did it all go well?" she asks. "Did the doctor take good care of you?"

"Yes, thank you," Hill replies.

"Good. If you would like to follow me, I'll show you to the library."

They leave the consulting room and continue through the rest of the medical suite, passing doors to other consulting rooms.

Mrs. Schiller leads him to an elevator at the other end of the medical corridor. Two camera domes are affixed to the ceiling, and the control panel is fitted with a card reader. Mrs. Schiller taps her card against the reader and presses the top button.

As the elevator rises, Hill steals a glance at the control panel. It has four floors. The medical suite is situated on the first floor, and the library to which they are now headed appears to be on the second floor.

But beneath the first floor there is both a third and fourth button, which suggests that Astroholm Manor has two subterranean levels.

A basement and a garage, perhaps?

Or an underground burial chamber where Bernhard Irving lies at rest? A complex of tunnels extending all the way to Boulder Isle?

The thought makes Hill's heart pound a few extra beats.

The elevator stops on the second floor. Mrs. Schiller swipes her card against a second reader to open a door.

"So, here we have Astroholm's great library," she says, her voice full of pride.

Hill can see why.

The contrast with the starkly modern medical facility beneath them is huge. The chamber that they have entered is at least a hundred feet long and thirty feet wide. On the floor lies a plush green carpet decorated with various mystical symbols that recur here and there in the wainscoting and curtains.

Along the walls and throughout the room stand row upon row of tall, dark bookcases with hand-carved adornments. The shelves are packed with books, files, and bound documents.

Judging by the interiors, Bernhard Irving must have been at least as taken with astrology as he was with astronomy. The vaulted ceiling that rises over the imposing gothic windows is filled with murals depicting constellations and celestial bodies. A kind of macro version of the bedroom ceiling in Villa Arcturus.

"In here you will find both Bernhard and Gunnar Irving's book collections," Mrs. Schiller says solemnly. "A sizable corpus, as you can tell."

She leads him past rows of replete bookshelves. The thick carpet completely absorbs the sound of their footsteps and the tap of Hill's crutch.

"And down here . . ." Mrs. Schiller says once they have reached the far end of the library, ". . . is the section concerning the history of the company. We have had a workspace set up for you over there, and we have taken the liberty of preselecting the most important documents. They are sorted in chronological order."

She points at a large desk with a reading lamp and printer, where three piles of files and books await.

"The printer has a scanner function, so if you need to take anything back to Villa Arcturus, then you can simply scan or copy it," she goes on. "But the originals must remain here. You will have access to the library between nine a.m. and eight p.m. each day. Coffee is served at nine thirty a.m., lunch at one p.m. and an afternoon coffee service at three. You may eat at your workspace. Simply leave everything on the tray and someone will come to collect it. You can find the bathroom and exit over there."

She points to a door that is so well hidden in the wainscoting it is barely visible.

"The door shuts automatically, so you can exit unescorted."

Hill is a little overwhelmed. He should probably ask her questions, but he can't think of what.

"The simplest way to book transportation is to send a message to me through the app. Or simply call me," Mrs. Schiller goes on. "You have downloaded the app, haven't you?"

Hill nods.

"Excellent!" She nods amiably. "I'll leave you here to familiarize yourself with the space in your own time, but don't hesitate to be in touch should you need anything. Oh, and one other thing . . ."

She pauses, as if to ensure she has Hill's full attention.

"Astroholm Manor is, as I'm sure you have observed, a very private place," she says gravely. "This is first and foremost Gunnar's home, which we must respect. Your mobile phone must be put on silent before entering the manor house, and I must urge you not to stray out of bounds. That would be most inappropriate."

She holds Hill's gaze for a few seconds, as if awaiting a reply.

"Of course," he says. "No problem."

"Good." Mrs. Schiller's facial expression softens again. "In that case I wish you luck with your assignment, Associate Professor Hill."

ASKER

By the time she reaches Hörby, a small town and municipality in central Skåne, it is after five and darkness has already fallen. The shapeshifting mist has turned into a bitter rain that is both so light and so irregular that the automatic windshield wipers struggle to find the right speed.

During the drive she tried to call Martin but reached only his voicemail. Normally she would hang up—she hates to leave messages—but on this occasion she made the exception and gave his voicemail a short rundown of her discoveries.

The down-at-heel Freedom Gym premises lie on the outskirts of Hörby, complete with peeling paint on the building's sheet-metal façade, cracked asphalt, and a drooping fence with more holes in it than the average golf course. The lights in the premises are on, and some cars are parked in its anemically lit parking lot.

Asker parks a little ways off and fetches her gym bag from her trunk.

Of course, she could march straight in there, flash her police ID, and ask to speak to the owner. Try to squeeze out of him whether he remembers Tord Korpi. But after doing some research on the place, she has decided on another tack.

The owner of the gym is registered as one Rune Andersson, a name he officially registered some five years before. This was, incidentally, the fourth time he has changed his name in the almost thirty-five years that he has lived in Sweden.

On an internet forum she has learned that the man, whatever his ID might read, goes by the name of Lalo, and that he originally hails from somewhere in the eastern Mediterranean region. According to the police databases, his various aliases over the years have been convicted of a number of minor offenses for dealing in stolen goods, which presumably means he is smart enough to avoid getting caught for the more serious crimes.

Which is why she suspects badge-flashing won't work here. Her remaining option is to visit the gym and pretend to work out while trying to find an in.

Not exactly a watertight plan, but she doesn't have anything better.

Pulsing music hits her as soon as she opens the door. The reception desk inside is unmanned, so she slinks straight into the ladies' changing rooms and puts on some sweatpants and a washed-out hoodie. Before leaving the city, she had let down her hair and taken off what little makeup she was wearing. Resisted the impulse to put on a cap, since no other garment in the world screams "undercover cop" quite as loudly.

The gym consists of a cluster of machines that have all seen better days, and an oversized area for free weights. A few bearded men with biker-gang vibes are standing around by the bench presses. They appear to be more interested in shooting the breeze than exercising. On the treadmill a middle-aged woman jogs almost on the spot while staring at her phone screen.

Asker hovers around the edge of the room, trying to look like a lost beginner while keeping an eye out for someone who could be the owner.

The bikers appear to have finished their session.

"I'm just going to swing by Lalo's office," she hears one of them say.

She watches him out of the corner of her eye while he walks over to a staircase and disappears downstairs. After a few minutes he returns with a paper bag in one hand and leaves the gym with his friends.

Over the music she can make out voices and irregular thuds coming from down in the basement. She walks downstairs. The damp air that meets her halfway down is giving off fifty shades of sweat.

The basement space is large, its floor lined with a blue wrestling mat on which a dozen people are practicing some kind of martial art. At the far end of the room she sees a door and some windows that look like they could belong to an office. But blinds prevent her from getting a good look inside: all that she can see is that the lights are on.

Asker stops for a few seconds while debating her next move.

Then she sees the movements on the wrestling mat stop.

"You here for the course?" someone yells.

"Huh?"

"Are you here for the self-defense course? Good, now we'll have a more even number."

The man addressing her is around her own age. He has a pony-tail and beard and wears a vest emblazoned with the word *Combat*. His muscular arms and legs are so chock-full of Viking symbols that he could quite easily moonlight as a runestone.

"Kneel down."

The walking runestone points at the mat, where the rest of the participants are kneeling with their legs wide apart. Asker follows suit. There are eleven participants besides her: seven men and four women, most of whom are between twenty-five and forty.

"Let's get going," says the walking runestone. "My name's Tyr and I'm a close combat instructor. In modern society people have lost sight of the most fundamental thing. The ability to defend themselves."

He sweeps his stern gaze over all the participants, until enough of them have nodded in agreement.

"In nature, the animals who can't defend themselves get weeded out," he goes on. "But our cushy modern society has undermined this natural order. To learn self-defense is to return to the natural order, to follow nature's laws."

In a Swedish littered with English clichés, Tyr reels off some quasi-philosophical guff about the importance of being able to fight for one's survival; about how men must be real men, but how women must also be warriors who can hold their own in the battlefield's shield walls.

Asker is only listening with one ear. With the other she is too busy trying to figure out what is going on in the office. Every now and then she catches movements inside that she guesses belong to two people.

"Class, listen up! Time for some sparring," says Tyr. "You'll find gloves and pads in the box over there. I'll come around and show you a few techniques."

Asker follows the others. Finds a pair of boxing gloves of the right size that smell only mildly rancid.

She is paired up with a skinny, slightly slump-shouldered man who looks around forty but is probably much younger. He hardly dares to make eye contact. She holds the pad in front of her rib cage while he clumsily pummels it according to Tyr's instructions.

Tyr himself struts around between the pairs, yelling abuse at the guys while flirting all the more openly with the girls. Every now and then he doles out a hard punch or kick to the pads while shouting commands in English.

Asker and her partner have just swapped places when it is their turn to endure Tyr's attention. The wiry man is holding the pad almost as though he is afraid it will burn him.

Asker gives him a few generous beginner punches that, even with her considerable attempts to rein herself in, almost knock him off-balance.

"Come on! Fight!" shouts Tyr, who has by now fully amped himself up.

Asker dishes out another couple of punches, all while flicking her hair and making an effort to look like she has no idea what she is doing.

"What's your name?" Tyr asks.

"Leo," she replies, because she can come up with neither a good fake name nor any reason why she should need one.

"OK, Cleo, here's what we're going to do," says Tyr. "Now, watch closely!"

He takes her place and deals a snappy right-left combo at the pad that the wiry man is gripping in front of his chest. The force makes the man totter backward.

"Again," Tyr commands. The beanpole looks terrified, but reluctantly steps forward. "Are you watching, Cleo?"

Asker nods, but she is aware of the office, the door of which has just opened.

"Watch this!" Tyr unleashes a different combo, which ends with a front kick that knocks the beanpole to the ground.

"You weren't ready!" Tyr shouts at the man on the floor while throwing a smirk at Asker.

"You always have to be ready. Are you ready, Cleo?"

She nods absent-mindedly.

"Come on then, up with your fists!"

Asker raises her gloves, but her attention is still on the office door.

Two stout men have stepped out. The more barrel-shaped of the two is in his sixties, wearing sweatpants, clogs, and a Freedom Gym T-shirt. He struts around like he owns the place, which presumably means he's Lalo. Besides, there is something faintly familiar about him. Perhaps they have met before, which isn't impossible given Korpi's links both to the Farm and this place.

Before her thoughts can get any further, Tyr throws a jab at her second-rate guard, sending her own boxing glove flying up to hit her in the face.

Asker gives a start.

"Come on, Cleo," he smirks. "You have to be able to take a blow. Now it's your turn!"

She shifts her attention to the heavily tattooed instructor. Tyr's gloves are held high, and his weight is on his back leg, with the other in front of him. He lifts his knee up and down, bouncing his toes off the mat, as if to show how dangerous he is.

"Come on, Cleo, gimme your best shot!" he yells with a big, sneering grin.

At his yell, the portly gym owner throws a glance in their direction. It's the closest thing Asker will get to an opportunity. She has to take it.

She whips around, sweeping her left leg along the floor in as wide a circle as she can while sinking down over her right knee. The movement creates a wide, powerful swing that strikes Tyr's supporting leg just above the ankle, downing him like a pile of bricks.

He lands on his back, so heavily that she hears the wind getting knocked out of him.

Asker straightens up. The gym owner has stopped short. He looks her up and down in surprise. And not just him. The entire group have cut short their exercises and are staring almost flabbergasted at her and Tyr.

The instructor bounces back up to his feet. His face flushes bright red.

He has a choice.

Either he can swallow the humiliation, force a laugh, and praise her for an excellent leg sweep. Maybe even ask her to show the others how she did it.

Or he can try to restore his wounded pride by doing something stupid.

He plumps for the latter option. Of course.

Tyr steps toward her with his guard raised. His eyes are black, his mouth compressed to a furious line. He lets loose a jab that she easily parries.

He follows it up with two or three identical jabs, before moving on to weightier combinations. Clearly he has figured out that all that standing-on-one-leg bullshit is a bad idea and has chosen to fall back on his fists.

Asker backs away, raises her gloves, and hides behind her guard while edging sideways. Blocks the few blows that she can't dodge in time. By this point Tyr the runestone should have cottoned on to the fact that she is no beginner. That he would do best to chill out.

Instead her effective defense only seems to rile him more.

He surges on forward, starts throwing more weight into his swings.

She is nearing the edge of the mat, and soon she will have her back against the wall, less able to dodge his carpet-bombs.

"Enough!" she says. "You win."

But Tyr pretends not to hear; he is too preoccupied with proving to himself and everyone else in this basement that he is the Viking chief.

Asker sighs inwardly. She lowers her guard on the left a few inches and raises her chin.

Tyr immediately takes the bait. She sees a brief, triumphant look as he spots the opening, followed by a twitch in his shoulder. His right hand travels toward her face in a wide roundhouse punch. She waits, pretending not to see it.

Then, just in time, she bends her knees as low as she can and takes a big step to the left. Feels the whoosh of air as his fist passes just an inch above her head. The air-punch throws Tyr off-balance. She adjusts herself quickly, twists her elbow, and lands a short but rock-hard left hook to the bottom two ribs on his open right flank.

The shock waves from the blow spread through his ribs, straight into the liver's rich nerve supply. In just a millisecond the organ releases the blood and toxins that it has filtered out straight back into the bloodstream, making the blood pressure plummet and the body's pain center go completely bananas. Or, as her father would always say when they would drill this particular blow: *Makes no difference who you are, Leo. A direct hit on your liver and it's good night.*

Tyr is no exception. His body shuts down, his legs turn to jelly, and he melts—rather than falls—straight onto the mat.

For what must be ten seconds, the room falls completely silent. Tyr is barely moving, his faint whimpers his only sign of life.

Around him the rest of the group gather, eyes wide and mouths agape. Asker puked the first time Per landed a liver shot on her. The second time, too. But at least Tyr escapes that kind of humiliation.

Asker lowers her fists and looks back at the gym owner. The man's eyes have narrowed, and he sucks his front teeth.

Then he gestures at her with a thumb over his shoulder in the direction of his office. Turns on his heels and walks inside.

Asker pulls off the stinking boxing gloves and drops them to the mat next to Tyr, then heads toward the office.

"Class dismissed," she says over her shoulder, mostly because she can't resist.

THE GLASS MAN

The door lock clicks. His compliance has paid off; the reward has finally come.

Freedom.

At least as much as the Father permits.

Within the barriers of the estate. Within the Servants' control.

"For your own good," as the Father usually says. "Because we care about you. Very much. You are unique."

As always, he seeks out the underworld. Works his way down into its dankest depths, and the dense, all-enveloping darkness that always awaits.

By this point he knows it like the back of his hand. Knows every tunnel, every cave. Recognizes every mite that lives down there.

Blind creatures that swim and crawl through water and mud.

Others that flutter through the darkness on brittle wings.

All just as hungry as him. They devour life whenever given the chance.

Predators, bloodsuckers, carrion-eaters.

All of them fear him. His strength; his power.

Down here in the depths, beneath the human habitations, he is once again a prince, if just for a few short hours.

The prince of the underworld.

But to Boulder Isle he can no longer go. The gate there is locked, his dominion restricted.

He knows that he has only himself to blame. What he did to those two young men.

He should have let them get away. Contented himself with watching them from afar. But then they broke into his observatory. His secret place, the spot they would visit as children, when he was still Prince Pollux.

He had decorated the observatory, filled it with treasures that he had found in tunnels, caves, forests, and ruins. Things that had numbered among the living as well as the dead.

Both men were intruders. They forced the door, sullied his most sacred place with laughter and camera flashes.

Destroyed his treasures.

So he punished them in the severest possible terms.

And as a result he has been locked off the island, punished in turn for his transgression.

The Father's almighty eye never rests.

He places his hands on the locked gate, shakes it a few times.

But even strength such as his is no match for the cold metal.

This makes him angry.

HILL

As promised by Mrs. Schiller, the afternoon coffee arrives punctually at three p.m. Hill has spent the time before then gaining an overview of the materials set out for him.

The piles mostly consist of annual reports, testimonies, catalogues, and copies of patent applications in a multitude of different languages.

Besides that, there are a number of books containing news clippings about the company.

Not exactly a literary gold mine.

While Nova Irving did want this book to look past the myths and focus on AlphaCent's breakthroughs, she would hardly have hired Hill for the job had she just wanted a traditional, sandpaper-dry anniversary tome.

So what does she want him to write about?

After all, it was Gunnar's 1965 close encounter on Boulder Isle that laid the foundations for the entire company, and there is no getting around that. That also happens to be the angle that interests Hill, the one he wants to build on further once the company book is published.

He needs a hook of some kind, a backbone on which to hang the narrative that will give him free rein later on. He just doesn't know what.

He decides to park all that for a while, drink his coffee, and then explore the large and—to put it mildly—fascinating chamber.

The tall gothic windows look out over both the front courtyard and the side of the building. The end of the hall that faces the back of the house does have windows, too, but they are smaller, positioned so high up that Hill can't see through them, which is frustrating. He would have hoped to get a glimpse of the lake and Boulder Isle beyond.

The lion's share of the library collection consists of scientific tomes. Astronomy, geology, architecture, and of course medicine. There are also some less scientific collections on astrology, running all the way from antiquity to the present day.

In an out-of-the-way corner at the far end of the library Hill even finds an impressive array of science fiction. The genre's more distinguished names are all there, but the richly ornamented bookshelves also contain a mass of well-thumbed editions of pulpy American sci-fi from the fifties and sixties. He pulls out a few and flicks through them.

The covers are colorful and dramatic, depicting mystical planets, flying saucers, and strange, humanoid creatures with large heads. Bernhard Irving has signed his name on the inside cover of many of the books, in the same swirly lettering as on the ceiling of the master bedroom at Villa Arcturus.

Hill thinks back to the elevator buttons. Could one of those underground levels house Bernhard's burial chamber?

He sweeps that thought aside for now, returns to the desk, and starts flicking through the books of newspaper clippings. Many are articles that he has already come across in his previous research into the Irving family, but some of them are new to him.

He takes out some paper and a pen and starts sketching a timeline of the company's history, as per the clippings.

They begin from the late sixties, with a few dry three-liners about young Gunnar Irving taking over as CEO from his father, Bernhard.

In those days Gunnar Irving is happy to be interviewed. He speaks at great length about his plans to take the company in a new direction, but he is granted little attention. Only when he mentions his UFO encounter do the journalists wake up.

By that point Gunnar has already launched his first med-tech inventions, including the obsidian scalpel.

UFO GUNNAR GETS IDEAS FROM SPACE! reads one of the headlines.

FROM SPACE ENCOUNTER TO STAR PATENT, reads another. The articles are mostly contemptuous, of course, but the mocking tone fades in line with the company's success.

By the mid-seventies the interviews haven't entirely lost sight of aliens and close encounters, but the focus is nevertheless more on growth percentages and market share. "Space-Case" Gunnar has transformed himself from a promising but eccentric youth into a successful inventor and company leader. When Gunnar turns fifty in the early nineties, long, fawning articles are written about him, in which the UFO encounter serves as no more than a bit of added spice.

From the turn of the century onward, Gunnar drastically reduces his number of interviews and public appearances. The last interview that Hill finds among the clippings is over ten years old. The article bears the headline THE KEY TO ETERNAL LIFE, and it discusses various cryonics technologies.

When I was a boy I heard about a tree frog that winters by allowing itself to freeze, Gunnar says in a passage that ends with a long tract:

> The frog's bodily functions cease completely for hundreds of days, before warmth returns it to life. This thought has fascinated me ever since; just imagine the opportunities if we could do the same with people! Astronauts could travel for years through space, frozen in deep sleep, and be woken just before reaching their destination, unaffected by age or the adverse physical and psychological impact of the long journey. Or if we could freeze time for the terminally ill and wake them up again in a future in which their conditions can be treated. A time-traveling journey into the future.

The tone of the interview is deferential, and not even when Gunnar himself raises the topic of space travel are any questions posed about UFOs or aliens. In spite of this, a fact box on the company still mentions the UFO encounter on Boulder Isle, and the nickname Space-Case Gunnar still persists.

Hill puts down his pen. Gunnar's journey from young whipper-snapper with a lively imagination to eccentric visionary is interesting.

But those elevator buttons give him no peace. The faint hint of two underground levels that could contain almost anything.

Hill turns his gaze up at the ornamented ceiling. Bernhard Irving was certainly eccentric enough to have planned a burial chamber for himself. Or to have a secret tunnel excavated all the way to Boulder Isle.

Besides: while Mrs. Schiller was certainly pleasant enough when she showed him around the library earlier, wasn't there something to her words that seemed to warn him against snooping around where he shouldn't?

He thinks back to the warning letter.

He who goes there in search of Irving secrets must tread very carefully.

He takes out his phone, logs back into the urban exploration forum, and finds his question about the two young men who drowned in Miresjön Lake.

This time he has received a reply, from a user who goes by the name of DeepGoat.

You mean Nick and Elis? Yeah, I knew them. Nick was completely obsessed with Boulder Isle. He was the one they found in the water that spring. In the papers they said he'd drowned, but I've heard there were inconsistencies. And they never did find Elis. Loads of weird stuff about that case.

What inconsistencies? Hill replies. Waits impatiently for a few minutes, but DeepGoat no longer appears to be online.

He gets up and does another lap of the library. The building is completely silent, and darkness has fallen outside the windows, which, when combined with the dim library lighting, makes the hall feel a little creepy. He is reminded of the warning letter again.

Astroholm is a haunted place.

Elsa Irving said the same thing, word for word. But it can hardly have been a visually impaired thirteen-year-old who posted the warning letter through his mail slot in the middle of the night.

So who was it?

Hill starts to feel tired, so he decides to head back to Villa Arcturus. He messages Mrs. Schiller via the app to request a lift, then starts packing away the materials on the desk. Two of the pages in one of the books of clippings have stuck together, and when he parts them he discovers an interview with Gunnar from a long-since defunct magazine, in which he speaks in detail about his close encounter.

Hill has read many other articles about the encounter before, but this one he has never come across. Judging by the date, it could even be the very first.

He photocopies the article to take back with him for some evening reading.

While the machine spits out the copies, he walks over to one of the tall windows facing the front courtyard to keep an eye out for his lift.

The outdoor lighting is on, but even that is unusually dim. The Glass Man stands just twenty yards from the window, and although the sculpture is illuminated, Hill can only just make it out through the darkness and fog that hangs heavy over the estate.

While standing there, Hill notices a movement down in the court-yard. Just below him a woman is slowly pedaling off on an old bicycle. She is wearing a coat and a wide-brimmed hat, and in the bicycle's basket sits a large, long-haired cat. The sight is so strange that Hill must fight the impulse to rub his eyes.

The woman with the cat slowly cycles away from the house. Disappears into the mists beyond The Glass Man.

The red glow from her back lights flashes for another few seconds, before it, too, disappears.

ASKER

The basement office at Freedom Gym is larger than expected. Besides a desk, it also contains a chunky TV and a cracked pleather couch. Sagging chipboard shelves holding files and presentation cups circle the walls, the upper sections of which are brimming with dusty diplomas, streamers, and martial arts certificates.

The portly gym owner who is apparently Lalo has sat down at his overloaded desk. With his hands clasped over his stomach he studies Asker from head to toe. His hair is thinning, and his teeth are a smidge too big and symmetrical to be real.

"So who are you and what the fuck are you doing at my gym?" he grunts. "Since you sure as hell aren't in need of any self-defense lessons."

Asker takes a deep breath. There would be several possible entry points into this conversation, but she chooses the most direct.

"I have some questions about Tord Korpi," she says.

"Who?"

"A northerner, around fifty, bearded, pretty well built. He was here one summer years ago, helping you to build something underground. This basement, perhaps?"

That Uncle Tord would have been here for a job is mostly just a guess, albeit an educated one: it's hardly likely that he would make the almost-two-hour journey from the Farm to Hörby just to work out.

Lalo sucks his teeth, still studying her closely.

She stares back at him. There really is something familiar about the gym owner, but she still can't place him.

He opens his mouth in a big grin that reveals his entire denture.

"You're Per Asker's daughter, aren't you?"

Asker gives a start.

"Yes, yes you are," he chuckles, while wagging his chubby index finger from side to side. "I'd never forget those weird-ass eyes of yours. I was skinnier back then, so you probably don't remember me."

She tries to keep up the front, but it's hard.

"You were maybe ten or eleven," he goes on. "Your dad invited me to the Farm to discuss a few things."

Asker can't help herself: since he already knows who she is, there's no point in her holding back.

"What things?"

Lalo throws his hands out to his sides in a shrug. The movement makes a hairy roll of fat peer out from between his sweatpants and T-shirt.

"Ah, this and that. I guess you could say we had a number of shared interests. Self-defense being one. Your old man was a real Krav Maga hotshot. That liver shot you just sank Tyr with was straight out of Per's handbook. The idiot should be happy he didn't shit himself, amirite?"

The gym owner flashes those dentures again.

"By the way, is he still around, your dad? Still squatting in the forests waiting for the end of the world?"

"Oh yes." Asker nods.

Lalo shakes his head in amusement.

"Per Asker's daughter, fuck me. I remember how hard he pushed you. Worked you like he was gonna make some sports prodigy out of you. Gold medalist at the doomsday Olympics."

He laughs at his own joke.

"Tord Korpi," Asker repeats. "What can you tell me about him?"

"It was Per who referred him. Korpi helped us to build our basement, just like you said."

"And when was this?"

Lalo leans back in his chair, looks pensively up at the ceiling. The gap between his T-shirt and sweatpants grows even more, as though his hairy belly were stretching out toward the light.

"The summer of 2006, I'm pretty sure. The first time he came was at Midsummer, to take measurements and all that. I remember that because he showed up on Midsummer's Day, when all of Sweden's normally hungover as fuck. Then he came back a few weeks later. That time he had a troop of foreigners with him, and they did the job. Fast guys, efficient."

"Do you remember anything else?"

"Only that they worked evenings and weekends. As I understood it, they had another job during the day and did ours on the side. Fuck knows when they slept, but that wasn't any of my concern."

"And you paid him in cash?"

The gym owner nods. "That's right."

"With money rolls?"

"Money rolls?" He frowns. "No, why go to the hassle?"

"How much money are we talking?"

Lalo shrugs again.

"A hundred grand, I think. Half up front, half later. A good price."

Asker thinks. Obviously Korpi could have rolled the bills himself, though that seems unlikely. And the amount isn't right either: Korpi's duffel bag contained far more than a hundred thousand kronor.

"Do you know who Korpi and his builders were working for during the day?" she asks. "Or where?"

Lalo shakes his head.

"Nope. They'd just show up in a couple of shitty vans in the evening, dig and drill fast as fuck, and disappear at some point after midnight. No funny business."

An unconscious micro-expression on his face catches Asker's attention.

"But something else happened," she says.

"Why are you asking all this?" he asks evasively. "It was decades ago, you couldn't have been more than a teen."

She doesn't reply, simply gives him her two-toned stare.

Lalo shifts position and tugs at his T-shirt, as though suddenly aware of his belly gap. At this movement the office chair groans faintly under his weight. Asker waits him out.

"OK, OK, something happened," he says, pulling a face. "A couple of kids who worked out at the gym got wind that Korpi had cash. They decided to jump him one night. I don't know all the details, but from what I heard Korpi pulled a gun and shot one of 'em in the leg."

Asker leans forward in interest.

"And then?"

"Seriously, I have no idea. The pigs weren't involved, at any rate, and Korpi never mentioned it to me. Soon after that the job was done, Korpi kicked up and left, and I never heard from him again."

"Do you remember their names?"

"One of them," he nods. "Linus Palm. The other two were his friends, but I don't remember their names. Anyway, that Palm guy's a local councillor these days. Cleaned himself up real good. But if you plan to go running after him, you didn't hear anything from me."

"Of course not."

Lalo leans back, clasps his fingers over his belly.

"So, you gonna tell me what this is all about?"

She blinks at him.

"Do you really want to know?"

Lalo lets out a laugh.

"You really are Per Asker's daughter. It's been years since I last thought about him. Years since . . ."

His face turns grave.

"Your dad and I had a falling out a year or so after the excavation," he says. "At one point we came close to blows. Back then I was younger and in better shape, and I never backed away from a fight. But with Per I actually did. I'm not saying he scared me, but . . ."

The expression on his face is difficult to read.

"Let's just say I was very happy our ways parted, if you catch my drift. Per would have killed me without a second thought."

Asker doesn't reply, simply turns and leaves the room.

HILL

Hill is back in Villa Arcturus, and after dinner and a cup of tea he has managed to gather his thoughts somewhat. Every now and then he still struggles to get his head around where he is: not just at Astroholm Manor, but in Bernhard Irving's very own home. Even so, for now it is still Gunnar who interests him most. Space-Case Gunnar Irving, the man who built a commercial empire out of an alien encounter on Boulder Isle.

Hill hobbles to the living room, sits down at Bernhard's enormous desk, and pulls out the magazine article he photocopied. It dates to the end of the sixties, and the journalist has relayed Gunnar's story so verbatim that you can almost hear his voice.

It was early winter in the year I turned twenty-three. My father Bernhard, who has always been very interested in astronomy, had built an observatory out on Boulder Isle in Miresjön Lake.

We were supposed to have spent that night stargazing together. But my father was taken ill, so I went there alone. It was just after midnight when I suddenly spotted a light gliding through the sky.

Initially I thought it was a plane, but its movements were far too erratic. And then the light grew brighter, and it drew all the closer to Boulder Isle.

In the end I was forced to shade my eyes so they wouldn't be dazzled.

I was scared, I'll happily admit. I was completely alone out there on the island. The light hovered over the observatory, and I ran outside to get to safety. But then it was as though someone spoke to me from inside my own head. The voice told me that I needn't be afraid, that they came in peace. So I stopped.

The light hung in the air above me, and I could make out the outline of a spaceship. Its body was made of a dark, shiny material that reminded me of glass. Then a door opened, and a creature stepped out.

He was tall—at least eight, nine feet—and humanoid in shape. In some way he traveled down toward me. The creature appeared to be made of the same material as the ship. I could scarce make out any facial feature, except his eyes, which glowed red.

The creature spoke to me through telepathy. He told me that he hailed from Alpha Centauri, and that he had traveled from afar to aid humanity. Then he reached out and touched my head. After that I don't remember anything until I woke up the next morning. Even though it was winter and I had been lying outside all night, I was quite warm, and I felt full of strength and vigor.

In addition, my head was churning with tremendous thoughts, thoughts I had never had before. Ideas of different inventions that might aid humanity.

Giddily I traveled back home to Astroholm, where I told my father everything. He was the only person in the world who might believe me.

And he did. My father understood what was required. Bernhard entrusted me with the entire family firm. Allowed me to build on the ideas the extraterrestrial had given me.

I shall always be deeply grateful to him for that.

Hill leans back in the desk chair. He has read different versions of the UFO encounter before, but this is the first time he has read Gunnar's version of events, narrated in his own words in one continuous sweep. Reading it has actually given him mild heart palpitations.

He spins a half-turn and gazes out through the back window. The garden behind Villa Arcturus consists of a three-hundred-square-foot lawn that then gives way to broad-leaved woodland. The faint outdoor lights on the façade reach only the first tree trunks.

Gunnar described a white light in the sky. And one winter long ago, Hill saw the same thing through his binoculars. At least that's what he *thinks* he saw—or what he thought at the time.

But it was what happened next in Gunnar's story that made the strongest impression on Hill when he first heard the account as a teenager: the description of an enormous, dark creature with glowing red eyes. He shudders.

For years before—and especially after—his journey to the shores of Miresjön Lake, that very creature had stalked his nightmares. Yet Hill's desire to visit Boulder Isle only intensified. He wanted to explore the place, find something to confirm what he thought he once saw. Now he has finally been granted that opportunity. Or at least he has been promised as much.

His phone starts to ring, and Nova Irving's name appears on the screen.

"I just wanted to check you're settling in well," she says. "Has Mrs. Schiller given you everything you need?"

On the phone Nova's voice sounds even deeper than in person. He wonders if it's natural, or if she puts it on for some reason.

"Thanks, I'm being very well looked after," he replies.

"Excellent," she says. "Between you and me, when it came to the importance of this book Gunnar wasn't easily persuaded. He's a very private person, you see. But he was very impressed by your eagerness to travel here and get started straightaway."

"Great . . ." Hill is unsure how to continue the conversation. "Well, I've been giving some thought to the book's angle. If I understood you correctly, you want to present the AlphaCent beyond the myths. What exactly did you mean by that?"

"That I want the book to focus on the company's achievements. Gunnar's achievements. His contribution to humanity."

Hill's thoughts turn to the interview with Gunnar that he just read.

"I agree, of course," he says. "But with corporate books, there's a risk that the text will get too dry and fact-driven. And then no one will read it. The investment is wasted, so to speak."

He pauses briefly, carefully weighing his words.

"If we want to catch the readers' attention—if we really want to get them to understand what Gunnar's achieved—then we also need to get to the heart of what makes him, the Irving family, and Alpha-Cent so unique. Draw the readers into the story."

His words hang in the air for a few seconds.

"Which isn't to say we have to focus on the past," he hastens to add. "But I think we should use it as our starting point, and then work forward from there. Gunnar hasn't given any interviews in years. And, of course, many people are interested in his account of what really happened on Boulder Isle. His own words instead of hearsay. How the encounter affected him, how it made him the man he is today."

Hill is getting into his stride. He toys with the idea of asking her about a possible visit to Boulder Isle while he's at it, but decides it's too soon.

"Interesting thoughts, Martin," Nova says. "I'm pleased to hear you're already so engrossed in the project. Let's let this sit for a day or two and touch base soon. In the meantime, just make yourself at home."

"OK," says Hill, in the absence of anything better to say.

"Excellent. Well, have a great stay, and don't hesitate to call me if there's anything you need. Good night in the meantime."

She ends the call, and Hill is left sitting there with the phone in his hand.

His superpower has always been his ability to get people to like him, and Nova Irving didn't reject his ideas outright, which is a good start, at least.

He navigates to the urban exploration forum.

DeepGoat has replied to his message in the thread about the drowning.

I heard Nick's body had strange wounds. His eyes were gone—completely gouged out. And Elis was never found, even though they dragged the whole lake. Fuck knows what happened on that island, but it was no accident.

Hill wonders whether to ask anything else, but then again Deep-Goat's story appears to be based entirely on vague hearsay. There must be a police report where he can sort fact from fiction. Which makes him think of Leo.

Only now does he see that she has left him a voicemail; presumably something to do with the shaky signal. He listens to the message and learns that she has discovered the identity of the dead body outside the Farm, that she had once met the deceased, and that she has gone to visit a gym in Hörby.

He calls her back, and she picks up immediately. Judging by the background noise, she is driving. As usual, the sound of her voice makes him happy.

"Hey," he says, "I just got your message, so I'm pretty up-to-date. Has anything else happened?"

"Oh yes."

She gives him a rundown of her visit to Freedom Gym.

"OK," he says, pausing a few seconds before going on. "So your plan is to talk to the local councillor tomorrow?"

"It looks like it, yeah."

"And you haven't wondered whether . . ." he pauses, but forces himself to go on, ". . . whether Per might be trying to manipulate you?"

Her reply comes a little too fast.

"Why would he do that?"

"Maybe because he wants you to help him get away with a murder he actually committed?" Hill offers. "Or because he's insane, or he wants revenge, or he still can't let go of you . . . Need I go on?"

"OK, I get it. With Per there's no ruling anything out," she admits. "But it's not like I have any choice."

She's defensive now, he notes. Just like she used to get whenever they would talk about Per as teens. As though, in spite of everything, Leo isn't prepared to accept how insane her father is, and so tries to defend him instead.

At the same time, he knows that pushing her won't help.

"Just be careful," he eventually says, which is of course just as idiotic as it is unnecessary.

But Leo seems to take it the right way.

"I promise!" she says with a quiet laugh.

The mood between them lightens again.

"So, how are things with you?" she asks. "Is Astroholm everything you dreamed of?"

"So far the answer's probably yes."

He tells her about his day: about Villa Arcturus, Samuel, and the Schillers; about his encounter with Elsa Irving, his visit to the manor house, and his conversation with Nova—even the lady on the bicycle with the cat.

"Sounds a little surreal," she says. "You must be loving every minute."

Now it is Hill's turn to laugh.

"Right you are. Though, as it happens, I was going to ask you for a favor. Two urban explorers drowned in Miresjön Lake three years ago while trying to get out to Boulder Isle. I got a tip that there were a bunch of inconsistencies around their deaths. One of them was never found, and apparently the other had a bunch of weird injuries to his body. I'd like to access the police report."

"Which of your book projects is this for?" she asks teasingly.

"The one the Irving family are paying you to do, or your next best-seller? *The Secrets of Boulder Isle*, or whatever you're going to call it?"

"No idea," he replies with a laugh. "Maybe both."

"OK, I'll get the report for you tomorrow."

"Great, thanks!"

They fall silent for a few seconds, as if neither of them wants to end the call. In the end it is Hill who does.

"Well, good night then, Leo."

"Good night, Martin."

For a brief moment their voices linger on the line before the call ends.

Hill gets ready for bed, turns in for the night, and switches out the light. Up on the ceiling, the constellations slowly begin to emerge, growing brighter and brighter as his eyes adjust to the darkness.

They must be made with some kind of luminous paint.

After a while even Bernhard Irving's swirly lettering is legible.

Ursa Major.
Cassiopeia.
Leo.

He thinks about Leo again. She flutters him to sleep.

ASKER

When she arrives back at the big house that isn't hers, Asker makes sure to immediately rinse off Freedom Gym's lingering sweat stench in the steam shower in the master bathroom. The feeling of normality that she got from her conversation with Martin has already dissipated, and after a while she turns off all the luxurious special features and just stands there with a hard torrent of water running over her head, in an attempt to clear her mind.

Hellman's gang have had all afternoon to do a deep dive on Prepper Per. According to her mother, they have already identified Tord Korpi, and if one of the sharper team members has been assigned to the case, then they may even have found the military connection between him and Per. That should mean that Hellman and his gang will start planning her father's arrest any day now.

She must find an alternative suspect before then.

Tord Korpi's links to the local area appear to have been work-related: bunkers for Prepper Per, a basement for Freedom Gym, and a third job for an as-yet-unknown employer.

Could Lalo have had something to do with Korpi's death? He knew Prepper Per and disliked him, which would give him reason enough to dump the body at the Farm.

But she doubts that.

Although the gym owner is undoubtedly shady, nothing in his criminal record suggests an involvement in any violent crime. On top of that, he voluntarily confirmed that he knew Korpi, something he would likely keep to himself if he was indeed trying to blame Korpi's death on Prepper Per.

Which leaves two possible lines of inquiry: the botched robbery that Lalo told her about, in which Korpi supposedly shot someone in the leg, and the unknown employer for whom Korpi and his team worked during the day.

For the first theory she at least has an entry point: the name of one of the men involved. Linus Palm, now a local councillor.

For the second theory she has so far only vague information: Lalo's statement, the wads of cash in the duffel bag, the phone call she happened to overhear. And those details aren't necessarily even linked.

Korpi could have rolled his own bills, and the phone call could have been with someone else entirely.

One of Prepper Per's favorite lecture topics was resource management. Water, food, fuel, medicine, ammunition—nothing could be wasted, especially when the supply was finite. Any decisions regarding resources had to be made based on logic and a statistical analysis.

Fail to plan, plan to fail, as Per used to say.

The only resources she has right now are basically herself and what little time she has left before Hellman tries to invade the Farm, when his entire tactical unit will get blown to kingdom come. Had she still been working at Serious Crime, she could have put a team on each theory. Made them work in parallel until they got to the bottom of each. But that is impossible now.

If Per were here, he would tell her to devote her time to where the potential for results is the greatest. That's to say on the botched robbery. There she has a name, a weapon, and a serious violent crime.

Yet her gut instinct faintly protests. She doesn't know why, has far too few facts to hang it on anything in particular. Perhaps it's just that she would somehow prefer it if Uncle Tord's death was linked to her own observations? That she is putting her feelings ahead of logic? Per would have punished her for that kind of arrogance. Wouldn't let her forget it in a hurry.

Her scar itches again.

She lowers the water temperature drastically. The shock of the cold makes her gasp, and she takes a few deep breaths to get her breathing back under control.

The itching stops, at least for now.

She turns off the water and stands up straight. Her body shudders a few times before adjusting to its new conditions.

Adapting, as always.

Tord Korpi, Lalo, the gym—all of it is Per's world.

In his shadowlands, all feelings must be put to one side.

You have to do things his way to survive.

And Per would have focused his resources on the botched robbery.

She dries herself, pulls on a dressing gown, and eats a microwave meal at the large kitchen island while googling Linus Palm.

Just as Lalo said, he is now a local councillor. He is thirty-six years of age, which means he would have been twenty when Korpi was murdered. Since Palm, like every politician, is overactive on social media, Asker finds plenty of images of him in various more-or-less staged environments.

Asker enlarges some of the images and studies them carefully. Linus Palm has blond hair and a side part. His eyes are blue, and when he wants to appear serious he wears glasses that he probably doesn't need. His general uniform tends to be a shirt and blazer over dark jeans, which makes him seem sufficiently down-to-earth. And he's smart enough not to pose in super-expensive oilskin coats and hunting boots, like the big-city politicians do whenever they deign to set foot on a dirt track or visit an organic strawberry farm. Instead he opts for a fleece jacket and regular boots when he is outside the urban planners' remit.

In every interview, Linus Palm labors the point that he's a salt-of-the-earth country boy at heart, just like the majority of his voters. That he is passionate about local issues and has no desire to up and leave for the capital, despite the rumors that certain people in high places would love to tempt him into national politics.

All in all, Linus Palm gives the impression of someone who is very careful with his brand. It's quite rare that he mentions his past, other than to emphasize how normal he is, but Asker does find one interview where he claims to have gone through a "difficult" phase in his young adulthood. In the next breath he makes it clear that he has never been suspected of any crime, and that he has learned from his stupid mistakes.

As far as she can tell, the police files appear to agree with him on that.

So how keen will Linus Palm be to talk to her about a robbery dating sixteen years back? Or a man executed with a shot to the back of his head?

Part of her wants to go straight over to his house to find out. But showing up on his doorstep in the middle of the night and trying to squeeze him for answers in front of his family is definitely a bad idea.

Still, she is far too restless to go to bed.

She switches apps, sends a message.

Are you home? Feel like company?

As soon as she gets an answer, she pulls on her jacket, locks and alarms the house, and takes the stairs down to the garage.

HILL

Hill is standing on the roof next to Bernhard's observatory. Above him the sky is filled with stars. Luminous dots that flicker faintly in the eternity.

Beside him stands a blind girl who points out the constellations for him, even though she can't see them herself.

"Boötes, Carina, Canis Major."

A white light flashes over the lake, so brightly that the stars pale.

The light starts to move toward them, turns into a shining spaceship reminiscent of a flying saucer on the cover of a cheap sci-fi paperback.

Elsa goes on reeling off the constellations.

"Canis Minor, Sagittarius, Cassiopeia, Leo . . ."

The spaceship hovers in the air above them.

A door opens and a big, dark creature with glowing red eyes appears in the doorway. Its arms are unnaturally long, its hands sharp claws.

"The Glass Man," Elsa gasps. "It's all about him."

The next second he finds himself in an elevator. A long corridor extends beyond its open doors. There are only two buttons, and he presses the lower one. The elevator doesn't move.

A sound makes him look up. The space creature is coming straight for him down the corridor, its claw-hands raised.

Its large eyes are burning red, its pupils like two black holes.

He presses the elevator button, hammers it again and again in an attempt to make the doors close.

The creature starts to move faster. It opens its mouth to reveal a jaw of black, glass teeth, then lets out a roar.

Finally the doors start to move. They shut just before the creature reaches him. The elevator descends at such a furious speed that Hill's feet lose contact with the floor. Just when he thinks it is about to crash, the elevator gently glides to a stop.

"*Please note*," says a dry elevator voice that sounds just like Samuel's. "*This area may under no circumstances be visited without express permission.*"

The doors slowly slide open.

Outside awaits total darkness of a kind that Hill has never experienced before. Like a wall where all light suddenly ceases to exist. Or perhaps a black hole?

Cautiously he extends one hand, and it immediately disappears into the darkness. When he draws it back in terror, his hand has transformed into black glass. The glass scales his arm like a living organism, spreading across his body and devouring all the light, until all that remains is darkness.

Hill wakes up soaked in sweat and needing to use the bathroom. The moon is shining down on his face through a crack in the curtains. The wound in his leg is throbbing, and he suspects that he has a fever. With some effort he manages to get himself to the bathroom.

He hasn't dreamed about the space creature since he was a teenager. He thought he had grown out of that kind of nonsense, but clearly not. Space-Case Gunnar's story must have triggered it all again.

He downs an ibuprofen, pees, and hangs his wet pajama top up to dry. Pulls out a dry T-shirt from his suitcase.

On his way back to bed he limps over to close the crack in the curtains.

The lawn outside glints with dew and moonlight. Behind it the forest looms, dense and dark.

The shadows around the trees at the edge of the lawn sponge up the faint light. As he is drawing the curtains Hill thinks he catches sight of someone standing between the tree trunks. He quickly opens the curtain again, but of course there is no one there.

His imagination, obviously. The remnants of a fever dream.

But for a brief second, amid the deep darkness of the trees, he could have sworn he saw a red glow.

WEDNESDAY

ASKER

She slips out of bed and grabs her clothes without waking the man sleeping naked beside her. His name is Viktor, he is a few years her junior, and they meet from time to time, mostly for sex. Viktor often travels for work, and he has neither a steady girlfriend nor a criminal past. She doesn't know much more about him, other than that he's hot and good in bed, which is enough for her.

She gets dressed in the bathroom, trying to make as little noise as possible, then sneaks out of his stylish apartment in the Limhamn district of Malmö.

The piercing wind takes hold of her jacket, and the sun still hasn't risen.

The morning traffic toward central Malmö flows drowsily.

Ideally she would have headed straight for the town hall in Hörby, to speak to Linus Palm. But according to his assistant, frustratingly enough the local councillor won't have time to speak to her until after lunch. But it gives her a chance to check in on her department.

Once she has reached police HQ and taken the elevator down to level minus one, she stops by Rosen's office and asks her to pull up the investigation into the double drowning in Miresjön Lake that Martin asked her about. Though she is aware that it's a breach of all kinds of rules, one of the advantages of working at the Department of Lost Souls is that no one is keeping an eye on small fry like that. Besides, she's happy that she can repay Martin the favor he did her by getting her into the forensic medicine division.

"OK," Rosen says once she has been given her tasks. "I'll see what I can find. By the way, here's the data you asked me for yesterday, about the area where the bog body was found. Police reports, incident reports, parking fines—everything logged for the time period that you gave me."

Rosen hands over a file with a look that is both satisfied and focused, as though the diminutive woman has actually started to develop a taste for real tasks.

"Amazing," says Asker, who hadn't counted on Rosen having it ready so fast. "Great work!"

She stops.

"By the way, how's your daughter in Australia doing? Have you been in touch lately?"

"We FaceTime once a week," Rosen replies evasively. "But the time difference makes it hard."

"Maybe you should give her a call," Asker says with a nod at the office landline. "Right now, before they go to bed over there?"

Rosen lights up. She has already started dialing the number when Asker shuts the door behind her.

She is halfway to her office when Virgilsson nabs her.

"I have a few papers that need your signature."

"OK." She signals at him to follow her to her office at the end of the corridor.

"So, what's new then, Chief?" he asks once she has signed her name on the right lines. "Any exciting cases in the works?"

"Exciting cases, down here?" she replies dryly.

The toad-like man gives the faintest hint of a smile.

"Well, exciting is perhaps the wrong word. Are you working on anything interesting?"

Asker knows exactly what Virgilsson is doing. He is out on a fishing trip, hoping to get a bite that he can then take to Hellman for some kickbacks.

"I'm still cleaning up after my predecessor," she says. "There was a lot that was left up in the air."

Virgilsson tilts his head to one side.

"Yes, I'm afraid Bengt Sandgren probably wasn't all that organized. Well, do let me know if I can assist you with anything."

"Of course," she replies.

"Oh, by the way, just so you know," he says when he reaches the door. "Kent's still off sick. I wouldn't expect him back for at least a week."

Asker straightens up. The time has come for her to find out what's wrong with Attila.

"Why not?" she asks.

Virgilsson pulls a sorrowful face. "Hasn't anyone said anything? I thought perhaps Rosen might have told you. After all, the two of you have been working together rather a lot."

She ignores his prying hint.

Virgilsson shuts the office door and sits down uninvited on the chair opposite her.

"It's a sad story, all in all."

Asker waits patiently for him to go on.

"Kent has never been married. But he did have a niece, Ella, who was also his goddaughter. Ella had some problems. A restless soul, one might say. Drugs, the wrong crowd. Almost ten years ago she passed away, all too young, of an overdose."

He tilts his head to one side.

"Apparently it was her boyfriend who was plying her with the drugs. Every time Ella's parents managed to get her back on her feet, he'd drag her down into the mire. The day after her funeral he disappeared."

"Disappeared? You mean he left town?" Asker says.

Virgilsson shakes his head.

"Disappeared. He was never seen again, and he hasn't been heard from since. By this point he might well have been officially presumed dead."

Asker grimaces.

"And they think Attila was involved?"

"The internal investigators questioned him a number of times," Virgilsson says with a nod. "But Kent refused to cooperate. They even raided his apartment, but they found nothing. After a year-long investigation, they eventually chose to transfer him."

"Here, to the Resources Unit," Asker summarizes. "So that he'd get bored and resign, or sit out the rest of his working life out of sight."

"Exactly. Normally Kent keeps a low profile, but when the anniversary of Ella's death starts to near . . ." Virgilsson throws his hands out to his sides in resignation, ". . . he calls in sick, shuts himself away, and drinks himself senseless for a week or so. After that he returns as though nothing happened."

"Has anyone tried to help him?" Asker asks.

"Oh yes, Sandgren tried. He went to see him and offered his

support, but Kent kicked him down the stairwell. After that the two never spoke to each other again. My advice would be to leave well enough alone. Kent will be back soon, and then it will all go back to normal."

Asker nods absent-mindedly. She has no intention of trying to save Attila. He's a grown man, after all; if he wants to drown his sorrows and what little remains of his career with it then that's his problem.

She has much more important things to take care of.

"I'm going to be out on a case this afternoon," she says.

"Where, if I may ask?"

Virgilsson smiles as though to suggest that the information he provided on Attila was part of a transaction, and he expects something in return.

"Why do you ask?" she replies curtly.

"Oh, no particular reason," he says. "Polite conversation, mostly." He raises his eyebrows, as if still expecting a response.

"Was there anything else?" she asks.

His smile stiffens, and his lips purse in disappointment.

"Oh no, I'll let you work in peace."

He turns around and stops by the door.

"Oh, by the way. Since you'll be out anyway, perhaps you could call in at Madame Rind's. It's Kent's turn, really, but someone will have to step—"

"I don't have time." She cuts him off. "You'll have to send someone else."

"Oh, that is a shame. You see, Rosen doesn't have a driver's license, and naturally we can't send Zafer." Virgilsson gestures at one of his ears. "He doesn't hear what Madame says. So in the past it was Kent, Sandgren, and I who shouldered the task between us. But now Kent's unwell."

"I see. Can't you go then? Like I said, I'll be out on a case."

"Normally I'd be happy to, but as it happens I've just changed medication and ought not to drive for a week or so. And if we don't make an appearance, then Madame Rind will start calling around. Normally she starts with the commissioner, before working her way down the ranks. The last time we missed our appointment with her, Sandgren was given a real rap over the knuckles. The commissioner didn't appreciate being hounded by an insistent fortune-teller . . ."

Virgilsson pulls a face that is equal parts apologetic and amused. Asker purses her lips. The crafty little sweater-vested toad has backed her into a corner, and he knows it. She has absolutely no time for this kind of nonsense. But under no circumstances does she want the commissioner breathing down her neck, or to risk any questions about what she was working on that was so important that she had no time for a routine visit to the medium.

"OK," Asker says through gritted teeth. "I'll stop by this afternoon."

"Excellent. A nice gesture to the department. Shows that the chief isn't afraid of mucking in and doing the work when necessary."

Asker simply gives a curt nod.

"Well, good luck with whatever you're working on!" Virgilsson says while slinking through the door.

Asker must resist the urge to hurl the closest heavy object to hand at his stubby neck.

HILL

Groundskeeper Ville collects him just before nine a.m. The fog has eased slightly, but the air is still piercing. After a restless night, Hill doesn't feel too good. His wound smarts more than it did the previous day, and he shivers when he takes a seat in the golf cart.

At the library he nevertheless manages to muster some enthusiasm and starts sifting through the materials more carefully, collating new information with what he already knows.

He is working on two fronts: on the one hand, he is trying to chart AlphaCent's and Gunnar Irving's business affairs, while on the other he is trying to gather information that might somehow relate to Boulder Isle or the rumors about the underground burial chamber. Every now and then he gets up and scans the bookshelves.

After an hour or so he finds a plan of Astroholm in an old file shoved between two thicker tomes. It even has annotations, in Bernhard's handwriting. But when he unfolds the map on the table, he notes, much to his disappointment, that the single subterranean level it details is in fact a basement that doesn't look remotely exciting, which dampens his fire somewhat.

He is still feeling feverish and out of sorts, and after this setback he no longer has the energy for work. Instead he takes a stroll to the sci-fi section. The bookshelves in this corner are even more elaborately ornamented than in the rest of the library, and when he steps back to admire them he notices that there are carved figures up at the top. Muscular human bodies, some with animal heads: a goat, a ram, a lion, and a bull.

The creatures resemble those from the small graphite drawings in Villa Arcturus, he realizes. And with that he recognizes what they are. The figures are constellations, but in human form: Capricorn, Aries, Leo, and Taurus. And, farther along, Virgo, Gemini, and Sagittarius.

Hill takes some of the most colorful sci-fi paperbacks back to his desk and sits down to flick through them.

Many of the books are illustrated, the imagery typically fifties in style, back when the atomic bomb and jet propulsion represented science's furthest frontiers. The depictions of both the future and space are fanciful, to say the least: by and large, the spaceships look like flying saucers, and the aliens traveling in them tend to have disproportionately large heads, glowing eyes, and long arms.

The drawings call to mind the creature from Hill's own nightmare.

He stifles a shudder and reminds himself that he is a grown man who has recently had a brush with true evil. A creature from a dream shouldn't affect him this much.

His reading is interrupted when the elevator door opens, and a woman in a white apron wheels in a trolley with his lunch. She doesn't even look his way, disappears before he can say so much as a thank-you.

Hill prods listlessly at his food while scrolling on his phone. Nothing more from Leo. He fires off a quick message to her.

How's it going?

He sees that she reads the message, then the flashing dots to indicate that she is drafting a reply.

So-so. Will call you later.

He sends an impersonal *OK* by return, then after some hesitation supplements it with a smiley face emoji. He sees new dots and waits for her to respond, only for them to abruptly disappear.

For some reason he feels a little disappointed.

After lunch he is fetched by Mrs. Schiller and escorted down to the medical suite. They take the same route as before. In the elevator he once again gazes at the two buttons below the slightly larger one that represents the ground floor. If one is for the basement he just saw on Bernhard's plan, where does the other one go?

In the consulting room Dr. Schiller once again inspects his wound.

"The tests showed that the infection doesn't quite seem to want to pass," he says. "I'll put you on a stronger antibiotic. I'll also give you a round of vitamins, to kick-start your immune system."

From a fridge he takes two filled syringes.

"If you could just roll up your sleeve."

Hill looks away while the doctor gives him the injections.

"There!"

The doctor puts a Band-Aid on Hill's elbow crease and clears away the needles. After that he wheels over the machine with the AlphaCent logo that was standing in the corner.

"This is one of our latest treatment methods," he explains. "Cryotherapies have proven very effective in aiding the body's recovery. First the machine will cool the wound to a very low temperature. This may feel a little uncomfortable. Then, once we have attained the right temperature, I'll treat the wound with a laser. The combination of deep cooling and heat both kills bacteria and stimulates the healing process. If you could just lean back on the bed and relax."

Hill does as he is instructed. Without any preamble, the doctor places a kind of pad over his wound, which he then connects to the machine.

"Now we'll get started. I'll leave you here for a moment while the cooling process is underway." He presses a button before leaving the room, and the machine faintly starts to hum.

Once it is working, the skin under the pad starts to feel increasingly cold. The chill works its way inward, and after a while it feels as though Hill's entire thigh is deep-frozen.

To while away the time he opens the chat forum for urban explorers. Nothing more from DeepGoat, but a new user has posted on the thread.

> Loads of weird stuff has gone down around Miresjön. It's been that way for years. I have a friend who swears he saw a UFO over the lake.
> And if you check AlphaCent's webpage it's right there in black and white that they work with NASA. They openly admit it!
> That thing about the flash of light in 2001 being a meteorite is just a government cover-up, when in actual fact it was a UFO landing on the island. Check the Göinge UFO Society's website! They have everything you need to know.

Hill opens a new window and searches for the UFO association's website. He has stumbled across the association before in his research. If he isn't mistaken, it's chaired by the same people who run, or at least ran, the down-at-heel café that he and Samuel passed on the way to Astroholm.

Indeed, the photo on the website's homepage is of the fiberglass flying saucer on the roof of that very café. The Göinge UFO Society's website isn't exactly user-friendly: the text is small, and its color palette hurts his eyes. At the top of the list of its most popular articles he finds one that bears the headline THE SECRET UFO LANDING ON BOULDER ISLE, JANUARY 6, 2001.

The headline of the second article is even more tempting: DROWNING OR COVER-UP? WE KNOW WHAT HAPPENED TO THE LOST URBAN EXPLORERS.

Hill clicks on the link. Nothing happens.

He tries the next, then another.

The result is the same.

All of the links are dead.

THE GLASS MAN

Despite their banishment to Villa Canopus, he continued to be a model of comportment. Continued to reap successes, meet every expectation.

He patiently staked out a smooth and impeccable path for himself, in the hope that the Father would one day take him back. Bring him into the light once more, raise him up as his prince and heir.

But the longer the Father delayed, the more he was hounded by thoughts of the night at the soccer club. How he had felt when witnessing Bure's journey into the darkness.

With time, these thoughts grew to longing. Then desire.

And then, finally—hunger.

He hungered to once again feel what Bure's death had given him.

The feeling of control.

Of absolute power.

One year after the banishment the Father remarried, which finally broke their mother. The cruelest part of it all was that they were forced to witness it all from afar. To watch on, powerless, as the Father moved another woman into the manor house; as he built a new family while their own slowly imploded.

That was when he made a decision.

He must still the hunger that tormented him.

But how?

One day he was out on a walk in the grounds when a thick branch came crashing down right beside him. He heard a voice shouting and looked up to see the estate's head gardener and a few other men pruning the trees.

"Are you blind or something—didn't you see the sign?" the man cried, pointing at a sign that he had evidently missed.

"Sheer luck it didn't knock your thick skull in!"

For a second he thought the head gardener must not have recognized him. Must not have seen to whom he was speaking. But then he saw the way the man smirked and exchanged glances with the other men. As though they knew that he had been banished. That they need neither fear nor respect him anymore.

The thought made him furious, but also determined.

In the weeks that followed he watched the head gardener through binoculars as he moved around the grounds.

Sometimes the man had his moronic son with him. He showed him the tasks, and appeared to be patient with his mistakes.

For some reason this only enraged him all the more.

After some weeks he had learned most of what there was to know about the man. Had discovered that sometimes—presumably without the Father's knowledge—he did small jobs on the side, beyond Astroholm's walls.

Perhaps it was that very impudence that decided it.

He prepared himself better this time. Acquired some dark clothes and gloves. Swapped his axe handle for a baseball bat that sat more comfortably in his hands.

Strangely enough, he wasn't even nervous. Only resolved.

Excited.

Ready.

The man was holding a chainsaw, didn't hear him coming.

He sneaked up closer, aiming for the nape of the neck, where all the body's nerves are gathered. Swung the baseball bat in a wide arc, striking him with full force.

The man crumpled without a sound. His bent legs jerked a few times, but after that everything was still.

He kneeled down next to his victim and turned the man's face upward.

This time the experience was even more powerful.

A wave of intense pleasure swept through him, intensifying as he watched the spark of life die out; as he watched the man slowly sink into the abyss, consumed by the eternal darkness from which no one ever returns.

At least that was what he thought at the time.

ASKER

Hörby town hall is centrally located, opposite the town's church. It is a large, modern, concrete building beside a local police station with scant open hours.

Linus Palm meets her in reception. He looks exactly like he does in his pictures: side part, blazer, jeans, and comfortable shoes. He asks her for her badge and takes a close look at her ID before shaking her hand.

"You can never be too careful nowadays," he says. "We live in uncertain times. Do come in."

He offers her coffee, which she declines, then pours a cup for himself and shows her to his office.

"So, how can I be of service?"

Asker has been wondering how to approach this conversation the entire journey here. She has booked the meeting under the pretense that she needs to ask a few routine questions regarding a police investigation, which at least isn't completely untrue.

But Palm is clearly no idiot. He has a certain sway and no doubt plenty of contacts, which means she needs to be careful.

"I'm working on a cold case," she says. "A dead man found up in the forests just on the other side of the border with Småland province."

"I see." Palm looks puzzled.

"The dead man's name is Tord Korpi." She pauses briefly, searching for any small micro-expressions that might betray that he knows exactly who she's talking about.

Instead Palm pulls an exaggerated face. He looks up at the ceiling, drums his fingers against the desk.

"Tord Korpi? Tord Korpi?" The tactic is smart; it buys him time while masking smaller, more revealing expressions. Presumably he's had training in how to sidestep thorny questions.

"I'm afraid it doesn't ring any bells," he says with a shake of his head.

Asker nods. The trick to questioning someone who is media-trained is to keep an ear out for whatever it is they *aren't* saying.

Palm isn't saying he *hasn't* met Korpi, only that the name doesn't sound familiar. A small, but crucial, difference.

"Do you think this Korpi man has any connection to Hörby?" he asks—as if straight from another page of the media training hand-book: make your opposing number answer questions instead of asking them. She counters this by simply ignoring his question and sticking to the point.

"Did you know him?" she asks.

Palm fidgets.

"Like I said, his name doesn't ring a bell."

"So you've never met?" she persists. "Korpi was a stocky man with a beard. He spoke a Norrland dialect. Pretty memorable around these parts. He used to hang out at Freedom Gym. You used to train there once upon a time, didn't you?"

"Uh . . ."

She can see Palm's brain feverishly flicking through the pages of that handbook.

"Yeah, that's right. I worked out at Freedom for a while. But that was many years ago. Now I go to Friskis och Svettis. Unfortunately not as often as I should." He pats his belly, attempts a smile. It doesn't have the intended effect.

"Did you meet Tord Korpi? He did some construction jobs there."

"I mean . . ." Playing for time again. "I haven't worked out at Freedom in at least ten, twelve years. When would this have been?"

"2006."

"Oh." He does the math. "I mean, that's sixteen years ago. My memory's not *that* good. My wife will tell you I can hardly remem-ber what I did last week . . ."

Another smile. Charming, personable, disarming. Asker leans in.

"You still haven't answered the question," she says quietly. "Have you met Tord Korpi? Yes or no?"

Palm squirms uncomfortably. He doesn't have many options.

Either he can lie and run the risk that she knows something he doesn't, in which case she will be able to throw it back in his face. Or he can tell the truth and run the risk of getting drawn into something he would rather avoid. But he finds a third option: counterattack.

"Why are you asking me all this?" he asks sternly. "Am I suspected of something? Do I need to call my lawyer?"

He raises his eyebrows, as though expecting the word *lawyer* to end the conversation.

Asker shrugs. "I don't know, actually. Have you done anything that would require a lawyer to be present?"

The question throws him. Palm searches for a new foothold, a way to take the initiative.

"Do you really, in all seriousness, suspect that I might have something to do with this Korpi person's death? I'll have you know that the police commissioner in Malmö is a good friend of mine . . ."

A mistake, he realizes, as soon as the words come out. Slinging threats around suggests guilt, or at least that he has something to hide.

She leans in even further, fixes her heterochrome gaze on his. Palm can't hold out.

"It's not impossible," he admits. "I met lots of people at Freedom Gym. Back then I was a little wild. Fell in with the wrong crowd, made a lot of stupid decisions."

He switches to a softer facial expression.

"But I got lucky. I met a girl, found a job, and got my life together. I've left all that way in the past."

He stops, gives her an imploring look.

"And I'd prefer if it could stay that way. Whatever happened to that Korpi guy, I had nothing to do with it. Absolutely nothing, I can assure you."

"So you and a couple of friends didn't try to rob him? He didn't pull a revolver and shoot one of you in the leg?"

Palm's face drains of all color. He purses his lips.

"I think . . ." His voice falters, and he gulps, clears his throat.

In a few seconds he will realize that the only way out of this is to shut his mouth and call his lawyer.

So she throws him a bone before he gets there. Pulls a pen and notepad from her jacket pocket and flicks through to a blank page. Looks down at it as though she is reading from some notes.

"As I understand it, you weren't the ringleader in the robbery, but more of a witness," she says. "It was the other two who were the instigators. You even tried to prevent the whole thing—is that right?"

Lalo said nothing of the sort, but technically the claim isn't a lie. Those four little words *As I understand it* magically free her from all responsibility.

Palm takes the bait.

"Yes, that's exactly what happened," he says quickly. "I tried to get them to leave him alone."

"And it was also you who saw to it that your friend got treatment after Korpi shot him in the leg?" she adds, thrumming her pen against the notepad.

Palm nods eagerly. "I bandaged Jon up and sat with him in the back seat to the ER."

Asker writes the name *Jon* in her notepad.

"But it wasn't your car," she says, as though she already knew as much. In actual fact she's going off the assumption that Palm would have driven had it been his car.

"No, it was Erik's," he confirms.

Erik, she adds.

"And when you were at the ER? How did you and Erik stop the doctors from calling the police?"

"The bullet had gone straight through the leg, so we said Jon had impaled himself on a reinforcing rod. The doctors bought it completely."

"Mm-hm," Asker hums, drawing a little doodle in the notepad, to make it look like she's adding to the pages of information that she already has.

"That was a real idiot move, the whole thing," he goes on. "I should never have been there from the start. Jon almost bled to death."

"I understand." She nods.

Palm appears to have calmed down. To make him relax even more, she adds:

"Fact is, it's your would-be victim that we're investigating. Tord Korpi. Did you or the others have any contact with him after what happened?"

Palm shakes his head. "Not me, at least. The experience was a bit of a wake-up call for me. I moved away to a relative in Norrköping for a while. Stopped hanging out with Jon and Erik, met a girl, like I said before, and got my act together."

He sounds sincere: now that she has stripped away the layers of media training, she finds no clear indication that he is lying.

"And the others?" she asks.

"Not a clue."

Palm's brain appears to catch up.

"So what is it you think that Korpi guy did, then?"

She makes an apologetic gesture.

"I'm afraid I can't go into the specifics. But your little stunt is outside the statute of limitations anyway, so you have nothing to worry about."

His shoulders sink, and his face relaxes slightly.

"Jon and Erik," she says. "Could you just confirm their surnames? Unfortunately we've had some conflicting information."

"Jon Danielsson and Erik Sundin." Palm nods. "But I have no idea what they're up to these days."

He forces a misplaced smile, which suggests to Asker that that last statement is a lie.

HILL

Once Hill has been lying on the consulting-room bed for around half an hour, Dr. Schiller returns. He removes the cooling pad and starts treating the wound with some kind of laser gun. The heat thaws the tissue, and once the treatment is complete, the wound does actually feel much better. It hurts less, too, and his mobility has improved.

This progress—perhaps aided by the vitamin injection—gives Hill a mental boost. Back in the library, he dives back into his work with renewed energy. As soon as he is a little more mobile, he will visit the UFO Café to find out more about the UFO association's theories, and why the articles on their website can no longer be accessed. But until then he plans to focus his energies on the information relating to Boulder Isle. After all, that's where both AlphaCent and the urban legends have their origins; the place where both of his book projects converge.

He ventures into the company side of the library, in search of anything to do with Boulder Isle. This time he takes a more methodical approach: working through one shelf at a time, he flicks through anything that might be of the slightest interest, then pulls out books and files to search behind them.

After roughly half an hour he strikes it lucky.

In a section containing quarterly reports he stumbles across a large, cardboard concertina file with different compartments stuffed full of yellowing pages.

Flicking through the documents, he realizes with growing excitement that he has found just what he was looking for.

The file is full of documents pertaining to Boulder Isle: geological surveys, purchase contracts, work orders, wage sheets, invoices, and various kinds of internal memos.

Hill takes his haul back with him to his desk and eagerly supplements his timeline with the new information that he finds from the documents.

According to the contract, Bernhard Irving buys the land along the southern shore of Miresjön Lake in 1944. Boulder Isle is included as part of the purchase. Even then Bernhard seems to have been aware that the island contained what is for Scandinavia an extremely rare type of rock: rhyolite, a rock formed either through volcanic activity or a meteorite landing. Bernhard decides to extract the rhyolite and use it for the construction of Astroholm Manor.

Artur Nilsson, an experienced mining engineer, is hired as the site manager. As part of his contract, he and his wife are granted residence in one of the guest villas on the Astroholm estate.

Bernhard has an extra-large mine hoist built over the mine shaft, and on the top of its headframe he constructs an observatory. To Hill's delight, in one of the compartments he even finds the invoice for the telescope, which makes his palms just a little clammy.

He scans the various documents governing production and working hours. Initially the mine operates only on a small scale, purely to supply the Astroholm Manor construction site with materials.

But in the early sixties all that begins to change.

Bernhard is consumed by the theory that Miresjön Lake wasn't in fact formed by a volcanic eruption, as most geologists tend to agree, but by a meteorite landing. According to the records, Bernhard instructs Artur Nilsson to employ more men and excavate all the deeper beneath Boulder Isle, in search of the remnants of the meteorite that Bernhard is convinced lies underground. But all they manage to unearth is black obsidian.

This glass is a clear indicator of volcanic activity, and, consequently, proof that Bernhard is on a fool's errand.

As the documents seem to attest, site manager Artur Nilsson grows increasingly hesitant about the entire project. Hill finds a memo in which Nilsson expresses doubt about the meteorite theory, voicing concerns that they are digging too deep and too fast: cracks have started to form, and at ground level subsidence has been observed. He is afraid of water ingress, which could flood the mine.

This discovery unsettles Hill. So Bernhard was well aware of the risks at Astrofield Mine, yet he allowed the works to continue all the same.

This is one piece of information that he hadn't come across before.

So obsessed was Bernhard with Boulder Isle that he ignored every warning. Hill, too, has his own fixation with the site; he dreams about it at night, and his thoughts are consumed by the possibility of visiting the place. Even now that he knows that the story is bleaker than it first appeared.

In the spring of 1965 disaster strikes. The mine collapses, just as Artur Nilsson feared. Three men perish, among them Nilsson himself. The mine is closed, and numerous investigations are opened into various infractions, but all of them more or less run into the sand.

Bernhard holes up in Astroholm Manor while All Preserves teeters on the brink of ruin. For the Irving family, all appears to be lost.

But then, one night that very winter, young Gunnar Irving sets out for the observatory on Boulder Isle to gaze at the stars. He returns with a fantastic story and a number of new ideas that he claims to have been given by an extraterrestrial.

Bernhard generously transfers the company into Gunnar's name and gives him free rein.

AlphaCent is born.

And the rest—as Gunnar himself put it—is history.

Hill leans back, clasps his hands behind his head, and straightens his back while gazing up at Bernhard Irving's starry sky in the ceiling. An insane amateur scientist whose obsession caused the deaths of three men, a mysterious estate, and a company saved by a UFO.

Each of which is the kind of yarn that Nova wants to avoid in their book. But how is he supposed to look past these things, especially in light of what he has just learned? Is he to simply skirt around it all and start from Gunnar's time at the helm? If worst comes to worst, he may have to.

He returns to his timeline.

The company's later successes are easy to follow, at least, through interim reports and various press releases.

In addition to different surgical instruments, AlphaCent were pioneers in the development of instruments and technologies for DNA analysis, in which they are still world leaders. Soon enough Hill will need to better acquaint himself with that side of the business, but for now he is more interested in Gunnar as a person. He flicks through the books of newspaper clippings, focusing on arti-

cles from tabloids and gossip magazines. He wasn't particularly interested in Gunnar's private life when writing *Forgotten Places*, so a
number of these articles are actually new to him.

Five years after taking over the company, in 1971, the then-twenty-
eight-year-old Gunnar marries nineteen-year-old Karin Nilsson,
daughter of the disaster-stricken mine's manager, Artur Nilsson. After
her father's death she and her mother were allowed to go on living on
the estate, so she and Gunnar know each other well. In 1976, Karin
gives birth to their son, Viggo, and, less than two years later, to their
daughter, Maud.

After twenty years of marriage, Gunnar and Karin divorce unexpectedly. Just one year later, in 1991, Gunnar remarries Yvette
Marchand, who works at the company's Luxembourg office. Almost
ten months to the day after their wedding, Gunnar's third child is
born, his daughter Nova. Shortly thereafter Gunnar Irving turns
fifty. He celebrates the occasion with a huge party, and most of the
business world's movers and shakers of the day are in attendance.

The magazines and tabloids are full of pictures of Gunnar with
his new wife and newborn daughter.

Hill photocopies a large article from *Kvällsposten* that bears the
headline: "SPACE-CASE" GUNNAR TURNS FIFTY!

In the article he finds a photo in which Gunnar is standing beside
two teenagers in party attire. On Gunnar's other side stands his new
wife, the infant version of Nova Irving in her arms.

Hill inspects the grainy image more closely. Gunnar, tall, stately,
and dominant, is the center of the shot. The focal point of the photo
as well as of the party.

Yvette must be significantly younger than him, and she looks almost impossibly good, her dazzling smile directed at the camera. In
her arms she holds little Nova, whose face is barely visible.

The teenager to Gunnar's immediate right is his son, Viggo, his
first-born, the caption reveals. The boy is around fifteen and tall for
his age, with strawberry-blond hair and blue eyes. He looks faintly
like his father. Beside him, out on the right of the image, stands
Viggo's sister, Maud, a few years younger than him. She looks almost
exactly like her daughter, Elsa, minus the dark glasses.

Something about the composition of the image doesn't sit right,
but Hill can't quite put his finger on what.

He flicks on through the articles but finds only confirmation of what he already knows. In 1996, Bernhard Irving passes away at ninety-five years of age, and Gunnar formally becomes the Irving family's patriarch. According to the few sources that Hill has managed to find, both in previous years and in the documents that now lie before him, the funeral takes place privately within the gates of Astroholm Manor, which naturally gives rise to some of the speculation surrounding a possible burial chamber.

Gunnar continues to lead AlphaCent until 2013, when at seventy years of age he steps down from his post as CEO and is replaced by his daughter, Maud. Gunnar goes on as chairman of the board for a few years before eventually taking another step back. Eight years after Maud takes the reins, Nova replaces her half sister as CEO. It would undeniably be interesting to hear the sisters' own account of that shift.

But it is another family member who has sparked Hill's interest.

He flicks back to the photo from Gunnar's fiftieth birthday.

This time he realizes what feels off about the image.

Gunnar has his right arm around his new wife and daughter, while his left shoulder juts forward, closing him off from his other two children. Viggo and Maud are also very close, but they are turned slightly in on themselves, almost like a counterweight to their father's pose. An empty space appears between Gunnar and his only son.

Hill takes out his laptop. The only thing he actually knows about Viggo is that he was involved in a car crash by Miresjön Lake in January 2001, the very same crash in which Maud's boyfriend was killed. After that, Viggo is mentioned neither in articles nor documents.

Hill hasn't questioned this in the past, since his research mostly revolved around Boulder Isle and Astroholm Manor, but now it strikes him as odd.

One of Gunnar's children seems to have disappeared off the face of the earth, and another to have fallen from grace, while the third is the company's rising star, just as her name would suggest.

Nova. *The big dog*, as Elsa put it.

Yet another detail is clamoring for his attention, though it takes a while for his brain to sift it to the fore.

January 2001.

He checks his research on Viggo.

The accident supposedly happened on a Saturday night, that's to say the night of January 6, 2001.

He has seen that date somewhere before.

Hill navigates back to the UFO association's website and returns to the link he was unable to open earlier. The headline alone makes his heart start to pound a little faster: THE SECRET UFO LANDING ON BOULDER ISLE, JANUARY 6, 2001.

Hill clicks back through his own old research to check he hasn't missed anything. He hasn't.

On the night of January 6, 2001, an unusually bright meteorite, also called a bolide, passed over Miresjön Lake. At least that's what all the established science suggests. Others, like the UFO association, claim that it was in fact a UFO landing out on Boulder Isle.

That very night, the teenage Viggo Irving happened to crash his car into the lake. His future brother-in-law perished, while he was swiftly written out of the family narrative.

Hill pushes his chair back and rubs his eyes.

Once again the Irving family's fate is inextricably linked with Miresjön Lake, Boulder Isle, mysterious deaths, and strange celestial phenomena.

And here he is in the middle of it all.

THE GLASS MAN

The blind girl sometimes appears in his thoughts. She is one of few among the estate's residents who interest him. He has wondered whether her disability is some kind of punishment. Retribution for her mother's sins. Or whether her blindness has something to do with the Father's all-seeing eye?

He would so love to see the girl's eyes to find out. But the dog protects her, keeps watch over her day and night. Besides, he has discovered something else. Something that interests him even more.

Or rather: someone.

The Servants have started to whisper about a Stranger.

Someone important.

He has seen him from afar. A man with black hair and dark skin who walks with a crutch.

This Stranger has moved into Villa Arcturus, and he spends his days in the library working on some kind of assignment. The Father must have invited him here.

That's unusual. New.

It piques his curiosity.

He must find out more. Find out who this stranger is, what he is working on, and who he meets.

Whether he presents a threat, or perhaps an opportunity.

ASKER

Finally her investigation is getting somewhere. She has two possible suspects for the murder of Tord Korpi: Jon Danielsson and Erik Sundin. Their former pal Linus Palm knows what they have been up to in recent years, and, given that he wants to distance himself from it, it's likely that they have been forging all the further down their old criminal paths.

She should be happy. Per's logic is gleaning results.

Perhaps that's where the rub is?

Why she can't put her mind at rest.

She calls Rosen for help digging up more on the two men, but gets no reply. Presumably she and Virgilsson have already clocked off for the day.

If it were up to Asker she would head straight back to the office and root around in the most obvious police databases herself, but first she has one job left to do. The visit to Madame Rind that Virgilsson foisted onto her.

She pushes the car hard, cuts her journey time to under forty minutes.

Madame Rind's dark, thatched Skåne longhouse looks roughly the same as it did last time Asker paid her a visit. The dream catchers and wind chimes dangling from the eaves are now joined by a rough-hewn chainsaw woodcarving that stands propped up against one wall, presumably intended to resemble a totem pole of sorts.

Another car is parked in the front yard, a red, freshly washed Fiat 500 that Asker is fairly sure doesn't belong to Madame Rind.

The front door opens and the medium steps out.

Black hair, pale skin, and homemade jewelry, just like before. But in contrast to the last time, no little blind pug comes hobbling out behind her: he has moved on to the happy hunting grounds.

"Oh, Leo, it's you," says Madame Rind.

"Hadn't you foreseen that?" Asker asks.

Madame Rind gives her a sour look.

"We'd thought Kent would be coming. It's his day today."

"Kent's off sick, so you'll have to make do with me."

The fortune-teller shows her through to the living room, where a coffee tray is waiting. On the sofa sits a woman in her sixties.

"Siw," she introduces herself. "I live a few miles away."

She looks surprisingly normal to be sitting in Madame Rind's strange abode. Her hair is styled in a neat bob, and she wears a blouse, jeans, and glasses with dark frames.

"Siw is one of my clients," the fortune-teller explains. "Kent had promised to look into a police case that she raised. How is he, by the way—is he seriously ill?"

Asker shakes her head.

"No, I think he'll be back in the office next week."

"I'm glad," says Siw. "I have a present for him."

She hands Asker a gift-wrapped bundle.

"It's an oven glove. I made it myself."

The woman looks expectant, and Asker doesn't quite know what she is supposed to say.

"OK, I'll make sure he gets it. What was the case he was supposed to be looking into for you?"

"Someone's been stealing my mail."

"Sorry to hear that. Have you spoken to PostNord about it?"

"Oh yes, a few times. But nothing's happening."

"And you're sure the mail is actually being stolen? That the deliveries aren't just running behind?"

The woman shakes her head.

"Kent asked the same thing. He suggested I do a test and send a few letters to myself. I followed his recommendation and mailed five letters last week. Only two arrived. The others are still missing."

"I see . . ."

Asker takes out her notepad and writes down Siw's full name and address.

"And you're not aware of anyone who might have some kind of grudge against you? An angry neighbor or similar?"

"Oh no. Not that I know of. And Madame Rind has used tarot cards and crystals to try to find leads."

"The spirit world had nothing to divulge," Madame Rind interjects. "The problem is likely earthly in nature. That's why we got Kent involved. He's been so very understanding."

Both women exchange glances, and Asker notes that Siw blushes. She looks at the clock.

With every passing hour Hellman's gang are closing the net on Per, and here she is discussing missing mail with an old psychic and her lovesick friend.

"I'll see what I can do," she offers.

She takes a sip of coffee from the cup that Madame Rind has set out for her.

"Is there anything else?"

Asker is expecting a wild medley of assorted tips, just like the last time she and Virgilsson were here. Instead Madame Rind simply shakes her head.

"No, the spirit world has been unusually quiet this week. That's not a good sign."

She makes a sad face.

"A storm is brewing again. The spirits are agitated."

Asker stifles a sigh. So she has come all this way to prevent Madame Rind from flooding the switchboard with tip-offs, only to find that the woman had none to begin with.

She drains her coffee cup.

"In that case I'd best get going," she says.

"Oh, by the way, there was one thing," says Madame Rind. "I was wondering if the information Garm gave you was of any use?"

"Garm—as in your dead dog?"

"Exactly!"

Asker doesn't reply, but for the briefest of moments she is back in the Mountain King's workshop, with the jar containing the mechanical butterfly before her. A *papillon*, just as Madame Rind—or Garm—had warned her to look out for.

And down in his lair, the Mountain King had had hundreds of real butterflies trapped in glass jars. Held captive deep underground, until their wings stopped fluttering and they shriveled into small paper mummies.

She shudders. But the Mountain King is dead, and, whatever happened in his workshop, that chapter is now closed.

"Something's troubling you," Madame Rind says with a frown. "Something important, something your mind just can't drop—no?"

Asker doesn't reply. She knows what Madame Rind is doing. The technique is actually pretty similar to the one she just used on Linus Palm.

First an assertion that sounds specific and personal, but which is in actual fact pretty vague. If the person in question confirms it, then it's simply a matter of digging deeper. Of slowly honing your assertions until you have narrowed them down to something that actually *is* unique and personal, thus making it seem like you knew it all along.

The fortune-teller observes her intently.

"It's someone close to you. Someone in your family."

Yet another wild stab in the dark, albeit one with a high chance of success.

Asker gives her head a little shake.

Madame Rind reacts exactly as Asker would expect: she raises her hands to her temples and shuts her eyes.

"No, no. Not your family. But someone you care about."

Asker throws a sideways glance at Siw. The woman looks completely entranced.

But Asker isn't nearly as impressed. Most people in the world will have some kind of concern that 99 percent of the time will relate to either themselves or someone they care about. Madame Rind is simply playing the odds.

"You doubt me," says Madame Rind.

A fairly obvious conclusion, given the look on Asker's face.

"So it is for some," the fortune-teller goes on. "But that's no problem. The spirit world doesn't take offense. They'll wait until you are ready."

"How nice of them," says Asker.

She makes a show of looking at the clock. "But if there isn't anything else, I really should get going. I promise to look into your problem with the mail."

"And give Kent his present," Siw adds.

"Of course."

Madame Rind gets to her feet. "I'll see you off."

Outside it is already getting dark. The wind is lashing at the bare treetops, making the windchimes tinkle eerily.

The medium stops by Asker's car.

"You may not believe in my methods," she says. "But the fact is, my work gives people great solace. It's comforting to think that there's something more out there, something we can't see or completely understand. Forces that guide us, or a life beyond this one. And I'm no charlatan. I'm not selling winning lottery numbers, miracle cures, or love potions. All I do is try to guide people."

Asker has neither the time nor the inclination to get into this discussion.

"I have to go" is all she says. "Kent or Virgilsson will be with you next week."

The medium nods.

"Thank you for coming, Leo. And thank you for your kindness toward Siw. You have far-seeing eyes; did you know that?"

Asker laughs.

"I've had many things said about my eyes over the years, but this is actually the first time I've heard 'far-seeing.' It has a nice ring to it."

She jumps into her car and reverses.

Just as she is about to pull off, Madame Rind signals at her to lower her window.

"The solution you seek is closer than you think," she says gravely. "The spirit world wants you to know that. You must simply dare to have faith."

"Thanks," Asker says, in as friendly a voice as she can muster.

Then she winds up the window and drives away.

HILL

He works in the library until after five o'clock, then sends a message to Mrs. Schiller to request a lift back to Villa Arcturus.

After a while he stands up and walks over to the bay window on the front side of the building, to keep an eye out for his ride. Instead he sees Samuel's Mercedes come gliding in and stop in front of the main entrance.

Samuel steps out and opens a back door to let out a gangly elderly man wearing a coat and a wide-brimmed hat. The outdoor lighting is so faint that his features are impossible to make out in the darkness.

Before the man has made it all the way up the steps, the copper doors open smoothly to let him in. Then they close again just as smoothly.

Hill catches himself gasping.

Although he may have only seen the man from the side, he couldn't be more certain. It must have been Space-Case Gunnar Irving in the flesh.

Hill stands there in the bay window staring at the front steps, but when the Mercedes sails away, he realizes that Gunnar won't be coming back out.

The app beeps. His lift is waiting outside.

Ville greets him with a curt nod and pulls off as soon as Hill's rear hits the passenger seat.

"I just saw Gunnar get home," Hill says, in another attempt at small talk.

Ville grunts inaudibly.

"He looked very sprightly for someone who's almost eighty."

No response.

When they pass *The Glass Man*, it strikes Hill that he is staring at the sculpture just like Ville does.

Something about it attracts the gaze, in the same way that the real and considerably older Gunnar Irving just did.

Something fascinating, something magnetic, and yet . . .
Something uncanny.

Hill is still wired when he gets back to the house. Whatever was in
those injections Dr. Schiller gave him, they have sure done the trick.
At the same time, he is still reeling from his discoveries about the
Irving family: that Bernhard was warned of the risk of a mine collapse, and that Viggo's accident happened the very same night the
bolide flew over Miresjön Lake.

His leg really is feeling much better, so he decides to explore the
house's second floor. Carefully he climbs the steep staircase, one step
at a time.

The space upstairs has been opened up to the very rafters, and it
consists of one large room. At one end stands a large drawing board
and a chest of drawers to store drawings; at the other, a couple of
easels and some shelves holding brushes and paints.

The middle of the room is taken up by a large telescope. It
looks completely out of place here, partly because of its size, and
partly because there are no skylights, so it can't be pointed at the
stars.

More things jump out at Hill as he steps closer. This kind of
telescope is motor-driven, and electricity is needed to change its
angle and adjust the focus. The model is also old-fashioned, with a
metallic green casing and solid handles and buttons. A plate at one
side gives the model number and year of production: 1947.

Suddenly Hill realizes what he is looking at: this is the telescope
from the observatory on Boulder Isle.

The teenage explorer inside him is overjoyed. Meanwhile, the
adult, more rationally inclined part of him is mostly baffled.

What is this telescope doing here, where it can't be used? Even
if access to Boulder Isle was closed, it would hardly be difficult to
find another place for it on the whole estate where it could actually
be used.

He walks over to the drawing board. It is roughly the same model
as those used in architecture courses: adjustable, with a light, and
movable rulers along both axes. A drawing is placed in the holders.

It depicts a three-story concrete tower on six supporting columns, with a large dome up on the roof. It must be the headframe

and observatory out on Boulder Isle. Hill feels his pulse quicken even more.

When he was writing that chapter of his book, both he and his publisher had searched frantically for a plan of the headframe, to no avail. They had even struggled to source a drone image.

And now here it is, before his very eyes, with Bernhard Irving's signature along the base. He pulls out his phone and takes a few photos.

Hill can't help but reach out and touch the paper. But it's not entirely smooth, as he expected: his fingers trace faint furrows running across the entire sheet.

Another sheet must have been placed on top of this, he thinks. One that someone drew on with such force that it left impressions on the drawing beneath.

He turns on the lamp. The furrows are so faint as to be barely visible.

Hill tilts the board up so that the light is parallel to its surface, rather than coming from above. Fiddles with the angle until the furrows cast faint shadows, and a word emerges across the drawing.

Six letters, drawn so many times that they have turned sharp and jagged.

Danger

A sound makes Hill give a start. He stands in silence for a few seconds. Wonders briefly if he is hearing things.

But then he hears the sound again. He recognizes it now.

Someone is knocking on his front door.

Carefully he makes his way back down the stairs.

"Hello!" says Elsa Irving when he opens the door.

The black dog is sitting beside her, still glaring suspiciously up at Hill.

"I came to ask if you'd like to have dinner with us at Villa Canopus. Mom would invite you herself, but she's too shy. Say yes!"

Naturally Hill can't pass up on the chance to meet Maud Irving.

"Thank you, I'd love to come."

"Good. Come by in an hour. It's just down the road, on the other side. See you then!"

"Uh . . ." Hill doesn't quite know what to say.

"That was a joke," Elsa says with a grin.

"Of course." Hill forces an awkward laugh.

Elsa turns around. The dog positions itself by her left knee and leads her back up the drive.

Hill stands there, watching her go. As she disappears into the darkness, the hidden word on Bernhard Irving's drawing flashes through his mind again.

Danger

For some reason it makes him think of Leo.

And of her father.

SIXTEEN YEARS EARLIER

It's early summer, and the chain on Martin's bicycle has popped off, leaving him stranded here on a narrow forest track out in the sticks. Around him lies only dense coniferous forest, and verges with sprawling greenery.

Had Leo been here, she would have fixed his chain right away, found some trick to get it back on its wheel. But today he is alone, and all he has to show for his tussle with the chain is filthy hands and a sweaty neck. To top it all off the wind has turned, kicking up bluey-gray thunderclouds on the horizon.

He buttons up his flimsy summer jacket and starts walking his bicycle home.

The broken chain clinks faintly.

It's at least an hour on foot, maybe even more.

The first drops fall sooner than he expected, and more follow suit, faster and faster. He is just about to drop his bike and run into the forest in search of a dense tree to take shelter under until the storm has passed, when he sees headlights approaching.

He leans his bike toward his body and waves both his arms to attract the driver's attention. Water sneaks in at his wrists, turning into icy tendrils that trickle all the way to his armpits. He shudders.

The car approaches through the rain. A beat-up pickup with a faded paint job.

Suddenly he recognizes the vehicle and lowers his arms.

The pickup slows to a crawl, pulls in beside him.

At the wheel sits Leo's father. He studies Martin through the side window, as though toying with the idea of driving on.

Then he stops the car and points his thumb over his shoulder at the cargo bed.

For a second Martin hesitates. He has never been alone with Prepper Per before, and the thought of getting into a car with him isn't appealing. But the rain is about to turn into a deluge, and he can hardly say no.

He grabs his bicycle and with some effort heaves it into the cargo bed. Its wheels hit a bundle, something long wrapped up in a tarpaulin.

The rain is lashing at his face, so he hurries back to the cab. The windows fog up from all the moisture he brings with him. The inside of the truck smells—something bad that he can't quite place.

"Thanks." He wipes the water from his forehead.

Per pulls off without a reply. Looks just as sullen and grave as usual.

Martin can't resist the impulse to say something—anything—to lighten the mood.

"It's real cats-and-dogs weather out there," he says with a hard-won breeziness. "Came out of nowhere."

No reply.

Per hits the fan to defog the windows. His hand is sinewy and rough, and the back of it is flecked with something brown.

Martin gulps. They travel in silence for a few minutes.

"What were you doing out here?" Per eventually asks.

His voice is dry, almost accusatory.

"Nothing." Martin gulps again, tries not to sound nervous. "Just wanted to see where this road led."

"Can't you read a map?" Per grunts.

"Oh, I can," Martin says with a nod, "but that's way less fun."

Per snorts.

"A map would have saved you from getting cold and soaked to your skin. Saved you from standing at the roadside like a drowned rat, begging for a ride. There's nothing out here but forest."

Martin wants to say that sometimes you have to dare to follow your gut if you want to learn new things, but he doesn't dare. Besides, he doubts Prepper Per would understand.

The smell in the cab prickles his nose.

"All good with Leo?"

He regrets the question the very second it passes his lips.

Per gives him a long, sideways glance.

"Leo's busy," he says curtly.

"Yeah, so she said." He clears his throat.

"What else has she said?"

"Nothing . . ."

"Nothing?"

Martin gulps, shakes his head. The rain is clattering against the roof, and the wipers are fighting frantically to keep the water off the windshield, but Per doesn't slow down. He seems to know this road like the back of his hand.

But what was he *doing out there? What was the bundle lying in the back? Martin stares at the brown flecks on Per's right hand, notices that they continue up his sleeve.*

He breathes in through his nose. That pungent smell that he noticed as soon as he got in. It could be blood.

He looks around the cab warily.

The pickup only has two seats, but in the space between the seat backs and wall lies a long rifle cover in a camouflage print.

Could the bundle in the back be a poached deer or roe?

Something that Leo once said echoes through his head.

Per's dangerous. Lethal.

His heartbeats become irregular. He squirms, tries not to glance over his shoulder at the back.

But it's hard. He can just make out the bundle in the wing mirror. Isn't it a little big to be a roe?

Suddenly the car starts to slow, without Per making any attempt to explain why. He stops the car at the side of the road, applies the hand brake, and turns to the passenger seat.

Martin gulps again, can't help himself, even though he knows that the sound betrays his fear.

"You and Leo are good friends," says Per.

His eyes are cold, but their gaze is incandescent. It feels as though they are boring straight through Martin's head.

Martin nods.

"Friends tell each other things. Confide in each other, don't they?"

He starts another nod, but stops himself halfway through.

"So what's Leo said about me? About the Farm?"

Martin feels himself contracting, melting under Per's laser eyes. It is as though his gaze is turning his brain inside out.

His mouth is bone-dry, and he can't utter a word.

Per leans in closer. The smell of blood in the cab grows even more intense, almost asphyxiating.

"So what's Leo said about me?" he repeats quietly.

Martin gulps again.

"Nothing," he almost whispers. "We don't talk about you."

A lie, and a bad one at that. Per's eyes cut straight through it.

One side of his mouth rises into a nasty, scornful smile.

"You don't talk about me. Not at all."

"N-no," Martin croaks.

Prepper Per stares at him for another few seconds. Then he shuts off his laser eyes, releases the handbrake, puts the car into gear, and starts driving again.

"Good!" he says, almost cheerily. "Just how it should be. Now, high time we got you back to your mom and dad, isn't it?"

Martin gasps for air, but he can't force out any response. He turns to the side window and wipes his nose, unable to stifle a sound that is a mix between a sniff and a sob.

The humiliation makes his cheeks flush.

He hates Leo's dad.

Hates him more than anything else in this world.

ASKER

She drives back to police HQ. Since it's after six p.m., the Department of Lost Souls is silent and dark, as expected.

Up in Serious Crime, however, the lights are still on, and every now and then she spots movements in their windows through her binoculars. She wonders how close they are.

She sits down at her computer and types in the names she was given by Linus Palm. Although far from any match for Rosen in database searches, after a little poking around she nevertheless finds both men. Jon Danielsson is registered in Hörby. His criminal record follows his previous trajectory. First petty crimes—shoplifting, vandalism, illegal driving. After that he moved on to drug crimes, did a few years inside for dealing.

According to the system, he is free again, and he is registered at his mother's small studio flat. Asker doubts he actually lives there.

Erik Sundin's story begins roughly the same way as Danielsson's, but in later years he has also found the time to add breaking and entering, robbery, and grievous bodily harm to his repertoire.

A history of violence, then, which makes him even hotter as a murder suspect. Unlike Danielsson, Sundin has no known address, at least not in the police data systems, and she has no access to the other authorities' systems. She needs Rosen's help.

Asker tries to call her mobile again, but it's still off. She groans, rubs her forehead in frustration.

She has to find Sundin and Danielsson.

If she can just press them hard enough, one of them will crack. That may not be much of a plan, but right now it's all she has.

She should go home and try to relax. Rally her forces ahead of the day to come.

Her phone starts to vibrate, and she hopes it's Rosen. Instead it's a message from a private number.

The message contains a short video clip, just eight seconds long, taken with what she assumes is a trail camera hidden in a tree. The time stamp is from just half an hour before. In the video, three hunched men are moving between some thickets. Two of them are dressed in SWAT uniforms.

The third she recognizes instantly, even without the bandage over his ear.

It's Eskil.

So not only have Hellman's gang found the link between Korpi and her father: they are also planning an operation to arrest him.

The tactical officers aren't dressed for combat, so it won't be happening tonight.

But soon—very soon. And her father will be waiting, following their every move. That's what he wants to show her by sending her this clip.

That her time is running out.

HILL

Exactly one hour after Elsa's visit, Hill lifts the boat-shaped door knocker to Villa Canopus. The house is just a little farther down from his own, on the other side of the road that runs through the entire estate. It is built in the same strange kind of hybrid architecture as Villa Arcturus but must be three times the size.

A few hundred yards separate the two houses, the longest distance that Hill has walked since being discharged from the hospital. But he still feels strong and limber after his treatment and doesn't even need to stop to rest.

The woman who opens the door is somewhere just north of forty. She is tall, with red hair styled in a bob, and the jeans and light blue shirt that she is wearing make for a refreshing change from all the black that Hill has seen in recent days. She is also attractive, Hill notes. Very attractive.

"You must be Martin," she says. "Come in!"

Maud's eyes are blue, but not quite as bright blue as her half sister Nova's. Her gaze is friendly yet somewhat guarded.

"I hope you didn't feel forced to come. It was Elsa's idea to invite you. Fact is, she didn't tell me about it until you'd already said yes."

"Oh, I hope I'm not causing any trouble . . ."

Maud holds up her hand. Her nails are short, painted with clear nail polish.

"Not at all. It's nice to have some company. Besides, I'm used to Elsa's little whims."

"She seems like a very independent young lady," says Hill.

"You have no idea," Maud laughs. "Let me take your jacket."

She shows him through the spacious hallway and into a large living room that boasts a dining table, bookshelves, and a large sofa suite.

At one end of the room a fire is roaring, filling the space with a pleasant aroma of birchwood intermingled with food.

"Hi Martin!" Elsa is sitting on one of the sofas in front of the open fire. When Hill steps closer, Orion rises from his post at her feet.

The dog stares at Hill, curling his lip to bare his front teeth. From his chest comes a faint growl.

"Quiet, Orion," says Elsa. "Lie down!"

The dog obeys, but keeps a careful eye on Hill as he takes a seat in an armchair.

In front of him stands a tray containing glasses and a bowl of chips.

"Help yourselves," says Maud, who sits down in the armchair next to Hill's. "Elsa, there's a glass of water at one o'clock on the table in front of you, and a bowl of chips at three o'clock."

The girl moves her hands as instructed and picks up her glass without spilling.

"Cheers and welcome, Martin!" says Maud. "Elsa and I are happy you wanted to come keep us company."

"Thank you for the invitation," he says, raising his wineglass. "Will Karin be joining us?"

Maud shakes her head.

"No, Mom prefers to keep herself to herself. She has her own annex with a separate entrance," she says, gesturing over her shoulder. Then she raises her glass and drinks.

"So, what do you think of Astroholm?" she asks.

"A fascinating place," says Hill. "I've never seen anything like it."

"Fascinating is a good word," Maud says with a snigger. "I'd probably go for bizarre myself. Do you have any other suggestions, Elsa?"

"Strange, creepy, weird," the girl says while stuffing a handful of chips into her mouth.

Hill thinks of the mysterious warning on the drawing board. Elsa isn't completely wrong there, but of course he can't say that.

"Elsa told me you've met Dr. and Mrs. Schiller. Anyone else?"

"Groundskeeper Ville," he says, and notes Elsa's snort when he does. "And Nova, too, a few days ago at her office."

"Ah, of course." Maud's smile stiffens at the edges. "The book project was her idea. Will it be about AlphaCent or the Irving family?"

She takes another sip of wine.

"Primarily about the company," Hill replies. "But AlphaCent's history is closely intertwined with your family's."

He wonders whether he should ask any questions about her time as CEO, but decides to hold off for now. After all, he has been invited here for dinner, not for work.

"And you've been allowed to stay in Grandpa Bernhard's old house," Maud goes on. "No one's lived there in almost thirty years."

"They say Bernhard haunts the place," Elsa adds while sneaking Orion some chips.

Maud clears her throat self-consciously.

"If you'll excuse me, I'll just check on the food. It's a vegan stew, I hope that's OK? Elsa's going through a vegan phase."

"For the thousandth time, Mom. It's not a phase. I *am* vegan."

Maud rolls her eyes at Hill before disappearing into the kitchen.

"So, did you call him Willy?" Elsa asks with a big grin.

"Yes," Hill chuckles. "I stepped right into your trap."

"Did he get mad?"

"A little."

"Good. He's always moaning that Orion poops on the lawns. I think he's afraid of dogs; you can hear it in his voice."

Maud comes back into the room with a pot that she places on the dining table.

"Food's up," she says. "Martin, I suppose you can sit next to me."

The food is surprisingly good. Not that Hill has anything against vegan food, generally speaking, but to be on the safe side he usually lowers his taste expectations by a notch or two. But tonight that adjustment isn't necessary.

Besides which, Maud and Elsa are great company. They chat and joke with each other in such a relaxed way that Hill sometimes forgets they are mother and daughter.

"So, Martin," Maud says once she is onto her third glass of wine. "I've googled you, and you certainly seem like a busy man. University lecturer, best-selling author. Why did you agree to something as boring as writing a company book on AlphaCent?"

She smirks teasingly, as though the question isn't meant in earnest. But Hill is fairly certain that isn't the case.

"Well, I guess the short answer is I'm getting paid well," he says jokingly. "Your sister can be pretty persuasive."

"Half sister," Elsa adds. "We normally call her my half aunt. When we're being nice, that is," she adds with a smirk.

The table falls silent for a few seconds.

"So what do you do for work, Maud?" Hill asks.

"Right now, nothing." She sips her wine. "I'm kind of between jobs, you might say. I'm sure you know I was CEO of AlphaCent for eight years."

She leaves the sentence hanging in the air, but it's far too good an opportunity for Hill to pass up on completely.

"Why did you stop, if you don't mind me asking?"

"Mom doesn't want to talk about that," Elsa cuts in sharply.

"Thanks, Elsa, but it's no problem," says her mother, in a tone of voice that suggests otherwise. "Truth is, I was completely burned out. Being the CEO of such an expansive, innovative company as AlphaCent takes its toll."

Maud's reply sounds rehearsed, and the mood has suddenly turned tense. Hill can see that now is not the time to try to press Maud for more information, but he isn't really sure if he is expected to change the subject or wait for one of the others to do so.

After a moment's silence he can't take the tension anymore.

"When I was a teenager, I lived not so far from here," he says. "We moved around a lot when I was a kid. My parents ran restaurants, and they were pretty restless back then. When I was around fifteen, we ended up in these parts. I was already into urban exploration, so when I heard the story about the abandoned mine, the observatory out on Boulder Isle, and the UFO story I was hooked."

He pauses, tries to read the room. Decides that the atmosphere isn't any worse than before, at least.

"One time I even came out here," he goes on. "Or, actually, to Miresjön Lake. I remember how exciting it was. I stood on the shore down by the Boy Scouts' cabin and watched the island until long after dark, just hoping to catch sight of something."

"And did you?" Elsa asks, adjusting her tight-fitting dark sunglasses.

"Only the silhouette of the observatory and the odd seabird," Hill lies. "But I stuck around a little too long and missed my bus home. This was in the early 2000s, so I had no cellphone. I had to walk miles before I found a house where I could call home."

He wonders whether he should mention the fact that back then he had heart problems, and that the walk had left him both cold and severely drained. But he decides to leave out that part of the story, in the same way that he avoided mentioning the light.

"My dad came and picked me up," he goes on. "I remember driving through the forest, just waiting for his lecture. But for the longest time we just sat in silence, and then he asked me: *Was it worth it?*"

"And what did you say?" Elsa asks. Even Maud appears to be listening with interest.

"I said yes. My dad just nodded, as though he got it. And there and then, in the car on the way home, I promised myself that someday I'd make it to Boulder Isle and see it all for myself."

He shrugs.

"So, there you have the real reason why I agreed to write the book. In short: I'm a nosy so-and-so."

He drinks up his wine while casting a cautious glance at his two hosts. Maud appears to have thawed out again.

Elsa's face is turned toward Hill, and her chin is slightly lifted. She gives a little nod, as though to praise Hill for what he just did.

Hill knows it's all in his head, and that she can't see him, but he still can't shake the feeling that the girl is studying him closely.

ASKER

After Per's video, Asker has shelved every thought of going home and resting. Instead she has spent some anxious hours scouring the files that Rosen compiled for her earlier. The police records from the area around the Farm for the summer of 2006 consist of a delightful medley of traffic accidents, break-ins, diesel thefts, drunk driving, and even a woman who claimed to have seen an alien.

But, much as she expected, nothing that in any way appears remotely related to either Tord Korpi or her father. Yet she still can't bring herself to go home.

The image of Eskil sneaking around the forests by the Farm is now etched in her mind, hampering her concentration. They are scoping out the area, which means the time frame for the operation itself must be within days. But she needs to know for sure. Must somehow figure out when Hellman's gang intends to strike.

By now it is almost nine o'clock, and police HQ is at least half-empty.

Should she try to sneak into Serious Crime and snoop around?

A risky venture that would cost her her job if she got caught. There are cameras everywhere, and the lights are still on up on the sixth floor, which means that at least one person is working tonight—maybe even all night. The risk of detection is way too high.

But how else will she find out what's going on?

She steps out for some coffee, not because she feels like any, but out of a need to do *something* to quell her frustration.

In the kitchen she unexpectedly runs into Enok Zafer.

Asker was certain that everyone in the department had gone home, but, much like his job description, it's impossible to make head or tail of Zafer's working hours.

When she says hello, he gives a start, sloshing coffee all over his hands.

"*Saatana perkele!*" he curses in Finnish. Mutters a few other curse words in other languages, of which at least one is Arabic and another perhaps Persian.

"I'm sorry, I didn't mean to scare you," she says. "I didn't know anyone was still in the office. All the lights were off."

"I'm working on an important report," he says, as usual five decibels too loud. "Have to have it in by Monday."

"What's it on?"

Zafer gives her a suspicious look.

"Do you have the right security clearance to be party to that kind of information?" he asks.

"I'm department chief," she replies in a cocksure tone. "Class A2," she adds, simply because the code sounds high-ranking and important.

Zafer glares at her some more.

"OK," he says eventually. "I'm running an analysis of the risks associated with cellphone-tapping technologies. The technology has come on in leaps and bounds in recent years. An apparently innocent app can, in the right circumstances, give a third party access to a phone's microphone and camera. The director of technology is very interested in my conclusions."

Asker nods. She has been hearing Prepper Per hold forth about the dangers of cellphones ever since she was a kid. Remembers the lead cabinet on the Farm where he would keep them locked away.

"Interesting," she says. "Are you working on anything else?"

Zafer stands an inch or two taller. Clearly the strange man isn't used to anyone taking an interest in his work.

"I'm also charting the force's use of specialist firearms. Submachine guns, assault rifles, sniper rifles. But that's a longer project that will run for some years."

"Mm-hm." Asker pours herself a cup of coffee.

Suddenly it hits her.

"So does that mean you have access to when firearms are booked out from the armory, and by whom?"

"What?" Zafer clasps his ear.

"Do you know when specialist firearms are booked?" she asks a little louder.

"Of course. I have access to the inventory logs."

"Can you also see bookings for future use?"

Zafer nods. "It's all in the logs."

Asker takes a sip of coffee, trying to conceal her excitement.

"You wouldn't be able to show me how it works, would you?" she asks.

"Certainly, follow me."

He shows her into his large office. Just like the last time she was here, the shelves are loaded with various gadgets, electronic devices, and charging stations whose uses she can in most cases only guess at.

Zafer has an adjustable desk with two modern display screens.

A stark contrast to her own sagging office chair and semi-antique computer.

"Here, take a look!" Zafer says, eagerly pulling up a database. "Every use of specialist firearms in the last two years."

"Impressive!"

Her comment makes Zafer puff himself up even further.

"And you said you can see future bookings, too?" she says.

"Naturally."

He clicks around on the screen. Asker holds her breath.

If Hellman is planning a raid of the Farm, he will need all the firearms he can get.

And if they have already decided on a date for the operation, then it should appear in Zafer's database. If his database isn't baloney, that is—yet another pretend assignment that no one asked him for. But Zafer's high-tech office equipment would suggest that he at least occasionally does some actual work.

"Here are the holds for the next six months. Drills, state visits, and the like . . ."

Asker leans in closer to the screen.

The window contains a calendar of blue blocks, the size of which appears to vary based on the number of weapons booked.

The largest block in the entire calendar is right at the start, and after that it is empty for weeks.

When Asker double-checks the date, she almost swears out loud.

The operation at the Farm is planned for the following night.

Shit!

HILL

Hill's evening at Villa Canopus has been much more pleasant than anticipated. His little confession about Boulder Isle lightened the mood considerably, and Elsa has asked him to tell her about other scary abandoned places that he has visited.

Maud has also relaxed, which could have as much to do with her wine consumption as his own disarming charms.

"So what's your first impression of the Irving family? Aren't we weird?"

"I'd sooner say fascinating," Hill replies. "Or unique."

"Good answer," Maud laughs. "Remember that if anyone else asks."

She holds his gaze a second too long.

"I grew up down in the manor house," she eventually says. "But when I was thirteen Gunnar left my mother and we moved up here, to Villa Canopus. A *unique* way of handling a divorce, wouldn't you say?"

Hill's mind is all questions, but he is also aware that he should tread more carefully than before.

"That must have been hard," he says. "My parents moved around throughout my childhood. As soon as I'd put down roots in one place, it would be time to move on to the next. But at least they didn't get divorced."

Maud drains her wineglass. Her fourth, if Hill isn't mistaken.

"We never really understood what happened," she says. "One moment we were living down in the manor house with Daddy. The next, all three of us were out. Banished, without explanation. He remarried the next year."

She gives a slow shake of her head. Hill casts a furtive glance at Elsa, but the girl's face gives nothing away.

"All three of you?" he asks cautiously. "You, your mother and your brother Viggo, you mean?" He has been wanting to broach this topic all night. Learn more about Viggo from someone who knew him well.

"It was Mom I felt most sorry for," Maud says. "To be replaced in that way. She'd loved my father ever since she was a girl. Worshipped the ground he walked on. She took it very hard."

"And his second wife, Yvette. I found very little mention of her while trying to iron out the family history, other than that she apparently worked for Gunnar. Are they divorced?"

Maud shakes her head.

"No, but they've been separated for years. Yvette lives in Spain, has a comfortable life there at Dad's expense. In return he's presided over Nova's entire upbringing."

She once again raises her wineglass to her lips, only to realize it is empty, upon which she slams it down again a little too hard.

"She's here, by the way," says Elsa. "Nova, I mean. I ran into her and Samuel this afternoon when I was out walking Orion."

"Of course she is," says Maud, pulling a face. "She wants to keep an eye on you, Martin. This AlphaCent book was her idea, and she won't dare risk it going sideways. And Samuel's always at her side; he does whatever he's told."

Hill notes that Elsa is fidgeting awkwardly, so he takes the opportunity to lead the conversation away from Nova. He can ask Maud more about the sisters' relationship and the CEO takeover another time, when Elsa won't have to hear it.

"Samuel drove me here," he says. "Clearly Gunnar takes security very seriously."

Maud shrugs.

"There's a whole load of lunatics out there. We've had problems over the years, mostly people trying to break into the estate to look for Bernhard's burial chamber or the tunnel they think leads to Boulder Isle. You actually fed those fires with your book, by the way."

Hill clears his throat. He is aware that his book has had that kind of effect, but this is the first time he has had it thrown back in his face.

"But it's not just the UFO dummies trying to get in," Maud goes on. "Medical technology is a sensitive field. The competition is brutal and the stakes immense, so industrial espionage is a real problem. Samuel's been in charge of AlphaCent's security for many years. He's one of the few people Gunnar trusts implicitly. And Nova, too. A little too implicitly, perhaps."

Her sour tone has returned.

"What do you mean?"

Maud falls silent, then gets up and starts to clear the table. Obviously Samuel wasn't as safe a topic of conversation as he had hoped.

"Don't listen to Mom too much," Elsa says quietly as soon as Maud has retreated to the kitchen. "She's mad at Nova because it's her fault that Mom had to step down as CEO. But Nova's OK, really. Samuel, too. Most of the time, anyway."

Hill hums in response. He searches for a suitable question, but finds none. They sit in awkward silence for another few seconds, until Maud's return.

She looks happier again, as though she has shaken off what they were just talking about.

"Can I get you some coffee, Martin?" she asks. Yet again she holds his gaze just a second too long.

Hill looks at the clock. His body suddenly feels heavy, and he realizes he ought to get home while he still has strength enough for the short walk up the lane.

"Another time I'd love to," he says. "But tonight I think I'd better get back to Arcturus before it gets too late."

He gets up, thinks he catches a look of disappointment in the faces of both mother and daughter.

"Thanks for a great evening," he adds. "I hope you'll let me repay you the invitation soon."

THE GLASS MAN

He has heard them talking up in Villa Canopus. Stood for a long while in the darkness of the basement, listening as their sounds descended through the floor and walls. Chatter, laughter. The clink of cutlery, glasses, and plates. The Stranger has made himself at home. Made some friends.

He hears them laughing, the blind girl and she who is always in his thoughts.

The Stranger makes them happy.

He doesn't like that. Not at all.

Jealousy is one of humanity's basest instincts, so the Father used to say. For a long time he hoped he had been freed from it.

But he was wrong.

The jealousy sinks its claws deep into him, sparking his anger.

So he returns to the dark depths and the silence. Finds his way through the underworld and all the way here, to the Stranger's house.

To learn more about him.

He cuts the power at Villa Arcturus's fuse box, then sneaks up the basement stairs. Listens carefully by the hallway door.

At first he thinks he hears sounds, so he stops dead. But after a while, once his heartbeats have calmed, he is certain that the house is empty.

He has always liked Villa Arcturus; has always felt more at home here than in Canopus or the manor house. Knows its every nook and cranny, every space, every smell.

Yet it all feels so different now. As though the Stranger's energy has disturbed the prevailing order even of this place.

He starts in the bedroom, opens the wardrobe and runs his hand over the Stranger's garments. Two shirts and a blazer.

The fabric is soft and well worn, and it smells good. Laundry detergent, aftershave, and then another note—the Stranger's own scent.

He holds the garments up to his chest in the bedroom mirror. The faint light of his protective goggles reflects back at him like two large, red saucers.

The Stranger's clothes look so small against his own hulking frame. He hangs everything up again carefully and in the right order, then moves on to the bathroom. The damp air inside smells of shower gel and aftershave.

The Stranger washed for dinner. Wanted to make a good impression.

He leaves the bathroom and steps into the large living room.

All around he finds traces of the Stranger. Furniture that has been moved, papers left lying around, impressions in the cushions on the seats.

Signs that the Stranger has made himself at home. Made himself comfortable.

He stops and sniffs the air.

For a brief moment he thinks he makes out another scent in the room.

A familiar one, one that doesn't belong to the Stranger.

Was someone else here before him? Did they sneak out just before he opened the basement door?

The scent is gone before he can be quite sure.

He returns to the bedroom and lies down carefully on the bed. The springs creak under his weight.

He likes to lie here and gaze up at the luminous starry sky. Imagine the universe as one endless, expanding darkness in which light is but the exception. Just small, flickering dots of stars, in some cases extinguished thousands of years before their glow ever reached Earth.

Eventually all the stars will die out. All life will cease, and darkness will prevail for eternity.

He likes that thought.

Before long the Stranger will start hobbling home in the darkness. Alone, vulnerable.

Shall he wait for him here?

Perhaps . . .

ASKER

She drives home way too fast. Slams her foot on the gas as soon as the traffic lights hit green, making her electric car shoot off like a rocket.

A pretty pointless exercise, given that she has to stop at the next light and repeat the procedure. But her aggressive driving is not about urgency, but about trying to manage her stress at the situation she finds herself in.

She has two alternative suspects for Korpi's murder. They have motive, opportunity, and violent pasts. But she has just one day to find them, question them, and get them to confess.

An impossible task, even for her, and right now she couldn't feel more alone. Neither Hellman, her mother, nor even Martin Hill seems to realize the magnitude of the looming disaster.

Her father was once prepared to blow both himself and her to pieces, simply because she was going to free herself from his clutches.

So what will he be prepared to do now, when the very authorities that he has hated with a passion for twenty years show up at the Farm to try to take him by force—and for a crime he didn't commit, at that?

On top of all that, she can't shake the feeling that she is wrong. That, for all her logic and resource management, there is something that she has missed.

She speeds up again, zipping from lane to lane in yet another futile attempt to outpace her frustration.

She is less than a hundred yards from the freeway on-ramp when she realizes she has zero desire to go home to that big, empty house. That either way she won't be able to sleep.

She slams the brakes and swings her car into the hard shoulder.

A silvery car behind her is forced to swerve around her to avoid a collision, but in spite of this the driver refrains from honking and making her even more mad.

One silver lining, at least.

She stops the car and pulls out her cell. For a brief moment she considers calling Martin, but he's far away and too taken up with his own boyhood adventures. Instead she pulls up Viktor's number.

"Are you home?" she asks without even a hello. "Good, I'll be there in fifteen."

As it happens, the journey takes her only twelve. He opens the door straightaway and she pushes him back into the apartment. Kisses him, almost tears off his clothes, before she makes him do the same to her.

The sex is wild, hard. Liberating.

Helps, at least for a while.

HILL

The damp night air outside Villa Canopus ushers the cold straight through his clothes. Hill shivers. A vintage ladies' bicycle is parked a few yards from the door. On its front, a basket big enough for a cat.

He guesses that the lady he saw on the bicycle the previous night must have been Maud's mother, Karin Irving.

The fog has thickened again, and after just a minute or so the lights of Maud and Elsa's house have disappeared behind him. Hill tries to make out the outside light of his own house, but even though the distance is only a few hundred yards, strangely enough he can't see it. Still, as long as he keeps to the gravel drive, there's no real danger of him going astray.

He goes on walking with careful steps.

His wound feels fine for now, but his energy levels are starting to flag.

His long day has caught up with him, and he stops to catch his breath and let his eyes adjust.

The fog is so humid that he can feel its touch on his skin, and between that and the darkness, the whole experience actually is a little creepy. He tries to tell himself that he is only a few minutes from his house, and that he has been in places far more sinister than a dark estate. A stupid idea, since the thought instead calls to mind the Mountain King's horrific lair. Takes him back to when he and Smilla Holst were running through the darkness, chased by a serial killer.

He gets a grip on himself, forces his brain down another track.

The Mountain King is dead, and he is here, at Astroholm Manor, in no danger at all.

He starts walking as swiftly as he is able, but after another fifty feet he feels unsure. Is he really going the right way?

He has no reference points with which to orient himself, and somehow, in spite of his best efforts, he has managed to stray from the gravel drive onto the lawn.

He takes out his phone and tries to use the flashlight to light his way. But the flat light simply rebounds off the fog, adding to his confusion, so he turns it off again.

Should he turn and go back? But soon he realizes that he isn't quite sure which way that would be.

Since his energy isn't boundless, he decides the better thing for him to do is to stop and try to gather his bearings. Normally he has a good sense of direction, and he can almost always give the rough position of each cardinal point. Which makes it all the more unsettling to have suddenly lost his way completely. To not even have the slightest idea of which way he should go.

He has read that this phenomenon can strike pilots in conditions of poor visibility. Make them not only lose sight of the cardinal directions, but also of up and down. What he is experiencing now is almost as bad.

A sound makes him flinch.

He squints, trying to make out where it came from. A bird, or at least he thinks it is.

Then he sees something through the darkness and fog.

A lamp has been lit a little way away. He walks toward the light.

After around twenty yards he recognizes where he is.

He is on Villa Arcturus's drive. He gives a sigh of relief. It was the house's outdoor light that he saw.

But why was it off just a minute before?

The light was on when he left the house—of that he is sure.

Of course, it could be on a timer that is set to turn off late at night, but if that's the case, then why would it have turned back on just a second ago?

The relief he just felt fades as he nears the front door.

He unlocks it, then stands in the doorway for a moment, listening.

All is quiet and still.

He turns on the lights in the hallway. They feel so dim, make no real dent in the oppressive darkness lurking in the house.

"Hello?" he asks. Clears his throat when his voice quakes.

He steps inside. The kitchen is empty, the living room, too.

Bernhard Irving stares down at him from the mantelpiece.

He walks on toward the bedroom but stops a few feet from the door.

The door is shut. He doesn't remember shutting it. Not that that means he didn't.

For some reason his pulse has started to race, preparing his body for flight. Why is he so jittery?

"Hello?" he says again. All is still silent.

He steps back into the living room.

Should he go outside, call the guard station, and say that he thinks there's an intruder in the house? Based on what?

A light that turned on, a closed door, and a tingling feeling down the back of his neck?

What would Leo do? That question is easier to answer.

He looks around the room. Grabs a poker hanging by the open fire and weighs it in his hands a few times.

His pulse is still racing, making his mechanical heart valve rattle in his chest.

Hill walks over to the bedroom door and places one hand on the handle while gripping the poker in the other.

He takes a deep breath, then rips the door open with the poker raised over his head.

The bedroom is pitch-black, and he fumbles around on the wall for the switch.

A faint click and the room is bathed in light.

Hill exhales and lowers the poker.

The room is empty.

He quickly checks the bathroom and the guest room on the far side, but the outcome is the same.

He is alone. No sign of any unwelcome guest.

Exhausted, he returns the poker to its place, then sinks down onto the sofa in the middle of the living room.

The new energy that his treatment gave him has finally ebbed out; perhaps the walks and dinner were a bridge too far. But he did have a nice time, and Maud Irving was both funny and charming, perhaps even a little flirty. Still, it was clear there were things she didn't want to talk about. Her brother Viggo, for example.

It's clear that Elsa is far more perceptive to her surroundings than people expect. She also protects her mother from questions relating to the CEO change and to Nova.

And yet both Elsa and Maud come across as pretty normal people, at least in comparison to all the other oddities that he has witnessed since being invited to Astroholm.

He stands up and hobbles into the bathroom.

Changes into his pajamas and brushes his teeth. Does one final round of the house to lock the front door and turn out the lights before climbing into bed.

Just when he is about to hit the lights, the feeling returns, the one he felt earlier when he was standing outside the door. A vague sensation that makes him toss uncomfortably in bed.

He can't say why, but he is convinced that someone has been in his house.

He gets out of bed again. Checks that all the windows are shut, the front door locked and bolted. Then he fetches the poker and props it up beside his bed.

Despite his weariness, it takes him some time to fall asleep.

THURSDAY

ASKER

She lies awake, staring up at the darkness. Viktor is asleep beside her. The worst of her frustration has lifted, and her mind has cleared.

Still, the problem remains.

In twenty-four hours the SWAT teams will storm the Farm to arrest Per. And that won't end well.

But this pleasant little interlude has at least allowed her to come up with a plan. An unexpected solution, but one that might actually work. Though it will require her to break a promise she made to herself.

She climbs out of bed and finds her clothes. Drinks a glass of water at the kitchen counter before heading for the door.

Viktor doesn't wake up; he never does when she is slipping out.

It is after two a.m. and the street is empty. She walks to her car and hops into the driver's seat.

Instead of immediately pulling off, she sits there for a minute or so, trying to foresee the possible consequences of what she plans to do.

The danger it involves.

Just as she is about to start the engine, another car comes crawling down the street. Only once it has passed and disappeared around a corner does Asker realize it looked familiar.

It resembled the car with the silver paintwork that was a little too close on her tail earlier that night.

It could just be a coincidence, but Prepper Per has taught her never to accept that as an explanation.

She starts her own car and tears off in the same direction that the silver car took. At the next crossing she ups her speed, thinking she glimpses a pair of rear lights. But when she catches up, the lights turn out to belong to a red Volvo, and the silver car has vanished without a trace.

She steers toward the freeway while trying to figure out who might have reason to tail her. Hellman could have tasked someone with keeping a tab on her, but the car didn't look like an unmarked police car.

So who else? She has no answer to that question. Which could suggest it was a coincidence, in spite of it all.

She tries to remember as many details as possible from when she saw the car by the freeway. She never got a glimpse of the license plate, but she does think she saw that there was only one person inside.

She looks in her rearview mirror. Whoever her possible shadow was, he or she is long gone, and there's not much that she can do about it right now.

Besides, she has a task to focus on.

She drives north through Skåne. The time is almost four a.m., the witching hour upon her, and outside the car windows the nature has changed. The forests have become denser, punctuated only by lone black boulders erupting from the ground.

The primeval bedrock of the Fennoscandian Shield.

She knows this kind of nature like the back of her hand. Can move through it as silently as a ghost. A pretty fitting likeness, given where she is headed.

To the Shadowlands; the ghost of her past.

The roads she is traveling on get narrower, as the forest creeps ever closer to the verges. The sky sinks almost all the way down to the treetops. She turns off onto the dirt track that she knows so well.

Once upon a time this road felt like an eternity, but now she covers it in a matter of minutes.

She passes the barrier to the old dump where Tord Korpi's body was found. The police cordon is already gone.

She continues another few hundred yards and stops the car. Sits there at the wheel while staring at the gate, the barbed wire, and the cameras, all clearly visible in the headlights' glare. The yellow signs warn trespassers against coming any closer.

She swore that she would never come back here.

And yet here she is.

Back at the Farm.

Her entire body is screaming at her to get out of here. To slam her foot on the gas and never look back.

Every one of her instincts is telling her that this can only end badly.

She turns off the headlights and looks at the clock. Four thirty.

She needs to gather her thoughts for a minute. Prepare herself mentally for what is to come.

But that's not easy. The door she once shut is suddenly wide open, releasing memories that she has long tried to repress.

She decides to try to focus on a happy memory. Find one small light to cling onto, to stop her from gazing down into the abyss.

She doesn't have many, but there are a few.

And one of them shines brighter than the rest.

Martin Hill.

She half shuts her eyes, and for a moment she thinks she can see two people cycling down the road. Two teenagers heading away from the Farm.

On their way—out.

SIXTEEN YEARS EARLIER

They have been cycling for almost three hours. On her own Leo could have made it in under two, but Martin needs to stop every half hour to catch his breath. Even though she is carrying the tent and most of their gear, he still walks his bike up any slope steeper than five degrees.

"The journey's part of the goal, Leo," he says with a laugh whenever she rolls her eyes impatiently when he needs to stop again.

He found their destination on a chat forum for urban explorers, made a pack list, and drew their route out on a map.

She has only a vague idea of what a chat forum even is.

Naturally Prepper Per forbids computers and cellphones from the Farm, so her experience of the internet is limited to the computers at school.

The last few miles follow timber roads that wend their way all the deeper into the spruce forest, ending at a waterway that flows past an old building made of stone.

"That's it—the waterfall and the sawmill," Martin says breathlessly.

Leo isn't quite as sold on abandoned buildings as he is, but she will take any chance she can get to spend some time away from the Farm.

While he scouts the outside of the abandoned building, she sets up camp in a sheltered spot that won't get flooded if it rains. Then she builds a big campfire contained by a ring of stones and gathers enough dry wood to last them the night.

Not that it looks like a storm is approaching—the summer sky is almost completely cloudless—but because Preparatus supervivet—Latin for "the prepared survive." It's one of Prepper Per's favorite maxims, one that must never go ignored.

When Martin eventually comes sauntering back, he hardly notices any of her efforts.

"I know how we're going to get inside," he says with a big smile. "Or almost, anyway. I need your help."

The windows and doors to the old sawmill have been nailed shut for many years. But he has found a loading hatch.

"I think it's how they got the logs in," he explains. "Maybe there was a belt here, or something like it. The hatch hasn't been nailed shut, but it's heavy. We need to find a way to lift it."

Ten minutes later, and with the help of an iron rod and a rusty oil barrel found in a shed, Leo has constructed a crude lever that solves the problem. She wedges the hatch open with a few old boards before they worm their way in.

As always, Martin wants to start in the cellar.

"That's what the real urban explorers do," he explains, clearly forgetting that he has told her the exact same thing many times before. "They start down in the cellar and work their way up toward the light."

Leo lets him have his way.

The cellar is cold and damp and contains nothing but rusty machine parts and impressive amounts of rat droppings.

The ground floor is more interesting. Although the water wheels have been removed, the mechanisms that transmitted the power to where the saw once stood look intact. Martin inspects them carefully.

"Get a load of this," he says, shining his flashlight on the wooden posts that support the mezzanine level. "The workers carved their initials here. JM 1948, AP 1952, FD 1958."

He pulls the digital camera that he got for Christmas out of his backpack and starts taking pictures.

"Do you think any of them are still alive?" he asks.

"Maybe. If they were in their thirties in '58, then they'd be around eighty now."

He lowers his camera, runs his fingers over the carvings.

"Still, their initials look just like they did when they carved them," he says. "Traces of lost moments. That's what I love about urban exploration."

A wooden staircase leads them up to the mezzanine level. There is nothing up there, but Martin takes more pictures anyway. He is good at finding beautiful shots: sunlight filtering in through boards; a rusty key in a window frame; a backlit cobweb.

As for her, she's just happy to have his company.

"So your dad let you off the Farm?" he says over his shoulder. "Is Prepper Per going soft?"

"I wish!" she says with a laugh. "But he does have a new friend visiting. Today they were building a bunker, and tonight I'm sure they'll be drinking beers and shooting cans on the range."

She could add that Per is pleased with her, that she has been a good girl; that she earned herself this trip by spying on Uncle Tord.

But she lets it pass. Martin would nod and listen. Even force a joke or some words of encouragement, pretend that her story doesn't worry him.

But Martin sees through her all the same. He stops, gives her a serious look.

"We should have a distress code," he says.

"A what?"

"A distress code. A signal for if one of us needs help but can't say it out loud. A secret Mayday, one that won't sound out of place but that the other will still understand."

Her instinct is to laugh it all off, but she stops herself when she sees the look on his face.

"Like what?" she asks instead.

"Double knot," he says, without hesitation. She realizes that he must have been thinking this over for a while.

"Double knot?"

"Yeah, like, 'don't go tying yourself up in double knots,' or 'this situation is a real double knot.' If one of us says it, the other will know we're in danger."

Leo gets what he is doing. He's trying to make it seem like the distress code is for both of them, when in actual fact he's certain the only one who will ever need it is her. One part of her wants to tell him it's unnecessary. That he needn't worry. But another, bigger part of her fills with warmth at his thoughtfulness.

"Double knot," she says with a nod. "OK."

"Good." He lights up with that smile that she likes.

They go back down to ground level. Martin stands in the middle of the room, his eyes half-shut.

She knows he is trying to work out if there's anything else to discover. Anything they missed on their first round of the building. He walks over to the nailed-shut windows and inspects the window frames.

Meanwhile she heads back to the wooden columns.

When Martin's back is turned, she takes out the pocketknife she always carries and carves a few characters into the old wood.

LA+MH 2006

She knows that this is against the rules of urban exploration, that Martin would be mad if he saw her. Still, it feels right to leave something behind in the time machine. A small trace of them that might remain long after they are gone.

Double knot, she thinks to herself, and she can't help but smile.

"Leo, come look!" he shouts, and she hastily puts her knife away.

He has pulled up one of the windowsills.

In the space beneath it lies a bottle of liquor and some glasses.

"You see, most buildings have their secrets," he says. "It's just a matter of knowing where to look."

He takes a few pictures of the liquor stash, then carefully puts the windowsill back in place.

She thinks of the secret that she just added to the column.

The message she carved, the proof that this moment ever took place.

That they once existed.

She and he.

ASKER

She must have dozed off, since a faint sound makes her jerk awake in her seat. Something is standing to the left of her car, a large gray silhouette that she can only just make out in the darkness.

A moose. A yearling standing with its front legs on the dirt track and its back legs in the safety of the forest. Its breaths hang like smoke around its head in the freezing air.

The moose ruminates mechanically while staring at her, as though trying to figure out whether she poses a threat. After a few seconds it turns and floats back into the forest.

Asker's heart calms, but the scar on her forearm has been reawakened. Has realized where she is, and what she is about to do.

She unbuttons her shirtsleeve to see the tattoo.

The scar beneath it burns and writhes, as though it were a living being.

Resisting the impulse to scratch at the skin, Asker instead traces the tattoo's letters with the fingers of her right hand. Repeats the word *resilience* again and again.

But it is as though the ritual no longer works like it used to.

She pulls down her shirtsleeve again, opens the door, and steps outside.

Takes a few breaths of the piercing morning air before walking over to the gate.

At the intercom she presses the bell. The signal illuminates a spotlight, and she turns her face toward the camera beside it.

She waits.

Breathes.

Her scar stirs faintly.

It's not too late to get out of here, it seems to want to say. Not too late to disappear into the darkness like the moose just did, avoid the double knot that she is drawing around herself.

But she stays there.

Waits.

Breathes.

After just a minute she hears the sound of an engine. After that, the headlights of an approaching quad bike on the other side of the gate.

Asker gulps her heart back down from her mouth.

The quad bike enters the light, and the driver glares at her.

He now has a big, bushy beard, from which his hawkish nose protrudes at a sharp angle. He is also thinner, more hollow-eyed.

His left eye is the color of milk. One of his hands is plastic. She is the one who did this to him. Who once defeated him.

And yet he still scares her.

Per Asker.

Prepper Per.

Her father.

He stops at the gate and turns off the engine. Casts his working eye over her a few times before opening his mouth.

"Welcome home, Leo," he says with a cold smile. "What could you be after?"

Asker inhales again. Her scar feels like a serpent beneath her skin.

"I have an idea," she says. "A very logical one, actually, but you're not going to like it."

Silence reigns for a few seconds.

"And why not?"

He stares at her with that uncanny gaze of his that makes him look like an apparition—which he also is, in a way.

Her apparition. Her ghost.

She breathes out slowly.

This is the weakest part of her plan. It all hangs on how much he hates her.

Her scar is twisting furiously.

"Because you'll have to trust me," she says calmly. "Are you prepared to do that?"

HILL

He makes himself breakfast in the kitchen of Villa Arcturus, eating with more appetite than he has had in a long time. Slices of bread topped with cheese and marmalade, all washed down with freshly squeezed orange juice. With the daylight his unpleasant feeling from the night before has started to fade, almost like a dream. Perhaps it *was* just a dream.

Once he has finished eating, he puts on a pot of coffee, and while it's brewing he steps into the living room. Stands there for a minute, trying to identify what it was that could have sparked his vague suspicion that someone was in the house. He is just on his way back to the kitchen for his coffee when he hears a knock at the door. He is half expecting it to be Elsa. So far she has been his only visitor.

Instead he finds Nova Irving standing there, Samuel at her side.

Her eyes are even more intensely blue than Hill remembers.

"Good morning," she says with her deep voice. "We just wanted to check how you're getting along. That you have everything you need."

She steps past Hill and into the house before he can even reply. Samuel indicates with a nod of his head that Hill is expected to follow her.

"Can I interest either of you in a coffee?" he asks. "I've just brewed a pot."

"I'd love some, thanks," says Nova. She is already in the living room, where she sits straight down on Bernhard's armchair, making herself at home.

Hill fetches coffee for them all, and after some hesitation he takes a seat in the armchair next to Nova's. Samuel, on the other hand, walks over to the window facing the garden and stares out watchfully.

"So you've made a start in the library," Nova says.

The black suit she is wearing is almost identical to the last one. Her pendant is the same, and the blood-red lipstick, too, but today she has her hair up in a ponytail. If possible she looks even more striking than at their last meeting.

"And Dr. Schiller says he's started treatment on your wound," she goes on. "And I also hear you've met my sister and niece."

"Yes, I had dinner with them last night," he says.

Nova nods in a way that suggests she was already party to that information.

"Maud's divorce really put her through the wringer a few years ago. She more or less hit the wall. That's one of the reasons why she had to step down as CEO. One that we didn't sing from the rooftops, for obvious reasons. But Maud blames me for everything. She thinks I had her removed."

Nova pulls a regretful grimace.

"Nothing could be further from the truth. It was the board's decision; I had nothing to do with it."

"I see," says Hill, for want of anything better to say. Nova's charisma is so intense and self-assured that he struggles to gauge the truth in her words.

"Well, it was nice to spend time with Maud and Elsa, anyway," he says. "Now I've met half the family, so to say."

Nova raises one eyebrow quizzically, so Hill hurries to finish his thought.

"Everyone except Karin, Viggo, and of course Gunnar himself."

Nova shakes her head.

"Karin pretty much lives in a world of her own, has done for many years. Besides, she's never had anything to do with AlphaCent, so I don't see what she would be able to contribute to the book."

"I understand," Hill nods. He mostly used Karin as a means of approaching the topic he would rather discuss.

"And Viggo, your half brother? He should at least get a mention in the book. Or ideally an interview."

"Oh, poor Viggo," Nova says with a sad shake of the head. "Now, there's another tragedy."

She crosses her legs elegantly.

"He sustained permanent brain damage in his car crash." She shakes her head again, more sorrowfully this time. "He needs a great deal of ongoing medical support, so he lives in a specialist facility abroad, where he can get the best possible care."

"How sad," says Hill. "He can't have been that old when it happened?"

"Twenty-five. Maud was twenty-three. I was only nine. My clearest memory of what happened is how furious our father was. Viggo was his only son, after all. As I'm sure you know, Maud's fiancé, Pontus, also died in the accident. So it was a double blow, not least for poor Maud."

She takes a sip of the coffee, then crosses her legs the other way, as if to signal that she has finished with that subject and that it is time to move on to something else.

"So, I've talked over your ideas with Gunnar."

"Oh, you have?" Hill fidgets.

"He has a number of thoughts that you might want to consider."

"Of course," Hill says with a nod.

She pauses, as if trying to weigh her words.

"Dad isn't so keen on the 'Space-Case' nickname. He thinks it detracts from his achievements. So he'd prefer that the book steer away from that story. Focus on the future."

"Yes, but the company's very name comes from his alien encounter, so I don't think it's possible to skip over it completely," Hill protests.

Nova chuckles.

"Gunnar isn't asking you to skip over it completely. But he doesn't want that to be where the emphasis lies. Enough has been written about that chapter already, and he'd much rather see the book have a new, more forward-looking focus, one that doesn't revolve around UFOs and mysterious space creatures. He doesn't want that to be his legacy."

"Of course. I'll bear that in mind," Hill says with a reluctant nod. Then he adds: "By the way, what's the situation with Boulder Isle? I'd really like to go out there as soon as possible. After all, that *is* where it all began."

Nova lets out another chuckle.

"It's great that you're so raring to go, Martin. But it's Gunnar who has final say on everything Boulder Isle related. You'll go there when he thinks you're ready. The best thing you can do right now is come up with a good angle for the book. After that I'm sure everything will fall into place. Oh, and preferably a great title, too—I know that would make Gunnar happy."

She holds his gaze.

"OK," Hill says. "I'll give it some thought."

"Great!" Nova gets to her feet. "In that case we'll let you get back to it. But before we go, Samuel also has something he'd like to tell you."

She nods at the security chief, who clears his throat.

"Yes, I'm afraid we've had some problems with intruders on the estate again. It happens every year around the anniversary of Gunnar's encounter. We've increased security, so you may notice a heightened presence of guards and drones around the grounds. And if you see anything strange, or anyone who shouldn't be here, we'd be grateful if you could raise the alarm via the app."

"OK," Hill says with a nod.

"All right then, Martin," Nova says in parting. "Gunnar and I look forward to hearing more about your progress."

Hill sees them to the door, then looks on as they climb into the large Mercedes. Nova gets into the front seat, he notes. Next to the driver and not in the back, like both he and Gunnar Irving had done.

Might it have something to do with what Maud insinuated the previous night? That Nova and Samuel are more than just colleagues?

Perhaps—that or Nova just gets motion sickness.

Once the car has pulled off, Hill goes back to the living room and starts clearing away the coffee cups, muttering irritably to himself.

He has no idea how to rustle up the kind of angle that Nova and Gunnar seem to be looking for. The UFO story is central to Alpha-Cent, the Irving family, and—not least—the book that he himself hopes to write in future.

But it is becoming all the clearer that without that angle he is never going to set foot on Boulder Isle.

By Bernhard's big desk he stops short. Something white is protruding from under the edge of the desk mat.

He lifts up the mat, and underneath it he finds an identical envelope to the one that was slipped through his door a few nights before. His name is written in rounded letters on the front.

Hill frowns.

Inside it lies a sheet of paper folded double. Not a letter this time, but a drawing.

A graphite sketch of a figure with a human body and an animal's head.

He feels his heart valve do a little drumroll.

Taurus.

He knows where he has seen this figure before.

At the top of one of the bookshelves in the great library.

HELLMAN

Hellman is standing at the front of the large incident room, which is full of police officers. A mix of his own staff from Serious Crime and tactical officers dressed in black.

The atmosphere is charged, expectant. Everyone knows what is coming.

He loves this part of the job. And on this particular day he loves it even more, for personal reasons. But he keeps his excitement in check. He must appear stone-cold, composed, competent.

A professional leader for a professional operation.

"Good morning, everyone," he says, to gain their attention. At the same time he starts up his PowerPoint presentation with a remote control. The words *Operation Eagle* slowly appear on the screen behind him.

He pauses for a few seconds, to make sure all eyes are on him.

"So, our suspect is Per Asker, fifty-five years of age. Formerly head of research at a large munitions company, he has long since withdrawn from both the job market and society. Just over twenty-five years ago he had a dispute with his employer. Asker sued the company and lost, which, in addition to essentially ruining him, reportedly also left him particularly bitter. It was around this time that he got divorced and moved up to the forests, to a place known as the Farm."

He clicks the remote control to display first a map, then an image of a plot enclosed by a double-barbed-wire fence. Within the enclosure some barracks and old trailers are visible.

"Asker became a prepper, or a survivalist as it is sometimes called. One of those people who devote all their time to preparing for a future catastrophe, and who want as little as possible to do with society at large. When the research unit he once managed was struck by a flash fire immediately after his final appeal was quashed, he was the prime suspect for the crime. Our colleagues at the Swedish Security Service surveilled him for months, suspecting that he had become something of a Swedish Ted Kaczynski, whose name I'm sure you all know."

"The Unabomber," Eskil interjects from the first row.

Hellman gives him an annoyed look.

"In any case," he goes on. "Despite a long and costly investigation, we were never able to pin the crime on Per Asker. No one doubted that he had both the means and the motive, but they came no closer than that. Asker was just too wily."

He clicks up a new image, taken from afar, depicting a tall, wiry man moving between a couple of trailers.

"So, here he is. Per Asker. A former reservist who trained with the paratroopers."

Some of the tactical officers whisper among themselves, presumably because they have a similar training background.

"Asker is extremely paranoid," Hellman goes on. "When a homemade bomb exploded in his face, he was left blind in one eye and now uses a prosthetic hand."

Hellman pauses briefly. He has considered whether to mention Leo in this briefing. Rumor that her father stands suspected of murder has no doubt already started to circulate in police HQ.

But he has decided to keep her name out of this—not out of consideration for her, however, but for purely practical reasons. The commander of the tactical unit or another one of his officers might get it into their heads to involve her, which is the last thing Hellman wants. Leo has already beaten him to the victim's ex-wife, and he doesn't want her to point out that little fact, nor anything else that might make him seem like the second-best detective in the room.

"Our intel suggests Per Asker probably knows he's a person of interest," he goes on. "He rarely to never leaves the Farm, uses a double-gate system for deliveries, and is very vigilant about his surroundings. It will also be very difficult to take him by surprise."

Hellman clicks up a new image, this time of an old driver's license photo.

"The murder victim is one Tord Korpi, also a former paratrooper. Both Korpi and Asker are, or were, members of the paratroopers' regimental association, which is likely how they met. Korpi's body was found a few days ago, buried a short distance from the main entrance to the Farm.

"He had lain there for sixteen years, but he was well preserved enough for us to be able to identify him using his dental records. From Korpi's ex-wife we have learned that he was a mining engineer, and that he worked as a project manager on underground excavations and constructions. Cellars, tunnels, you name it. Our working theory is that he did a job for Asker, they clashed, and Asker executed him with a shot to the back of the head."

He clicks up the next image, which contains autopsy photos of Tord Korpi's face and the back of his head.

"All in all, Per Asker is violent and paranoid, and he has considerable expertise in weaponry, explosives, and close combat. In addition, he has a license for a total of seven firearms, although he may have access to further unlicensed ones. We have every reason to believe that he is extremely dangerous, so the operation must take place with a great deal of power and grit."

He nods at the commander of the tactical unit, who is sitting in the front row. He immediately stands up, clicks up a map of the Farm, and starts going through the details of the deployment scheduled to take place at four a.m. the next morning.

Just as he is explaining that the fourth team will be lowered in by helicopter, the door to the incident room is opened. A colleague pokes his head in, seemingly trying to get Hellman's attention.

Hellman shakes his head to show that he is busy, but the officer in the doorway won't budge.

"Is this something we all need to know?" Hellman asks.

The man in the doorway's gaze flits between Hellman and the commander of the tactical unit.

"Leo Asker's here," he eventually says. "She says she has important information to share regarding the operation."

"Oh, bring her straight in then," the tactical commander says irritably.

"That's probably not such a good idea," Hellman protests while stepping forward. "Leo Asker's presence creates . . ."

Before he can say any more, Leo is in the doorway. She looks determined, and Hellman must make an effort to keep his cool.

"As I was just explaining, Asker, your presence here creates a serious conflict of interest. A potentially life-threatening one."

"Because you're planning to arrest my father tomorrow morning." She nods. "Yes, I'm quite aware of the problem."

"Good," Hellman says dryly, to silence the whispers now circling the room. He feels the commander of the tactical unit looking at him, perhaps questioning how he runs his department.

"If you'd be so kind, Asker . . ." Hellman says, signaling at the door.

"I just have one thing to add," she interrupts. "About my father, I mean. A small but rather important detail that I thought you might want to know before kicking up this shitstorm."

Hellman is fighting hard to keep his cool. He feels every eye on him now, their gazes transformed into a faint vibration that suggests his authority has been rocked.

He must remain stone-cold, take back control. Show them who is boss.

"And what might that be, may I ask?" he says, with just the right dose of irony. "What do you think you could possibly offer us, Leo?"

Asker points her thumb over her shoulder.

"Per's waiting for you down in reception," she replies. "All you have to do is go downstairs and fetch him. If you dare, that is."

THE GLASS MAN

After the head gardener he stayed calm for many years. Graduated from high school, moved to Malmö to study. Started working at the company part-time. The Father hardly saw him; he was too busy with other things.

With other people.

A whole new family.

Still, he managed to convince himself that what the Father was doing was a test. A trial of his own strength of will, of his devotion. In those years he lived almost like a monk.

Studied, exercised, worked. Built a body and a mind worthy of an Irving.

Worthy of an heir.

Occasionally the hunger would make itself known, tormenting him with nightmares that he would hold at bay with sleeping pills.

Or with violent desires that he would repress through exercise, pushing his body to the brink of blacking out.

The method worked, at least for a while.

But then his grandfather died, and at the funeral he, his mother, and sister were forced to sit in the pew behind the Father and his new wife. He saw how that wounded his mother. How she steeled herself for his and his sister's sake. Swallowed her pride, her disgrace.

That evening he went to the gym, pushed himself until his muscles throbbed. Stayed there until the premises closed and he was forced to go home.

But this time it didn't help.

The hunger burned inside him. The desire to punish someone. Repay the disgrace.

He knew who it would be: the Father's new wife, the one who had replaced them.

He shadowed her all the closer, observing her; fantasized about taking her neck between his hands and watching her journey down into the darkness.

But somehow the Father must have realized what he was planning.

Overnight he was sent away. Enrolled without warning at an exclusive university in the USA and packed off across the Atlantic.

A fantastic opportunity, for anybody.

And yet he felt banished, yet again. Cut off from his loved ones.

The thought chipped away at him: Did the Father's all-seeing eye extend all the way to his own mind? To his innermost thoughts, his very darkest desires?

Or was there another explanation?

Namely that someone he trusted—the only person in the world with whom he had shared his secrets—had betrayed him.

ASKER

Her father is sitting on a bench in reception, straight-backed but with his eyes shut, as though meditating. He doesn't look up until they are near.

"This is Detective Superintendent Jonas Hellman," Asker says. "He and his colleagues are going to question you. After that the prosecutor will decide whether you should be detained. If you are detained, they will have three days to request that you be charged and remanded in custody; otherwise they have to let you go."

"Thanks, I'm aware of how the Swedish justice system works," Per says brusquely, sizing Hellman up with his ghostly gaze. "I see you brought an entourage, Hellman."

He nods at the three burly tactical officers who have encircled him.

"Stand up!" Hellman commands sharply.

Per remains seated, gives his daughter a long look.

Then he stands up demonstratively slowly, turns around, and places his hands behind his back.

A brief moment of confusion arises when the tactical officers can't agree on who should cuff Per.

Followed by another when the officer who finally takes on the task discovers the detainee's prosthetic hand. After a little wrangling they eventually get the cuffs in place.

The first part of Asker's plan is now complete. Many aspects of it worry her: that she won't manage to find Danielsson or Sundin, for example. Or get them to admit that they murdered Tord Korpi.

But what worries her most is how easily Prepper Per was persuaded.

As though he already had the whole scenario planned out long ago and was simply waiting for her to put it into action.

Waiting for her to break every promise she had made to herself.

The thought latches on and takes root as she watches Per get marched off between the tactical officers. Wasn't it all a little too easy?

"Thank you for your help, Asker," Hellman says through gritted teeth. "But for the record, let me stress how important it is that you keep out of this case going forward."

Asker nods.

"Just one piece of advice: don't underestimate Per. Assume he knows at least as much about you as you do about him. That he's thought out every possible scenario and is always two steps ahead."

Hellman gives her a cold smile.

"Thanks for the tip. Now, if you'll excuse me, I have a department to run. As do you, I suppose?"

He gestures down at the ground, then turns on his heel and marches off toward the elevator.

On level minus one a drowsy stillness reigns. Virgilsson's door is shut for a change, so Asker can slip inside Rosen's office unseen.

"I was trying to reach you all evening," she says irritably. "Why didn't you pick up?"

The diminutive woman avoids meeting her eyes.

"My phone's acting up a bit. I should probably get a new one . . ."

Asker is just taking a breath to say that Rosen is a terrible liar and that it's part of her goddamn job to be reachable, but at the last minute she checks herself.

"OK," she mutters grudgingly.

She hands Rosen the papers with the information she managed to dig up on Danielsson and Sundin.

"I have two men I need you to help me locate immediately."

"OK!" The woman takes a seat at her computer. "I'll see what I can do."

She logs onto the system.

"By the way, you asked me for some other information the other day, on the drownings in Miresjön Lake. Here it is!" Rosen hands her a file. "A tragic story. I remember it, actually. One of the bodies is still missing. There have been lots of strange goings-on around Miresjön. UFOs, fatal accidents, meteorites, God knows what else."

"Mm-hm," Asker grunts.

She had almost forgotten the favor she promised Martin. Suddenly she is struck by something akin to a guilty conscience: although Rosen did avoid taking work calls the previous evening, the little woman has completed every task Asker has given her. Not to mention with a level of ambition that far exceeded her expectations.

Asker swallows the last of her irritation.

"You can tell your friend at *Sydsvenskan* that the police have just brought in a suspect for the murder on the border with Småland," she says, as warmly as she can. "Milk it a little, get him to take you out for a nice dinner."

Rosen's face lights up.

"I'll find those men for you, don't you worry!" she says. "Give me one hour, max."

Asker nods, leaves Rosen's office and sets off in the direction of her own. Attila's door is still shut, and the small traffic light on the wall outside that indicates whether he is in or busy is off. Still off sick, then.

Zafer rounds the corner from the kitchen. He is wearing a white lab coat, and as usual he is in a hurry. Walks in short, jerky steps, almost sloshing the coffee over the rim of his cup.

"No time to talk," he mutters. "Have something urgent."

A second later he disappears into his double-size office and shuts the door behind himself.

Asker fetches a glass of water, takes it back to her office, and slumps down heavily on her desk chair. She stuffs the files for Martin into the backpack beside her desk, but as she does she accidentally topples another object balanced on a stack of documents.

It's the gift-wrapped oven glove that Madame Rind's friend, mailless Siw, knitted for Attila. She picks it up off the floor, slings it onto the nearest flat surface, and sinks back down in her chair.

The status report reads as follows:

Prepper Per is safely in custody—for now, at least—which buys her a little more time to try to clear him of murder.

But the price she has paid for this is that the door to her past has been flung wide open, bringing Prepper Per back into her life.

On top of that, Hellman is furious—no—*even more* furious at her.

And then, to add insult to injury: her and her department's actual cases comprise a medium and her mail-less friend who knits oven mitts as a token of her love.

Asker pinches the bridge of her nose. She has a headache, which isn't so strange given that she only slept an hour or so last night.

She leans back and shuts her eyes.

Treats herself to a few minutes' microsleep to recharge her batteries.

A knock on the door wakes her up. How long was she out for? Half an hour, according to her watch.

"Come in!" she says, while rubbing the sleep from her eyes.

It's Rosen.

Asker signals at her to shut the door and take a seat.

"So, I think I've found something on Danielsson and Sundin," Rosen says eagerly. "You have their mug shots here, for starters."

She places two enlarged photos on the table.

Jon Danielsson is thin, with long, greasy hair and a middle part. His eyes are slightly bloodshot, and he looks jumpy.

Erik Sundin gives an entirely different impression: his head is shaved, with tattoos coiling all the way up his neck. He glares spitefully at the camera.

"Two real gems," Rosen summarizes. "You're right that neither of them lives at their registered addresses. Both the enforcement agency and the bailiffs have tried and failed to track them down. And of course they aren't on social media either—or at least not under their own names. But I think I might have found something."

She sets down another piece of paper.

"I found an old intelligence note that stated that Sundin and Danielsson had been traveling in a Volvo that was stopped at a checkpoint. They weren't suspected of any crime, but the officer who pulled them over recognized Sundin from an earlier case and wrote down the information."

Asker straightens up. This sounds interesting.

"I checked the license number, and the Volvo is registered to a woman who lives on an old farm up in the north Göinge area."

Asker gives a start. That's near Per's Farm. If the two men can be linked to the area around where Korpi was found, her theory is suddenly much stronger.

"She has no criminal record," Rosen goes on. "Though she does have a few records of nonpayment of debts in her past. I've checked her social media, and in a few instances she's mentioned her boy-friend E, who doesn't like being in photos."

She sets down an enlarged profile shot of a thirty-something woman with a nose ring and sunglasses.

"Look at that!" Rosen points at the sunglasses.

In them she can make out a faint reflection of the photographer. The image is small and not particularly sharp, but there is no mis-taking the shaved head and what appears to be a neck tattoo.

"Erik Sundin," says Asker. "Good work, Rosen!"

HILL

Hill's mind is on the strange envelope and sketch the whole golf-cart ride down to the manor house, though he tries to play it cool. In the elevator he avoids looking up at the cameras in the ceiling. Strangely enough he hasn't given them much thought before, but now all of a sudden he feels watched.

When Mrs. Schiller lets him into the library, his first instinct is to head straight for Bernhard's sci-fi shelf with the ornately carved figures, but he stops himself. There is a camera on the wall right next to the library entrance, which means there may be others. He must go on pretending that all is business as usual until he has had a chance to scope the place out.

So he takes a seat at the desk. Puts his crutch to one side, flicks through some papers, clatters on his keyboard. Tries to make it look like any other day at the office. Thinks that perhaps he should use this time to come up with an angle for the book—one that will allow him to write about what he wants to write about, while also appeasing Gunnar enough to let him travel to Boulder Isle.

But he finds it impossible to concentrate. His mind keeps jumping back to the sketch, and to who could have planted it on his desk. The handwriting and envelope suggest it was the same person who tried to warn him against going to Astroholm in the first place.

Hill had sat at that very desk the previous afternoon, and he is completely certain the envelope wasn't there then. Which means it was either placed there in the evening, overnight, or early that morning.

He knows of two people who were in his house in that time frame. Both Nova Irving and Samuel were in his living room that morning, in the vicinity of the desk. Either one of them could have easily taken the envelope out of an inner suit pocket and slipped it under the desk mat in a matter of seconds. Still, the thought of either of them turning to mysterious letters feels almost absurd. Which means he must also have had a more secret visitor.

Mrs. Schiller has the key to Villa Arcturus. Could she have let herself in while he was at dinner with Maud and Elsa? Could it be her whose presence he thought he sensed? Though theoretically possible, he still has his doubts. Mrs. Schiller made it clear that he shouldn't stray out of bounds, while the letter seems to be encouraging him to do just that. The identity of the mystery letter-writer will remain unknown for now.

He is almost as intrigued by what the drawing might mean. That much at least he hopes to be able to figure out shortly.

So as not to arouse any suspicion, he decides to wait until after the morning coffee service before approaching the bookshelves. He takes out his phone and messages Leo to kill some time.

I've stumbled across something exciting, he writes. Waits for her to read and reply, but nothing happens, which only adds to his impatience.

The coffee lady finally appears. He drinks his coffee, and once she has retreated with her trolley, Hill waits another ten torturous minutes before getting to his feet.

He browses here and there in various bookshelves, and, once he is sure the only camera is the one by the door, he strolls over to the corner that houses Bernhard's sci-fi collection.

He stops in front of the innermost shelf and slips the drawing out of the inside pocket of his blazer. Unfolds it in front of him and compares it to the wooden figures at the top of the shelf.

He was right. The drawing clearly matches the sculpture to the far right, the one with the bull's head that represents Taurus.

At the same height, but on the left, stands a similar figure that is supposed to represent Aries.

The sculptures' bodies and poses are identical; only the different animal heads distinguish them.

Hill examines them closely. As it happens, there is one other difference.

Taurus's wood is slightly lighter in color—at least on its lower section. As though the varnish has been worn by repeated touch.

He props his crutch up against one of the shelves, reaches out, and takes hold of the carving. His hand covers the lighter field on the wood exactly.

His heart pounds all the harder as he gently pulls the figure toward him. At first it refuses to budge, but then suddenly it folds down, as though affixed to a hidden hinge.

Something clicks.

A slit appears between the bookshelf and the wall, and a puff of cool air wafts over Hill. Carries on it an all too familiar scent of dust, damp, and cement.

The scent of the abandoned.

Hill pokes his fingers inside and discovers that the entire shelf swings open, just like a door. The stone wall behind it contains a narrow opening, through which he glimpses part of a spiral staircase leading upward.

With a pounding heart Hill steps through the opening, then turns on his cellphone flashlight at the bottom step of the spiral staircase.

The staircase is made of wrought iron with a blackened finish, and it looks old. Judging by the thick layer of dust that covers it, it hasn't been used in many years. He tries to make out where it ends, but the staircase spirals beyond the short reach of his flashlight.

Hill tries to get his excited breaths under control.

A hidden staircase behind a secret door. Why would someone want him to find this place? He takes a few cautious steps onto the staircase, testing its solidity. It sways faintly but feels relatively stable. The staircase is so narrow that two people would be unable to pass each other. The banister is cold and sticky with dust.

He follows the spiral upward, slowly, so as not to strain his wound. One round, two, three. By now he must be almost level with the library ceiling, but the elevator didn't suggest that there was any third floor. So where is he going?

After yet another spiral, the staircase ends at a platform before a wooden door.

The door is covered in carvings of humans with animal heads. Taurus, Capricorn, Aries, and Leo, just like the wooden sculptures on the bookshelf. But also Sagittarius, Virgo, and the Gemini twins.

The door handle reminds him of the bear knocker on Villa Arcturus.

Hill presses it down and hears a faint creak. The door moves slightly, but then catches. Hill leans forward to put his weight behind it.

"Hello? Associate Professor Hill?"

He gives a start.

The voice is coming from down in the library, ringing its way up the stairwell.

It sounds like Mrs. Schiller. If she finds him here, it will no doubt spell the end of his secret investigations.

He turns off his phone flashlight, grabs the banister, and races down the stairs as quickly as he can. His wound protests, and he grimaces in pain.

"Associate Professor Hill?"

The voice is closer now.

He reaches the opening behind the bookshelf and carefully pokes out his head. No one is there, but he can hear the faint crunch of carpet from approaching footsteps. Hill slips out, puts his shoulder to the bookshelf, and pushes it to. It closes with a faint click.

Straightening up, he grabs a book at random from the shelf, while with his other hand he wipes the cold sweat from his forehead. As he does so, he notices a big, white patch of dust on the elbow of his blazer, and only just manages to hide his arm behind his back before Mrs. Schiller rounds the corner with an anxious look on her face.

"Oh, there you are, Associate Professor Hill. Didn't you hear me calling?"

"Sorry." He flashes his most charming smile. "I must have been somewhere else entirely. Bernhard's collection really is fascinating."

He waves the book in his hand before putting it back on the shelf.

Mrs. Schiller's face softens.

"It certainly is," she says with a faint smile. "Well, the reason I'm interrupting you is that a space has come up in Dr. Schiller's schedule. He was wondering if you had time to come down for your treatment straightaway?"

"Of course," Hill replies. "After you!"

He chivalrously gestures at her to lead the way. As soon as her back is turned, he pats the dust off his sleeve.

HELLMAN

He has left Per Asker to sweat in a bare cell for an hour, then alone in an interview room. The man's nose protrudes from his furrowed face almost like the beak of a bird of prey. His dead eye is white, which, along with the beard, calls to mind the wizened face of the god Odin. All that is missing to complete the likeness is two giant ravens and a flying, eight-legged steed.

He tries to find some resemblance between Per and Leo Asker but doesn't quite succeed. Perhaps because Per's face is completely static.

Fact is, his entire being is almost completely static.

In the fifteen minutes that he has been watching the man through the cameras, Per Asker has sat there with his back poker-straight, his eyes closed, and his arms on the table. Hasn't slouched, sighed, or looked around the room.

There is something uncanny about that level of self-control.

"So," he says when he enters the room with Eskil at his heels.

He places a thick case file on the table in front of him and sits down opposite Per Asker.

The man slowly opens his eyes, watches him while he turns on the recording equipment and states the formalities.

He nods at Eskil to take a seat on the chair over by the wall, so that he is just on the outskirts of Asker's field of vision. A classic trick to up the stress in the suspect; make them feel watched.

Per Asker doesn't even throw a glance Eskil's way.

"So, Per, before we begin, I'd like to inform you that you have the right to have a lawyer present at this interview should you so wish."

He consciously avoids asking a direct question. Another trick picked up in his almost twenty years on the force, one that fulfills his legal requirements while reducing the risk of the suspect actually asking for legal counsel.

"Thanks. I think we'll get by without a lawyer," says Per. "What do you think, Jonas?"

Hellman gives a wry smile. Asker is trying to show that this is a conversation between two equals. A delusion that he will soon rid him of.

"As you already know, this interview concerns the murder of your old friend Tord Korpi, whose body was found just outside your property. What can you tell me about that?"

"Nothing," says Per Asker. He still hasn't looked away.

"No? You did know one another, didn't you?"

"That's right. But you didn't ask if we knew each other; you asked for details about his murder. I don't know any."

He goes silent again.

"OK."

Hellman changes tack. This isn't his first rodeo, and Per Asker is far from the first suspect who has tried to be a smart guy.

"How long did you know Tord Korpi before he died?"

"I couldn't say, because I don't know when he died," Per says with a smile.

Hellman maintains the façade.

Leo might not take after her father in appearance, but it's clearly from him that she gets her talent for winding him up.

"Tell me about when you first met Tord Korpi," he says calmly.

"It was in 1998, at a paratroopers' get-together. We got talking, and he told me what he was working on. I took his details. We kept in touch now and then. A few years later he was down in my neck of the woods, and I invited him to come stay with us."

The sentences come thick and fast; they sound rehearsed.

"What was he doing in the area, beyond staying with you?"

"No idea. I didn't ask any questions, and Tord wasn't the type to give me an answer even if I had."

"Was he working, do you think?"

"That's what I assumed."

"And he helped you with some kind of construction work, too?"

"I'm not commenting on hypothetical building works on my land. That's my business alone."

"Did you have planning permission?"

Per Asker tilts his head to one side.

"Oh, now you disappoint me, Jonas. Are you really investigating planning and construction violations?"

Hellman tries to keep his cool, but it's harder than expected. He sees Eskil throw him an uneasy glance.

"When was the last time you saw Tord Korpi?" he tries.

"August 16, 2006. In the afternoon."

"And you remember that in detail?"

"No, I don't. It's sixteen years ago, after all. But I keep a calendar, so it was easy to look it up."

"What were the circumstances of that meeting?"

"He'd stayed with us for a while, and he was moving on."

"Where to?"

"No idea. As I said, Tord wasn't the talkative type. It's one of the reasons I liked him."

Hellman chooses to change the subject again.

"I hear you're very skilled at the martial art of Krav Maga?"

He taps the thick case file, as if to show that they have plenty of intel on Per Asker. That they know basically everything worth knowing about him, right from the very day he was born. In actual fact he has padded it out with stacks of irrelevant documents—yet another trick that usually puts pressure on the person being questioned.

Per doesn't look the least bit concerned.

"That's right. When I was young, I spent a summer at a training camp in Israel. I got a pretty certificate—I hope you have a copy of it in that jam-packed file of yours?"

Hellman ignores his mocking tone.

"And you're a paratrooper and have therefore received weapons training."

"That's correct."

"Are you a good shot?"

Per Asker observes him closely. His dead, blind eye is unpleasant to meet.

"Ah," he says eventually. "So poor Tord was shot. Interesting."

His smile needles Hellman. So far the interview has consisted of questions that the other man has clearly anticipated and prepared for. He needs to shake things up, seize the initiative.

"In 2007, the year after Korpi disappeared, you almost killed yourself and your daughter in an accident. Blew your own hand off, blinded yourself in one eye."

Per's smile goes out like a light. Hellman immediately amps up the pressure.

"What could have caused you to make a mistake like that? An old bunker fox like you, getting sloppy with explosives? That doesn't sound right."

Per's working eye narrows, but he doesn't respond.

"Was it your conscience catching up with you?" Hellman goes on. "Old sins that distracted you? Or was it about Leo?"

A small muscle twitches on Per Asker's upper lip, but still he says nothing. Hellman hasn't planned any of this; he is running on intuition alone. Leo is Per's weak point; he needs to exploit that.

"You built yourself a fort out there in the forest," he says, before Asker can collect himself. "You hate the authorities and want nothing to do with society. And yet you handed yourself in as soon as Leo turned up at your gate. Do you trust her so blindly?"

Per Asker shakes his head.

"No. I don't trust anyone. But unlike most other people, she interests me. In a lot of ways you could say she's my likeness."

"Because you kept her prisoner in your little two-person sect? Made her believe she had to prepare for the end of the world, which, strangely enough, still hasn't happened?"

Per Asker doesn't respond, but instinctively Hellman can tell that his words have hit a nerve.

"Have you ever wondered why she stuck her neck out for you like that? Risked what little remains of her career?"

"You should probably ask her that."

Hellman shakes his head.

"I think we both know the answer, Per. We know why Leo wants you here, in this chair. Because she knows the truth, or at least suspects it. She lived on the Farm, so she must have met Tord Korpi. But above all, she knows better than anyone else what you're capable of."

Hellman pauses just long enough to see Per Asker's working eye start to wander.

"Leo knows how you work," he goes on. "Because, as you say, she's your likeness. A better, smarter version of you. She wanted to get you in this chair, and here you are."

Per's Adam's apple bobs up and down in his throat.

Hellman can smell it now. The scent of weakness.

"Leo knows," Hellman says quietly. "She knows what you did. She was there, she saw you with Korpi. She wanted to give you the chance to unburden yourself."

He fixes his detective's gaze on the man across from him. Thinks he can see Asker contract in his chair. He is close now; he can feel it in his whole body.

"Isn't that so, Per?" he almost whispers. "Korpi posed a threat to you and Leo. You simply did what you had to do. Protected what was yours. Protected your daughter."

The room is completely silent, the air so charged that he can almost taste it. Eskil is leaning so far forward that he is about to fall off his chair.

Per Asker looks down at the table. His cockiness is gone; he looks utterly deflated.

Just the death blow left now.

"You were only doing your duty, weren't you, Per?" Hellman says softly. "Your duty, that's all. Isn't that right?"

Per Asker clasps his hands on his lap and inhales slowly. His head lowers in what looks like a faint nod.

Here it comes, Hellman thinks.

Eskil looks like he has stopped breathing.

Then Per Asker lifts his head and straightens up. Goes back to his former, stiff posture while a smile spreads over his lips.

"Not bad, Jonas," he says. "Almost straight out of the FBI's interview manual. You must seem like a genius around here."

He signals at Eskil with his remaining hand.

"But the truth is, you only do what you've been trained to do, which makes you predictable. Hardly surprising Leo got bored with you."

Hellman tries to stop himself from pulling a face, but it's impossible.

"You do your research; I do mine." Per's smile widens. "The only difference is I don't need a stack of fake documents."

He leans forward and taps his index finger on the file.

"I know everything about you, Jonas. School grades, military service, where you live, where your wife works, how long you cheated on her with my daughter for, how you harassed my daughter when she dumped you. You got Leo demoted from Serious Crime because you're afraid of her. Afraid that she's a better detective than you."

He contemptuously waves his finger in the air.

"And after this bungling display I'd say that fear is completely warranted. Leo's everything you're not . . ."

Hellman slams his fist on the table. The sound makes Eskil jump, but Per Asker doesn't move a muscle.

"You think you're so fucking smart," Hellman splutters. His face is hot, and his pulse is pounding in his temples. "Yet here you are, suspected of murder. All while we turn your whole life inside-out. If you've missed anything—one tiny fucking speck—we're going to find it and then you're done for. It'll be life, if you're lucky, or else back to the psych ward, and this time for good."

Hellman stands up and grabs the file from the table.

"But maybe you're hoping your daughter will get you out of this. In that case you'd better cross those fucking fingers of yours," he says coldly. "Or at least the ones you have left. Because at this point I don't see what she could do to help you—if she even wants to, that is."

ASKER

The drive from Malmö to the address Rosen dug up takes less than two hours. Asker feels like she has spent the last twenty-four hours in the car, but the adrenaline keeps her going. Every now and then she glances into her rearview mirror in search of the silvery vehicle from the previous night, but so far she has seen no sign of it. She still has no idea who could have been following her: Hellman's shock at her handing Per over makes it seem even less likely that it was one of his gang. But in that case, who else could it be? Internal Affairs? A journalist who somehow got wind of her involvement in the Holst case? A private detective?

None of those answers seems credible.

The farm where she hopes to find Sundin and Danielsson lies a good way out in the countryside. The last mile or so of her journey is down a frost-damaged dirt track that coils through dense forest.

According to the Google Maps satellite images that Rosen supplied her with, the farm consists of one brick house and a wooden barn.

But, as she notes when she arrives, what the images didn't show is that both buildings are in a state of extreme disrepair. The spruce trees creep in on them from either side, the barn's roof ridge is covered with a green tarpaulin, and the window frames on the squat farmhouse are so rotten that you can barely tell what color they once were. Up by the chimney, a satellite dish and TV antenna are competing to see which one can tumble down first.

A cat is slinking around the front steps, but it shies away when Asker comes near.

Instinctively she reaches for where her holster belt should have been. But her firearm is still in Forensics, and day by day she has come to suspect that Hellman may be behind the long delay in it being released. She would have happily borrowed a colleague's weapon for this outing, but the only person in her department besides herself who is authorized to bear arms is Attila, and he's still off sick. So her only form of defense is an expandable baton that she keeps in one of her jacket pockets.

Asker knocks on the front door. No response.

She knocks again, louder this time, but still with the same result.

She walks over to the barn and peers in through the gaps in the planks. There is a car inside—the same Volvo station wagon that Sundin and Danielsson were stopped in just a few months back.

She returns to the farmhouse and walks around to the back of the building. From a rusty drying rack hangs a T-shirt that probably wasn't greenish-gray when it was hung up last summer.

Farther away, by the edge of the forest, stand a few greenhouses that appear to be in slightly better shape than the rest of the farm. When Asker draws closer, she sees that the glass walls have been lined with sackcloth. Through them she glimpses cables and grow lights over a green carpet of plants. She can tell what she is looking at even before the smell hits her. The door is wide open, and a faint sound is coming from inside. Regular thuds, as though someone is doing some kind of labor.

Asker takes the baton out of her pocket.

The stench is overpowering. A hot mix of skunk, sulfur, and garlic, emanating from the hundreds of small cannabis plants crammed inside.

Sundin has enough cannabis here to go down for serious drug offenses, which means she now has some leverage. Hopefully that will be enough to make him talk.

All that's left is to find him.

The greenhouse is traversed by two parallel paths. Choosing one, she cautiously creeps along it. The thudding continues.

The plants stand in beds raised up off the ground, making them tall enough to block her view of the other path. As she works her way down the path she stumbles slightly on a watering hose, and her shoe scrapes in the gravel.

The thudding stops abruptly.

Asker swears inwardly. She presses on ahead, gripping the baton even tighter. Stops suddenly when she thinks she spots a movement to her right. Turns toward it and raises her baton, preparing to whip it out to its full length.

But before she can, someone leaps out from between the plants with a loud cry.

Her assailant tackles her in the chest and shoves her backward, straight onto the nearest plant bed. The impact knocks the wind out of her, but she pulls herself upright and totters to one side, protecting her head while trying to regain her balance.

Instead of attacking her again, her assailant has darted away. She glimpses a flash of a shaved head and a neck tattoo.

It's Erik Sundin.

She sprints after him, extending her baton.

Sundin has given himself around a forty-foot head start. On top of that, he is quick as a whippet and knows exactly where to place his feet. He races through the overgrown garden while Asker tries to work up her speed.

He rounds the corner to the main house, disappearing out of sight.

Asker slows down, preparing to take the corner in a wide curve, just in case he is waiting for her there.

But when she hears a car engine splutter to life, she throws all caution to the wind.

By the time she has rounded the corner, the door to the barn is open and the Volvo is waiting in the drive. Sundin tears open the passenger-seat door and jumps inside. The car takes off, sending gravel spraying around the wheels, but Asker manages to catch a glimpse of the driver. Jon Danielsson.

She runs over to her car, jumps inside, and steps on the gas.

She can see the Volvo up ahead of her on the gravel road. It drops out of sight every now and then, over the crest of a hill or around a bend, but the distance between them is shrinking fast. The Volvo is no match for her zippy electric car.

When a sharp corner nears, she sees the Volvo's brake lights come on a little too soon. Now is her chance to catch it. She presses the accelerator harder, taking the curve as widely as possible while keeping her speed up.

Suddenly her wheel claps, and her car lurches to the left. She tries to turn it back, but nothing happens.

Before she knows it, the car is flying off the road.

For a brief moment she is weightless.

Then comes the bang. The airbag deploys with an ear-splitting crack, up and down lose all meaning, and Asker is flung around the cabin like a ragdoll while her car somersaults through forest.

Spin after spin, until it crashes into a tree trunk, and all goes quiet and still.

HILL

The forest is flying past the windows so fast that it all melts together into a grayish-green wall. The car isn't his, but a fast loan that Mrs. Schiller helped him to procure. It doesn't behave remotely how Hill expects it to, yet even so, he drives faster than he really dares. Every now and then he curses—at the car and everything else that is preventing him from getting there fast enough.

The anxiety is gnawing away at him.

A car crash: that was basically all that Leo said when she called him to ask for help. But he could tell from her voice that she was hurt. And Leo isn't one to complain about pain.

The journey takes him just under half an hour, the last stretch driven in total disregard for the law, his cell in his hand, its GPS guiding him to the dropped pin that marks his destination.

The first thing he sees is a path of leveled greenery leading straight into the forest. At the end of it, a car lying upside-down, more or less totaled.

His heart sinks like a stone in his gut.

Leo is sitting on a boulder. Hill screeches to a halt and jumps out, without a thought to the car that he leaves standing in the middle of the road.

"Are you OK?"

Leo gets to her feet with some effort. Her hair is wild, she has a gash on her forehead, and her left arm is folded over her chest in a makeshift sling that she has fashioned from a scarf. Her face is pale and dogged.

"I've felt better," she admits. "I've dislocated my shoulder, and I think I may have concussion. Plus I'm a little black and blue all over."

Hill helps her into his passenger seat and then limps around to the driver's side, without the help of his crutch.

Her phone call came just after he had finished his treatment, and right now he is much more mobile than she is.

"Thanks for coming so fast," she says. "I'm sorry for bothering you."

"Don't be silly. Astroholm's just around the corner."

She gives a faint smile.

"I didn't know what to do. If I'd called an ambulance, they'd have sent a police car out, and I don't want my colleagues getting involved in this."

"Because you're investigating solo," he adds.

"Exactly," she says and nods. "The car I crashed is one I use privately, so I'll call a wrecker later and have it discreetly towed. The police won't ever need to know."

"Sure, but first we need to get you to the hospital and get you seen to."

He hits the gas, sending gravel spraying against the car's undercarriage.

"So, what the hell happened?" he asks once they have rejoined the highway.

"Well, I was checking out a couple of guys who might have something to do with Tord Korpi's murder, and stumbled across an illegal weed plantation while I was at it. They tricked me. One of them tampered with the screws on my steering wheel before they took off. I went after them, and when I took a hard bend—bang!"

She does a circular motion with her uninjured hand.

"Shit," Hill says. "That could have ended really fucking badly."

"Uh-huh." Leo grimaces, pinches the bridge of her nose.

"Does it hurt a lot?"

"I've had worse."

"I don't doubt that."

Silence, though they are both probably thinking about the same thing.

Or, rather, the same person.

"So you're literally risking your life to save Prepper Per now?" Hill asks dryly.

Leo fidgets.

"It's complicated."

"Is it really, though? Per controlled you your entire childhood, forced you to live in an isolated doomsday camp, and then tried to murder you when you chose to leave. Stop me if I'm wrong."

His voice sounds madder than it should—Hill knows that—but what he's saying is still the truth. Per is definitely not worth this kind of risk.

Leo gazes through the side window. He recognizes her body language, knows that she has shut the door on herself and that he won't get any more answers.

"Prepper fucking Per," he mutters to himself.

The emergency room is half-empty, so they get to wait for a doctor in a consulting room.

In the meantime Leo quietly recounts what has happened over the past few days. Tells him about Korpi's work on Freedom Gym's basement, his bag of cash, and the botched robbery.

Goes on to tell him about how she contacted Prepper Per and got him to hand himself over.

Hill feels his breaths becoming more agitated.

"So you went back to the Farm?" he asks. "In spite of everything that's happened?"

"I had no choice," Asker says. "It was the only way to stop the bloodbath. And now he's in custody, where he can't do any more harm."

For some reason Hill isn't convinced by this latest assertion. Leo doesn't seem to be, either.

She seems to want to change the subject, and he is about to oblige and ask if she managed to find the investigation into the two urban explorers who drowned. But instead the doctor appears.

Hill chooses to excuse himself while Leo is examined. He takes a seat in the waiting room and fiddles with his phone, tries to strong-arm his thoughts back to his discovery at Astroholm.

The staircase that leads to a mysterious door on a secret level. What lies behind that door, what is he onto, and who is the one leading his way?

He wants to solve these mysteries more than anything else.

Or, more than *almost* anything else, since in spite of it all he is sitting in the ER instead of opening the door at the top of that staircase.

It takes a good while before Leo returns.

Her arm is now in a proper sling, and her face looks less pained.

"Light concussion," she says. "And the doctor fixed up my shoulder. It's already feeling better."

"Morphine?" he asks.

She nods. "Good stuff. If you could drop me off at the train station that would be great. I don't want to disturb you anymore."

"Not a chance! You can't have eaten all day, and as it happens neither have I. Besides, I'm not having you bumping around on a train in your condition, or being at home on your own. You're staying with me at Astroholm tonight. I have a guest bedroom, and we can pick up some food on the way. Tomorrow I'll drop you off wherever you want to go."

Leo looks as though she means to protest. But then her expression changes.

"So I won't be disturbing your work?"

"Hell yes," he says with a smirk. "You're a huge disturbance. But there's not so much we can do about that."

She gives him a long look.

"Thanks, Martin," she says softly.

HELLMAN

He is still in the office. Not because he has to be—he's the boss, after all, he can do whatever he wants—but because for once he is reluctant to go home.

He would rather not admit it, not even to himself, but there is a risk that he has been manipulated. That Leo Asker and her psychopath dad have simply backed him into a corner. Forced him to reveal his hand long before he should have.

Although the prosecutor has agreed to keep Per Asker in custody, that also means the clock is ticking. Now they have only three days to get their hands on enough evidence to secure a charge.

And right now it all looks, to quote the same prosecutor, "a little thin on the ground." He lacks any technical evidence or witness testimonies to link Per Asker to the crime.

Per's link to Korpi is beyond all doubt, but since the old fox was sly enough to admit as much willingly at interview—even freely offering up that Korpi stayed at the Farm from time to time—that fact is now less significant than had he tried to dodge or deny the question, as Hellman had hoped. Now it's just circumstantial evidence, without any definitive weight.

That Per Asker has a violent past and knows his way around a firearm is of course another circumstance that speaks against him. Add to that the shallow grave right on the Farm's doorstep, and there is definitely some chain of circumstantial evidence. But for now that chain is too short.

They need something more, or else the prosecutor will decline to file charges and will let Per Asker be released. Let him win. And then malicious tongues at police HQ will surely start to question not only Hellman's competence, but also his motives, having devoted so many resources to a single suspect in a cold case. Perhaps they will go so far as to hint that he was out for some kind of petty revenge against the woman who once reported him for harassment.

A woman who perhaps should have had the job that he snapped up for himself. A woman about whom he still nurses secret fantasies.

It's the kind of failure that he can under no circumstances afford.

Despite that car crash of an interview, Hellman is certain he was right on one front: Per Asker's weak point is his daughter, and the reverse seems to be true of Leo. Per wants Leo's help to evade suspicion of murder. And Leo is prepared to help her father, even though doing so means risking what is left of her career.

Even so, it's clear that neither trusts the other. Per Asker spoke of his daughter as though he both admired and despised her.

This quagmire of contradictory feelings and strange loyalties is where Hellman's opportunity lies.

Because there is a third party in this equation. Someone whose presence neither Per nor Leo has bargained on, since they are too busy keeping tabs on each other. He picks up the phone and dials the number.

HILL

When they reach Astroholm's gates, Hill opens his window to reach for the intercom, but before he can hit the button the gate glides smoothly to one side. A uniformed guard steps out of the guard station, signals at Hill to stop, and shines a flashlight in his face. Only then does it hit Hill that he might need permission to bring a guest with him onto the grounds.

"Good evening, Associate Professor Hill," says the guard, who then points the flashlight at the passenger seat.

Hill curses inwardly, but the guard turns off the flashlight.

"Sorry for the trouble. We've had some issues with intruders on the grounds," he says.

"No problem," Hill says in relief before pulling off again.

"Intruders?" Leo asks.

"It's almost the anniversary of Gunnar's close encounter," he explains. "Apparently a bunch of UFO believers think the date has some special significance. Maybe they're hoping for another landing, or something like that."

"Oh, I see. Sounds like you're going to be busy."

"Yeah, you can probably say that," he laughs.

"So how's it been going? You said you'd found something exciting. Sorry I didn't reply to your message."

"No problem," says Hill. "You've had a lot going on yourself."

As he parks the borrowed car outside Villa Arcturus, Hill tells her about the hidden door in the library, the warning on the drawing board, and the mysterious messages that he has been receiving.

"And you have no idea who's behind it all?" she asks.

"No, not yet. But maybe that'll become clearer once I find out what's on the other side of that door."

Leo appears to be thinking.

"Whoever it is, they're trying to both help *and* warn you. Just keep that in mind before you go racing off on some voyage of discovery, OK?"

Hill is about to point out that he's not the one fresh out of the ER with his arm in a sling, but he checks himself. Even with all that she is going through, Leo is worried about him, which feels strangely nice.

She opens the car door.

"Shall we go inside? I'm starving. You can tell me more while we eat."

Over dinner at the large dining table in the kitchen they share information and ideas. After a while Hill decides to tell her the story of the light he thought he saw over Boulder Isle as a teenager.

"You never told me that before," she says.

He shrugs.

"Maybe because I thought you'd laugh at me."

"And you still believe in the UFO," she says with a smile. "Even now that you're a grown-up."

"Well, I'm not sure if *believe* is the right word," he says, dragging out his answer. "Let's just say I'm trying to keep an open mind."

"And all the stories? The people who claim they've been kidnapped, had their cars beamed up into the sky, or met aliens—like Gunnar the Space Case?"

Hill throws out his hands in a shrug.

"The way I see it, I believe in the experience, if nothing else. That the person has been through something upsetting and maybe inexplicable, whether or not I buy all the details."

"In other words, you believe in people."

"Yeah, I guess you could put it like that."

She shakes her head. Hill knows why. Leo was raised to look out for number one, to treat everything and everyone with suspicion, and never to place her trust in anyone.

Mere days ago, Hill would have thought it unthinkable that Leo would be sitting in his kitchen back in Lund. But this moment is even more surreal: the two of them in a guesthouse inside Space-Case Gunnar Irving's estate, not so many miles from where they first met.

"I almost forgot," she says. "I have something for you."

She fetches her backpack and hands him a case file.

"It's the investigation into the double drowning you asked me about."

He opens the file. It's full of different documents.

"Can you help me figure out what's what?"

"Sure." She shifts her chair closer to his. Points with her good hand. "Here's the original report. Then you have witness interviews, a memo to state that a body was found, and then, finally, the autopsy."

Hill tries not to stare at her as she skims the documents, but her eyes are almost impossible for him to look away from.

"The investigation was pretty basic," she notes. "Two men were reported missing, their car was found at the Boy Scouts' cabin, and a rowboat was gone. The police were granted access to Boulder Isle to search the island and the water, but nothing was found. A few months later the body of a man turned up in the lake. They dragged it again, but the other one's still missing."

"Who was the man they found?"

She flicks through the pages.

"Nick Holmstedt, twenty-seven years old, from Malmö. The other guy, Elis Brorson, was never found."

"Is there anything about a cause of death?"

Leo leafs through more pages. Her arm brushes against his.

"Suspected drowning."

"Suspected?" Hill asks.

"Yeah, but that's not strange in itself. According to the autopsy, the body was badly decomposed after three months in the water. I've seen bodies pulled from water myself, and it's no pretty sight. The cause of death is always difficult to establish."

"Anything else?"

Leo turns the page.

In spite of the macabre subject, when Hill catches the scent of her shampoo he can't help but edge a little closer.

She notices this shift and casts him a furtive glance. Turns over a page, accidentally brushing his hand. Or is it intentional?

A hard knock on the door makes them both give a start.

Hill gets to his feet, feeling strangely self-conscious.

When he opens the door, Maud Irving is standing outside. She is dressed up, smells of perfume, and has a bottle of wine in her hand.

"Hi Martin! I thought you might like a little company."

Before he can say anything, Maud is already in the hallway, heading for the kitchen.

In the doorway she catches sight of Leo and stops short.

"Oh," she says sheepishly. "I didn't know you were busy."

For a few awkward seconds no one says a word.

"Maud Irving," Maud eventually says with a curt nod. "I live over the road. Martin had dinner with us last night."

"Leo Asker," says Leo, waving with her good hand.

"Are you . . . ?" Maud gives Hill a meaningful look.

"No," he replies, a little too quickly, though he doesn't quite know why. This whole situation is putting him on edge. As though he has been caught with his pants down.

"We're old friends," Leo jumps in. "I was in a car crash not far from here, hence the sling. Martin was kind enough to help me."

"Oh, I'm sorry to hear."

Another few seconds' tense silence.

"Well, in that case I won't bother you," Maud says. "Nice to meet you, Leo."

Hill walks her to the door. He still has a lot he wants to ask Maud—about the family as well as AlphaCent.

"I'd love to have a glass another night instead," he says, attempting to smooth things over. "If you have time, that is?"

"Sure, that'd be nice. Bye then."

He isn't completely sure, but he thinks he catches disappointment in Maud's voice.

"Say hi to Elsa for me!" he says, a little too loudly, as she walks away.

He heads back to the kitchen.

"Sorry," Leo says with a smirk. "I didn't mean to cramp your style."

"You didn't."

"Come on, clearly I did. I thought you were with Sofie?"

"I am . . . uh . . . It's complicated."

He wonders if he should tell her that Sofie is married, but he doesn't see how that would make things any better. So he lands on a grimace and a shrug.

"Wow, Martin. You really are making up for your nerdy teenage years," she says with a chuckle.

Hill has no good response. She isn't completely wrong, but he still feels like he wants to explain himself.

Her phone beeps. She checks it quickly, then puts it away.

"Everything OK?"

"Sure!" Leo yawns, suddenly looking tired. "If it's OK, I might turn in for the night."

"Of course. You'll find toothbrushes and a few other toiletries in the bathroom cabinet. And if you'd like to borrow a T-shirt or something to sleep in just let me know."

"Thanks. I really appreciate all of this."

"Anytime," Hill replies. "Are you sure everything's OK?"

"Yeah, definitely. I'm just a little shaken, that's all."

He looks her in the eye. That heterochrome gaze that he has thought about so much over the years. The one that can turn from stony to soft like the flick of a switch.

She really does look shaken.

"It's just . . ." she says, then stops herself.

"What?"

He can see her hesitation; Leo has been fending for herself for years now, never confiding in anyone. He wants to tell her that she isn't alone anymore; that she can let him in.

But Leo doesn't work like that. The best thing he can do is just keep his mouth shut and let her see that for herself.

Pensively she fiddles with her sling.

"Sundin and Danielsson clearly had motive to kill Korpi, and some link to the area around the Farm. And, as I've now learned the hard way, they also have the capacity for violence. All logic points to them being the guys I'm looking for."

"But . . ." Hill raises his eyebrows.

"But they were hardly twenty when Korpi was murdered. Besides the murder itself, that means they would have had to keep their mouths shut about it for sixteen years. Not accidentally let slip to some bigmouth pothead who'd blab to the police."

She shakes her head doubtfully.

"So you don't think it was them? But then why else would they try to kill you today?"

Leo rubs her forehead in frustration.

"That's just it. I showed up in a private car, and I never took out

my badge. Sundin and Danielsson can't have known I'm a detective—
they could just as easily have thought I was a competitor out for their
crop."

"Maybe Linus Palm warned them. Told them you were digging
around in the murder."

"Doubtful. Palm was keen to distance himself from them as much
as possible. Besides, even if he did, would their first reaction be to try
to murder a police officer, rather than just take off?"

Hill realizes she has a point.

"So what are you going to do now?"

She sits up straighter, and her voice changes again.

"I still have to keep my focus on Sundin and Danielsson. I have
nothing else to go on right now, and I need to manage what few
resources I have."

"Now you're sounding like . . ."

Hill bites his tongue before the name *Prepper Per* can pass his lips,
but Leo hears it all the same.

She sits in silence for a few seconds.

"You know what my upbringing was like, and how it all ended,"
she says quietly. "But, however crazy it might sound, it's partly thanks
to Per that I'm the detective I am today. All the things he taught me,
his logic . . ."

She throws her good hand out to one side.

"A lot of that is the kind of stuff that helps me in my work."

Hill wants to protest, tell her that Per's logic almost cost her her
life, but he knows that would be a mistake. Leo doesn't want his advice. Right now she just wants him to listen.

"Normally I'm so clear about what I need to do," she goes on.
"But right now it feels like I don't know where to turn. Like I've lost
my way a little."

Her voice is tired, sad.

They sit in silence for a few seconds.

For a few brief moments they are both teenagers again, both trying to come to terms with a world they don't understand or cannot
control.

He wants to say it. Wants to tell her she isn't alone, that they are
in this together.

But before he can open his mouth, Leo shakes her head vigorously.

"Sorry, Martin, that's the morphine and the tiredness talking. I should really get to bed."

She stands up quickly and does an exaggerated yawn.

The moment for Hill to say something has passed.

He watches her as she slips off to the bathroom. Somehow her father has managed to get back inside her head.

Last time, all those years ago, Hill didn't do enough.

Just sat waiting for her to call from hundreds of miles away; waiting for her to say their distress code, as agreed.

She never did. Still, he should have done more.

Much more.

This time he will. This time he is going to help her get rid of Prepper Per.

He just doesn't know how.

ASKER

She doesn't take out her phone again until she has shut the door to the guest bedroom and climbed into bed.

The message is from her mother.

Please call me as soon as possible Leonore, it's important.

As though she were a subordinate in need of a slap on the wrist. In this case it can't be about anything but Per.

Should she tell Martin?

She appreciates his support—she really does—but chances are that he would agree with Isabel, say that she should back off and let Hellman and the gang at Serious Crime try to put Per away.

Just like when they were teenagers, she wants to keep Martin as her counterweight to Prepper Per and the Farm. An antidote, a lifeline to stop herself from getting dragged down into the mire. And back then she also didn't tell him everything. Didn't tell him that she both loved and hated her father.

Yet Martin seemed to understand.

Would he understand her now? Does she even understand herself?

Is she a detective helping an innocent man get justice?

Or is she just a little girl who can't let go of the father she once loved?

Who, deep down, still believes he can be saved.

She takes those questions with her into her sleep.

She is woken by a sound. A faint scraping outside her window. After that, something that sounds like whispers. She creeps out of bed and over to the window, where she carefully opens the curtains a crack. It is almost pitch-black outside, and the sky is covered in clouds that swallow up most of the moonlight.

Thirty feet away she sees a small light from a flashlight.

It flits back and forth over the ground, then abruptly goes out.

Two shadow figures float across the small lawn between the house and the forest.

They can't be security guards; they would have no reason to sneak around like that.

She should raise the alarm—but that would mean having to wake Martin.

Before she can decide, she hears a hum from up in the sky. After that there comes a powerful beam of light. A drone illuminates the spot where the flashlight just was.

She makes out the backs of two people in dark clothes scurrying toward the forest. One of them is slightly heavy on their feet; they trip and fall headlong right on the edge of the trees, before scrambling to their feet again and rushing after the other one.

The drone tracks them from just above the treetops, but after a while it returns, drifting this way and that, as though it has lost them.

Asker stands there for another minute or so, until the drone disappears from view. Whatever freak show this is, it's hardly her problem.

THE GLASS MAN

Villa Arcturus is completely silent. Above him the Stranger sleeps soundly in his bed, completely unaware of what has risen from the darkness.

The hunger within him grows with each passing day, carving out a void within him that sooner or later must be filled. Perhaps that is why he is here.

To determine whether the Stranger is the right person to feed him. Or if the man sleeping upstairs has another purpose to serve.

Increasingly he has come to believe that the Stranger's presence means something; that it signals some kind of change.

Which is why he must learn more about him.

Carefully he sneaks up the cellar steps, avoiding the third step, the one he knows to be creaky.

He opens the door with the utmost caution. Cracks it just an inch, enough to pick up his scent.

The Stranger's fragrance is clear, as expected. He also smells some pungent food.

But then he notices another, unfamiliar scent.

It takes him a moment before he realizes what this means.

The Stranger isn't alone.

Someone else is in this house, another stranger, one whose presence concerns him. He should sneak in and find out who this visitor is; who the Stranger has invited into his home.

Instead he hovers on the threshold, exploring the scent. Sniffs cautiously; opens his mouth to taste it.

He thinks it belongs to a woman. With time he is quite sure of it.

But there is something else to the scent, something he doesn't like.

Something alarming and sinister that makes him turn and shut the door behind him. Silently withdraw to the darkness.

To go on biding his time.

FRIDAY

HILL

By the time he is awake and out of bed, in his dressing gown and slippers, he finds Leo in the kitchen. She is already dressed, and she looks much perkier than the previous day.

"I put on a jug of coffee, hope that's OK?"

"Of course," says Hill, noting that she isn't wearing her sling. "How's your arm?"

"Better. And you?" She nods at his leg. "I noticed yesterday that you've stopped using the crutch."

"Gunnar's doctor's giving me a special new treatment. It's exceeded my expectations. Cryotherapy, real sci-fi stuff."

"Speaking of sci-fi," Asker says. "I think I saw some of those UFO hunters the guard mentioned last night."

She tells him what she saw from the bedroom window.

"It was pretty funny, actually. One of them hit the deck right at the edge of the lawn. Must have really hit the ground hard. And let's just say they didn't look like spry teenagers. Still, I think they managed to get away."

"Damn. And I didn't hear a peep. Where did this all happen?"

Leo turns and points through the terrace door behind her.

"Over there, around the oak. It looks like they tore up a tuft in the grass, do you see?"

Hill stands beside her and looks out, too.

"By the way, I just spoke to my insurance company," Leo says. "They're arranging a rental car for me, so if you could just drive me to the nearest train station, I can take it from there."

"Of course."

His eyes are still fixed on the lawn. So UFO hunters really are sneaking around the estate. What exactly are they hoping to find? And why are they breaking into the estate but not trying to get to Boulder Isle?

When he glances over at the tuft again, he thinks he spots something twinkling in the grass nearby.

He opens the terrace door and steps outside. The air is piercing, and the grass soaks his slippers.

The tuft does indeed form one end of a huge skid mark. A few feet beyond it, an object lies half-trodden into the grass.

He bends down to pick it up.

A bunch of three keys on a flying-saucer key ring. On the saucer are the letters *GUS*.

He takes the keys with him and shows them to Leo.

"Göinge UFO Society," he says. "I'd been meaning to go speak to them anyway, so I guess now I have a concrete reason to stop by."

"It's good to see you so energized," Leo says with a smile. Then she looks at her watch. "Hey, there's a train in half an hour, and it'd be really good if I could catch it. Sorry to hurry you—it's just I have a few things I need to take care of."

"Like finding the guys who tampered with your car?"

"Exactly," she says, with a grim resolve. The previous day's reservations appear to be a thing of the past.

"Surely you aren't planning to go back there alone?" he asks.

She pulls a cryptic face that doesn't mean no.

Hill stifles a sigh.

"OK, just give me a second to get dressed and I'll drop you off at the station."

He goes back to the bedroom. Leo's plans concern him, but he knows there's no point trying to talk her out of them.

Just as he is finishing getting ready, his phone buzzes. A message in the Astroholm app.

Due to an overnight incursion onto the estate, the manor house, great library, and medical suite will be closed until further notice. An expanded security detail remains in place at the main gate.

Hill curses. He had counted on being able to explore the room at the top of the secret staircase that morning. Could that be why they have closed it? Are they onto him?

Still, given that the intruder explanation sounds at least plausible, he isn't too concerned.

Since he won't be getting into the library anytime soon, he might as well explore another aspect of the mystery. He grabs the keys he found on the lawn and goes back to the kitchen.

"All right, shall we go?"

At the main gate, two uniformed guards are standing in conversation with a third man in civilian clothes. As they draw closer, Hill sees that it's Samuel.

One of the guards waves down their car and signals at Hill to wind down his window.

He does as he is instructed.

"Is there a problem?" he asks.

"Increased security, that's all," the guard replies.

Samuel walks over to them.

"Good morning, Martin," he says briskly. He stoops slightly and looks at Leo in the passenger seat.

"I'm Samuel. Head of security here at Astroholm. And you are?"

Leo looks irritated, as though the question is interrupting her thoughts.

"What do you mean?" she asks.

Samuel's face stiffens.

"This is my friend, Leo," Hill says quickly. "She was in a car crash yesterday, so I let her stay over at my house."

"Ah." The security chief curls one side of his mouth into a smile. "Which must make you Detective Inspector Asker. I've heard about you."

Samuel stares intently at Leo, who in turn glares back at him.

Neither of them says anything, and once the silence has lasted a second too long Hill realizes that something is afoot. Some kind of mutual sizing up, or a test of strength that he doesn't quite understand.

"Can we get going?" he asks. "We're on our way to the train station, so we're in a bit of a hurry."

The staring match goes on for another second or two.

"Of course," says Samuel. He steps back and nods at one of the guards. The gate clangs and slowly starts to open.

"Till next time," Samuel says.

Hill can't quite figure out if the man is speaking to him or Leo. He shuts his window and drives through the gate. In his rearview mirror he sees the security chief still watching their car.

Neither he nor Leo says much on the drive to the station. She mostly gazes through the window.

Her thoughts are already somewhere else; that much is clear. Prepper Per is back in her head, pouring venom into her ears, drawing her back into the Shadowlands. It can only end badly.

He parks the car at the station.

"There's one thing I've been thinking," he says, before she can grab the door handle. "What you said yesterday, about you not being completely convinced you're on the right track with those weed farmers and the robbery."

"Yes?" Her gaze is present once again.

"Well . . ." Hill fidgets uncomfortably. "I wonder if it might be because you're tackling this problem like Prepper Per would have done. With logic and resource . . ." He searches for the right word.

"Resource management," she says, helping him out.

"Exactly." Hill takes a deep breath. He knows that what he's about to say probably won't go down well.

"Well . . . Maybe you should just put logic to one side and trust your gut," he says. "Use your intuition. Less Prepper Per and more Leo, so to say."

His wording is far from perfect, he knows that, but he had to get it out.

Leo looks at him. For a few seconds he thinks she is going to tell him where to shove it.

But then her gaze softens.

"Thanks, Martin," she says while opening the door. "Thanks for everything. I'd better go now, my train's coming. We'll be in touch."

She steps out of the car.

"Take care of yourself," he says, but she has already slammed the door shut and luckily doesn't hear.

Hill swears to himself. His Caribbean grandmother usually claims he has the gift of the gab; that he can smooth-talk his way into—or out of—almost anything.

But sometimes that gift deserts him when he needs it most.

Hill drives back to the small town. Passes the square with its library and handful of stores before arriving at the UFO Café. He parks on the cracked asphalt outside the entrance, steps out of the car, and stands there.

It is impossible not to be intrigued by the red fiberglass UFO on the roof—so like the flying saucer that appears on the covers of Bernhard's sci-fi novels. It is around six feet in diameter and, rather than a saucer, looks more like two enormous soup plates placed one on top of the other. The construction is supported by three rickety steel legs and topped off with a chain of Christmas lights that blink sporadically.

WELCOME VISITORS reads a sign on the door, so Hill draws the conclusion that they are actually open this time. Above the sign is a green alien with a giant head and big eyes, one long, luminous E.T. finger extended in a space greeting.

He opens the door to find the premises decorated in the same style. A curious mix of flea-market finds, plastic toys, and American kitsch. On the walls hang posters of sci-fi films that Hill has never heard of.

The room is almost empty of people, save for a couple in their fifties who are playing chess at one of the tables. They look up in surprise when he steps in.

The couple resemble each other in both appearance and style, in the way that people who have been married a long time sometimes do. Pear-shaped bodies, identical haircuts, matching sweatsuits.

"Hello," says Hill. "Are you the owners?"

When the couple nod in unison, Hill holds the bunch of keys up in the air.

"I think these are yours."

The couple stare at him, then give each other a meaningful look, as though wordlessly trying to agree on a strategy.

Hill places the keys on the table.

"Any coffee?" he asks, pulling out a chair.

The couple exchange another look. The man gets to his feet and fetches him a mug.

"I'm Martin Hill," he introduces himself. "AlphaCent have hired me to write a book about the company. I'm staying on the estate, in Villa Arcturus. It was my house you were sneaking around last night."

He holds up a hand to preventively silence their protests.

"I'm not looking to get you in any trouble," he goes on. "But what I would like to know is what you were looking for."

Hill takes a sip of coffee while the couple once again exchange looks.

"I saw a beam of light over the lake as a teenager," he says, in an attempt to get them to relax. "I've been interested in Boulder Isle and the UFO story ever since."

"The story!" the woman snorts. "It's no story. Miresjön is an important site for Visitors."

"Visitors?" Hill asks, although he has some idea what she is getting at.

"Extraterrestrials." The man steps in. "Visitors from another galaxy. The lake and Boulder Isle serve as a kind of terminal. The crater prevents their signals from being detected."

"OK, I see," Hill says with a nod.

"No, I don't think you do," the man says. "You think we're nutjobs. But it was actually Bernhard Irving who invited the Visitors here to begin with. He built a secret facility for them beneath his estate. We believe it to be a workshop for spaceship repairs. All that stuff about the mine was just a cover. People have died trying to prove—"

The woman places a hand on her partner's arm, and he abruptly silences himself.

"Died?" Hill asks. "Do you mean the drownings three years ago? Nick and Elis?"

The couple replay their two-person game of charades, and after some face-pulling they appear to reach a decision.

"Oh, there have been many more deaths than that," the woman says. "At least four that we've managed to trace. Even more if you count the 1965 mine collapse. The Irving family are trailed by death."

This drastic statement makes Hill give a start.

"OK, but if we begin with the drownings," he says. "Someone recommended that I check your website, but the links to your articles were dead."

"We shut them down," the woman says with a glance over her shoulder. "We think someone's watching us, that we got too close to the truth."

Hill is about to point out that in that case the best thing to do would be to take down the headlines entirely, or perhaps even the entire website, but the couple appear to have their own way of reasoning.

"So what do you know about the drownings?" he asks instead.

The couple look at each other. Then at Hill.

"What did you say your name was again?" the woman asks.

"Martin Hill."

"The author?"

"That's the one," Hill says. "I wrote a book called *Forgotten Places and Their Stories*. It contained a chapter on Miresjön Lake and Boulder Isle."

"Yeah, we know . . ."

She stands up and walks over to a large bookcase brimming with UFO literature.

When she returns to the table she places a copy of *Forgotten Places* in front of Hill.

"Oh, you have it," says Hill.

The couple take another look at each other, this time as though trying to make some kind of choice.

The woman opens the book and points at the title page.

The book is signed, but not by him.

To Tom and Krystal at the Göinge UFO Society. Many thanks for all your help. The truth is out there! Greetings from Nick and Elis

Hill gulps loudly.

"Go on," he says.

The man, whose name is apparently Tom, stands up and refills their coffee cups. On the way back he locks the front door and flips the open sign. Peers out through the window, as though concerned that someone is watching them.

"Your phone," he says. "Have you downloaded the Astroholm app?"

"Yes."

Tom tut-tuts in disappointment.

"Then they're tracking him," he says, turning to his partner. "Get the box."

Krystal with a K bustles off and soon returns with a metal box.

"Turn off your phone and put it in here," she orders.

At first Hill thinks she is joking, but nothing about the couple's gravely serious faces suggests anything of the sort. He does as he is told, upon which Krystal shuts the lid and carries the box away.

"It was in March three years ago," Tom begins once his partner has returned. "We'd exchanged emails and been chatting with Nick for some months. He became super-interested in Boulder Isle and the observatory after reading about them in your book. They weren't the first urban explorers to try to make contact, so initially we were a little hesitant."

He fiddles with his coffee cup.

"But Nick kept at it. He'd done plenty of research into the Irving family and the mine, and he'd read basically everything we'd ever posted on our site about various observations around the lake. So he convinced us to help him . . ."

"In short, he talked rings around Tom," Krystal interrupts.

Her husband shrugs sheepishly.

"Krystal and I had made it out to Boulder Isle one summer long ago, so we had some tips. I sent him a map I'd drawn and told them they could use the little plastic rowboat the Scouts club use for life-saving practice. But, as you know, they never came back."

"Elis has been taken," Krystal adds gravely. "Kidnapped by the Visitors—that's why they haven't found him."

"Have you spoken to the police?" Hill asks.

Krystal shakes her head.

"No. We were afraid of attracting the Visitors' attention. Or the Irving family's. And the police would only have laughed us out of the station anyway."

Hill is once again close to putting it out there that their website and café with a UFO on the roof don't exactly fly under the radar, but he bites his tongue.

"And you don't think it could have just been an accident?" he asks instead.

The couple shake their heads, almost in unison.

"We think . . . no, we *know* that Nick and Elis found something on the island," says Tom. "Something they shouldn't have seen. And now they're dead."

"How can you be so sure?" Hill asks.

Krystal leans in and lowers her voice.

"Because when Nick's body was found, the police discovered that the Visitors had done something to him. Something terrible, but typical of them."

"What's that?"

Krystal points at her face with her index and middle fingers.

"They'd taken his eyes. Gouged them right out of his skull."

ASKER

Lunch has passed by the time Asker is back at police HQ. The November wind is flinging an icy drizzle against the façade, but within the dim internal atrium next to level minus one neither the weather nor the surrounding world makes its presence known.

She thinks about what Martin said—that she shouldn't go back to Sundin and Danielsson alone. But she has to. Of course, she could tell some colleagues about the weed farm. Let them make their sweep in exchange for a chance to interview the suspects. But that process will take days, maybe even a week, and she doesn't have the luxury of time.

Besides, the more people involved, the greater the risk of something going wrong.

What she needs is a chance to speak to the men on their own, without lawyers or prying eyes.

She is pretty sure they will still be on the farm. A plantation of that size can't be moved in a hurry, and if it's as she suspects—that they don't know she's a detective, but instead assumed she was there to spy on a rival's behalf—then they wouldn't choose to fly like the wind. Instead they would up security around the crop until they are ready to move.

She isn't in top condition—her shoulder kills, and she can't take any more painkillers if she wants to stay alert. So she needs to get herself a real upper hand, which calls for a battery of tools. But all she has is an extendable baton.

She needs more gear—ideally a real firearm—all at short notice and also on the sly.

The only person with those kinds of contacts at police HQ is the little toad Virgilsson. While the likelihood of him running straight off to gossip to Hellman is high, it's a risk she has to take.

When Virgilsson's office door turns out to be closed, she walks on to the kitchen, where she finds Rosen sitting on her own eating lunch from a Tupperware box.

"Do you know where Virgilsson is?"

"N-no," Rosen says with an anxious shake of the head. "Or, wait, yes I do. It's Friday today. Virgilsson has choir practice on Fridays."

"Choir practice?"

"The police choir. They're in the auditorium."

Asker takes the elevator to the right floor and makes her way to the auditorium. Carefully opens the door a crack.

On the stage stand twenty people at most, almost all of them women. She slips inside and takes a seat in the back row.

Virgilsson is standing with his back to her. Today's sweater vest is black-and-white, and it takes her a few seconds to see that its pattern is made up of piano keys and treble clefs.

"Attention!" Virgilsson says. "Let's take it again, from the top!"

He blows a note from something that sounds like a small harmonica.

"And a one, two, three, four . . ."

The choir strikes up in a straggly interpretation of "White Christmas" that would have Bing Crosby turning in his grave.

Virgilsson, however, pretends not to hear. He conducts with enthusiasm and little cries of joy, and when the song is finally over his face is flushed, his forehead sweaty with exertion. There is a happy look on his face that Asker has never seen before.

"A big round of applause to you all. Very well done," he concludes. "See you next week!"

Asker stays where she is until the choir has dispersed. Virgilsson is returning the stage to its former setup, and he doesn't see her until she is beside it.

"Are you here to join the choir?" he asks breezily.

"I need your help."

Virgilsson looks surprised.

"Oh, I see. May I ask why the sudden change of heart? Earlier this week you seemed somewhat averse to collaboration."

Asker doesn't reply.

"Well then, how might I assist the chief?"

He smiles one of his usual toady smiles.

"I need a firearm, today. Mine's still in Forensics."

"Hm . . ." He looks pensive. "I don't have any firearm to lend you. I saw no point in practicing down on the range myself, so I requested to be excused. But I do have an acquaintance down in the armory. Let me see what I can do."

"Thanks. I'll also need some tear gas, and those cable ties that we use for mass arrests."

"Well I say, this does sound dramatic," he says with a smirk. "Should I ask what they're for, or is it safest not to?"

Asker doesn't reply, which makes Virgilsson smile even wider.

"Say no more. I know just the person you can speak to while I pop down to the armory."

HILL

They are onto their third cup of coffee, and Tom has just set out a plate of prewrapped chocolate oat balls that they are demolishing between them.

"It goes without saying that we don't dare set foot on Boulder Isle anymore," says Krystal. "But we haven't given up our search for the underground terminals. There should be an entrance behind Villa Arcturus. That's why we were searching there last night. But the guards chased us away."

"And why do you tend to search for it around the anniversary of Gunnar's UFO encounter?" Hill asks, wiping stray flakes of desiccated coconut from his mouth.

They both look at him as though he's stupid.

"Because that's when it all began. Gunnar revealed the Visitors' existence to humanity, which he shouldn't have. He has paid dearly for that mistake."

"Ah."

Hill is battling hard to stay neutral, but without success. This interview is confusing, to say the least.

"Don't believe us?" Tom says irritably. "Then how do you explain all the deaths around Gunnar?"

"Yes, you mentioned there were more deaths," says Hill. "The only one I know of besides the mine collapse in 1965 is Viggo Irving's car crash in 2001, the same night the meteorite passed."

"Meteorite," Krystal snorts. "That's what they want us to believe. It was a message from the Visitors to Gunnar. A warning. They made the car crash into Miresjön. Viggo Irving almost died, and Gunnar's future son-in-law Pontus Ursvik was beyond saving. There were irregularities with his body, too—just like with Nick's!"

"What kind of irregularities?"

Tom looks around, as though to check yet again that no one is listening.

"I have a cousin who's a fireman," he says quietly. "He told me that Viggo was found in the water outside the car. He was clinically dead, but at the hospital they managed to bring him back to life. But the strange thing was that Pontus's body was in the back seat and not in the front, where you would expect him to be. As though a mysterious power had moved them."

The couple nod in unison, resembling two graying, oversized owls.

"Or they both tried to get out of the car when it hit the water?" Hill suggests. "Viggo succeeded, but Pontus got stuck in the car and drowned?"

Tom shakes his head.

"My cousin said that Pontus's body was beaten to a pulp. Almost unrecognizable. And it looked like someone had tried to gouge out his eyes, just like the Visitors did with Nick's."

"Maybe he wasn't wearing a seatbelt?" Hill objects. "Got thrown around when the car crashed? That could explain his injuries."

He doesn't know why he is debating this; it would be far simpler to just hum along to their claims. But the signed book has put him on edge. Either way, the couple pretend not to hear him.

"Not to mention the other death," Krystal goes on. "Björn Knudsen, the old head gardener at Astroholm Manor, who was beaten to death in the nineties. Had his skull smashed in."

Hill raises his eyebrows. Didn't Groundskeeper Ville say that his surname was Knudsen, and mention something about taking over after his father?

"Knudsen's murder is still unsolved, and there's no known motive or lead on the murderer," says Tom. "But Knudsen would sometimes work out on Boulder Isle, felling trees and the like. And Pontus died in Miresjön itself, so it all fits together. We believe that both Knudsen and Pontus, just like Nick and Elis, stumbled across some secret. They saw something they shouldn't have seen and were silenced by the Visitors. Study it more closely and you'll see for yourself!"

"OK . . ."

Hill writes down the head gardener's name. Adds a note about mysterious injuries on Pontus Ursvik's body.

He sneaks a glance at the couple. There is no doubt that Tom and Krystal are a pair of oddballs. Their theories have more holes in them than he can count, and it would be all too easy to just laugh it all off.

Still, the story troubles him. Perhaps the message in the book above all. As though he bears some kind of responsibility for what happened to Nick and Elis—whatever it was that did happen.

The words from the warning letter suddenly ring in his ears.

He who goes there in search of Irving secrets must tread very carefully.

ASKER

A few minutes after she and Virgilsson part ways, Asker is back down in the Department for Lost Souls, knocking on Zafer's door.

He opens her her third attempt. His hair is on end, and his glasses with in-built hearing aids are perched on the end of his nose.

"Yes?" he asks irritably, as though she were a stubborn Girl Scout peddling cookies, as opposed to his head of department.

She decides to skip the small talk.

"Virgilsson said you could hook me up with some tear gas."

"What?" He cups his hand around his ear.

"Tear gas. And some other gear. Cable ties, that kind of stuff."

Zafer goes on glaring at her irritably. Only now does it hit her that Virgilsson could have made it all up. Zafer is an indoor cat, after all. He hasn't taken up any front-line duties in years, so why would he have that kind of gear on hand?

But then his expression softens up.

"Come in," he says, a wily look on his face. "And shut the door."

He leads her between some shelves and over to a metal cabinet with a combination lock.

When he opens the doors, she can't help but gasp. The closet is so full of ancillary weapons that even Prepper Per would be impressed: batons of different models and lengths, nunchucks, blackjacks, cable ties, knuckle-dusters, knives, and a whole drawer full of small, more or less legal self-defense, pepper, and tear-gas sprays. On the top shelf there is even a charging station with different Taser models.

"I'm working on a report," Zafer explains. "Assessing effectiveness, dangers, countermeasures, etcetera, etcetera . . ."

He waves at the cabinet.

"Take whatever you need."

She starts grabbing what she thinks might be of use: some small cans of self-defense spray, a bundle of thick cable ties, and one of the tasers.

Meanwhile she can't help but smirk. Here, in the very bowels of the police organization, stands a cabinet full of very much illegal weapons and arms. It makes her wonder what he might have in the other cabinets in the room.

"You wouldn't have any guns, would you?" she asks, in the hope of being able to avoid owing Virgilsson a favor.

Zafer gestures apologetically.

"Not anymore. There was an unfortunate incident . . ." He gives a rueful look and points up at the ceiling, as though that explains the rest of the story.

"But do tell me what you think about the products. A field test will look good in my report for the technical director."

"I'll have a write-up with you next week," she says.

Zafer lights up. "That would be perfect. Thank you!"

Asker returns to her office to find that Isabel has sent her yet another message. She decides to take the bull by the horns, but before she can call her mother, Virgilsson knocks on the door.

In his hands he holds a cardboard box.

"One firearm, as requested," he says. "You can keep it until you get your old one back. I took the liberty of making some arrangements for ammunition, too. It's all in the box."

"Thanks." Asker braces herself for the inevitable. "What do you want in return?"

Virgilsson holds up one hand modestly.

"Nothing at all. I suppose we can call it a peace offering. A fresh start."

Asker gives him a long look, but as usual the little man is hard to read.

"Though, since you ask . . ." he says, ". . . we do have a gap in the police choir—"

"I can't sing." Asker cuts him off, only to realize her mistake almost immediately.

"As I'm sure you noticed at rehearsal, you're hardly alone there. We need all the help we can get for the Christmas concert next month."

Virgilsson tilts his head to one side and lets the question, which is really no question at all, hang in the air.

Asker takes a slow breath through her nose. Caroling in front of the entire police HQ is probably as close to the fires of her own personal purgatory as she can get. But the little smirker has backed her into a corner.

"OK," she sighs. "I guess we have a deal."

HILL

He goes back to his car, turns on his phone, and decides to start googling the information the UFO couple gave him.

He stops himself before hitting the search button.

Locking his phone away in a lead box, as Krystal and Tom had instructed him to do, felt like an overreaction, if not absurd. But now that he thinks about it, it is true that he has installed an unknown app on his phone without the slightest clue how deep its digital tentacles might go, or what information it might be sharing. On top of all that, he often makes use of Astroholm's Wi-Fi network.

If he is to start delving into conspiracy theories about his employer, might it not be a good idea to do that in a more anonymous way, just to be on the safe side?

He drives back into the small town center, parks by the square, and steps into the small library branch.

The librarian, a short-haired woman in her sixties with big, red glasses, proves very helpful. He is given access to a computer workspace, where he searches the name "Björn Knudsen."

The head gardener's digital footprint consists of no more than a gravestone by a nearby church. The year of his death is 1992.

Hill stands up and walks back over to the librarian.

"Do you keep any old newspapers on microfilm?" he asks.

She lights up.

"Normally only in the main library branch, but they've had some water damage there, so we're holding some of their archives down in the basement for now. You may be in luck, but it depends what you're looking for."

"Any north Skåne newspaper from the nineties."

"Let's go down and take a look."

She shows him down a staircase and into a big, dark basement full of chipped bookshelves brimming with old books, files, and box files.

The librarian walks over to a shelf loaded with cardboard boxes and searches for a while.

"No, nothing specifically from northern Skåne," she eventually says. "But I do have a Malmö newspaper, *Arbetet*, for that time period; might that work?"

"Let's take a look," says Hill.

The librarian brings him a box labeled *Arbetet 1990–2006* and shows him to a corner where a microfilm reader is waiting beneath a cover.

After a bit of fiddling, she manages to get the machine started, then helps Hill to feed the right film into it. She hovers over his shoulder.

"Thanks, I think I can take it from here," Hill says.

"Certainly, of course." The woman heads back upstairs while Hill starts skimming through the issues published in the days after the head gardener's death.

It doesn't take long before he finds an article with the headline MAN FOUND DEAD IN WOODLAND.

On Tuesday evening, a sixty-four-year-old man was found dead in an area of woodland south-west of Miresjön Lake.

The deceased man had held the position of head gardener at Astroholm Manor. He was said to have been in the area felling trees for another landowner, and his relatives raised the alarm when he didn't return home.

The police are treating the death as suspected murder and are urging the public to contact them if they have any information to share.

The brief article is accompanied by a photo of a few trees and a police cordon, together with a map that shows the spot where the body was found. It is only a mile or two from Astroholm, Hill notes.

Yet another death with a link to the Irving family.

Hill decides to seek out articles from January 8, 2001: the Monday after the meteorite landing and Viggo Irving's car crash.

Almost the entire front page is dedicated to the light phenomenon, but, having already read all the information on the meteorite, Hill quickly skims those pages.

Toward the middle of the newspaper he finds the article that he is looking for: ONE DEAD IN TRAFFIC ACCIDENT BY MIRESJÖN LAKE.

Beneath it is an image of a car, a black BMW, being winched from the water. The article relates the events summarily:

One person was killed and another seriously injured in a traffic accident on Saturday night. The cause of the accident remains unknown.

Not much to work with. He looks at the image again. The lakeshore is steep, and in the foreground emergency services are working hard to recover the car.

He is just about to reach for the switch when he notices something else in the background.

At the very edge of the image, a figure is looking on. A tall, dark silhouette that doesn't appear to be remotely involved in the recovery operation.

Hill zooms in as far as he can with the microfilm reader. The silhouette belongs to a man who appears to be shading his eyes with one hand to see better.

The image is grainy, the man scarcely more than a handful of pixels, but Hill recognizes him almost immediately. The posture, the coat, the hat.

It's Gunnar Irving himself.

Hill leaves the library a little while later, still preoccupied with his discovery. He returns to the parking lot and unlocks the car with his key fob, only to find someone standing beside it: an older woman of around seventy dressed all in black, with a hat on her head and a bouquet of flowers in her hands. He recognizes her right off as the woman he saw on the bicycle at Astroholm.

"You're the Bear Guardian," she says when he reaches her.

"Uh, yes."

"Good, I need a lift home to Astroholm."

Before Hill can react, the woman has opened the door and sat down in the passenger seat. He has no choice but to hop in.

The woman simply stares straight ahead while clutching the bouquet.

"You're Karin Irving, aren't you?" he asks. "Gunnar's first wife, and Viggo and Maud's mother?"

She curls her lip in confirmation, but still says nothing.

"I saw you the other evening from the library. You had a cat with you on your bicycle."

"Perseus," the woman confirms, without making the slightest effort to go on.

Hill decides to expand on the cat theme.

"My grandmother had cats," he says tentatively. "Two Siamese. I was always a little afraid of them. What breed is Perseus?"

More silence.

"A Norwegian forest cat," she says eventually. "Calmer than Siamese."

"And how does he get on with Orion? That's his name, isn't it, Elsa's dog?"

"Perseus doesn't care for dogs."

"I'm sure he doesn't."

Hill tries to keep the faltering conversation alive. Karin Irving has lived at Astroholm her entire life; she must know at least some of the estate's secrets.

"I was at dinner with Maud and Elsa the other night."

"Yes, I heard."

Karin turns toward him and studies him closely.

"Maud said you were kind. It's been a long time since she's had a good word to say about anyone." She goes on studying him. "Are you married?"

"No," he laughs. "Why, are you flirting with me?"

She breaks into something that could be considered a smile. The ice appears to be broken, but Hill still tries to keep his curiosity in check.

"Has Maud lived with you long?" he asks gingerly.

"Six months. She needed rest, and so it suited her well to come home to Villa Canopus. Our sanctuary after the Fall."

She goes quiet, staring ahead yet again. Once the silence has lasted a while, Hill's thoughts drift back to the newspaper photo from the accident. Why was Gunnar standing there in the forest, watching his son's wreck of a car being salvaged? Surely Viggo must have been at the hospital long before then?

By now they have arrived at the main gate to Astroholm, and just as before, it opens before Hill needs to do anything.

The guard is still standing at his station, but he simply waves them through. When they are approaching the turnoff to Villa Canopus, Hill slows down, but Karin Irving raises her hand and points straight ahead.

"Continue down to the manor house," she says.

Hill does as she says.

"You must know Astroholm like the back of your hand," he says, steering the conversation in his desired direction.

Karin nods.

"I was born and raised here. When I was a girl, we lived in a house over there, where the annex now stands. My father died in the mine collapse, as you may know, but Bernhard allowed Mother and me to go on living here. And then I married Gunnar."

They cross the bridge, then pass *The Diviner of Stars*.

"And here we have The Glass Man himself," he says, pointing at the sculpture.

"Yes," Karin mumbles. "Gunnar is eternal. Immortal."

"But not unbreakable," says Hill.

He gets an unexpected laugh in response.

"No, you're right there."

Hill drives toward the main entrance, but Karin Irving gestures at him to go on.

"Keep going," she directs him.

"Where?"

"We're going to pay Bernhard a visit."

THE GLASS MAN

By day he sleeps. A light sleep, scarce deserving of the name. Not like the one he is used to.

He rarely dreams.

But sometimes the Father's tale of Castor and Pollux comes into his mind. The immortal Pollux who split his time between Olympus and Hades—heaven and hell—so that his brother might return to life.

The story could be his own, as the Father also likes to remark.

"You and I will both be immortal, Prince Pollux," he often says. "Together we'll take over the world!"

Normally he agrees. Contents himself with that explanation.

But sometimes, in his darker moments when hovering between sleep and waking, he can nevertheless have his doubts.

Doubt that there is any Olympus, any heaven.

That all of his sacrifices and torments are not in vain.

The thought makes him anxious.

Angry.

So he pushes it aside.

Instead turns his thoughts to more pleasant pursuits.

To the soccer player Bure; the old head gardener Knudsen; the two young men on Boulder Isle whose names he doesn't know.

But he does remember what he did to them.

Their journeys down into the darkness.

Most of all he thinks of the Stranger.

Of Martin Hill.

HILL

They park the car in a small lot next to a tall, wrought-iron fence and gate just beyond the west wing of the manor.

Hill tries not to let his eagerness show. Could Karin be about to show him the underground burial chamber?

He steps out of the car and opens the passenger door for the elderly lady.

"Can you walk?" she asks, pointing at his leg. "You were using a crutch a few days ago."

"A little, at least," Hill says. "Dr. Schiller's treatment has made it much better."

Karin snorts. "Schiller? That ass just does what he's told. It's Gunnar who's choosing your treatment. Gunnar makes all the decisions at Astroholm. He sees and hears everything!"

She gestures at the dark manor house that looms over them.

"Well, *almost* everything. Come on!"

She walks over to the wrought-iron gate, takes a key from her handbag, and unlocks it.

"I don't think I'm allowed to visit this part of the estate," Hill says dutifully. "It said in the app that this area was off-limits."

"Nonsense!" Karin Irving gestures at him to step through the gate.

Hill happily follows her orders.

The elderly woman takes him by the arm and guides him down a small path that appears to lead to the water. At a fork she takes a left, away from the manor house. They continue another few hundred yards, until they reach a small headland.

At the bottom of a steep bank, just feet away, Miresjön Lake begins. The water glitters, black and shiny, reminding him of the material that *The Glass Man* is made of. Out in the lake, just over half a mile away, Boulder Isle lies dark and still.

Hill has never been this close to Boulder Isle before, and in other circumstances his pulse would surely be racing by now. But his excitement is dimmed by a tall, rhyolite memorial stone that stands before him at the edge of the lake.

When they step closer, he sees the inscription: BERNHARD IRVING 1901–1996.

Karin Irving removes the paper wrapping from the bouquet of flowers, then places it at the foot of the stone. She stands there for a moment with her head lowered, her hands clasped before her.

"Bernhard was a great man," she says. "A visionary." She points at Latin engraving on the stone. "*Per aspera, ad astra.* That was his motto."

"Through adversity to the stars," Hill says.

He has come across this saying a few times before, but here it feels particularly apt, with Boulder Isle within sight. If he squints, he can even make out the observatory amid the treetops on the middle of the island.

But right now that isn't where his primary focus lies.

"Is this Bernhard's grave?" he asks.

He hopes that her answer will be no. That she will give him a response that at least implies the existence of a burial chamber.

Instead Karin Irving nods.

"Gunnar had him cremated and buried here," she says. "He got some sort of special authorization, don't ask me how. Gunnar always gets what he wants."

Hill is disappointed. Of course, it could be the case that the chamber remains a secret even from close family. But that is probably wishful thinking on his part.

"Gunnar seems to have idolized his father," he says tentatively. "He speaks so well of him in all the interviews."

Karin Irving slowly shakes her head, without tearing her gaze from the memorial stone.

"Gunnar hated his father," she says. "The shame he brought on us all." Her eyes fill with tears. "But I don't believe Bernhard knew what he was doing."

"What do you mean?"

No reply.

"What was it that Bernhard did?" he tries again, with a softer tone of voice this time.

They are interrupted by brisk footsteps on the gravel behind them. Hill turns to see Samuel approaching on the path. Behind him Mrs. Schiller.

"Didn't you read the rules of conduct?" Samuel asks angrily. "This part of the estate is off-limits to visitors."

"I did," Hill protests, "but Karin asked me to come with her to Bernhard's grave."

"Karin isn't well," Samuel says, cutting him off. "Mrs. Schiller, would you please see to it that Karin immediately returns home. And Martin, it's time that you got back to Villa Arcturus. This way."

Samuel escorts Hill back to the parking lot.

"We have certain rules here at Astroholm," he says once they are out of carshot of both women. "It's important that the rules be respected. For everyone's safety. Not least your own."

His tone is polite, but Hill thinks he can make out a threatening undertone. At the car Samuel stops, turns to Hill and looks searchingly in his eyes.

"One more thing. You brought a guest onto the estate without informing me," he says.

"Leo? Yes, but that was an emergency. And I didn't actually know—"

"How much do you tell her about your work?"

The question—or perhaps the accusatory tone of it—makes Hill flustered.

"Nothing," he says defensively.

"Nothing?" Samuel looks at him with a gaze that seems to penetrate his skull.

Hill gulps.

"Nothing," he says. Samuel's words remind him of Prepper Per's, and for a split second he is that same terror-stricken teenager again.

"Good," says Samuel, in a friendlier tone of voice. "I remind you that you signed a confidentiality agreement. Next time you want to bring a guest onto the estate I'd ask that you contact me first."

He gives Hill a friendly pat on the shoulder.

"It's starting to get dark. High time we got you home—what do you say, Martin?"

Hill nods. Samuel waits while he jumps into the car, then gives an outwardly friendly wave as he pulls off.

ASKER

She has found a good vantage point on the edge of the forest around the drug farm. The temperature is teetering around thirty-two degrees, but the wind sweeping through the trees makes it feel even colder. She is dressed for the task, in a winter jacket, long johns, and boots, her face covered by a ski mask with openings for her eyes and mouth alone.

Smoke is pouring from the chimney over at the farmhouse, and the lights are on in the windows. The Volvo is parked out front, now in the company of a Jeep.

The latter seems to belong to two burly men with Viking beards who remind her of the biker hooligans she saw back at Freedom Gym. Maybe they are actually the same men? But it's too dark, and she's too far away, to tell that through the binoculars.

Asker has been here long enough to map out their routine. Every half hour one of the bearded Vikings emerges from the main house. He does a lap of the buildings with a shotgun in one hand and a flashlight in the other. Trudges over to the greenhouses to check the weed plantation before returning to the warmth of the house.

Sundin and Danielsson are there, too, but neither of them is doing the rounds. Perhaps their green fingers are too sensitive for guard duties?

Asker chews on a protein bar, washes it down with a few swigs of water. She is used to waiting. Prepper Per made sure to give her plenty of practice in that particular field.

The trick to taking someone by surprise is to wait for the right moment. The point when the target lowers their guard. When tiredness and convenience get the better of their vigilance.

She is tired, too. By this point she has zigzagged back and forth across Skåne province more times than she can count. Besides which, she still has a nagging pain in her injured shoulder. On the plus side, that pain is keeping her awake and alert.

She thinks of Martin Hill. It was nice to spend time with him. In that brief moment when their hands touched, it had almost felt like they were teenagers again. And at the same time not.

While standing here she has had time to ponder what he said to her earlier about following her gut. Her first impulse was to laugh it all off; to just be happy that he cared, that he listened to her. After all, police work is almost exclusively about being methodical, using logic, and making the most of the resources at hand.

But with every passing hour she can't help but wonder if there isn't some truth to what Martin said. Ever since Per made his unwelcome comeback in her life, it has felt like she has lost something of herself; like she no longer trusts her instincts, for fear of going astray.

She shakes the thought out of her, steers her brain in another direction.

Something else has been preying on her mind.

Samuel, the security guard who stopped them on their way out of Astroholm, the one who knew who she was. The two of them have never met before, but she has come across his type in other guises. On shooting ranges, in incident rooms, and during operations. She recognizes his body language, his patterns of movement, the way he scrutinized her. How he wore his jacket open, his hand at belt height, so as to quickly be able to access the concealed weapon at his hip. The self-confidence, the conviction that he is the most dangerous person in the room.

Should she warn Martin? Tell him to be careful?

She doesn't think so. Martin is flicking through books, exploring secret passages. The worst thing that could happen to him if he snoops too much is lose the assignment and get kicked off the estate. Unlike her; she's currently risking far more . . .

She waits for another hour before she makes her move. By now the night is almost coal-black.

She sneaks down to the greenhouse containing the weed plantation. The door is locked with a padlock. Beside it stands an open toolshed, so she slips inside and stands in wait in the darkness, among tools and sacks of soil.

After around five minutes she hears one of the bearded Vikings come lumbering out. She pulls out the Taser she borrowed from Zafer and readies herself.

The man rounds the house. He shines his flashlight over the lawn, and she shrinks deeper into the shadows.

The Viking trudges over toward the greenhouse. His shotgun is slung over his right shoulder, which means he's right-handed and will therefore spin to the left if taken by surprise. So his blind spot will be diagonally over his right shoulder blade.

Surreptitiously she sneaks to that side. The wind and the earflaps on his hat mean he doesn't hear her coming.

Just as he reaches for the padlock on the greenhouse, she pulls down the collar of his jacket and presses the Taser's metal points to his meaty neck, at the very spot where the nerve pathways between body and head meet.

The Taser emits a short, electric crack. The man flinches as though in a spasm, letting out a gurgling noise. After that his knees buckle, and he drops to the ground like a sack of potatoes.

Asker puts the Taser away, uses the thick cable ties to gift-wrap the Viking's ankles and wrists securely behind his back, then tops it all off by stuffing a rag in his mouth and taping it over with duct tape. She drags him into the toolshed and leaves him behind a pallet of soil.

She picks up the shotgun, unloads the cartridges with a practiced hand, and takes the weapon apart. Throws the pieces in different directions in the darkness while making her way toward the house.

She has one adversary neutralized, but there are three more in the house, and in just a few minutes they will start to wonder where their buddy has gone. Which means she has no time to lose.

She finds the ladder that she saw through her binoculars and loads it onto her good shoulder.

At the house she leans it against the roof ledge. She climbs it as quickly as her sore shoulder will allow, then sneaks as quietly as possible over to the stone chimney.

From here she can feel the heat through her ski mask. The dudes inside must have the fire roaring, which suits her just fine.

From her jacket pockets she pulls two handfuls of small teargas and pepper spray canisters. Drops all the cartridges down the chimney, hears them rattle as they land in the fire, then quietly starts counting to herself while climbing back down the ladder.

She has less than a minute, but she reaches the ground in good time. Crouching beneath the windows, she rounds the house and takes position in front of the door. Draws her firearm with one hand while unfurling the extendable baton with the other.

She is ready. The indoor firework display ought to start any second.

No sooner has she thought that than she hears a powerful bang from inside the house, followed by a second and then a third and a fourth. It sounds like very loud popcorn.

The sounds intermingle with the howl of voices and heavy footsteps, until the door is flung wide open.

A cloud of stinging smoke pours out, through which three men in loungewear stagger in stocking feet. They are coughing, spluttering, and retching so much that they have no choice but to walk bent double.

The largest of them, the remaining Viking, is rubbing his eyes while flailing a large revolver in the air, clearly with no idea where his target is.

Asker takes two quick steps toward him. Cracks a sharp baton blow to his wrist that sends the revolver flying across the gravel. In the same movement she strikes another blow to the point where the man's right thigh muscle meets his knee. This meeting of steel with muscles, nerves, and bones is extremely painful—that much she knows from experience.

Now the Viking knows it, too. The man crumples to the ground with a howl, grabbing his knee with his good hand. She strikes him again, over the kidney this time, just to make sure he won't be able to get up.

The Viking turns himself into a ball.

Sundin and Danielsson have started running off to the barn, as though trying to get to their car.

She raises her gun and fires a shot in the air.

Both men throw themselves headlong.

"Noses to the ground!" she commands. "Whoever looks up gets his skull blown off."

Danielsson and Sundin do as they are told. All she can hear is their coughs.

Asker holsters her gun and retracts the baton. Uses the cable ties to wrap up the whimpering Viking in the same way she did his clone just minutes ago.

Then she moves on to Sundin and Danielsson and does the same to them. Finishes by dragging the three men into the barn. By the time she has finished, the sweat is dripping down her back and inside her ski mask despite the chill in the air, and her injured shoulder is protesting loudly.

She sits down on an old bale of hay and rests for a few minutes while studying the three men tied up on the floor before her. The Viking she struck with the baton is glaring at her, but his duct-tape gag prevents him from saying anything. His face is red with rage and pain. But he's not who she's interested in. He blusters and hisses, lurches angrily with his body when she anchors him to a pillar inside a stall.

The other two men are much meeker. Sundin and Danielsson look terrified. Asker sits them upright against a wall and lets their imaginations run wild while she fills two buckets with water from a tap.

"W-who are you?" Sundin splutters. "Who do you work for?"

Asker doesn't reply. Instead she casts a bucket of water over him. After that she does the same to Danielsson.

Both men scream in shock, then reel off a torrent of four-letter words into the air.

Asker returns to her seat. Inside the barn the temperature is maybe forty degrees, and the air is biting. She sits in silence, watching the men.

After just a few minutes the men stop swearing, the curses replaced by the chatter of their teeth as they sit there in the cold in their soaked clothes.

She waits until their lips have turned blue.

"So," she says without standing up. "I want you to tell me about Tord Korpi. Everything, right from the start."

HILL

He eats dinner alone, heats up the leftovers from his and Leo's Thai takeout while scrolling on his phone. She was only here one night, but the villa feels strangely empty without her.

That, or he just isn't used to being this isolated. Astroholm is exciting, but at the same time dark and very quiet. Right now far *too* quiet. He still feels uneasy after his conversation with Samuel. The security chief scared him, stirring up memories and events that he had hoped to never have to relive.

But more than that, he is probably disappointed; now that Karin has shown him Bernhard's real grave, he will have to dismiss the underground burial chamber as pure urban legend. What will that mean for the book he wants to write about Boulder Isle and the Irving family?

Perhaps not so much, as it happens. It's not like there is any shortage of mysteries beyond those tired old conspiracies.

He flicks through the case file on the drownings that Leo brought him. Lingers for a while on a memo detailing the police efforts to drag the lake again for Elis's remains once Nick's body was found at the start of spring. Neither his body nor the wreck of the rowboat turned up then either. The latter is a little peculiar, notes the police officer writing the memo, since plastic boats are hard-wearing; it would take a great deal to make one sink all the way to the bottom and stay there.

The last document in the file is the autopsy.

It states that Nick's body was in a very poor condition, having lain in the water for three months. The tissues were more or less dissolved, and a number of fractures were observed, mostly to the upper body.

Hill discovers that the UFO couple were indeed right on yet another point: Nick's eyes were completely gone.

The forensic examiner, however, reacted with no great surprise to the injuries, instead noting that they could have occurred in the lake, and settled on the cautious conclusion of *suspected drowning*, just as Leo said.

On the whole, Hill can see that the information he was given by the UFO couple has, at least in point of fact, been proven correct: Nick and Elis's fateful excursion, the murder of head gardener Björn Knudsen. Add to that Viggo's car crash in which Maud's boyfriend Pontus met his end, the site of which Gunnar would for some reason choose to attend.

In summary, four deaths, all apparently different, yet with one thing in common: a link to the Irving family or to Astroholm Manor, Miresjön Lake, and Boulder Isle.

Naturally this could all be coincidence. Things happen over time, and the greater and longer the course of events, the more correlations are likely to be found.

It's the very lifeblood of conspiracy theories.

Still, he can't deny that it's all fascinating. And when he throws in his own experiences since his arrival at Astroholm, it does feel like he is onto something. A secret, or perhaps even several. Plenty of material for his book, and even more that simply piques his curiosity. Fuels his obsession with Boulder Isle.

Though he won't get any further than that tonight. He will have to wait till tomorrow and hope the library opens again, so that he can explore the space behind the secret door.

He still has no idea where the door fits into the puzzle, but someone has put a whole lot of effort into helping him to discover it.

Whatever lies behind that door, it must be something that will bring him closer to at least one of the Irving family's secrets.

But, despite his own excitement, he has an uneasy feeling that has been creeping up on him ever since Tom and Krystal placed *Forgotten Places* on the table in the café.

Nick and Elis had read his book and been inspired by it. They tried to reach Boulder Isle because of what *he* had written about it. An uncomfortable part of his conscience maintains that that makes him complicit in their fates.

He tries to persuade himself that, ultimately, Nick and Elis were grown men who made their own decisions. Still, the guilt nags at him, fostered by the horrible details he just read in the autopsy.

He needs to occupy his mind, somehow.

The UFO couple said they were searching for an entrance to the underground terminal around Villa Arcturus. He could always stretch his legs and take a look for himself in the forest around the house.

He looks for a flashlight and finds a rechargeable one on the wall just inside the basement door, next to the fuse box.

He turns it on and shines it down into the darkness of the basement. A strange smell wafts up from below. Damp, underground, and then something else. Something faintly unpleasant that he can't put his finger on, but that he feels the need to investigate. He takes a few steps down the stairs. One of the steps creaks loudly.

Once he is down there, he shines the flashlight around the room.

A washing machine and a tumble dryer, just like Mrs. Schiller said. A few shelves with boxes on them, and in the far corner a metal door with DISTRICT HEATING written on it. Nothing exactly exciting.

He goes back up to the hallway and shuts the basement door carefully behind him.

Outside, the air is cold and windy. Hill does up his jacket and pulls his hat down over his forehead, then rounds the house to reach the little garden behind his bedroom window. Once he reaches the spot in the grass where he found the bunch of keys, he keeps walking, steps in among the trees.

The flashlight picks out a narrow path that he decides to follow.

The wind whistles in the treetops as he presses on deeper into the forest.

He sweeps the flashlight from trunk to trunk, on the hunt for a structure that could constitute a shaft of some kind.

All he sees are tree trunks and bushes.

After twenty minutes of idle searching he starts to get cold and decides to head back to the house.

A faint hum makes him look up. A small, dark craft is hovering just above the treetops. For three seconds his brain thinks he is looking at a UFO, but then sense catches up with him. It's a drone, just like the one Leo told him about that morning. Presumably it's part of Astroholm's security system. The craft floats completely still, as though observing him. When he starts to move, it follows.

Hill can't help but think about what the UFO couple said about his cellphone. He carries it with him and has the app installed, which connects him to Astroholm's Wi-Fi network. Sure, the drone could have detected the flashlight and headed toward it. But what if that isn't it? What if he is being tracked by his phone?

Was that how Samuel knew he was at Bernhard's grave?

The thought is an unpleasant one.

He steps off the path and cuts through the trees, in the direction of Villa Arcturus. The drone goes on humming above him, but as the forest becomes denser, he loses sight of it.

He changes direction, moves deeper into the woodland. Eventually he stops, presses up against a tree trunk, and tries to listen out for the hum of the drone. After just a minute or so he hears it again: it whirs closer, only to stop just above him.

Then there comes a beam of light so powerful that Hill must instinctively raise his hand to cover his eyes.

The drone hovers there for a few seconds, illuminating him.

Then the light goes out abruptly, the drone's motor revs up, and it disappears off over the treetops.

Hill stands there in the darkness.

The drone didn't find him by chance—that much is clear.

Someone wants him to know they are keeping an eye on him.

ASKER

Both men's teeth are chattering like maracas. The sound echoes between the walls in the old barn.

"Tord K-Korpi?" Sundin stutters. "Who the f-fuck is that?"

Asker isn't in any hurry to reply. The moron still hasn't figured out that time isn't on his side. For every minute he drags out his responses, his and Danielsson's worries will only be the greater. Their lips are already blue, and soon the shakes will set in.

All she has to do is wait.

"W-what the fuck do you want?" Danielsson's voice is breaking. He is skinnier and weaker than Sundin, and he appears to be much closer to cracking.

"Tord Korpi," she says again. "You tried to rob him a long time ago. I want to hear the whole story."

Danielsson whimpers. His greasy middle part makes him look even more pathetic, if possible.

"I'm f-freezing my fucking ass off . . ."

"Then I suggest you talk quickly," says Asker. "Take it from the top."

Danielsson and Sundin exchange glances.

"OK," Danielsson eventually puffs. "We saw that Korpi had cash and decided to try to jack it."

"You two and who else?"

"L-Linus Palm," Danielsson gasps. His slender body has started to shake uncontrollably.

Asker knows that it looks worse than it is. The shakes are the body's way of trying to keep the muscles going. Unpleasant, but not all that dangerous. It's when the shakes stop that you need to start to worry.

"We tailed him." Sundin jumps in. Even he appears to have given up. "Waited till he left Freedom Gym and followed his pickup. Got ourselves some ski masks and baseball bats."

"Go on!" she commands. "I want details!"

"He drove north for a while, then turned off straight into the forest," Sundin chatters. "Went to an old gravel pit. Another car was waiting for him there. A woman who jumped into Korpi's pickup."

"And then?" Asker urges him on impatiently, wanting him to get to the point.

"At f-first we thought they were going to fuck; it stank of a hookup from a mile away, so we almost called the whole thing off. But then she got out again after just a few minutes and drove away. So we decided to do him. B-but it all got out of hand. Korpi pulled a rod and shot Jon in the leg."

Danielsson nods to confirm. His skin has turned a chalky white. "He held the gun to my head. Y-yelled at us to tell him who we were working for. We were shit-scared, told him we were just small fry. Begged for our lives . . ."

He sobs, and Sundin takes over again.

"K-Korpi took off. We panicked, threw Jon into my car, and drove straight to the ER. He was bleeding like a pig."

Danielsson nods jerkily.

"It fucking killed . . ." he gasps.

"And then?" she asks again.

Both men look at each other.

"What do you mean, then?" Sundin asks. "Korpi took off and we never saw him again."

Asker doesn't reply. Instead she stands up, walks over to the tap, and starts filling one of the buckets with more water.

"W-wait!" Sundin cries.

Asker fills the bucket and sets it down a few feet in front of them.

"What happened next?" she repeats.

The men stare at her.

"Jon got sepsis. W-was in for months," Sundin chatters.

Danielsson nods eagerly.

"Almost lost my leg," he attests.

Asker raises the bucket.

"So which one of you murdered Korpi?"

The men stare at her.

"Murdered?" Sundin chatters. "What the fuck are you on about?"

Asker raises the water bucket even higher. Danielsson lets out a little whimper.

"No no no, fuck no, no more. We didn't touch him, I swear, I swear."

Asker looks at Sundin. He, too, is shaking his head.

"W-we were only kids," he splutters between shakes. "Korpi scared the shit out of us. Jon almost fucking died. Linus took off to some relative up north."

"And you? What did you do after the robbery?"

"I w-went to Denmark," Sundin shivers. "I have cousins there."

"Tell her everything, Erik," Danielsson whimpers. "I can't take this anymore . . ."

His shakes are starting to subside.

"I got put away for breaking and entering," Sundin says quickly. "I did a year."

"In Denmark?"

Sundin gives a shaky nod.

"When was this?"

"The same summer. Like, three weeks after the robbery."

"So you were in prison from August for one year?"

Sundin nods.

Asker thinks through this claim. A Danish prison sentence wouldn't appear on any Swedish registers, which would explain why Rosen didn't come across that information in her searches. Still, that's an easy thing to check—which Sundin must reasonably know. So chances are he is telling the truth.

Asker turns to Danielsson.

"And you were in hospital? For how long?"

The man can barely produce a nod.

"Till October. C-came home on my birthday."

"What happened to Linus Palm?" she asks.

Sundin shakes his head. His speech comes in fits and starts.

"We stopped hanging out. He met some girl. He's a politician now, doesn't want to know us."

Asker puts down the bucket, trying to take in what the men have told her.

By this point, Sundin and Danielsson are too cold and too scared to lie convincingly.

Korpi was murdered at some point between mid-August and September 9, when the last pile of trash was unloaded and the barriers were installed at the dump.

By then Sundin was in prison in Denmark, and Danielsson was still in the hospital. Theoretically Linus Palm could still be involved, but she doubts that.

Which leaves only one conclusion. A really crushing one.

Palm, Sundin, and Danielsson had nothing to do with Tord Korpi's murder. The botched robbery, however logical it might seem, is just a red herring.

She has wasted her limited resources on the wrong information.

And now her investigation has reached a dead end.

Shit!

SATURDAY

HILL

The uneasy feeling Hill felt the previous night is still hanging over him at breakfast. Yet again he briefly toys with the idea of simply packing up and quitting the job, only to reach the same conclusion as before: he is far too fascinated by the whole story to be scared off by a mere reprimand, however unpleasant it may have been.

Besides, the Irving family have pretty good reason to be on their guard after the intruders the other night. And, at the end of the day, he did break the rules by visiting Bernhard's grave.

The app beeps, informing him that the manor house is open once again, which puts paid to his final reservations.

He immediately requests a lift to the library.

Then impatiently drinks his morning coffee while waiting for Ville to appear.

Instead it is Mrs. Schiller who appears at the wheel of the golf cart.

"Good morning, Associate Professor Hill," she says in greeting. "Did you sleep well?"

"Good morning, Mrs. Schiller," he says in an exaggeratedly friendly voice. "Yes, thanks, I did."

Hill has decided to try to put right yesterday's little overstep. Conduct himself in an exemplary manner so that he can explore the secret stairwell in peace and quiet.

"About yesterday," she says after a while, smiling her usual, mild smile. "Samuel was probably a little short with you, for which I do beg your pardon. You must understand, Mrs. Irving isn't quite herself. We're very protective of her."

"Of course," Hill replies. "As I explained to Samuel, I'd given her a lift from the florist in town. She more or less insisted on me going down with her to Bernhard's grave, and I didn't want to seem rude."

"I understand. What were you doing in town?"

The question sounds innocent, but it still puts Hill on his guard.

"I gave my friend a lift to the train station, and on my way back I took the chance to pop by the library."

He wonders whether he should mention the UFO Café, too—not least because he suspects that they are tracking him. Still, he decides to keep mum.

Mrs. Schiller sits in silence for a few seconds, apparently concentrating on the road.

"As I said, Mrs. Irving isn't quite herself. Sometimes she can seem entirely lucid; at others she is in a whole world of her own. You have to take everything she says with a pinch of salt."

"I understand," says Hill.

"Did she say anything to you?" Mrs. Schiller asks. "Anything you thought seemed strange?"

"No," says Hill, in as innocent a tone of voice as he can muster. "She mostly talked about how much she admired Bernhard. Called him a great man."

Mrs. Schiller nods.

"Yes, Mrs. Irving and Bernhard were very good friends. She cherishes his memory, as we all do."

She brakes in front of the door to the medical suite.

"So, here we are."

The woman steps out and opens the door to the facility with her pass card, then escorts Hill to the elevator and up to the library.

But instead of leaving him alone as usual, she takes a seat in an armchair and starts fiddling with an iPad.

It takes all of Hill's self-control not to glance over at the bookshelves where the secret door stands. As long as Mrs. Schiller is here, he has no other choice but to work.

Besides, he has promised Nova some kind of angle for the Alpha-Cent book, and until he can present one that they approve of there will be no trip to Boulder Isle for him.

Having seen Bernhard's grave and heard Karin speak about the man, he decides to return to the articles in which Gunnar speaks about his father.

It takes him about an hour to sift out the most interesting comments. Almost all of them relate in some way to Gunnar's experience on Boulder Isle.

My father understood what was required. He had vision and courage
enough to see it through. Bernhard entrusted me with the entire
family firm. Allowed me to build on the ideas the extraterrestrial had
given me. I shall always be deeply grateful to him for that.

This text doesn't contain the slightest hint of the hatred Karin claimed
he felt.

Hill flicks on, reading article upon article. He makes notes, tries
to compare sentences and words.

Certain phrases return, while others change.

To begin with, Gunnar's UFO story is more detailed, but as the
years pass it becomes shorter, briefer. In addition to that, a number
of details change: how high up in the sky the light was, how big the
spaceship and creature were. In one description the creature is shiny
and black, while in another it is matte. In some instances Gunnar
even describes various sounds, which are left out of other versions
of the story.

The description of Bernhard, however, remains a striking constant over the years. The father is a visionary who has the courage to
take action and allow Gunnar to follow his calling; one who dares to
let go of his life's work and entrust it to his son.

But in the early nineties something else changes in this narrative.
A 1992 article marks the first time Gunnar uses the phrase *when I
took over the company*.

Although the distinction may be slight, as far as Hill can tell Gunnar has until this point always used words like *handed over*, *passed on*,
or *entrusted* when describing the process. Stressed that it was Bernhard doing the action, not he himself. But from that interview onward Gunnar instead starts describing himself as the active party. It
becomes he who *took over*, who *stepped in*, who *took care of things*.

This shift in narrative is so subtle that it only becomes clear when
you actively look for it.

The gratitude that Gunnar so often expressed in regard to his
father is also entirely absent in later articles.

Hill rocks on his chair.

So what happened in the early nineties that made Gunnar's attitude to his father change? He goes back and checks the timeline he
compiled the other day.

Gunnar divorced Karin in 1991, just a few months before that interview. He remarried the year after, and had a daughter, Nova.

At around the same time, AlphaCent presented new advances in DNA analysis. Hill shakes his head, struggling to see any link between these events and Gunnar's apparently altered relationship with his father.

Mrs. Schiller coughs, disturbing his train of thought.

This time he can't help but steal a glance at the sci-fi bookshelves. His whole urban-explorer soul would like nothing more than to go to it.

But until Mrs. Schiller leaves him alone, he has no choice but to sit tight. He must let it all go for now, focus on finding an angle for the AlphaCent book instead.

He flips to a blank page in his notebook and drums his pen against the paper a few times.

His gaze is once again drawn to the bookshelves.

What lies on the other side of that door?

What secrets await him?

ASKER

She allows herself a few extra hours' sleep before doing her usual run, all the way from the big house to the golf course. On her way back she pushes her body hard, in an attempt to clear her head.

Prepper Per is in custody, and both of her prime suspects have proved innocent. The only interesting information she gleaned from that entire lead was Korpi's meeting with a mystery woman, perhaps an illicit affair. But since Sundin and Danielsson couldn't give her any more details—not even the make of the woman's car—she will be impossible to trace all these years later.

Still, the situation isn't completely hopeless, at least not judicially speaking. That Per and Korpi knew each other, or that Korpi spent time on the Farm just before his murder, isn't enough to hang any kind of case on. The courts could never bring charges on those details alone, especially not for a sixteen-year-old murder case. Both the prosecutor and Hellman know that.

They need more—more circumstantial evidence or hard proof, or at the very least a clear motive that can make Per seem much more suspect.

Failing that, Per should be free again by Monday—still a suspect, of course, and pretty mad at her, to be sure, but without having caused any bloodshed.

Maybe the best she can do now is just sit on the sidelines and hope that both Hellman and Per run out of steam?

An appealing thought.

When she gets back to her front yard, a racer-green sports car is waiting in the drive.

Isabel's car.

Her mother steps out. As usual she is impeccably dressed, even though it's a Saturday morning. She is wearing a suit, coat, scarf, and fur hat, which, combined with her body language, enhance the impression of British monarch with a hint of apex predator.

Meanwhile Asker is sporting soaked running clothes, worn far beyond the critical point at which the smell of sweat refuses to quite wash out.

"Good morning, Leonore!" Isabel says, exaggeratedly cheery. "I thought I'd treat you to breakfast. I've brought some rolls."

Asker doesn't know what concerns her more: the fact that her mother has turned up unannounced, or that she is trying to be friendly.

Asker takes a quick shower while trying to figure out exactly what Isabel could want from her, but she fails to come up with anything beyond it reasonably having something to do with Hellman and her father. Still, with Isabel you can never be entirely sure. That very uncertainty is one of her most formidable weapons.

When she steps into the spacious kitchen, Isabel has laid out a spread of breakfast rolls, croissants, and freshly squeezed orange juice, which only adds to Asker's worry.

"I tried to make coffee, but that espresso machine must need some kind of engineering degree to operate," her mother says, in that same cheery tone that Asker doesn't quite know how to handle.

Asker makes them two coffees, sits down at the table and tucks into the rolls.

"So, Leonore, how are you?"

"Fine."

Clearly they are expected to chitchat for a while before Isabel will cut to the chase, so Asker throws in an "It's busy."

"You don't feel like getting a place of your own in town?"

Her mother makes a little hand gesture at the enormous house.

"Your sister and Fredric have bought a house in Bellevue, so their apartment will soon be available."

Asker is on the brink of saying exactly what she thinks of that idea, but she bites her tongue.

"I'm pretty happy here," she says. "It's quiet, and nice. The train into town doesn't take long."

"Oh, yes, well, you do as you like, of course. But if you need any help, we're only a phone call away, you know that."

Asker tries to stop herself from flinching. Warning flag number two has just been raised. Not only is her mother acting friendly, she is also offering her help. Whatever it is she wants to talk about, it must be serious.

"Is Junot all right?" Asker asks.

"Oh yes." Isabel bats away the question. "He's on Mallorca playing golf this weekend."

"And you?"

"I'm fine."

Isabel takes a sip of coffee, as though collecting herself. Asker waits in suspense. They have danced around the subject for exactly as long as politesse demands.

"Look, there's something I need to tell you," her mother says.

"OK?" Asker says, in a tone of voice at least intended to convey surprise.

"It's about your father. As I understand, you've continued to help him with his . . . legal issues."

Asker groans inwardly. The topic isn't unexpected, of course—but why come all the way out here just for that?

"Jonas Hellman contacted me again," her mother goes on. "He told me you'd managed to get Per to hand himself over to the police. A very wise move, Leonore."

Asker doesn't quite know what she is expected to say. Praise from Isabel is such a rare occurrence that she has no stock response. All the same, she doesn't like the fact that Hellman and her mother appear to have running contact.

"But according to Hellman, that maneuver caught him and his colleagues a little off guard," Isabel goes on. "They would have liked more time to prepare."

Asker tries to stop herself from smirking. What had sounded like praise was of course nothing more than beautifully veiled criticism. Order is restored.

"That's too bad for Hellman," she says caustically. "It must be hard to have your prime suspect dropped into your lap for free, without having to lift a finger."

Her mother pretends not to hear.

"Hellman also said that they will probably be forced to release Per again after the weekend. That he's concerned about what that might lead to—not least for you."

Asker clenches her teeth.

"So you've come all the way out here to tell me how worried Jonas Hellman is about me? You do remember I made an official complaint about him, don't you?"

Isabel ignores the question and takes a delicate bite of a croissant.

"Think what you will of Jonas Hellman," she says once she has finished chewing, "but he's a strategically minded person. And he has an excellent reputation within the police authority. A future candidate for police commissioner. Or even higher."

Asker's temples have started to pound.

"And you intend to help him with those ambitions?" she asks with a hard-fought calm.

Her mother gently purses her lips.

"My prime concern right now is actually to help you, Leonore. It worries me a great deal that your father has managed to insinuate his way back into your life."

"But he hasn't!" Her protest comes automatically, which is never good.

"Oh, hasn't he?" Her mother raises one of her perfectly plucked eyebrows. "So then why do you think Per agreed to hand himself over to the police, just like that? The man who hates the authorities, who hates being locked up?"

Asker has long grappled with this question herself.

"Because it was his only way out."

Her mother laughs.

"Per's had years to plan and think through possible scenarios. It's all he does. Plan and prepare for the worst. And of all his possible options, he chose to kindly let himself be apprehended." Isabel shakes her head. "No, Per has something in his sights. Something to do with you. And whatever it is, I can't stand by and let it happen."

She opens the briefcase that she has placed under the table and takes out some papers.

"You don't know this, but for a while after our divorce I helped Per to get his affairs in order."

Asker frowns.

"Why? I thought you were enemies."

"Actually, the divorce was unexpectedly civilized. I had nothing to gain from a long, drawn-out process that might affect Lissander and Partners' standing, and Per for his part had other things to focus on. So we came to an agreement. As part of that agreement I under-took to handle some of his affairs. Or, *conclude* would perhaps be the more accurate description."

She pushes the papers across the table.

"Among other things I helped your father to pay a tax debt. You'll see the payment here."

Asker suddenly sees where her mother is going with this.

"When was this?" she asks, though she already knows the answer.

Isabel taps a well-manicured finger on the page.

"The Tax Agency registered the payment on September 25, 2006. I remember it well, since your father turned up with the entire sum in cash. I was forced to pull a whole lot of strings to get the tax authority to accept the payment."

Asker tries to gather her thoughts, but it's almost impossible.

"Where did he say he'd gotten the money from?"

"A loan from an acquaintance. And I didn't ask any more questions."

Asker's brain does the math. Her father conjures up hundreds of thousands of Swedish kronor in cash out of nowhere, in the very same time frame that Tord Korpi is murdered and buried next to the Farm.

"This cash," she says, as calmly as she can. "Do you remember how it was packed?"

Her mother nods.

"Oh yes, as I said I remember it all very well. Per was carrying a dark duffel bag that he placed on my desk. It was full of rolled-up bills."

Asker hears the rest as though through a crash of waves.

"Yesterday I shared this information with Jonas Hellman," her mother says. "In all likelihood it means that Per will be detained further. My advice to you . . ."

She pauses. Her voice softens.

"My *appeal* to you, Leonore, would be to keep as far from all of this as possible."

HELLMAN

Hellman is back in the interview room. Per Asker is sitting in the chair opposite, with Eskil over by the wall, just like before.

But this time everything is different.

Having just placed the Tax Agency's records on the table between them, he watches Per Asker's smug smirk pale away.

"We've spoken to Tord Korpi's ex-wife," Hellman says. "She told us that Tord always used to carry lots of cash. And that the last times she received money from him, it came in rolled-up bills. Much the same as the bills you gave to your ex-wife when she was clearing up your tax debt."

He pauses, savoring the moment.

"The timing of the tax payment is also a perfect match for the time frame of Korpi's death, which you yourself helped to establish. By September 25, Tord Korpi lay in a shallow grave just outside your property, while you used his money to pay off your debts. That's how the prosecutor and I view the facts, and he is convinced that the court will agree. So you can look forward to being remanded for some time to come."

Hellman pauses to let the words sink in. In the meantime he throws a quick glance over at Eskil, who looks just as impressed as he should.

"You've been locked up until further notice before, Per, haven't you?" Hellman goes on softly. "Pretrial detention's worse than the psych ward. No visits, no activities. Just four walls and an hour in the yard each day, while we'll be busy turning your den up in the woods inside out."

He leans in. This time he has the upper hand for real.

He knows it, too, Per Asker. Hell, even Eskil has twigged.

Maybe by now Leo also knows the lay of the land. Has come to see which of the two is leaving the game victorious; that she has been beaten.

That he has beaten her.

The thought excites him, strangely enough. Even turns him on. He shakes off the feeling, returns to his professional role.

"Of course, a confession from you could speed the whole process along. But you don't plan to do that, Per, do you?" he says quietly.

"You're not the kind of guy to confess. You'd rather sit in a cramped little cell for months than make the slightest peep. And, you know what? That suits me just fine. Bite your tongue all you want, either way you're fucked."

Per Asker chews his top lip. He doesn't look at all as cocky anymore, Hellman notes with some satisfaction.

"So, is there anything you want to add, Per?" he says.

The man glares at him with his functioning eye.

"I . . ." he says thoughtfully, ". . . I'd like to confer with my legal representative."

"Of course," Hellman nods. "Would you like a public defense, or do you already have a lawyer?"

Per Asker shakes his head.

"Not a lawyer. My legal representative."

This pedantry should irritate Hellman, but he can afford some magnanimity, let the old man have his nonsense attempts to retain at least a shred of his dignity. After all, they both know who has won. Which one of them is running the show.

"Of course. Eskil here will help you to contact them," Hellman says with an exaggerated friendliness. "What's your representative's name?"

Only when he sees the man's little smile does Hellman realize two things. One: that Per Asker is the person he hates most in this world. And two: that this fight is far from over.

"Leonore Asker," says Per. "I believe you already have her number. Let her know I'd like to speak to her as soon as possible."

HILL

Hill tries to wait out Mrs. Schiller, but once lunch and the afternoon coffee service have passed, it becomes clear that the woman intends to spend her entire working day keeping an eye on him. Clearly his little excursion to Bernhard's grave has dented trust in him more than he had hoped.

But he will have to get rid of her somehow, if he wants any chance of investigating the staircase and the mysterious door. So he has spent the last hour devising a plan to put his superpower to use—only in reverse.

He gets up and walks over to Mrs. Schiller.

The woman looks up from her iPad as he approaches.

"I have a few questions," he says.

"You do?" She takes off her reading glasses.

"Gunnar's divorce from Karin. That seems to have happened quite hastily?"

Just as he hoped, Mrs. Schiller gives a stiff smile, as though the topic flusters her.

"That is a private matter. I should hardly think it material for an anniversary book on the company," she says.

"One could see it that way," Hill replies. "But on the other hand, it *is* the daughter from Gunnar's second marriage who is currently CEO. Without the divorce, Nova would never have existed. So it would be hard not to mention it at all in the book."

Mrs. Schiller retains her stiff smile.

"So what is your question, Associate Professor Hill?"

"I was wondering if Gunnar might have experienced some kind of change in the early nineties? Divorce, a new family, a young wife, a new baby—it all sounds like a classic midlife crisis to me."

"I don't think so," Mrs. Schiller replies evasively.

"But it could be," Hill persists.

Mrs. Schiller looks away, as though she would rather not answer the question.

Hill almost feels bad for pestering her like this.

"And then, ten years later, his son and heir Viggo is gravely injured in a car crash, and Maud's boyfriend is killed," he goes on.

"Yes . . ." Mrs. Schiller fidgets uncomfortably, just as Hill hoped.

"At that point Gunnar is both CEO and chairman of the board. And yet he finds it in himself to go on."

She clears her throat, straightening her already-erect back another few degrees.

"Gunnar has never let anything hold him back. Not even private tragedy. Naturally Viggo's accident was traumatic for the family, and no one wants to see it raked up again. Besides, Viggo hasn't had anything to do with AlphaCent in many years, so it should hardly be important to the book."

"Perhaps not, but the crash must have affected Gunnar—and *he* is very important to the book."

Mrs. Schiller is fighting all the harder to retain her smile.

"Nevertheless, my advice would be to refrain from devoting any more time to matters surrounding the accident."

She makes a show of looking at her watch, and Hill delivers the knockout punch.

"Where's Viggo these days?" he asks.

"Abroad," Mrs. Schiller replies. "Where he can get the best possible care."

She looks at her watch again and stands up, a little too hastily.

"If you'll excuse me, I must leave you now. Use the app if you need a ride back to your accommodation."

Hill strains to hide his relieved grin.

"I might walk," he says. "My leg's feeling much, much better after my treatments. So you needn't wait for me to contact you."

Mrs. Schiller observes him for a few seconds.

"Naturally that's your decision. But there'll be more fog again tonight, so do keep to the road. One can easily go astray."

"Thanks for the tip!"

Once Mrs. Schiller has carefully shut the door behind her, he waits patiently for five minutes before heading to the nook with Bernhard's book collection and opening the hidden door.

The wooden door at the top of the spiral staircase sweeps open with a faint creak. Hill is enveloped by a musty scent. The loft space inside is dim, but not pitch-black, as he had expected.

The room is upward of 250 square feet, under rafters and a low, pitched roof. At the far end of the room is a round window, through which the faint afternoon light still filters. Here and there, where the ceiling allows, hang shelves topped with ornaments. Most are metal toys that look handmade. Space rockets, planes, and UFOs, all painted in garish colors, just like on the book covers in the great hall below.

Midway along the room there is a wood-burning stove, and at the far end, by the window, a drawing board stands alongside a chest of shallow drawers for architects' drawings. The workspace reminds Hill of the one upstairs at Villa Arcturus.

He shines his flashlight on the drawing board. Just as in Villa Arcturus, a sheet of drawing paper is held across the surface. The paper is dusty, slightly warped with damp, and yellowed with age.

He studies the paper for a while to see if it contains any message from his anonymous friend. Another warning, or a clue. A reason why he has been led here. But the paper is completely blank.

So instead he checks the chest of drawers.

The drawers contain a multitude of plans and drawings of the manor house and guesthouses alike. There are also designs for decorative details and furnishings. He finds one of the door knocker for Villa Canopus, and another that represents the starry sky in his own bedroom. On the whole, the contents of the drawer constitute a fantastic collection, one deserving of a better fate than to lie up here in oblivion. But he must reluctantly accept that it is not his place to take care of them.

In the very bottom drawer he finds what at first glance looks like another collection of drawings. When he cautiously flicks through the delicate sheets of paper, he realizes that they are in fact several different maps.

The top one appears to cover Boulder Isle and Astrofield Mine.

The mine shaft that bores down through the island is represented. From the shaft, tunnels extend beneath the lake, like uneven spokes, or rays of light emanating from a star. One of the longer ones extends back toward Astroholm, which makes the click of Hill's heart valve pipe up in the quiet little room.

A first suggestion that there might indeed be an underground connection between the island and the mainland.

He leafs carefully through the other maps.

At the very bottom he finds one that is in rather poor condition. The paper is yellowed and brittle, the folds so worn that the sheet is hardly intact.

The lines are so pale that at first he struggles to make out the map, but after a few seconds he realizes that it is of Astroholm's grounds.

The old mine, reads Bernhard's characteristic handwriting.

The mine tunnels here are considerably less symmetrical and deliberate than the ones on Boulder Isle. They appear to coil and interconnect more or less by chance, winding under almost the entire estate. One of the passages appears to extend some way out under the lake.

Hill can barely believe his eyes.

So there *is* an underground system of mine passages beneath the Astroholm estate, one that might even extend all the way out to Boulder Isle!

That discovery alone is enough for a follow-up to *Forgotten Places*.

Hill's hands shake when he fumbles for his cellphone camera. He takes a few deep breaths to calm himself down.

Then suddenly it hits him that taking photos might not be such a good idea.

What if the Astroholm app is secretly monitoring not only his communications, but also his image gallery?

After a little consideration, he decides to throw caution to the wind and take photos of both maps. In theory he could have found them down in the library, after all.

However, he decides not to take photos of the loft itself, nor of anything else that might reveal its existence.

Once he is finished, he closes all the drawers, straightens up, and turns toward the round window.

The panes are set back quite deeply into the roof, and it is hidden by pitched gables and chimneys, which presumably make it difficult to spot from the ground.

The treetops conceal most of the garden below, but the view down to the boathouse and jetty in the private area of the estate is unobstructed.

In clear weather all of Miresjön Lake must be visible from here. But the November days are getting all the shorter, dusk has already started to fall, and a dense bank of mist is forming out on the water. It has already consumed Boulder Isle on its rolling course toward the mainland. Mrs. Schiller's weather prognosis appears to be coming true.

When Hill leans toward the glass, his hand hits a flat object on the round windowsill that he hadn't spotted in the shadows. It falls to the floor with a muffled thud.

He bends down and shines his flashlight on it.

The object turns out to be a small sketchbook with worn, brown leather covers.

Bernhard Irving, reads the gold-embossed lettering on the front.

Hill opens it with curiosity, only to find that the sketchbook is filled from cover to cover with drawings and small notes in Bernhard's swirly handwriting.

Close the old mine! The first page says, and the exclamation mark has been traced many times, followed by the sentence: *Boulder Isle = greater chance of finding the meteorite.*

After that come several drawings that must be from Astrofield Mine itself: the headframe under construction; some men chatting by a mine cart; a first sketch of the observatory.

Hill once again feels the excitement rise as he flicks through at random to different pages in the book. One drawing depicts a woman's hand holding black pieces of glass. Another is a sketch of a young man who is shading his eyes with one hand while gazing up at the sky.

Gunnar, 1961 is written below it.

This could definitely be a first sketch of what would ultimately become *The Glass Man.*

Hill shuts the sketchbook. He should put it back on the sill. Yet part of him wants nothing more than to take it back with him to Villa Arcturus, where he can peruse it properly, in good lighting.

While he wavers with the book in his hands, it strikes him that all the objects in the room are covered in dust, while the sketchbook is completely clean. Not one speck of dust mars its covers, and the pages are untouched by damp.

Besides, it was balanced on a round windowsill—a not entirely obvious place to store a flat, rectangular object.

He shines his light down at the floor. No dust there either. It is almost as though someone has recently swept it, perhaps to clear their own footprints.

Someone has been here, and recently, too.

Probably the same person who led him here, and who has now given him yet another clue to Astroholm's secrets.

He looks at the sketchbook again. Puts it in his inner jacket pocket.

Outside the window, the bank of mist has almost reached the mainland, making the faint glow of the lights down by the boathouse start to flicker.

Hill gives a start. Someone is standing down there.

A tall man in a hat with his hands in his coat pockets.

Just as the mist reaches the jetty, the man turns and lifts his gaze, almost as though he were looking straight up at Hill.

The next second the mist sweeps in, and the man is gone.

THE GLASS MAN

He waits patiently for the Stranger, beyond the statue, where the darkness and fog shield him from the faint lights of the manor house.

He likes the fog; likes how it unseats the light and dampens the air. How it bears a scent that reminds him of underground and rot.

And on this particular night it also helps him to hide.

Draw closer. All too close.

He still doesn't know what the Stranger's presence means, but he wants to find out.

Yet the hunger claws at him.

Vies with his curiosity.

Which of the two will win out?

That he doesn't know.

All he knows is that he must wait here in the darkness and fog.

Wait for Martin Hill.

ASKER

On her way to the detention center Asker tries to figure out why the hell her father would appoint her to be his legal representative instead of asking for a good lawyer.

Though she does hold a law degree, she is hardly a suitable representative to defend him on charges of murder.

Which means that Prepper Per must have other reasons to speak to her—in a room that can be neither recorded nor bugged, since it would cost Hellman his job to even try it.

The move is so well calculated that she suspects Per has had it in his back pocket all along. That he has even planned for it.

She finds Hellman and Eskil waiting for her at the entrance to the detention center.

"I don't know what you're playing at, Asker," Hellman says through gritted teeth. "I made it clear that you were to stay as far from this case as possible, but you give me no choice. I'll be forced to report this to the police commissioner."

"You do that," she says. "But I doubt there's anything in the rules that makes it possible to punish me for a suspect requesting me as their legal representative."

"You could have refused." Eskil jumps in.

"Which I will do," she replies. "In just a little while."

"After you've spoken to him," Hellman says insinuatingly.

She shrugs.

"Rules are rules. I did warn you not to underestimate Per, didn't I?"

She heads for the elevators. Hellman has sense enough to let her pass, but Eskil isn't so smart.

He blocks her way, flicks a finger out at her face.

"You better watch your fucking back," he hisses.

"Or what?" she asks. "Are you and some beefed-up colleagues

going to jump me down in the garage again? As I recall, last time you ran off with your tail between your legs . . ."

Eskil's gaze falters, and he reluctantly steps aside.

"Always lovely chatting to you boys!" she says.

HILL

Hill doesn't dare linger in the secret room too long, in case Mrs. Schiller returns, so he heads back down the spiral staircase and shuts the fake door behind the bookcase. Listens out carefully to make sure the library is empty.

Everything is silent and still.

He walks back to his workspace, straining to get his pulse under control. His shirt collar is sweaty, and his hands are still faintly shaking from the excitement.

Cautiously he fingers the sketchbook in his inner pocket, but he doesn't dare take it out. Once he has calmed, everything starts to fall into place. He now has proof that there is a system of mine tunnels under both Astroholm Manor and Boulder Isle. The two might even be connected.

But right now he sees no way that he can explore this possibility from the mainland. The map reveals no entrances, and he can't search for one without the drone following him.

He needs to get to Boulder Isle somehow.

The mine tunnels, Gunnar's UFO encounter, the drowned urban explorers—even his own alarming childhood memory—all of these strands converge out there.

But in order to get there he must impress Gunnar.

He rubs his face, stands up, and walks over to the large window that looks out over the front courtyard.

Just like the other night, the lamps over by the fountain are barely visible. The *Glass Man* sculpture appears as a silhouette against the darkness and the mist.

Hill thinks of the sketch in the book, the one depicting the young Gunnar that must be the original study for the sculpture.

Suddenly he has an idea.

He stands there for a while, thinking it through.

That might actually work.

Nova picks up after two rings.

"So, I've done some thinking about the angle for the book," he says.

"Oh, exciting."

"I think we should build the narrative around Gunnar. He's AlphaCent's backbone, which means he should also be the book's."

"Interesting." Nova sounds like she is contemplating the idea.

Hill takes a deep breath. He might as well go all out.

"I have an idea for the title, too," he says. "What do you think of *The Glass Man*?"

Nova is silent for a few seconds.

"*The Glass Man*?"

"Yes, after the sculpture you have here at Astroholm and at AlphaCent's HQ. You see, Gunnar took the obsidian glass—the very symbol of his father's fall—and with it he created the extremely sharp scalpel that would become the company's med-tech breakthrough. In doing so he not only saved the company, he also made a contribution to humanity. He transformed something as worthless as a piece of glass into something fantastic, in the same way that he transformed All Preserves into AlphaCent. So, *The Glass Man*."

The line goes silent for a few seconds while he waits for her reaction. Hill catches himself holding his breath.

"An exciting idea," she eventually says. "I'll pass it on to Gunnar straightaway. Thanks for calling, Martin, and have a good evening."

She ends the call.

Hill stands there with his cellphone in his hand for a few seconds, trying to make sense of Nova's reaction to his proposal.

She sounded almost a little amused. He hopes that that bodes well.

Hill puts his phone away, walks over to the desk, and packs up his things.

Rounds it all off by checking that the sketchbook is still safely in the inner pocket of his blazer.

It's high time that he got home and explored what else is hidden on those pages.

When he steps out of the manor house, he realizes that the darkness and fog are even thicker than the other night, when he almost got lost on his way home from Maud and Elsa's house.

He briefly toys with the idea of calling for a ride in spite of it all, but he could do with some exercise, and there is something mesmerizing about this thick fog and darkness.

Besides, unlike last time, tonight he has a flashlight on him. He flicks it on and starts walking up the road.

By *The Glass Man* he stops and lights up the sculpture. The dark glass glitters, almost like a living material. But just as before, there is something faintly eerie about it.

Its facial expression and body language appear to be constantly changing, depending on how the light falls. From one angle *The Glass Man* looks frightened and uncertain, from another self-assured and arrogant.

Hill thinks back to the sketchbook again, and wonders whether Bernhard envisioned that effect even while designing the sculpture.

Did he see all those sides to Gunnar?

He starts walking up the road in the direction of Villa Arcturus. The fog is so thick that the light of his flashlight bounces off it, dazzling him.

He angles the light downward, which helps with the glare, but he can still only see six to ten feet ahead. In any case, the only thing he needs to keep an eye out for is the turning to Villa Arcturus, and he must have a good way to go till then.

His mind drifts back to the sketchbook.

Who is the secret friend who wanted him to find it? Who has been feeding him these little clues to the Irving family's secrets?

And why?

In his distraction he pushes himself a little too hard, so stops to catch his breath. After two of Dr. Schiller's cryotherapy treatments his thigh feels almost good as new, but his fitness still isn't quite up to scratch.

A faint sound behind him makes him whip around.

The manor house has long since disappeared behind him, and he is surrounded by darkness and fog. Could it have been a bird?

Hill pricks his ears to have his theory confirmed, but the sound doesn't return.

He keeps walking up the road, but after just twenty yards he feels the hairs rise up on the back of his neck. He stops and turns around. He can't quite explain why, but suddenly he feels like he is being watched.

As though there is someone out there in the fog.

Someone whom he doesn't see—but who does see him.

ASKER

"OK, Per," she says once the guard has shut the door behind him, leaving them alone in the small room. "What the fuck am I doing here on a Saturday night?"

"You mean you don't get it?" He raises his eyebrows. "You're the one who convinced me to give myself up voluntarily. You said you were about to solve the case. That they didn't have enough evidence to keep me in custody, that at worst I'd only be in a couple of days. And now I hear they're working up a charge."

"And that's somehow my fault?" she hisses. "You gave Mom Korpi's money to settle your debts—a fact you chose not to mention to me."

"I don't owe you any explanations!"

Prepper Per stares at her with his functioning eye.

There was a time when she would have been terrified of that gaze. It is still unpleasant, especially combined with the dead, white eye that stares fixedly ahead.

Bores its way into her.

"It was Mom who sold you out," she says defensively. "I had nothing to do with it."

"You're wrong there." He shakes his head. "Isabel wouldn't betray me like that without a very good reason. I can only think of one: a mother's instinct to protect her child. Isabel wants me locked up because she's scared I'll hurt you. So you do, in fact, have quite a lot to do with it."

Asker is sick of this game.

"Why did you have Korpi's money?"

He pulls a face.

"It was a loan. Tord was the one who suggested it. He'd been chased by the tax man's vultures himself."

Asker doesn't rise to the bait. As a child she heard Per rail against the big, bad tax men more times than she cares to recall, and she has no desire to do it as an adult, too.

"And it didn't strike you as odd that Tord never showed up to re-claim his money?"

"Of course it did. But that was hardly my problem."

"Not until his corpse landed on your doorstep," she interjects.

He pulls the corners of his mouth into a bitter grimace.

"So, have you found an alternative suspect?" he asks.

Asker fills her lungs and slowly exhales.

"Not yet."

"Please elaborate."

His tone is scathing, and she repeats her breathing exercise.

"Everything pointed to Korpi's murder being linked to a botched robbery connected to Freedom Gym in Hörby. Since my resources are limited, I decided to focus on that . . ."

Even she can tell that she has shifted into a defensive mode. Has shrunk slightly, as though she is once again that scared teen trying to justify a mistake. She is even using his words.

"But after following that lead and questioning the suspects, I've found it was a red herring," she concludes.

"Is that all?" he says.

She tries to shake his disappointment.

"That's quite a lot given that this is a sixteen-year-old case that I have no way of accessing, and that I'm working alone."

Per drums the table with the fingers of his remaining hand.

She knows that tic all too well.

"I had such high hopes for you, Leo," he says coldly. "Your sister's a nice girl, but you were something else. Someone who shared my strengths. Maybe even surpassed them, at least when I wasn't at my best."

He gives his prosthetic hand a gentle tap.

"But now you're telling me that you, in spite of your assurances, are still at square one. That I'm risking weeks—probably months—in a bleak little cell. Is that how I'm supposed to see it?"

His tone of voice makes her furious. Either that or her apparent regression to the person she once was.

"See it however you want," she snaps. "The reason you're being detained is because you used Korpi's money to pay off a tax debt, which gives you motive. And because you didn't mention any of that when you had the chance, which makes you look like a liar."

His eyes blacken, but Asker refuses to stand down.

They sit in silence for a few seconds, glaring at each other.

"Thank you for coming," he says eventually. "Now I know what measures I need to take."

He stands up, walks over to the door, and presses the bell. Stands demonstratively with his back to her.

After ten to fifteen seconds the guard reappears and leads him away.

Just before the door closes, Per glances over his shoulder. His cold expression makes Asker's gut turn to ice.

She has seen that expression before.

Knows that it's a sign.

A warning that something bad is about to happen.

HILL

Hill stops again, and this time he is sure of it. There is someone there, out in the fog, just a few feet beyond the flashlight's milky wall of light. Someone who makes his heart rise into his throat.

"Hello?" he says. He can hear himself how scared he sounds.

He walks on up the road, constantly casting glances over his shoulder.

To his right and left, cloaked in darkness and fog, lie only lawns, trees, and flower beds.

Another sound, this one behind him to his right.

"Hello?" he says again.

The rational part of his brain is starting to struggle to make itself heard. It is being drowned out by another, more primal part of him, one that warns him of danger.

How far is it now to Villa Arcturus? He doesn't know, is disoriented yet again. Could he have missed the turnoff, in spite of it all? He hears the sound again, somewhere to his right, now level with him.

Footsteps. He is certain of it.

Someone is moving out there.

He shines the flashlight in that direction, but the fog dazzles him. So he turns off the light.

And suddenly something emerges from the darkness and fog.

Two enormous red eyes with coal-black pupils that stare straight at him.

Terror grips Hill's chest, and he gasps for air.

The surge of adrenaline that follows is so powerful that he almost trips over his own feet. He turns the flashlight back on.

The rational part of his brain has lost control, and suddenly he is a terrified fourteen-year-old running for his life.

The light of his flashlight bounces here and there, his shoes crunch on the gravel, and his mechanical heart valve rattles in his chest. He can taste the adrenaline in his mouth.

He hears his pursuer moving in the darkness. Sees the red eyes approaching from out of the corner of his eye.

Hill ups his pace even more. Surprises even himself with how fast he is, despite his injury and the laptop bag that he is carrying in his hand.

The red glow disappears, as though he is outpacing his pursuer. Instinctively Hill turns his head, only to realize his mistake when his foot suddenly meets air.

The road has rounded a bend, and he has kept going straight ahead.

Straight into a bed of roses.

He trips and lands on his knee, elbow, and head. The sharp rose thorns catch in his clothes, cut at his forehead.

He drops his laptop bag, and his flashlight flies to the ground.

When he rolls over onto his back, his heart is close to stopping. It is as though someone has opened a door inside his skull and unleashed his teenage nightmares.

An enormous creature with glowing red eyes emerges from the mist, coming straight for him.

ASKER

After her meeting with Per, Asker returns to her office down on level minus one. Calls the prosecutor and tells him that she has no intention of being Prepper Per's legal representative, and that her father needs a real public defense.

Per will be charged on Monday, there is no doubt about that. Hellman's investigation has the wind in its sails, and he will have plenty of time to piece together a watertight case against her father.

At least that's what Hellman thinks. Her own feeling is that Per has other plans. Plans that are far more ominous.

The question is what she is going to do now.

Should she follow her mother's advice, stand back and let Hellman and Per slug it out? She helped Hellman by getting Per to hand himself in, which means her career is in no immediate danger. And Per can't reasonably orchestrate any great catastrophes from a detention cell.

So in theory she should be able to sit tight while the two of them destroy each other.

Ironically enough, Per would have done the same, had it concerned anyone but himself.

At the same time, her thoughts keep coming back to what Martin said. That she should think less like Per and more like herself. Follow her instinct. And her instinct is telling her that she can't drop this, not yet. Not until she knows what Per has in store.

Besides, it's not like her to sit on the sidelines.

So, with the botched robbery struck off, what threads does that leave for her to untangle around Korpi and his violent death? The mysterious woman Sundin and Danielsson saw with Korpi is impossible to trace without more information, and she has no way of finding that.

Which leaves only the fact that Korpi, besides the gym, had another employer in the area, where he and his team worked during the day. That employer also paid him with bags full of notes, which means they either had plenty of black money to spend, or they wanted to keep their underground construction off the books.

The only problem is, even if it *was* the unknown employer who she heard Korpi on the phone to when he said he was just an hour away, that's still far too little to go on. She needs something that can point her in the right direction.

But how can she rustle up more leads after sixteen years?

There comes a knock at her door, and Virgilsson unexpectedly pokes his head in. Apparently he works weekends. Or—far more likely—he is here on some private matter that she would rather not know about.

"I heard about your father. So sad. Do let me know if there's anything I can do to help."

"Thanks."

She isn't really sure where she and Virgilsson stand anymore. Although he did help her to procure a firearm with the sole demand that she join his choir in return, she is still a long way from trusting him.

"Just so you know, I've tried calling Attila to see how he's doing. He told me to go to hell, but at least we know he's alive."

"OK," Asker sighs. "Is there anything we should do? Speak to HR, see that he gets some help . . . ?"

The little toad rejects her suggestions outright.

"Oh no, HR won't go near Kent. No one will, especially not after he threw poor Sandgren down the stairs."

"OK, noted. Thanks for the update."

She makes an effort to sound appreciative. Virgilsson has extended an olive branch, and the least she can do is take it.

"No problem, Chief," he nods.

As soon as Virgilsson has shut the door behind him, she puts her feet up on the desk, sinks down a little in her chair, and massages her sore shoulder. She accidentally kicks over a stack of papers, sending the gift that Mail-less Siw knitted for Attila toppling to the ground.

Asker bends over, picks up the package, and sits with it in her hands.

The solution you seek is closer than you think—apparently that was the spirit world's message to her. And the only tool her meeting with

Madame Rind gave is a fucking oven mitt—which isn't even for her, but for Attila.

Something clicks in her head, and she leaps up off the chair.

Attila.

Why the hell didn't she think of him before?

Attila used to work in the reconnaissance unit of the secret police. He told her just weeks ago that for a while the secret police had been interested in Prepper Per and the Farm. That he had spent an entire summer staking them out in the forest while the mosquitos ate him alive.

That could well have been the summer Korpi visited the Farm. If it was, there must be documentation: intelligence memos, photographs, something that could lead her further.

She pulls on her jacket and shoves the gift into her pocket.

It's time to pay Attila a home visit.

HILL

In panic, Hill tries to scramble to his feet. He slips, but in the end he manages to get himself onto his knees, his body tensed. Any second now the creature will launch at him. Plunge its glass claws deep into his back.

Two white beams suddenly pierce the mist, instantly transforming the whole world into dazzling, milky-white light.

Hill instinctively covers his eyes with one arm, then starts waving them both. He doesn't dare look around for the creature, but instead puts all his energy into trying to stagger toward the light.

He hears the screech of brakes and the crunch of tires on gravel, before the car stops less than a foot from his leg.

Hill rests his palms on the hood to regain his balance. Blood is running from his forehead. The car door opens, and someone steps out.

"What happened? Did you get lost in the fog?"

The voice belongs to Maud Irving. She doesn't sound scared, but rather slightly amused. Doesn't appear to see the seven-foot-tall monster that must be heading straight for them.

Hill spins around.

But the creature is gone.

"You have a nick in your forehead that needs seeing to," Maud goes on. "I have some stuff at home—get in and I'll drive you."

She bats away his feeble protests, and before long he is sitting in the living room at Villa Canopus, while she retrieves an unusually well-stocked kit.

"No need to worry," she says. "Before I became CEO of Alpha-Cent, I actually trained to be a doctor. I may be a little rusty, but I'm definitely qualified to patch you up."

She cleans the wound on his forehead before closing it with skin glue and surgical tape. Then she does the same with the nick in his right hand that he had hardly noticed.

"Now, tell me how you managed to face-plant in Ville's rose bed," she says while checking his eyes. "You looked completely insane, with blood dripping down your forehead."

"I . . ."

Hill has collected himself somewhat, but he still hasn't managed to get his head around what he actually experienced. Nor is he sure how much he should say.

"I got disoriented in the fog," he says, throwing in a sheepish smile. Her hands are warm and soft, her touch calming.

"Easily done," she says. "The fog out here really is something. The humidity from the lake gets trapped in the crater when there's no wind, though I'm sure you already know that."

She takes out a digital blood pressure monitor and places it on his wrist. Presses a button to make it inflate.

From this close he catches the scent of her perfume. Her skin is white, almost porcelain against her deep blue eyes.

The monitor beeps, interrupting his thoughts.

"You don't have concussion, but your pulse is still pretty high, and your blood pressure, too."

He wonders if he should tell her that he thought he was being chased by a space monster drawn straight from his childhood nightmares. That the adrenaline is still coursing through his veins because he was running for his life.

"You need a glass of wine," she says before he can decide either way. "Doctor's orders."

She disappears into the kitchen and returns with a bottle and two glasses. Sits back down next to him and pours wine for them both.

Hill takes a big glug.

"Where's Elsa?" he asks.

"At her dad's. I'd just been out to get some food to eat on my lonesome."

"Don't you eat with Karin?"

Maud shakes her head.

"Right now my mother's a little . . ." she searches for the right word, ". . . insular, one might say."

Hill takes another sip. His body is now starting to relax.

"I met her yesterday," he says. "Gave her a lift back from the florist."

He tells her about their encounter and trip to Bernhard's grave. Maud raises her eyebrows.

"Wow! Mom idolized Bernhard. If she took you to the grave, she must really have liked you. Though I suppose you're quite used to women liking you—aren't you, Martin?"

She gives him a teasing smile.

"That tall, broad-shouldered woman you had over the other day was pretty."

"Leo? We're just friends."

Hill doesn't really know why he stresses that fact. True though it is, something about this whole situation draws it out of him: the way Maud touched him, the wine, the endorphins, the dissipating tension.

"Fact is, I have plenty of food for two. If you feel like staying for dinner?"

Hill takes another sip of the wine.

"I'd love to," he says. "If it's not too much trouble."

"Of course not. I'm just happy for the company," she says. "It can get pretty lonely out here."

Hill can't help but glance at the window.

At the darkness and fog pressing against the glass.

They eat dinner together, washed down with more wine. Then move over to the sofa. As Hill already noted, Maud is both funny and whip-smart.

They get onto the topic of Elsa, and Maud talks about the challenges of having a daughter with a visual impairment, but in a light-hearted way.

"Fact is, Elsa's probably more independent than most girls her age. She doesn't see any barriers, only opportunities. A fantastic quality, one I wish I had. Among many other things."

She swirls the wine in her glass.

"If you could redo your life," she asks, "knowing everything you now know, would you do things any differently?"

The question is unexpected and at the same time not: they are onto their second bottle of wine, which usually tends to raise the philosophical bar a little.

"Sure," Hill says. "I'd be better at keeping in touch with people, for one." He thinks of Leo. He hasn't spoken to her since yesterday. On the other hand, she hasn't contacted him either.

"And you?" he asks.

"Plenty of things. I'd have built my own life, for one. And I'd have been more careful with regard to my brother."

"How do you mean?" Hill asks gingerly, but he gets a shake of the head in response.

"A subject for another night," she says. "Right now I'm too busy thinking about the future."

"Will you stay on at AlphaCent?"

Maud tops up their wineglasses again.

"I'm actually not so sure. But AlphaCent is still paying me a salary, and Gunnar certainly doesn't want me going to any rival. He's very guarded with his secrets."

She winks at him over the rim of her glass. Hill is starting to feel slightly tipsy.

"And you haven't given any thought to becoming a doctor again?" he says.

Maud laughs.

"My medical career is behind me. I dropped it as soon as Gunnar came calling. I always have been a good girl. Always tried to please my father. And yet . . ."

She downs the contents of her glass and pours herself another.

Then shifts a little closer to him on the sofa.

"How about we talk about something else?" she says. "I'd love to get my mind off my family for a while. Why don't you tell me something about yourself, Martin?"

Her eyes are soft and enticing.

Her lips, too.

ASKER

Attila's apartment is situated in one of Malmö's grayest districts. The functional sixties architecture that once was the very essence of modernity now feels mostly dark and drab. Asker presses the button on the intercom, but of course she gets no response. She tries another few times, then waits patiently in the dark for another resident to appear.

It takes seven minutes before a man with a beard and stocking cap heads her way with grocery bags in his hands. He fumbles with the code, and she helps him with the door. Throws in what she believes to be her most charming smile. The man looks a little sheepish, but he doesn't question her slipping in behind him.

Attila lives on the top floor. K ATTERBOM is written on his door, along with a sticker for a regional newspaper.

She cautiously peers through the mail slot.

No rotting smell—that's a good start. The doormat is empty, which suggests Attila was home as recently as that morning, otherwise the day's paper would still be lying there. She tries to peer further into the apartment, but all the lights are off. No flicker of a TV, no sound, no nothing.

She rings the doorbell while cupping her hand over the peephole in the door, trying to glimpse the faint changes in light caused by someone moving inside.

Nothing.

She tries again.

And again.

But everything is still.

Either Attila is sitting in silence in the darkness, without the slightest interest in who is ringing his doorbell, or he simply isn't home. Asker curses inwardly.

She goes back down to the street, and by force of habit casts her gaze back over the parked cars. None of them is Attila's black Ford.

So where the fuck is he? He must have someone to spend his Saturday night with. The thought nettles a little; that even someone as antisocial as Attila has someone to spend his Saturday night with, while she has zero plans.

She unlocks her car, thinking she should give Viktor a call. She decides to text him instead: she has already called him once this week, and she doesn't want to seem needy.

She gets into the driver's seat. A glint of light makes her look in her rearview mirror.

A car parked around fifty yards behind her has just started up, at pretty much the same second that she got into the car. As though the driver was waiting for her, was getting ready to pull off behind her.

She sits there, staring in the rearview mirror. The car behind her still doesn't move. Keeping her head low, Asker wriggles into the back seat. Makes sure the ceiling lamp is off before inching open the rear, right-hand door, just enough to get onto the sidewalk.

Bent double, she sneaks toward the car, shielded by the darkness around the other parked cars.

The car stays put, its headlights still on.

She keeps moving toward them, edging closer, one car at a time.

When she is roughly halfway there, she stops again and peers up cautiously through the windows of a parked Volvo.

Just as she makes out the driver's silhouette, the person suddenly moves, the engine revs, and the wheels swerve to one side.

Asker straightens up and starts to sprint.

With a screech of tires the car shoots out of the parking space and does a U-turn.

Asker runs out onto the street. She just manages to catch the first digits of the license plate before the car speeds away from her, its engine howling. The letters CL and a 1, or maybe a 7.

But there is one thing she is completely sure of.

It's the same silvery car that she saw the other night.

THE GLASS MAN

He sits in the rocking chair in her bedroom, as he has done so many times before. Watches her as she sleeps, sees her dream her pleasant dreams, unaware of his presence. Unaware that he is watching over her, as he always has done.

The room smells different from the way it usually does.

The primitive, age-old scents of two people.

Endorphins, sweat, bodily fluids.

Martin Hill is sleeping beside her. He looks calm and relaxed.

His heartbeats are audible in the silence. Not like a muffled pulse; rather, a faintly metallic click. As though his heart was constructed in a different way from others'.

This discovery fascinates him, and for almost a whole hour he sits there quietly in the darkness, listening.

Still, Martin Hill is a Stranger. Someone in a place where he doesn't belong. Who brazenly takes liberties with what isn't his.

This makes him angry.

He rocks slowly on the chair while watching them both sleep.

With every minute that he sits there, steeped in the scents of their coupling, hearing Martin Hill's heartbeats, his wrath grows.

And with that—his hunger.

Perhaps his decision is already made.

His decision to help Martin Hill down into the eternal darkness.

To silence that strange, telltale heart.

Not here. Not in her house.

But soon.

SUNDAY

HILL

He wakes up with a gasp and sits up. For a few seconds he has no idea where he is. Then, slowly, the room's contours emerge from the darkness. The double bed, the vaulted ceiling, the rocking chair in one corner. The clothes lying strewn across the floor. His and hers.

Maud Irving lies asleep beside him, her breaths heavy and even. Hill toys with the idea of sneaking out of bed, pulling on his clothes, and going back to Villa Arcturus. Making a not-so-gentlemanly exit to avoid the obligatory, and certainly awkward, small talk at the breakfast table. But just sneaking off isn't his style, and he doesn't really feel like setting off on another walk in the darkness.

Sleeping with Maud wasn't part of the plan. He intends to blame it on a dangerous cocktail of wine, endorphins, and relief at having survived.

But having survived what?

What actually happened to him earlier that night? Who was following him? Or, rather, what?

He creeps out of bed and finds his way to the bathroom.

His body is a little sore, but now in new places.

After peeing he surveys his face in the bathroom mirror.

The wound on his forehead is nicely dressed.

He had no idea Maud was a trained doctor. Perhaps a way to try to win Gunnar's approval?

I always have been a good girl. Always tried to please my father. And yet . . .

Those two words stick in his head.

And yet . . .

The old Glass Man won't be winning Father of the Year anytime soon, that's for sure.

Fact is, the more Hill learns about Gunnar Irving, the less he likes him. Genius entrepreneurs rarely tend to be sweethearts.

Though of course that impression could change once he has

finally had a chance to meet the man in the flesh. Hear his side of the story.

Hill opens the bathroom cabinet. He doesn't know why, really, or what he hopes to find. But Maud is still something of a mystery to him, and he can't help but snoop, just a little.

The cabinet contains the expected: toothbrushes, perfume, makeup.

But also prescription bottles.

Two different kinds of antidepressants and a bottle of strong sleeping pills, both prescribed by Dr. Schiller.

The discovery pricks at his guilty conscience, so he puts the bottles back and carefully closes the cabinet. In the hall he suddenly thinks of Bernhard's sketchbook.

He was carrying it in the inner pocket of his blazer. What if the book fell out when he landed facedown in the rosebush?

He roots around in his blazer.

Gives a sigh of relief when he finds the sketchbook is still there.

He opens it and surveys the pages in the dim light that seeps in through the hallway window.

In the middle of the book he finds a drawing that makes him stop short. A drawing of a woman lying asleep in a bed.

Her head is half-turned away, her back and one leg sticking out from under the sheets. There is something fragile and intimate about the image.

Freddie, 1951, reads the text beneath the drawing.

Hill scours his memory. Bernhard's wife and Gunnar's mother's name was Alma, and she died in 1947.

So who is this Freddie? A passing flame, a colleague, a lover?

That gives him something to get his teeth into for the next day's research, at least.

He puts the sketchbook back in his blazer pocket and returns to the bedroom. Maud is still asleep.

Hill stands in the doorway for a few seconds, watching her. In the faint light she almost reminds him of the woman in the drawing: the leg sticking out from under the sheet; the soft curve of her hips; the hair splayed out over the pillow.

The thought is almost staggering: over seventy years ago, and certainly not far from here, Bernhard Irving took pencil to paper and drew a sketch of a woman he was clearly fond of. A moment that meant something to him; one he wanted to preserve.

And here he stands, experiencing almost the same thing.

Freddie.

He must find out who she is.

ASKER

At five, she is already up. Downs a cup of coffee before getting started on her first task of the morning.

Ever since she spotted the silvery car outside Viktor's house, she has kept her eyes open. And she hadn't seen so much as a trace of anyone trailing her until last night.

So how did he find her? How did he follow her to Attila's place without her noticing?

There is only one answer to that question.

She walks downstairs to the spacious garage beneath the house.

Plugs in a work light, pulls on an old pair of overalls, and shoves a cap on to contain her hair. Lies down on her back, turns on the light, and slides under the car. Once there, she methodically works her way around the car's undercarriage.

It doesn't take her many minutes to find what she is looking for.

A small, flat object affixed with a magnet—not under one of the mudguards, like an amateur would do, but on the car's back wheel, where it is much harder to detect.

She twists and turns the object, examines it carefully under the work light.

A tracker.

At first glance it appears to be one of the kinds that can be ordered online. But the screws are slightly worn, as though someone has opened the casing.

She takes the tracker over to the workbench by the wall and finds the right size screwdriver.

When she lifts the casing, she finds that someone has made changes to the tracker itself. Has re-soldered a couple of cables, switched to a more reliable battery.

It has been many years since she has seen anything like it, yet she recognizes the handiwork and the intent behind it all the same.

The person who made these changes leaves nothing to chance. He wanted to be certain that the tracker not only worked, but worked *better*.

She herself was taught to make exactly the same kinds of modifications. Would sit with magnifying glasses and a soldering iron for whole nights through, until she could complete the task in her sleep.

In another time; another life.

In the workshop on the Farm.

HILL

Breakfast with Maud isn't at all as awkward as Hill had feared. Without either one of them saying it in so many words, they both seem to agree that the previous night was just a one-time thing. That aside, Villa Canopus is much more beautiful in daylight.

"Where did you live in the manor house, before you moved here?"

"In the west wing. As I'm sure you've noticed, the house is enormous. Gunnar had his own floor up top, and we lived below him."

"His own floor?"

She nods.

"We were almost never allowed up there. He'd come down to see us when he wanted a taste of family life, which wasn't all that often. Gunnar is a very private person."

Maud sips some of her coffee and gestures ironically at the tasteful kitchen.

"Mom called the move to this humble abode the Great Banishment."

"And Canopus was your sanctuary after the Fall," Hill adds.

"Exactly," Maud replies. "I see Mom's already told you the story."

"Yes, and her choice of words stuck with me. What did she believe caused this 'Fall'? It rings almost like original sin."

She shrugs.

"No idea. Like I said, Mom's pretty eccentric."

Hill thinks of the sketchbook.

"What about Bernhard, what do you remember of him?"

Her face lights up.

"Grandpa Bernhard was so kind. And Mom loved him. She looked after him like he was her own father."

Hill nods. "At his grave Karin said something about Gunnar and Bernhard not getting along. That Gunnar hated his father."

Maud pulls a face.

"Grandpa Bernhard took our side in the divorce. He and Gunnar fell out badly in the process. But *hated* is a pretty strong word."

Hill wonders whether to come out and ask Maud if she knows who Freddie is. But if he does that, he will also have to explain how he came to be in possession of Bernhard's sketchbook, and where he found it. Tell her about the drawing on his desk that led him to the secret chamber.

"I read in a book that there are supposed to be old mine tunnels under all of Astroholm," he says instead.

"Oh, you did?" She raises her eyebrows teasingly. "And here I was thinking you were only looking for an underground burial chamber with poor Bernhard lying in a glass coffin."

Hill almost chokes on his coffee.

"I read your book," she smirks. "No wonder you were so keen to come here. Sorry to disappoint, but I've never heard mention of any secret burial chamber. Besides, Mom's already shown you Bernhard's grave, so that mystery can probably be marked as solved, no?"

Hill wipes the coffee from the corners of his mouth with the back of his hand.

"And the only underground system I'm aware of is the district heating network," she adds. "But I suspect that's hardly what you're after?"

"No," he says with an exaggerated sigh. "I guess I'll just have to make do with the UFO."

She chuckles. Hill does, too. He likes her laughter.

"I've already told you I was fascinated by that story ever since I was a teenager. But what do you make of it? Did Gunnar really see a UFO?"

Maud shakes her head.

"I mean, when my brother and I were kids, Gunnar would sometimes tell us the story. About the spaceship that came swooping in, and the creature with the red eyes that gave him all these ideas. Back then we believed it all, hook, line, and sinker."

"And now, as adults?"

She grimaces to herself.

"As an adult I've learned that what Gunnar says is always right. Even when it isn't."

"Which means?"

"Which means you should probably be thinking less about urban legends and focusing more on the kinds of things that will make the company seem as serious and as grounded as possible. I mean, that's what Nova's paying you to do, isn't it? And believe you me, you *don't* want to disappoint her."

"How do you mean?"

Maud suddenly turns serious.

"Nova's Gunnar's favorite. She gets everything she wants . . ." Maud checks herself, shakes her head. "Forget I said that," she mutters. "Sibling bickering, that's all."

Hill puts on what he believes to be a sympathetic face.

"Speaking of siblings," he says once enough seconds have passed. "Your older brother Viggo lived here in Villa Canopus, too, didn't he?"

"Yes."

She looks away, as though the subject is a touchy one, but Hill has far too many questions to concede so easily.

"I read an old newspaper article about his accident," he goes on. "That he drove into the lake the same night the meteorite passed. And the passenger—"

"Was my boyfriend, yes," she says. "A horrific night, as I'm sure you can appreciate. I lost both Pontus and my brother."

"But Viggo survived, didn't he?"

"Yes, he survived. Or a version of him, you could say." She shakes her head. "I know you're only doing your job, Martin, but I don't want to talk about this anymore. Viggo's accident has nothing to do with AlphaCent."

Hill nods. But he has one question left.

"Where is Viggo these days?" he asks.

"Abroad." The response comes quickly, almost before the question has passed his lips. "In a place where he can get the best possible care," she adds, while getting to her feet and starting to clear the table.

Hill has heard this same response almost to the letter from both Mrs. Schiller and Nova Irving, said in almost exactly the same tone of voice. It's why he asked. It is as though the response is rehearsed. Part of a script.

"Now, if you'll excuse me, I have a few things to do," Maud says with a suggestive nod at the door.

"Of course. I have a book to write, myself."

She walks him to the door. Kisses him on the cheek.

When he steps outside, he sees that the wind and the pale November sun have dried out the mist, at least for now. But even in the daylight he still can't help but shudder. He is none the wiser about what happened to him last night. Could he have imagined it all?

Slowly he starts walking up to Villa Arcturus. When he reaches the small slope where the rose bed lies, he stops short. He sees his footprints in the soil, and a depression from what he guesses was his knee. The rose stems are long and full of thorns: he's lucky he got away with just a scratch to his forehead and a nick to his hand. He could easily have lost an eye.

He walks around to the other side of the bed and examines the soft ground. Around fifteen feet from the roses he finds a big footprint. He kneels down to take a closer look.

The impression is from a thick sole, with a tread that reminds him of a tractor tire. He compares it to his own shoe. The impression is much larger than his own size tens, and it is far too big to belong to Groundskeeper Ville.

So what happened the night before wasn't in his mind. Not that he had exactly believed that theory.

Someone was chasing him through the fog. A giant with glowing red eyes and heavy boots. What would have happened to him if Maud hadn't turned up?

Hill shudders again, then sets off at a stride as fast as his legs can carry him.

Back in Villa Arcturus he takes a shower and changes clothes. He is a little ashamed of himself for cross-examining Maud, but Astroholm is brimming with secrets, and if he doesn't ask questions, then he will never get any answers.

And right now the questions are only growing in number. The mysterious deaths, Viggo, who seems to have vanished off the face of the earth, and the mining tunnels under the estate. Not to mention the mysterious letter-writer who led him to the sketchbook.

Now that he has showered and changed, he sits down in Bernhard's worn armchair and pulls out his sketchbook again.

He can only leaf through a few pages before his cellphone starts to ring. Nova Irving's number.

"Hello, Martin," she says in an exaggeratedly chirpy tone of voice. "Are you very busy today?"

"No, why?"

"We thought we'd take you on a little outing to Boulder Isle. In an hour, if that's convenient?"

"Sure," Hill says in surprise.

"Great, see you soon. And wrap up warm, it can get pretty chilly out there."

The call ends, and Hill is left sitting there with the phone in his hand.

An outing to Boulder Isle.

Finally!

HELLMAN

The kids have just eaten the pancakes he made for their Sunday breakfast and taken their iPads over to the den. Lina, his wife, will be in bed for another half hour or so since it's her turn for a lie-in, and he intends to spend that time flicking through the newspaper while sipping his morning coffee.

The phone interrupts his plans. It's the police switchboard.

"Jonas Hellman," he answers.

"Hello, this is the duty manager at the detention center. I just wanted to let you know that we've just transferred Per Asker to the hospital. It was looking touch and go there for a little while."

Hellman slams his coffee down on the table.

"Wait, what did you say?"

"Well, Asker was taken ill overnight. His skin was pale, his pulse uneven, and he was complaining of chest pains. We contacted the on-call doctor, and he thought it was a heart attack. We had no choice but to call an ambulance."

"OK." Hellman makes for the bedroom. "And there's no way Asker could have been putting it on?"

A short pause, as though the man on the end of the line is trying to convey by his silence just how stupid the question is.

"Look, we do get the odd faker, but this was for real. The doctor was very concerned, and Asker was pale as a ghost and half-conscious by the time the ambulance arrived. But since he's likely to be charged soon, we didn't want to take any chances. I sent a supervisor and two guards with him."

Hellman has already ripped off his dressing gown and thrown it on the bed.

"How long ago was this?" he asks.

"Around half an hour—I had to call in new staff to fill the gaps in our schedule first. But I thought you'd want to know, since it's your case and all . . ."

"OK, thanks."

Hellman asks the duty manager to send him the phone number of the supervisor who accompanied Asker to the hospital, then ends the call and tears off his pajamas.

"Was that work?" his wife mumbles from bed. "Don't they know it's a Sunday?"

Hellman doesn't reply, simply throws his clothes on as quickly as he can. A sneaking suspicion has started to spread through his gut.

A nasty feeling that the shit is about to hit the fan.

ASKER

She spends the drive to Attila's apartment pondering the tracker. She picked up the rental car on Friday, which means the tracker can only have been there for a few days, max.

She is pretty sure the tracker must have been fitted when she left it parked on the streets around police HQ. Her tail must have known that sooner or later she would turn up at her workplace, and that's how they managed to identify her new car. Getting the tracker in place takes only a few seconds for someone who knows what they are doing. And the tracker is the exact same kind that Per used to make at the Farm, so one way or another it all comes back to him. But Per is locked up in custody, which means he must have an accomplice. Someone who has been keeping an eye on her, making sure she is doing what he asked. That she is being a good girl.

The thought makes her furious, and she skids into the parking spot outside Attila's building.

An old lady with a small dog is so intimidated by Asker's aggressive parking that she holds the door open for her without her even having to ask. Seconds later she is ringing Attila's doorbell nonstop. The newspaper is gone from the doormat again, so she knows that he is at home.

Still, he doesn't open.

So she goes on to pounding, then to shouting through the mail slot.

"It's Leo Asker. Open the door, Attila, I know you're there!"

Still no response.

"If you don't open up, I'm calling a locksmith," she cries. "I'll tell them I think you're dead in there, so they'll have to unbolt the door. A nice Sunday show for the neighbors."

She stops talking, listens.

Hears something that could resemble a heavy sigh. After that, the sound of footsteps.

She shuts the mail slot and takes a step back. The door opens a crack, with the security chain on. Attila is dressed in an undershirt and pants pulled at least five inches too high. He is barefoot and unshaven, his eyes bloodshot, his expression angry.

Very angry.

"What the fuck do you want, Asker?"

"Here!" She shoves the parcel with the oven mitt through the crack in the door. "From Siw, Madame Rind's friend. She's worried about you."

He raises his eyebrows, and after a second's hesitation he takes the parcel. His face softens a little.

"Look, I don't need your fucking help, OK?"

"Good!" she says with a shrug. "Since I'm not here to help you. But *you* are going to help me. Open the door and let me in, and I'll explain what it's about."

Attila glares at her angrily, but Asker is not in the habit of losing staring contests—with him or anybody else.

He slams the door with a bang.

All is silent for a few seconds.

After that, the security chain rattles and the door opens again.

"Come in," he mutters.

Attila's apartment is like stepping straight into the seventies: dark wood furnishings, heavy wallpapers, even beaded curtains. Not one speck of dust to be seen. A faint, almost sweet scent of boozy nights and hungover mornings hangs between the rooms.

On the coffee table in the living room stand a few half-empty liquor bottles and a single glass. He doesn't offer her any coffee, simply points at one of the armchairs. Asker takes a seat, looking around her as she does. The walls are full of photographs, most of which are of a young Attila, in groups and on his own, more often than not in some kind of uniform.

In the biggest photo he has his arm around an elderly woman with the same angular chin as his.

"Your mother," Asker says with a nod.

"Mm," he mutters. "So what's this help you need?"

She turns to look at him.

"You told me you were gathering intel on the Farm one summer when I was around fourteen. Could that have been 2006?"

He stares at her for a few seconds, then appears to think for a while.

"Could be," he says. "Why?"

She explains as concisely as possible her reason for being there.

Attila listens without asking any questions.

"So what I want to know from you," she sums up, "is if you and your friends in the secret police came across Tord Korpi, and if you did, if you saw anything else that might help me?"

Attila sits in silence for a few seconds.

"Are you really sure you want to help your father?" he eventually asks. "Wouldn't it be better to just let him sink in his own swamp?"

Asker bites her lip.

"I can't," she replies.

Attila studies her in silence for another few seconds.

Then he nods.

"I understand. Give me a minute."

He leaves the room, and Asker stands up and takes a closer look at the photographs. She finds one where Attila actually isn't in uniform. In it, he is standing with a young woman in a student's cap. In true graduation tradition, she is holding a poster collage with a picture of herself as a child.

It must be the niece Virgilsson mentioned. The one who died all too young, and whose boyfriend mysteriously disappeared. The reason for Attila's sad, one-man blowout.

Attila returns to the room carrying a cardboard box. He appears to have splashed some water on his face while he was gone.

He casts a glance at Asker and then at the photograph, but says nothing. Asker walks quietly back to her armchair.

"I know there were people coming and going around the Farm, but I'm afraid I don't remember all the details. It was quite a long time ago, after all. But I still have my notes."

He shoves the liquor bottles aside and sets the box down on the table.

"Now, let's see." Attila puts on a pair of reading glasses and opens the lid.

The box is filled with black notebooks, with small tabs to indicate the year.

Asker raises her eyebrows.

"Shouldn't you have handed those in when you transferred?" she asks.

He looks at her over the rims of his glasses.

"Of course I should. But my bosses were in such a hurry to see the back of me they overlooked standard procedure. I saw no reason to remind them—which I guess is lucky for you."

He turns back to the box.

"2006 . . ." Attila fishes out two books and starts to flick through them. "Oh yes, that's right, here it is. *Reconnaissance Mission: the Farm.*"

Asker tries to contain herself. This is her best lead—her *only* lead. It has to give her something if she is to have any chance of progressing with the case.

"And here we have Tord Korpi." Attila puts down the book and runs his hand over the well-thumbed pages. "The first time we meet him is June 27. I've noted his license number."

Asker feels her pulse start to rise. A license number is a good start. Something to unpack a little further.

Attila leafs through a few more pages, humming slightly to himself.

"Korpi appears to come and go. Sometimes he stayed with you for a few nights, like you said. Here, look." He points at a line in the book. "*TK speaks to LA in the gym.*"

She is about to ask who LA is, but stops herself.

Leonore Asker.

Her teenage self, scrawled as an entry in a notebook. It's almost like meeting a ghost.

Attila flicks on through the pages.

"OK, so our good friend TK seems to come and go. I've made a note about a gym in Hörby, so at some point either I or one of my colleagues must have tailed him there."

"Freedom Gym." Asker nods. "Is there anything else? Anyone else Korpi met?"

Attila flicks on.

"Here's a note about an MH who visits the Farm, but I can't find the full name," he says. I have the impression it was a young kid."

"Martin Hill," she quickly adds. "He has nothing to do with this case."

"OK." Attila gives her a glance before moving on. "I mean, Korpi wasn't our main target, so . . . Wait, here's something."

He taps one page.

"Korpi shows up in the middle of August. Clearly we decided to tail him again."

"And where did he go?" she asks impatiently.

"I might actually remember this . . ." Attila mumbles while turning the pages. "Yes, here's the name. That's right, I do remember it, now that I read the notes. Strange how memory works."

"Where did he go?" Asker repeats.

"To an estate called Astroholm Manor, about an hour's drive from the Farm."

THE GLASS MAN

In his years in America he managed to contain himself. Suppressed every forbidden thought, every wish, every desire. Locked and bolted them away behind a door deep in his mind.

With time it grew easier, perhaps because he was living his own life, far from that watchful eye.

In America he was an exemplary student, he won internships and forged contacts. Did everything the Father had wanted him to do and more. Played the perfect son.

A real Irving.

And finally, after years of silent, patient endeavor, he was rewarded. He was summoned back to Astroholm.

January 6. Old Christmas, as the Father called it. But also the Festival of the Magi—the astrologers—and of the Epiphany. The symbolism was clear: Prince Pollux had returned from his time in the wilderness. The prodigal son who had followed the star all the way back to his father's household.

All of them gathered for dinner. The Father, his new wife and daughter.

Nova. The new.

The rest of his family were also present. His mother, who by this point lived largely in her own world. His sister, who, unlike him, had been allowed to remain on the periphery of the Father's orbit.

Who maybe, just maybe, had bought herself that honor through treachery.

He could have forgiven her that lapse were it not for the man she had with her.

Pontus.

He was tall and blond, not too unlike himself. Worked for the company. Called the Father Gunnar, as though they were old friends.

A Stranger who had infiltrated his family. Who had brazenly taken his own seat at the table.

And yet he said nothing. Behaved, waiting patiently for the moment when the Father would make his announcement. Declare that he was once again Prince Pollux, the special one, the one who would change the world.

Who would with time become the head of the Irving family.

But dinner came and went without a word on the matter.

The Father was pleasant and charming. He discussed the firm with Maud and Pontus, looked upon Nova with pride.

But upon him he hardly deigned to throw a glance.

After dessert the Father called him into the smoking room. Asked him to take a seat in one of the old armchairs that Grandpa Bernhard had designed, while he lit a cigar.

His heart was pounding. Finally it was time.

The announcement. The reunion. The epiphany.

"You will behave, won't you?" the Father asked.

He swallowed, nodded, and waited for him to go on.

The Father took a deep puff on the cigar and turned to the fire.

"Good," he said. "After all, you can't help who you are. Whatever's broken inside you. The fault isn't yours, but your genes."

The Father flicked his hand in his direction, without even looking his way.

"You can go now, Viggo."

And in that moment it was as though the final floodgate burst.

His last little shred of humanity was flushed away, killing him hours before the cold, black waters ever did.

HILL

At nine a.m. on the dot Hill's doorbell rings. Nova Irving is standing outside, dressed in cargo pants and a black shell jacket. On her head she wears a baseball cap with the AlphaCent logo.

"Oh, what happened to you?" she asks, pointing at the dressings on Hill's forehead.

"I stumbled on the road back here last night," he says. "Still a little clumsy."

"Ouch. Do you think your leg's up to a little urban exploration?" she asks.

"Definitely," Hill replies eagerly.

It is like he has been on tenterhooks ever since her phone call earlier this morning. He hasn't been able to concentrate on the sketchbook, or even give much thought to the previous day's drama.

Nova drives them down to the manor house in a golf cart. Makes chitchat about his successful treatment, stresses once again that AlphaCent is at the cutting edge in cryotherapies.

She opens the wrought-iron gate with a key, just like Karin Irving did a few days before, and drives straight into the restricted zone. Clearly Nova can go wherever she likes.

She veers right and drives them all the way down to the boathouse, where Hill glimpsed the man in the coat the previous evening.

With hindsight he is pretty sure it was indeed Gunnar Irving he saw. But what would he be doing out here in the darkness and fog?

A boat is moored at the jetty, and Samuel is waiting beside it. He, too, is dressed in black shell clothes, which make him look like a soldier.

Hill hasn't fully gotten over the security chief's threatening demeanor at their last encounter, but he does his best not to let on.

Samuel gives Hill a polite nod in greeting and hands them each a life jacket.

"What do you say, Martin?" Nova asks. "Shall we get going?"

Hill tries to contain his excitement, but it's not easy. Boulder Isle awaits them, just a few hundred yards away.

They hop aboard while Samuel loosens the moorings. The boat isn't particularly big, but it does look very modern, full of angular edges. In the glass wheelhouse there is enough space for four.

Once Samuel has jumped aboard, Nova pulls the throttle.

The boat glides almost soundlessly from the jetty, and the water shimmers blackly beneath the overcast sky.

Hill lowers himself onto one of the seats, but Nova stays by the wheel.

"So, Martin, how's your first week been?" she asks once they are a little way from the jetty.

"Interesting," he replies.

"Interesting?" Nova gives Samuel an amused look. "How so? Have you made any exciting discoveries?"

Hill is thrown by the question.

Does she know that he has found the hidden door, secret chamber, and sketchbook, and wants to see if he plans to tell her? Like some kind of test?

Nova appears to tire of waiting for his response.

"I hear you've seen Maud again."

A statement, not a question.

Hill is once again at a loss for words. How can Nova know that? He fiddles uncertainly with the phone in his jacket pocket.

Nova pulls the throttle even more, making the bow of the boat rise out of the water.

"Don't get me wrong," she says without turning her head. "Maud's very attractive and nice to be around. But she's just been through a difficult time. The divorce, her job . . ." She doesn't finish the sentence.

"Besides, it's not easy having a visually impaired child," Samuel adds.

Hill studies them more closely. There is plenty of space in the wheelhouse, and three empty seats. Yet both of them stay standing, almost a foot closer to each other than the space requires. There is also something strange about their energy. They seem keyed up, raring to go. Like teenagers on an outing.

"So, here we are!"

Nova reduces the speed, and the bow sinks back into the water. The boat glides on toward an old concrete jetty with a dented sign that reads PRIVATE LAND, NO TRESPASSING.

Hill can hear his heart valve click excitedly.

He has dreamed of this moment for more than fifteen years.

And now he is finally here.

On Boulder Isle.

Once they have disembarked, Hill stops on the jetty and tries to take in his surroundings.

The air is raw and damp, carrying with it the scents of lake and spruce. The concrete jetty is cracked, unleashing tendrils of rusty reinforcing steel.

"Welcome to Boulder Isle, Martin! We'll go this way."

Nova takes the lead, and Hill follows her. Samuel hovers a few feet behind.

A rickety hut is perched just between the end of the jetty and the edge of the forest.

"This way," Nova says. "That's where the old mining road begins."

She points at a spruce that someone has marked with a white line around the trunk. Beside it, two wheel tracks carve their way through the dense woodland.

They follow the old road. Above them the treetops lean in toward one another, concealing most of the sky. All around them on the ground, rhyolite boulders peer out from moss cover and thickets.

"Boulder Isle sure lives up to its name, huh?" says Nova.

Hill nods. "Do you come here often?"

"My dad brought me here a few times when I was a kid. When I got older and learned to drive a boat I'd sometimes come here alone when I needed to think."

"A sacred place?"

"Yeah, maybe," she chuckles.

"Do your siblings feel the same way?"

Nova takes a few long strides away, as if evading the subject.

One of Hill's bootlaces has come undone, and he puts his foot up on a big rhyolite block on the side of the road and starts fiddling with the laces.

Just as he is about to straighten up, he spots a carving on the surface of the boulder, half-hidden behind a fern.

GUS

He knows what that acronym stands for: *Göinge UFO Society.* Tom and Krystal mentioned that they had made it to the island many years ago, and here is the proof.

But below that inscription there is another.

Newer lettering, in a different, more sprawling style.

URBEX 2019

Hill has seen the abbreviation carved or tagged a number of times in abandoned buildings. He doesn't really like it: vandalizing sites is against the urban explorers' code.

But this time the inscription has real significance.

It must have been Nick and Elis who carved it, which means they made it to the island, just as the UFO couple claimed.

The thought is both thrilling and disturbing.

So the accident must have happened on their way back to the mainland.

Nova is some way ahead by now, but Samuel has stopped next to Hill.

"What are you doing?" he asks.

"Just tying up my shoelaces," Hill lies, returning his foot to the ground. "I've never seen rhyolite this close before. Fascinating."

"We have to go," Samuel says with a glance at his watch.

He waves impatiently at Hill to follow.

"OK?"

Hill is expecting some kind of explanation as to why they are in such a hurry, but when none is forthcoming, he follows Samuel's lead.

Nova is waiting for them up ahead.

"Not far now," she says. "How's the leg?"

"Surprisingly good," Hill replies.

"Great." She points up the road. "Then let's go on."

"A cheeky question," Hill says once they have walked a little farther. "If I may, that is?"

"Shoot!"

"Do you really believe Gunnar saw a UFO and spoke to aliens?"

Nova doesn't reply, so he decides to press further.

"The reason I ask is because I've noticed the story changes over the years. Certain details have been added, while others have dropped away. The creature he meets gets scarier the more time that passes. Yet the alien is helpful, which doesn't really fit . . ."

Hill stops abruptly. Nova still hasn't replied, and he thinks he can feel Samuel's eyes burning into the back of his head.

"I think . . ." says Nova, ". . . that Gunnar is one of the great geniuses of our time. That he has faculties most people can only dream of. But I think you'll get answers to your questions sooner than you think."

"There it is," says Samuel, interrupting their conversation.

A large metal gate with the text ASTROFIELD MINE arching over it suddenly appears out of the forest. Both sides of the gate are open.

Hill gulps a few times. Suddenly his mouth is parched, and his pulse has started to pound in his eardrums.

Nova leads them through the gate, past thickets and mature birches, into a cracked asphalt yard. To their right stands a tall factory building, and to their left a squat row of workshops, but Hill hardly sees them.

On the far side of the yard the mine's headframe towers up before them. And, behind the railing on its roof, someone is staring down at them.

A tall man in a dark coat and a wide-brimmed hat.

"Surprise!" Nova says excitedly. "Gunnar wants to meet you!"

HELLMAN

When he is less than a mile from the hospital, his phone rings again. It's the supervisor from the detention center who was sent with Asker to the hospital, the one he spoke to just minutes ago.

"Look, the fire alarm just went off," he says. "They're saying we have to evacuate."

Hellman's blood runs cold.

"No, not a chance!" he says. "Where's Per Asker now?"

"In a consulting room with the doctor."

"Make sure he doesn't move till I get there. You can meet me outside."

When Hellman screeches to a halt outside the ER, the place is a hive of activity. An alarm is blaring, and a couple of security guards are trying to conduct the evacuation. Hellman hangs his police ID from a lanyard around his neck and starts making his way to the entrance. On his way there he meets a man in the prison service uniform.

"Take me straight to him!" Hellman commands.

They fight their way through the stream of people exiting the building. A security guard tries to stop them, but he steps aside when Hellman shows him his police badge.

In the waiting room the alarm is still shrieking.

"We have to evacuate, too," the supervisor says anxiously.

He points at some hospital employees who are busy rolling out hospital beds.

"Just take me to Asker," Hellman hisses. His stomach has hardened to a tough knot.

The supervisor opens a door and leads Hellman into a corridor. The doors are open, and the staff are evacuating the patients. But one of the doors is still closed. Outside it stand two stout men in the prison service uniforms.

"Is he in there?" Hellman asks, pointing at the door.

"Yes, but the doctor went in just before the alarm went off," one of the men says. "We can't go in there while he's being examined. It's an invasion of his privacy; we'll get reported on the spot."

Hellman takes a deep breath.

"How long have they been in there?"

The guards exchange glances.

"Five, six minutes maybe. But we've double-checked. The window can't be opened without tools, and we're too high up to jump. Besides, like I said, the doctor's in there."

"Could you describe the doctor?"

The guards shrug almost simultaneously.

"A woman," one of them says. "Pretty tall. White coat . . ."

"Move!" he says to the men.

"But we can't . . ."

"Move!"

The guards look at each other, then step to one side.

Hellman rattles the door handle. It's locked.

The knot in his belly turns to a lump of ice.

"Get this door open!"

One of the guards stops a passing orderly.

"Open the door," Hellman commands, pointing at the lock.

The orderly fumbles with a bunch of keys and eventually opens the door.

The consulting room is empty, and the window is ajar. A rope is tied to the radiator below it.

"Shit!"

Hellman runs over to the window.

The rope is fastened to a lightweight rope ladder that is dangling down the side of the building. The ladder ends on a lower roof, and at its base lie some detention clothes and a doctor's coat. One of the guards also sticks his head through the window.

"Fuck," he cries. "He's escaped!"

He and both of his colleagues race off down the corridor.

As they do, the alarm stops ringing.

Hellman stands there by the window. For a brief moment his vision blurs. Then he collects himself and pulls out his phone.

Eskil picks up after two rings, almost as though he was expecting the call.

"Per Asker's escaped from hospital. He had a female accomplice. Find out where Leo Asker is. Right now!"

HILL

Hill slowly climbs the grated staircase that winds around the headframe, stopping at every platform to catch his breath. His bad wheeze reminds him of his teenage years, when his defective heart turned the slightest exertion into an ordeal.

The steps appear to have been refreshed and repaired fairly recently. Some sections of railing and some of the treads look new, and there is a big welding seam between two of the sections.

His heart is pounding hard, from both exertion and excitement. Finally, he is here. In the place he has been dreaming about ever since he was a child.

And to cap it all off, he is about to meet the mysterious Space-Case Gunnar Irving himself.

"Dear Martin!" Gunnar says once Hill has reached the roof. "Welcome to Boulder Isle, and to Astrofield Mine."

He shakes Hill's hand as though they were old friends.

"Thanks," Hill manages to get out.

"So, what do you think? Isn't the view magnificent?"

Gunnar Irving stretches out his other hand toward the lake.

Hill can only agree. From here it is clear that they are at the bottom of a crater, surrounded first by the black waters of Miresjön Lake, and then the tree-lined hills that enwrap the lake on all sides, guiding the gaze upward, to the sky.

Yet that's not where Hill's eyes are drawn, but to Gunnar Irving himself.

He recognizes every one of his features from the images in the newspaper articles that he has trolled: the high forehead, pointy nose, and pronounced chin. Meeting Gunnar in the flesh feels both familiar and unreal.

"You must call me Gunnar, of course," he says.

Hill nods mutely. He isn't used to feeling starstruck.

Gunnar Irving doesn't look anywhere near his almost eighty

years of age. His movements are free and brisk, his gaze piercing and intense.

"My daughter speaks very highly of you, Martin."

For a brief moment Hill thinks Gunnar means Maud, but he corrects that impression when the man gestures at the ground below, where Nova and Samuel stand waiting for them.

"She told me you wanted to change the direction of the book and call it *The Glass Man*. I should very much like to hear your plans."

Gunnar nods encouragingly.

"Uh . . ." Hill searches for the right words. "Well, my main thought was that AlphaCent's story is in fact your story. It all begins with you—how you used the very proof of Bernhard's failure, the volcanic glass, to create something new. Transformed something worthless into something valuable."

Gunnar smiles with satisfaction.

"I do like that description, Martin. And it also happens to be one hundred percent true. See that field, there?"

He points back down at the ground, this time at a plot diagonally below the headframe, beyond the asphalt. A large field of sharp, black stones is visible through the dead grass.

"That's the remains of a pile of obsidian that Bernhard had dumped on the ground, because he thought it was precisely that: worthless."

He smiles at Hill. Gunnar's presence is so strong it practically radiates from him.

"Come now, Martin, let's take a look at the observatory! I hear you've waited years to see it, no?"

He gestures at Hill to follow him toward an open door.

Inside it the room smells of damp and tar. The observatory walls are made of concrete, the dome itself made of wood painted black. The floor is empty, as are the shelves that line the walls.

"I'm afraid there's not much to see here," says Gunnar. "The observatory has been blind for many years. The telescope was removed, and the roof hatch for the lens can't be opened anymore."

"Yes, I saw the telescope upstairs in Villa Arcturus," says Hill. "How did it end up there?"

Gunnar shrugs.

"Arcturus was my father's home. The telescope was his."

The words are said in a throwaway fashion, as though the subject were of little interest to him.

"Is it all right if I take photos?"

"Certainly."

Hill takes out his cellphone. As expected, he has no signal. His hands tremble slightly as he snaps a few shots, and, to be on the safe side, a short film clip, too.

"Nova mentioned that you didn't want the book to focus on the UFO encounter," he says once he is done. "That may be difficult, since it's there that your story as a company leader begins in earnest. Or, I suppose I should say, here."

He points up at the dome.

Gunnar studies him for a few seconds, then turns and walks back out to the roof of the tower.

Hill follows him.

Gunnar stands by the railing, gazing out over the lake.

"Gunnar the Space Case," he says. "That's how I've been known to the world ever since the sixties. To begin with I couldn't care less. I suppose I thought the name would fade as the company flourished."

He gives a gentle shake of the head.

"But instead it stuck. Regardless of the fantastic inventions and advances we made, to the media I remained Space-Case Gunnar Irving. They would weave references to space, aliens, and science fiction into every single report."

Another shake of the head.

"In the nineties we were trailblazers in DNA analysis. This represented a great leap forward for humanity, and a fantastic team effort from many gifted scientists. Yet several different reporters asked if I'd gotten that idea from aliens, too. Made a mockery of our discoveries."

Gunnar sighs.

"However much I've tried, the UFO narrative has haunted me. It has always carried with it a hint of mockery or ridicule. And it's all my own fault."

Hill nods, though in fact he has no idea what Gunnar is referring to.

"You see, Martin," he says in a quieter tone of voice, "my father was on his way to dragging the company to rock bottom. He had lost grip of reality completely. All he cared about was this mine and his madcap theories about space and meteorites. Even when they were digging up the obsidian by the buckets, he refused to give in."

He falls silent, his gaze apparently tracing a bird's flight over the lake.

"I was only twenty-three, studying medicine," he goes on.

"But I had an idea after I cut myself on a shard of obsidian out here. The incision was so incredibly fine, so clean that I hardly felt any pain. It made me start to wonder if that worthless glass could actually serve a purpose in medicine. But I needed money to develop it.

"Bernhard wasn't interested. He refused to listen to anyone, least of all me. And then the accident happened. Artur and the other two men died. I realized the end was near. So I did what was necessary to save both the company and my family."

Gunnar gestures up at the sky.

"I created a tool that saved us. A narrative, or, perhaps more accurately, a legend."

Hill's brain seizes up for a few seconds.

"You . . ." He tries to get the pieces of the puzzle to fit. "You made up a UFO encounter to get Bernhard to hand over responsibility to you. To give you the chance to develop your inventions."

Gunnar nods.

"I had no choice. Without the story, the Irving family would have gone under."

Hill tries to digest what Gunnar has just told him.

As with all similar narratives about alien encounters, he has always had the impression that at least Gunnar himself believed what he was saying. That his experience was at least real for him.

And now he reveals, without batting an eyelid, that it was all sheer fiction.

"And you want me to put that in the book?" he asks dubiously.

"No, of course not. Quite the contrary, I want us to put as little focus on that particular chapter of the company's history as possible. Because a new and exciting time is just around the corner."

Gunnar's face lights up.

"You see, in the near future AlphaCent will make yet another breakthrough, this time within the field of cryonics. A momentous discovery . . ."

He studies Hill for a few seconds.

"Perhaps you're aware of how cryonics works? You see, when you freeze tissue to minus three hundred and twenty degrees Fahrenheit, all chemical processes come to a halt. No life exists anymore. Nor time, for that matter. Everything stands still."

Hill's brain is still stuck on the fact that the UFO story was all a hoax. But he does remember this topic from Gunnar's last known interview, and he has seen a few instances of AlphaCent's interest in cryogenics and cryotherapies since his arrival at Astroholm. Plus of course his own successful treatment.

"People have been experimenting with cryopreservation a long time," Gunnar goes on. "Many people have already had themselves frozen after death. The problem is, the freezing process causes ice crystals to form in the body's fluids, destroying tissue and nerve pathways. Only one creature in the entire world has solved this problem: an insignificant little frog that winters in a deep-frozen state. This frog transforms its bodily fluids into a kind of antifreeze. We mapped its DNA in the early 2000s, and after years of experiments we have finally managed to produce a similar fluid for human tissues. Even so, the freezing process itself is actually the easier part of the procedure. What we, thanks to this little frog, have in fact managed to do, no one has done before . . ."

Gunnar leans in closer. His eyes are almost luminous.

"We have managed to thaw those tissues again, to full functionality. To restore life. Literally reawaken the dead. It's a groundbreaking medical advance, and a great prospect for humanity."

Gunnar wraps his arm over Hill's shoulders.

"And that's where you come in. You see, Martin, when you replace blood and other fluids with our invention and then flash-freeze the tissues, a very interesting process occurs. Are you familiar with the term *vitrification*?"

Hill shakes his head.

"It means glassification—that's to say the transformation of tissues into glass. A man who is vitrified thus becomes a . . ." Gunnar raises his eyebrows.

"Glass man," Hill says.

"Exactly, dear Martin. Which is why your book title is so brilliant. It describes both AlphaCent's origins and its future. And at the same time also my own. You see, AlphaCent and I are to continue our journey long into the future."

His expression turns grave.

"I have cancer, you understand. Today's medical expertise has given me one year, two at most. Far too little time to achieve the spectacular things that still lie ahead. So I intend to buy myself more time. Or stop time, if you will, before the disease defeats me."

Gunnar pauses for effect, as though waiting for Hill's brain to process what he has just said. It takes him a few seconds.

"You . . . you plan to freeze yourself?"

Gunnar flashes a big smile.

"We prefer the term *vitrification*. And you're going to tell my story, dear Martin. Transform me from Space-Case Gunnar Irving into The Glass Man."

ASKER

She gets back home, plugs the car in to charge, and wolfs down a frozen dinner while processing her conversation with Attila. So Tord Korpi, an expert on underground constructions, visited Astroholm Manor. According to Martin, legend has it that the estate houses some kind of underground facility, one that he hopes to find over the course of his work on his book. Add to that the fact that the drive from the Farm to Miresjön Lake is just under an hour, and the conclusion isn't all that far-fetched.

The employer who paid Korpi in bags of cash was Astroholm Manor.

However, the follow-up questions are fuzzier.

Are the motive and assassin also to be found within the estate's walls? What might Korpi have seen or done in there that cost him his life—and who took it from him?

She needs to speak to her own insider, Martin Hill.

She has tried to call him several times, but her calls keep going straight to voicemail. So she fires off a text message and waits impatiently for him to call her back.

A notification makes her look up. The house's security system informs her that a car has entered her drive. Then another one, and another.

She looks through the window to see two unmarked police cars and two riot vans stop on the granite slabs in front of the entrance. That can't be good news.

When she steps through the door, Hellman is already halfway up the front steps, with Eskil and two other colleagues from Serious Crime in tow. Behind them, tactical officers are busy unloading their vans.

"What the hell is this?" she asks.

"What does it look like?" Hellman says measuredly. "We're here to conduct a search of this property on the hunt for your father."

Asker raises her eyebrows.

"Per's escaped? When did that happen?"

Hellman and Eskil look at each other. Suddenly Asker cottons on.

"Don't fucking tell me you think he's hiding here," she sighs.

"Where were you at eight thirty this morning?" Eskil yaps.

"With a colleague. Kent Atterbom, to be precise. Here's his phone number."

She pulls out her cellphone and shows them the number.

Eskil and Hellman exchange glances. It's clear they both know who Attila is. Eskil signals at one of their other colleagues to take the phone number and call him to confirm Asker's story.

"And what were you doing with Atterbom?" he then asks.

"That's the least of your fucking concerns, Eskil," she replies. "So tell me, how did you geniuses manage to lose Per?"

"He got heart palpitations, and the doctor sent him to the ER," says Eskil, who is clearly shouldering the role of intermediary. "From there, he managed to climb through a window and escape. We're still trying to piece together the details."

"Yet you came straight here. Why?"

Eskil fixes his eyes on her.

"Per had an accomplice at the hospital. A woman. She set off a fire alarm to create a diversion and then helped him to escape while everyone else was busy evacuating."

A woman. That detail is interesting.

"And you seriously thought it was me?" she asks.

Neither of them responds, nor do they need to. The tactical unit on her driveway speaks loud and clear. What a pair of morons.

She has no difficulty inferring how it all played out.

"Clearly he prepared it all in advance," she says. "The heart palpitations must have been real, presumably brought on by some pills he managed to smuggle into detention. If I were to guess, I'd say he stashed them in his prosthetic hand. Meanwhile his accomplice waited coolly and calmly for him to be taken to the ER, at which point she set off the fire alarm. A doctor's coat, a stethoscope, and a confident demeanor—that's probably all it took."

Hellman looks at her skeptically.

"So how did Per contact his accomplice? How did she know it was time to activate the escape plan? He was locked up with full restrictions, and the only person who visited him is you."

Asker looks him in the eye.

"Are you suggesting I played messenger?" She shakes her head. "In your eagerness to kick down doors, you brainiacs seem to have forgotten that I'm the one who handed Per over to you in the first place. And I did that because I wanted to stop you from playing Wild Wild West up at the Farm and causing a bloodbath. With Per in detention there was no risk of anyone getting hurt, so why the hell would I suddenly help him escape?"

Hellman and Eskil look at each other again, as if each waiting for the other to answer the question. Neither of them does.

Asker grimaces in frustration.

"Look, Per's not your average thug. Getting information out of a detention cell isn't all that hard for someone who has planned ahead. But if you really suspect me of leaking something, I suggest you arrest me right now and get me straight down to the station."

She holds her hands out willingly.

Hellman glares at her angrily; he actually appears to be toying with the idea of cuffing her. For a few seconds they stand face-to-face.

The colleague tasked with calling Attila interrupts their staring match.

"I spoke to Atterbom," he says. "He confirmed that she was at his place of residence earlier this morning."

Asker gives a slight wave of her outstretched hands.

"Well?" she asks. "What's it going to be?"

Hellman doesn't reply; he simply purses his lips, as though to stop himself from saying something rash. The tactical officers on the drive have stopped, awaiting orders.

"So what are we doing?" Eskil asks his boss.

"Nothing," Asker jumps in, dropping her arms to her sides. "Since I have an alibi, there can't be any reasonable suspicion against me, so I'd say a search is not in the cards. Right, Jonas?"

Hellman simply stares at her. His eyes are black, his face white as chalk.

"OK, boys," she says. "Thanks for stopping by. I trust you can find your own way out."

She walks back inside and shuts the door behind her.

Her father is free again, and when you know how Per works, it isn't so hard to map out his thinking in hindsight. Per never leaves anything to chance. When Korpi never showed up to reclaim his money, Per must have already deduced that he was dead, and that he himself risked falling suspect of murder.

And, though it may have taken a whole sixteen years for that scenario to play out, when it did he was neither surprised nor unprepared.

First, Per gets her to help him by threatening her with a police bloodbath.

He figures that sooner or later she will suggest he hand himself in, which he agrees to, since he knows it will put pressure on the investigators, forcing them to show their hand. The evidence to support his detention is weak so far, and if they are forced to release him, the investigation will face a real uphill struggle.

Besides, his detention puts pressure on Asker to find an alternative suspect.

Meanwhile, Per knows that Isabel is sitting on information about his debt, information that could get him charged and at worst convicted, so he creates a backup plan in case his ex-wife should choose to hand over that evidence, or should Asker be unable to prove his innocence.

Asker knows exactly what the starting shot for that backup plan was; knows how Per managed to communicate with his accomplice. She should have guessed the very second she found the tracker on her car. Per's whole request for her to be his legal representative was just a smoke screen: what he really wanted to achieve was to get her to visit him at the detention center. To set off a chain reaction that the accomplice could follow via the tracker. Her journey there must have been the agreed signal. As soon as Asker stepped through the door of the detention center, the accomplice would have known it was time to trigger the escape plan.

Prepper Per used her and manipulated her, just as he always has.

Just as Martin warned her that he would.

Hellman and her father are on track for a violent collision.

And all the while a murderer has walked free for sixteen years, one she might finally have found a real lead on.

Tord Korpi worked for Astroholm Manor, an estate filled with secrets. That's as good a place as any to start.

But to investigate it further she needs to change tack.

To think less like Per and more like Leo, just as Martin suggested.

And to get herself some more resources.

HILL

They walk back to the boat by the same route they came. Gunnar Irving talks the whole way. Enthusiastically draws up a framework for the whole book, chapter by chapter. A *squaring of accounts*, as he describes the project.

Samuel hovers in the background, as usual, but Nova listens attentively, apparently lapping up every word. To begin with Hill does the same. Gunnar Irving has a magnetism that is almost impossible to resist.

But then they pass the rhyolite boulder with the barely visible engraving, and it is as though some of the magic fades.

Two young men came here because of Gunnar's tall story.

And on the way home they drowned in the cold waters of the lake.

The thought suddenly makes him feel sick.

Now Gunnar has made him complicit in that lie.

Not because of a bad conscience, and not because he wants to apologize for the lies he has spun for over fifty years, but because he doesn't want to be remembered as Space-Case Gunnar Irving.

To crown it all, Gunnar now wants to replace that old yarn with a new narrative that is even more eccentric, not to mention narcissistic. To become the father of cryonics. He who defied nature, who gave humanity eternal life.

Does Hill even want to write a book with that agenda?

Once they have reached the jetty and boarded the boat, Nova rustles up a bottle of champagne from a cooler and fills three glasses. Meanwhile Samuel unmoors and slowly steers the boat back to Astroholm.

"Here's to our book project, dear Martin!" Gunnar exclaims. "To *The Glass Man!*"

Hill forces a smile and sips the champagne. Gunnar appears to be in high spirits. As they cross to the mainland, he tells a long anecdote about AlphaCent's research process, and how they developed the artificial heart valve that Hill carries in his chest.

"I'd long dismissed the idea of any book project," he says. "But when Nova told me that you have one of our valves in your chest, I changed my mind. I felt that we had a connection. And now, having met you, I can only say my instinct was right. You're one of the AlphaCent family, Martin. One of us."

Gunnar pats him on the back, and Hill tries his hardest to get caught up in the happy mood. But it's not so simple as that.

"More champagne?" Nova asks when Hill can't bring himself to respond to Gunnar's long exposition. She tops up their glasses. "Daddy, didn't you have a gift for Martin?"

"Oh, that's right!" Gunnar's face lights up even more.

Nova puts the bottle away, opens a cabinet, and pulls out a wrapped package that she hands to her father.

"This, dear Martin, is for you," says Gunnar, handing him the gift. "A little piece of inspiration, one might say. But you're not allowed to open it until you get home."

Hill takes the gift. It is cylindrical and rather heavy. Glugs faintly, as though it contains water.

Back at Astroholm's jetty, Gunnar bids him farewell.

"We'll be in touch soon! Take a few days to digest it all, and I look forward to hearing your thoughts now that you can see the bigger picture."

Gunnar shakes Hill's hand enthusiastically, ups the ante with a friendly pat to his elbow.

Nova gives Hill a lift home in the golf cart.

"So, Martin, what do you say?" she asks once they have set off.

Hill doesn't know where to begin. He wants to ask her if she knew that Gunnar had made up the UFO story, but after a few seconds' thought he decides to steer clear of it.

"How long does Gunnar plan to be frozen?" he asks instead.

"We prefer the term *vitrified*," Nova replies. "Until we've found a cure for his illness. It's my task to lead that work, and right now we have no time frame. It may take ten, twenty years. Maybe even longer."

Hill is still trying to get his head around the situation.

"And in that time he'll be waiting in a freezer tank somewhere?"

"That's a fairly crude description of what is an extremely complicated process, but to answer your question as concisely as possible: yes, his body will be preserved in a cryonic chamber, where the conditions can be meticulously monitored."

"Where?"

She laughs.

"In a secure, controlled facility. You'll have to make do with that."

"But what if Gunnar can never be cured? Why risk what little time he has left to live, instead of making the most of it?"

"Good question, Martin," Nova replies. "There's a trade-off, of course, a price to be paid. But the fact is, any price is pretty low if the reward on the other side is eternal life, no?"

"Hm."

Hill sits in silence while they pass the fountain with *The Glass Man*.

Gunnar is eternal. Immortal.

Karin Irving said those words to him just a few days ago.

Back then he had thought them just the ramblings of a confused woman.

"Gunnar sees the world differently," Nova goes on, as though she has observed that Hill's brain is still grappling with it all. "He thinks in bigger, bolder ways. From an early stage he asked himself why humans should allow themselves to be constrained by death. To just meekly accept that our time is limited. Cryonics offers the hope that not everything simply ends. That we can return, reawaken, live on."

She slows down a little and turns to Hill, as though she wants to make sure that he understands what she is saying.

"When you think about it, these are exactly the same thoughts that made people turn to religion for millennia. The hope of a life beyond this one. A light beyond the darkness. The only difference is, the hope that Gunnar offers isn't one built on faith, but on science."

"And you genuinely believe that it'll work? That he can be reawakened?"

Nova gives a wry smile.

"Gunnar's been researching cryonics since the nineties. We don't believe it, we *know* it!"

Nova parks the cart outside Villa Arcturus and goes inside with Hill. She places Gunnar's gift on the table in the hallway.

"I understand how you're feeling, Martin. Meeting Gunnar can be overwhelming. Mrs. Schiller has arranged dinner for you so that you can gather your thoughts in peace and quiet. You'll find it in the fridge."

She gestures toward the kitchen, appears to be preparing to leave.

"Oh, one last thing. It may sound obvious, but I must remind you that you signed a confidentiality agreement, and that nothing you heard today can be published or disseminated beyond the framework of this book project. Not to anyone."

"Of course not," Hill confirms.

"Great! Have a nice evening, Martin, and do rest up. Tomorrow's the start of an exciting new week!"

Hill has just had time to say goodbye to Nova Irving and down a few glasses of water and a pain reliever when he gets a text message from Leo.

I think Tord Korpi worked at Astroholm. Can you talk?

Hill gives a start. He is about to call her, but then stops himself.

The drone the other night; Samuel and Mrs. Schiller turning up at Bernhard's grave; Nova's comment about his seeing Maud.

All of this together builds on his suspicions that the app truly is spying on him.

Not right now, he writes reluctantly. *Lunch tomorrow? I'll call you an hour before.*

He can see the dots appear on the screen. They flash for a little while, as though she is drafting a long reply, and Hill feels the need to stop her.

Shady network, he writes. It's cryptic enough—it could mean many things to an outside reader—but he hopes that Leo will catch his drift.

The dots vanish immediately. Then briefly appear again.

OK is all she writes.

Hill deletes the messages.

He goes into the kitchen and opens the fridge door. Inside it stand a few aluminum trays with his name on them. Evidently Mrs.

Schiller entered his house without asking him, which further reinforces his feeling of being watched.

A knock on the door disturbs this train of thought.

Maud Irving is standing outside. Behind her, a black car he didn't hear coming.

"Hi, how's the forehead?" she asks with a smile.

"Better, thanks." Hill touches the dressing. "Good thing there was a doctor to hand."

"Isn't it just?"

He hesitates for a few seconds.

"Would you like to come in?" he eventually asks, even though in reality he is far too tired to entertain.

"Thanks, but I need to run a few errands. I mostly wanted to ask if you'd like to come over for dinner a little later. Last night was fun . . ."

Hill sighs apologetically.

"Normally I'd have loved to, but I'm beat. Mrs. Schiller made dinner for me. I was thinking of getting an early night."

"I see." She sounds disappointed.

"But how about tomorrow?" he adds quickly. "I'd really like that."

"I'm going down to Malmö tomorrow to pick up Elsa," she says. "I don't know if we'll be back in time for dinner."

"OK."

Hill feels a pang of guilt, and wonders if he should agree to dinner tonight in spite of it all. But right now he's so tired he can hardly think straight. His head feels like a tumble dryer of thoughts and emotions.

"Well, I guess we can see how things go tomorrow," he says. "I'd really like to see you, I've just had a long day."

"Yes, I saw Nova drive you home," Maud replies. "Did she take you out on an adventure?"

"We were on Boulder Isle. Gunnar was there, too."

"I see." He sees that she is trying to play it cool. "Was it how you'd imagined?"

Hill shrugs.

"It was an exciting trip, in any case. Informative. Gunnar's pretty special . . ."

"Did he mention me?" she asks hastily, as though in passing.

Hill hesitates to reply. Should he tell her the truth—that Gunnar only talked about himself? That all he seemed to care about was his own immortality?

He glances at Maud. The expression on her face is almost pleading.

"Uh, oh yes, he did," he says in the end.

"What did he say?" Her face is at once tense and expectant.

"He said you did a good job as CEO. That he's still thinking about your future role."

"He did?"

Maud's face lights up, and Hill realizes he needs to end this conversation before he gets tangled up in too many white lies.

"I think I'd better take a shower and get to bed . . ." He gestures over his shoulder.

"Of course," she says. "You actually do look pretty drained. Let's keep in touch tomorrow!"

She steps in and kisses him softly on the cheek. Lingers there for a few seconds too long, enough time for him to smell her fragrance and almost regret his choice.

Hill stands there, watching her car pull off down the drive. It can't be easy to be Gunnar Irving's child. Just like Nova, Maud seems all but obsessed with her father. Gratefully laps up the slightest hint of validation, even if it's just a passing mention.

Despite Gunnar disowning her and her family when she was a child, and despite his removing her from her post of CEO, she's still here: still lives on Gunnar's estate, having moved back into her childhood home; still holds out hope of once again being invited back into the warmth.

He shuts the door and locks it with both the latch and the deadlock. Rattles the handle a few times to make sure it's locked.

On the dresser in the hallway stands the cylinder-shaped gift he was given by Gunnar.

He takes it with him into the living room and tears off the wrapping paper. The package contains a large glass container with a sealed lid.

Inside the jar, weightless in a formalin bath, floats a small frog.

Its eyes are closed, its body extended. The skin on its abdomen is so thin that you can see straight through it. Glimpse the tiny frog heart inside its chest.

It looks like it is sleeping.

At the base of the jar there is a small label.

Glass frog, Centrolene geckoideum.

Hill can't help but shudder.

THE GLASS MAN

He stalks the passages in the dark depths. Crosses the underground stream, hearing the sounds of the blind creatures that slither through it.

As always, they are smart enough to stay out of his way.

The hunger is clawing at him, giving him no peace.

Part of him regrets not doing anything about it last night. When he saw them together in her bed, it had taken all of his self-control to restrain himself. But he can't hurt anyone in front of her. That mistake he can never repeat.

But tonight she isn't here.

He follows the passage that takes him in the right direction, feeling his way along the rock wall. Knows every projection, every stone, every crack.

The gravel crunches quietly under his boots. Everywhere, the scents of damp and earth and rock.

Of darkness.

He is at home here. Safe.

His eyes are now so sensitive to light that not even the deepest darkness is any impediment to him anymore.

The prince of the underworld.

He reaches the staircase, follows its cold metal upward until he is standing by the steel door.

Turns the handle and opens it.

Night reigns, and in Villa Arcturus all is quiet and still.

He creeps up the cellar steps, carefully cracks open the door to the hall.

By the scent alone he can tell that the Stranger is home. That he is alone. That there is no threat, no danger.

Finally.

Cautiously he sneaks through the dark living room.

He can hear the Stranger's breaths from the bedroom; can make out the muffled sounds of his heart.

All while feeling his own heart pound all the harder.

Soon he will witness that journey again.

Follow the Stranger's journey into darkness.

Still his hunger.

But he stops short.

There is something on the coffee table in the living room. A familiar object that shouldn't be there. Yet there it is.

The glass frog that the Father once gave him, back when he was still Prince Pollux.

He walks over to the container and kneels down before it.

Comes so close that his breath frosts on the glass.

The frog inside it is still asleep, its minute heart visible through its glassy abdomen.

For a brief instant he feels like a boy again.

Fascinated. Innocent.

Happy.

And then, out of nowhere, its heart suddenly starts to pulse. The frog gives a start and opens its eyes. Stares straight at him with its black pupils, its heart clicking mechanically.

In terror he leaps back, knocking a chair that scrapes against the floor. In the bedroom the Stranger snuffles, as though he is waking up.

He stares at the glass frog. It is still again. Lifeless.

Perhaps it was all just a figment of his imagination.

That or it was a sign.

A warning from the omnipotent eye.

From the one who sees all.

MONDAY

ASKER

Have faith. That was what Madame Rind encouraged her to do.

And Martin tried, in his slightly unsubtle, yet thoughtful way, to get her to trust her own instincts more.

Less Prepper Per, and more Leo.

Per never trusts anyone, not even his own intuition. He believes in planning and control. In logic and probability, not humanity. And she has been running in that same direction all too long.

She came in early to level minus one and cleared out the empty office at the end of the corridor. The same office that Sandgren used as his secret investigation room when he was hunting the Mountain King.

Only a few weeks have passed since she found the place, but it feels like much longer.

She has kept the whiteboard in place, with a row of folding chairs arranged opposite. Has warmed up some cinnamon buns in the microwave in the kitchen, walked them up and down the corridor, spreading their sweet scent throughout the department.

The trick works.

Flocking to the aroma, her colleagues trickle in one by one, coffee cups in hand. First Virgilsson, then Zafer, and finally Rosen. The Lost Souls look in confusion first at one another and then at her, before they each grab a bun, and, after some hesitation, take a seat.

At eight o'clock on the dot Asker clears her throat.

"Good morning, everyone. I thought it was high time that we started having real morning meetings here in the department. That we shared what we're working on, trying to focus our resources where they can do the most good."

Asker stops and looks around for signs of agreement, but finds none. There is a sound in the corridor. A second later Attila appears in the doorway. He has shaved and brings with him a waft of aftershave and mints.

"Sorry I'm late," he mutters, then takes a seat at the back.

Asker starts again.

"So, I'm working on two bigger cases where I need some help." She looks up at her small cluster of colleagues. "Where I need *your* help."

She draws two columns on the board.

One for Tord Korpi, Astroholm Manor, and the Irving family, and one for Prepper Per. Then she explains how both cases fit together, and where she comes into the picture.

"So you want us to help you, not only by finding your father, but also by tracking down whoever really committed the murder of which he is suspected," Virgilsson sums up. "All while our other colleagues pursue him with every resource available to the force?"

Asker throws her hands out to her sides.

"In short: yep."

Virgilsson's eyebrows shoot to the sky.

"And you are aware that this kind of . . . operation . . . could cost us all our jobs?"

"I'm the department chief," Asker replies firmly. "You're acting on my orders, which means the only one risking their job is me. For all of you this is simply a chance to put your skills to something useful. Not pretend tasks, but a sharp hunt for a fugitive and a murderer. When was the last time you did that?"

Her four colleagues exchange sly glances.

"In exchange for your help I'm of course prepared to be . . ." she pauses, having given this particular part of her briefing some extra thought, ". . . flexible regarding how you want your work arrangements in this department to look going forward. I'd be happy to take on suggestions for improvements."

More silence, more glances. The department hardly seems enthusiastic, but Asker decides to go all in. It's sink or swim.

"To start with, I'd like some help finding a car that was likely used for Per Asker's getaway from the hospital yesterday morning. It's a silver car, possibly a Kia. The first letters on the license plate are CL, and the first number is a one or a seven. There are surveillance cameras in a few locations at the hospital, so if it's possible to get hold of those recordings . . ."

"No!" Zafer interrupts sharply, and, as usual, a few decibels too loud.

Every eye in the room turns to him.

"That . . ." he crosses his arms over his lab coat, ". . . is not a good use of our time."

He sternly prods his glasses up toward the bridge of his nose.

Asker feels her heart sink a few inches.

"There's a better way," he goes on. "Those hospital parking wardens are on the ball, everyone knows that. Mean little scamps. We'll start by checking what cars got parking tickets on Sunday. Parking is paid via an app, so if the fines don't get us anywhere, it means the driver must have used the app to pay for their parking. Time, license number, et cetera, it'll all be there in the app."

"If we can get access to the vehicle data, then I can do a cross-reference against other databases," Rosen adds. "Should be easy to find the right car."

"But can we access the data we need?" Asker turns back to Zafer, who gives a shrug.

"If the parking company helps us. We can, of course, go the official route, though that may raise a few eyebrows."

They fall silent for a few seconds.

Then Virgilsson clears his throat.

"Ah, ahem. Here I might perhaps be of some assistance," he says thoughtfully. "I have an older brother who happens to work for that very parking company. I can contact him, discreetly."

"Great!" Asker tries to stop herself from smiling.

"While we're waiting for that, I'll do a database check for Astroholm Manor, the Irving family, and Miresjön Lake," says Rosen. "And I'll try to figure out what happened to the car Tord Korpi was using when he disappeared. The one Kent made notes about."

"Good."

Asker sneaks a glance at Attila. The angular man is the only one who hasn't yet said a word. When he looks up and meets her gaze, he seems to realize as much himself.

"I can check with my old colleagues at the secret police," he offers. "Ask if anyone remembers any more about Tord Korpi and Astroholm. It's a long shot, but it's worth a try at least."

"Very good," Asker sums up. "It sounds like we've all got our work cut out for us. We'll do another review during our afternoon coffee break. There'll be pastries. Thank you all!"

She closes the meeting, and the Lost Souls retreat to their offices while making small talk with one another.

She, too, knows exactly what she needs to do.

Have lunch with Martin.

HILL

Despite his previous night's exhaustion, Hill slept badly. He dreamed of Boulder Isle, of the creature, of the carvings in the rhyolite block that are the last trace of Nick and Elis.

The questions crop up again, thick and fast: Should he step back from the whole book project? Can he? Does he even want to?

Even though the UFO story was pure fiction, there are still so many mysteries to be solved.

The red-eyed giant who chased him, the secret chamber, the tunnels beneath Astroholm. Bernhard's old sketchbook.

He flicks through the book over his morning coffee, examining it more carefully this time. Why did his secret friend want him to find it?

While the pages are largely filled with sketches, much of the content is made up of thoughts and small reflections. Reading it is almost like a sneak peek into Bernhard Irving's brain.

Hill searches for the drawing of Freddie, who in 1951 lay sprawled in bed in such a way that Bernhard felt compelled to draw her. The portrait is executed with such delicacy that you can sense that this was someone about whom Bernhard cared deeply.

Hill still wonders who she is.

In the last quarter of the book, the drawings become fewer. They are replaced by small tables of numbers, most of which with a minus sign before then.

Scrawled in the margin in one place is

They're laughing at me! But they're wrong. The meteorite is down there!!

On the final pages his handwriting has changed. More straggly, more fraught. The notes are cluttered with capital letters and underlinings, and the few drawings depict dark tunnels and waterlogged mine passages with wooden props supporting the ceiling. Written not far from the end is

Leak—Artur concerned

And that's followed by the words

Risk of collapse!

On the very final page Bernhard has written a few disconsolate sentences.

> *All is lost. The mine has collapsed, Artur is dead, the money gone.*
> *My final duty is to take care of his Fredrika and little Karin.*
> *I owe that to Artur.*
> *He was a good friend, and I betrayed him in the lowest possible way.*

The words ring in his head.

Fredrika and little Karin. Artur Nilsson's wife and daughter.

Karin, who would go on to marry Gunnar and give birth to Maud and Viggo. And her mother, Fredrika.

Freddie.

Hill gasps.

It all suggests that Bernhard Irving had an affair with Artur Nilsson's wife.

He thinks of what Karin Irving said about Villa Canopus. Her unusual, yet ominous choice of words.

Our sanctuary after the Fall.

HELLMAN

The scene in the briefing room is almost exactly the same as a few days ago: his own staff are in place, as well as the tactical officers dressed in black and their commander. The map of the Farm is up on the big screen. But the expressions on their faces are harder, more resolved.

No more mollycoddling, no more objections, no more civility.

Per Asker is going to find out the true cost of fucking around with the police.

That the man is a sociopath is crystal clear, and he is also sneakier than most perps. But he is no superior foe.

Even Per Asker has his weaknesses. The man should have fled the country. But Hellman's cop instinct tells him the old fox wouldn't do that. That he would instead slink back to his den.

So he posted someone to watch the Farm, very much on the sly, and that has proved a good move. Per Asker is currently lying low in his homemade bunker, hoping this will all blow over.

Maybe waiting for Leo to come to his rescue yet again.

Hellman still hasn't really gotten over yesterday's confrontation with Leo on her driveway. She provoked him, tried to trick him into making a mistake.

The thought of cuffing her and forcing her into submission was extremely tempting. Bordered on some of his nighttime fantasies.

But at the last second he came to his senses. Didn't let her get to him.

And now it's payback time.

"Ladies and gentlemen," he says. "The target for this operation is Per Asker, who is to be considered armed and extremely dangerous. We have intel to suggest he may have mined parts of the Farm, so to help us we've brought in some of our friends from the armed forces, who have more experience with explosive ordnance in particular."

He gestures at two men in green uniforms who are seated at the front. Then he turns to the screen and pulls up a paused film sequence recorded the previous night. The image centers on some of the barracks in the middle of the Farm.

"As you can see, the entire place is blacked out. But the scouts picked this up at around three a.m."

He presses play. In one of the windows a faint light briefly appears, as if from a phone screen, before it all goes dark again.

"In addition to the light leak, we also got a reading on one of the thermal image cameras at the same time. It's likely that Per Asker is hiding in an underground bunker to avoid detection. But as you can see from this film, he must have been forced to fetch something from one of the barracks and accidentally took out his phone."

He changes the image to a slide again, back to the map.

"Before handing over to the commander of the tactical unit, I want to stress that Per Asker is a dangerous adversary and suspected murderer. He knows that we're coming and has had time to prepare. In other words, we're taking no risks."

Hellman stops. In reality he wants to instruct every officer to shoot first and ask questions later, but that would be unprofessional.

Besides, he doesn't need to.

They already know the score.

ASKER

She and Martin meet at a roadside diner roughly halfway between Astro-holm and Malmö. Asker gives him the full rundown, first about Prepper Per's escape, and then about how she managed to link Tord Korpi to Astroholm.

Martin listens carefully, without interrupting her.

"OK," he says once she has finished talking. "Do you have any idea who Per's female accomplice is?"

"No. But whoever she is, she made the arrangements for his escape from the ER and placed a tracker on my car. And she wasn't averse to driving around in the middle of the night, tailing me. Those things take skills as well as motivation."

"A new member of Per's mini sect?"

"Exactly. And there may be others—I don't know."

"But you're still digging around in the murder? Why not just let Per go to jail?"

"Because I genuinely believe someone is trying to frame him, which means I'd risk letting a murderer walk free. And I think it may all have something to do with Astroholm."

She tells him about Attila's observations while anxiously waiting for his reaction. Martin is working for the Irving family, and he seems to be well in with Maud. He might not be all that happy about Asker accusing his employer—or someone in their circle—of an assassination.

But Martin doesn't appear to be fazed by it.

"OK." He frowns. "You mentioned that Korpi did jobs for both Per and that gym. What kind of jobs?"

"I don't know, exactly, but his specialty was underground constructions. According to the owner of the gym in Hörby I spoke to a few days back, he had a whole gang of Poles with him who likely came from his daytime job. I now suspect that that was at Astroholm Manor, so whatever they were building, it was probably pretty big."

Martin looks doubtful.

"And this was in 2006, right?"

"That's right. Could it be the burial chamber you wrote about in your book?"

He shakes his head.

"Bernhard died in 1996. If there is any burial chamber, it would need to have been built way earlier. Besides, I've seen Bernhard's gravestone. But I did find information to suggest that there's a sub-basement floor level in the manor house. That could be what they were building."

"Can you look into it on the sly, do you think? Ask around if anyone maybe remembers Korpi?"

"Sure." He nods. "I have a few more eyes on me than usual right now, but I'm seeing Maud Irving tonight. She's a little outside of the inner circle, so I might be able to fish around and see if she knows anything."

"Great." Asker dials down her enthusiasm a touch. "But be careful. I don't want you to risk your book project."

Those last words make him grimace. Something is troubling him, that much is clear.

"You haven't told me how things went on Boulder Isle," she says. "What was the Space Case like in real life?"

Martin looks over his shoulder before leaning in toward her.

"He doesn't want to be called Space-Case anymore," he says quietly. "Gunnar told me he made the whole story up, to get his father to hand over the reins of the company. It's all just a lie."

Asker whistles.

"Wow, what a scoop. Are you going to write about it?"

"No, Gunnar just wants me to tone it all down. He has other plans for the book."

"OK, but either way you've still solved the UFO mystery. Aren't you happy?"

He shrugs.

"I've personally helped to disseminate that UFO narrative. Two guys read about it in my book, and it cost them their lives."

"You mean the guys who drowned in the lake?"

"Yeah. Gunnar doesn't seem to care that his lies have had consequences. All that matters to him is his legacy. Who cares if he's lied for fifty years, it was for a good cause. Like, nothing to kick up a fuss about."

She watches him for a few seconds.

"Are you sure that's what's bothering you? That it has nothing to do with your teenage fixation? That something you've been obsessing over for years has turned out to be a sham, and that your faith in humanity has taken a knock?"

He throws his hands out to his sides in resignation.

"You definitely have a point there. In some strange way I feel both disappointed and complicit. Either way, Gunnar seems to think we're besties. And that my job is to more or less make him out to be some kind of god. Fact is, it's put a downer on the whole project. And my own book idea, for that matter."

Asker squirms. If Martin leaves Astroholm, then she will lose her only insider, which would be a real setback. On the other hand, she doesn't like how unsettled he seems.

"If that's how you feel, then you should probably pack your bags and get straight out of there," she says. "The sooner, the better."

"No, no." He shakes his head. "Astroholm still has plenty of mysteries that I want to get to the bottom of. And you've just brought me another one."

"But I don't want you staying on for my sake. Besides, snooping isn't entirely without its risks. Especially if they're keeping an eye on you."

He gives her a long look, then smiles from one side of his mouth.

"OK. I'll do some fishing on Korpi for you. Then I'll have a long, hard think about the book project. Does that sound good?"

Asker exhales.

"It would be really great to get confirmation that Korpi did actually work at Astroholm."

"I'll do my best," he says, and he actually does look a little happier.

She looks at the clock.

"Sorry, I need to get going soon. My department's on the case, and I've promised them pastries for this afternoon's briefing."

"Your department? I thought it was just a bunch of HR nightmares and deadbeats."

"I did, too," she smirks. "But you never know when people might surprise you."

He grabs his ears in mock astonishment.

"What's that I hear? Has Leo Asker started to doubt she's stronger on her own? Maybe even started to believe in *other people*?"

His comments draw a chuckle out of her.

"Maybe," she says.

They stand up, and as usual neither of them quite knows how to say goodbye.

"Be careful, Martin," she says. "If Korpi's death is linked to Astroholm, then it means there's a murderer inside."

"I promise," he says with a smile. "By the way . . ."

He appears to be thinking.

"There's another couple of deaths loosely linked to Astroholm. You may want to take a closer look at them, too."

HILL

As soon as he gets back to Villa Arcturus, Hill sits down at the desk and takes out Bernhard Irving's sketchbook. The drawing in the middle gives him no peace. It might even be the main reason why he has chosen to stay on at the estate.

Bernhard Irving had an affair with Artur Nilsson's wife. The drawing in the book is dated to 1951. The year after that, Karin Irving was born, and she in turn would go on to marry Gunnar and then have Viggo and Maud. The family that Gunnar would banish to Villa Canopus in the early nineties.

Our sanctuary after the Fall.

And it could be because of his much-needed breath of fresh air away from Astroholm's grounds, or because Gunnar Irving has lost some of his former shine in his eyes, but all of a sudden Hill thinks he understands what Karin was trying to tell him.

A truth she both fears and wants to share.

He checks his timeline. It's just as he thought.

In the early nineties, AlphaCent presented groundbreaking findings in DNA analysis, a field of research that was in those days only in its infancy.

And at the same time Gunnar's old family is expelled from the manor house.

Banished to Villa Canopus, while he starts afresh.

He remarries, has a daughter whom he prizes higher than the other two children.

Nova—the new star. She who will preside over Gunnar's frozen body. Reawaken him to life.

Hill is feeling all the more uneasy.

He must speak to Karin Irving. Find out whether his suspicions are grounded.

His phone has connected to the Astroholm network, and he places it on a shelf before slipping out through the kitchen door.

He takes a roundabout route to Villa Canopus, looking over his shoulder several times along the way. Instead of going to the front door, like the last time he was there, he walks around the house. After a little searching, he finds another, smaller door. On the front steps sits a large, fluffy cat that Hill believes to be the same animal he saw a few nights before, whose name is apparently Perseus. The cat stares at him searchingly, then stands up majestically and loops around his legs a few times.

Hill knocks at the door. He hears movements inside.

The door opens slightly. Karin Irving observes him suspiciously through the crack.

"Hello, Karin," he says, holding up Bernhard's sketchbook. "I'd like to speak to you about this."

Silence for a few seconds. Then the door opens another few inches.

"Come in, quickly," she says, looking around suspiciously. "Did anyone see you come here?"

"No, I took a detour."

She lets in both Hill and the cat, then shuts and locks the door.

"Good. Dr. Schiller has forbidden me from speaking to you. He says it's bad for my heart. But in fact it's Gunnar who's behind it all, of course. They've given me a new medicine that makes me . . ."

She twists her fingers in circles around her head.

Karin's annex is in actual fact her own separate apartment, complete with kitchen, living room, and a small bedroom that Hill glimpses through an open door.

Perseus has settled on the kitchen banquette.

"Take a seat," Karin says, pointing at the seat beside the cat, then pours coffee into two mugs.

"It's you who warned me," he says. "Who posted the letter through my door, who wrote *danger* on Bernhard's drawing board. Why?"

Karin stares at him for a few seconds, then sighs.

"So that you would know what you were getting yourself into. Be on your guard, not let Gunnar cast his spell on you."

"But then you also led me to Bernhard's secret chamber, so that I'd find this."

He opens the sketchbook to its middle spread.

"Freddie," he says. "That's your mother, isn't it? She and Bernhard had an affair before you were born. Bernhard is your biological father. Which makes you and Gunnar half-siblings."

Karin Irving looks down at her coffee cup sadly.

"No one knew it, not even Bernhard. He thought Artur was my father, swore it to the very end."

"But Gunnar didn't believe him, did he? He disowned you all when the DNA tests brought it all to light. Expelled you, the children, and Bernhard. Cast you all out of the manor house and stripped Bernhard of his observatory and telescope."

Hill has hardly had a chance to think through all of this, but the more he talks, the more things seem to fall into place.

"You and the children were his shame. His tainted family that he was forced to replace."

Karin Irving sobs, pulls a handkerchief from one sleeve of her cardigan.

Hill fears that he has been too hasty, has pushed her too hard. He gets up and fetches her a glass of water from the kitchen. She gratefully drinks a few sips.

"It wasn't our fault. We had no idea," she whispers.

"Did you tell the children?"

She shakes her head. "Gunnar made me stay silent. Threatened to cast us all out of Astroholm entirely if I said so much as a word. I'd lived here my whole life; I knew nothing else."

"So you've kept this secret for thirty years? That must have been awful. Especially when Gunnar started a new family in your home."

Karin sobs again.

Hill is struck by an impulse to hug her. What a terrible thing to have to shoulder all on her own. To not even be able to explain to her children why their father cast them out without warning.

In that instant Hill realizes that he can never write this book. After this revelation he won't even be able to look Gunnar Irving in the eye.

He waits until Karin has composed herself a little.

"There was a man here on the estate around 2006," he says softly. "Tord Korpi. He was a mining engineer, just like Artur."

Karin wrings her hands, then gives a faint nod.

"Do you remember what he was doing here?"

Karin goes on wringing her hands, as though there is something between them that torments her.

"He was building for Gunnar, but he promised to help us," she says, so quietly that Hill can hardly hear.

"Who? You and Maud?"

"Viggo," she whispers. "He was going to help Viggo. But then something happened—Tord told me to be careful and then he just disappeared. I never heard from him again."

Hill sits up straighter. He doesn't know what answer he was expecting, but it certainly wasn't this.

"Is Viggo here, at Astroholm? I thought he was abroad?"

Karin shakes her head.

"Gunnar has him. He . . ."

Suddenly there are sounds outside, followed by a hard rap on the door. The cat shoots up off the sofa and darts out of the room.

"Mrs. Irving? Martin?"

"They're here," Karin gasps. "They know what I've done!"

A key is placed in the lock.

Before Hill can say anything, she leaps out of the chair, claps her hands to her ears, and starts to scream.

The door is flung open, and Dr. Schiller and Samuel come running in. Samuel grabs Karin's hands and forces them down, while the doctor fumbles with his bag.

"Please, Mrs. Irving, there's nothing to worry about. We're here now," says Samuel, looking daggers at Hill. "Sit down and you'll get something to calm you."

He guides Karin Irving back down onto her seat, apparently without any effort. She stares up at him in terror.

"No," Karin gasps when Dr. Schiller takes a syringe from his bag, but she makes no further protest when the doctor pulls her cardigan off her shoulder and inserts the needle into her upper arm.

"There," he says. "You'll soon feel better, Mrs. Irving. But just to be sure, we'd like you to come down to the clinic with us so that you can relax."

Karin's eyes are already glassy.

"I've already explained to you that Karin Irving isn't well, Martin." Samuel's voice has assumed the same menacing tone as a few days before. "To turn up at her house without prior warning is extremely inappropriate, not to mention a direct breach of the rules."

Hill throws his hands out to his sides.

"I'm sorry, I really didn't mean to . . ."

But Samuel turns his back on him. Dr. Schiller has managed to get Karin Irving to her feet, and he steers her cautiously toward the door.

Hill stands up and goes after them.

On the threshold to the hallway Karin stumbles. The doctor loses his hold of her, and she falls almost straight into Hill's arms.

"Viggo," she whispers in his ear when he catches her, and he feels her slip something into his blazer pocket.

The next second Samuel has lifted her off him.

"It's best that you go home, Martin," the security chief says sternly. "I have no choice but to report this to Gunnar. I'd like you to remain in Villa Arcturus until further notice—is that understood?"

"I'm really sorry that this all happened," says Hill.

He follows them outside and stands on the doorstep, while Samuel and Dr. Schiller sit Karin Irving in the car and drive her off in the direction of the manor house.

Only once they have disappeared out of sight does he take from his blazer pocket the object that Karin slipped him. It is a key ring with two keys attached to a small plastic tag.

District heating, it reads.

ASKER

The Lost Souls turn up punctually on the dot of two p.m. Presumably this is thanks to the pastries that Asker picked up on her way back to the office, but part of her hopes that it has at least something to do with the job itself. The opportunity to do some real police work. If they have managed to come up with the goods, that is. She estimates the odds of that to be around fifty-fifty.

"So," she says. "What have we got?"

Her four colleagues look at one another.

"Uh," says Rosen. "Maybe I can start, then?"

"Please do," Asker nods.

Rosen flicks through a few papers on her lap.

"I have a hit on the car that Tord Korpi was using at the time of his disappearance. A dark-blue Isuzu, a nineties model. At that time, that's to say in the fall of 2006, the car was registered to someone in the Kiruna region who is a reputed dummy vehicle keeper. This fits in with the profile of Korpi as someone who wanted to go under the radar."

She leafs through to another page.

"The car turns up again in the spring of 2007, when a known petty thug is pulled over in the car just outside Kristianstad. When asked what he's doing in a car registered to someone who lives over a thousand miles north, he gives the slightly unexpected response that he had simply found the car with the key in its ignition in October of the previous year. The police don't believe him, the car is seized and eventually scrapped, so unfortunately we can't subpoena it anymore."

Rosen makes an apologetic gesture.

"But what is interesting is where the man claimed to have found the car: at a turnout next to Miresjön Lake, very close to Astroholm."

"OK," says Asker. "So that means someone could have dumped the car with the keys in it, intending for it to get stolen?"

"Sounds likely," says Attila. "Let's assume Korpi was murdered at

Astroholm. The assassin could then have used the car to transport the body to the Farm, buried it at the dump, and then returned. Abandoned the car at Miresjön Lake and walked the last stretch back to Astroholm."

The other three nod in agreement.

"But that of course presupposes that the assassin knew Korpi had a link to the Farm," Virgilsson adds.

More nods.

"OK," says Asker. She takes a whiteboard pen and writes the information about the car in the Astroholm column.

"Thanks, Rosen, that was a good start. Have we found anything else?"

"I spoke to an old colleague who was involved in the reconnaissance operation on the Farm," says Attila. "He remembered that Korpi was seen in the company of a woman when they tailed him to Astroholm. There may even be images. He's trying to dig them up."

Asker stiffens. That could be the same mysterious woman who Sundin and Danielsson saw just before they tried to rob Korpi. They had assumed that she was a secret affair, but what if she was more important than that?

Asker writes the words *Unknown woman* in the Astroholm column and takes a step back.

The board already contains more information than she would have been able to access that morning. Against the odds, the Resources Unit is actually living up to its name. She should have done this long ago.

"Anything else?" she asks.

"Zafer and I have checked what cars were ticketed in the hospital area, but unfortunately that gave us nothing," says Virgilsson. "My contact at the parking company was going to see if he could help us with data from the app, but apparently it was a little complicated. So no real news to take us forward so far."

"OK." Asker writes the words *Parking app?* in the column relating to her father.

"But we have dug up a more concerning tidbit," Virgilsson adds. "In all likelihood there will be a raid on the Farm tonight. They're going all out, with a helicopter, drones, snipers, and dogs. Apparently they've received indications that Per is there."

Asker takes a deep breath.

Never in her wildest dreams would she have imagined Per being so stupid as to return home. Clearly she was wrong.

But this does make the situation all the more dangerous. If Per is already so irrational that he would hide out at the Farm, there is probably no limit to what he is capable of when the tactical unit shows up at his door.

The room falls silent, for several seconds too long.

"I can set you up with the radio channels," Zafer eventually says. "If you want to listen to the operation, that is?"

"Thank you. I'd like that, as soon as we're finished here."

Silence falls again. Her colleagues fidget, as though they realize what thoughts are running through her head.

She takes a deep breath.

"OK," she eventually says. "I've received some new information that we need to look into. There are a few other deaths that may be linked to Astroholm and the Irving family. Björn Knudsen, the head gardener at the estate, who was found beaten to death in 1992. And on top of that, a car crash at Miresjön Lake in the winter of 2001, in which one AlphaCent employee died. We're looking for the lowest common denominator for each incident."

She assigns tasks, all while feverishly scrabbling to come up with a way to prevent the impending disaster.

HILL

Despite Samuel's orders, Hill leaves Astroholm and drives to the library in town.

"Welcome back!" says the librarian. "Is there anything else I can help you with?"

"Uh, yes, I was wondering if I could borrow your phone. Mine's stopped working."

The librarian gives him a puzzled look, then points at a phone on her desk.

"Be my guest!"

He waits until she has stepped aside, then dials Leo's number. Leo picks up straightaway.

"It's Martin," he says. "I just spoke to Karin Irving. She confirmed she met Korpi. Said he promised to help her."

"Help her how?"

"I didn't get any real clarity on that, but she said something about her son, Viggo. Then people from the estate showed up and she got terrified."

Hill quickly recounts his conversation with Karin, and then tells her about Samuel and Dr. Schiller's abrupt appearance.

"So they took her away?" Leo asks.

"More or less. Karin clearly isn't quite herself, so she probably did need looking after. Even so, it felt off."

"It sounds like they turned up because they knew you were there. But how could they know?"

"No idea—I left my phone in Villa Arcturus. Maybe they're keeping an eye on Karin after our little trip to Bernhard's grave the other day. In any case, it's clear they didn't want her to talk to me anymore."

He can almost hear Leo thinking.

"We have information from multiple sources to say that Korpi was seen and even photographed with a woman in the vicinity of Astroholm," she says. "We're trying to dig up the photos."

"It must be Karin," he says. "They seemed to be close."

"What did she say Korpi was even doing on the estate?"

"She said he was building for Gunnar."

"Building what?"

"I didn't get a chance to ask before the doctor and Samuel showed up."

"Shame, but given Korpi's specialty we can probably assume it was something underground, right?"

Something Nova said pops into Hill's head.

In a secure, controlled facility.

"I think I might know what it was," he says. "An underground laboratory where Gunnar's frozen body will be stored."

"Huh?"

He quickly summarizes his theory.

"Wow. So how can we confirm if that holds?"

Hill's mind turns to the key he was given by Karin Irving.

"I'll go back right away and try to find out more," he replies.

Asker falls silent.

"Is that really a good idea?" she eventually says. "Samuel and the doctor have already caught you asking Karin questions. If they find out you've been poking around into Tord Korpi's death, you could be in danger. Wouldn't it be better if you went home to Lund and let me take care of it from here?"

"Are you really going to get a warrant to search Astroholm on such weak grounds?" he asks.

"No," she admits.

"So then you still need my help from the inside. And if there really is an underground cryonics lab, then I want to see it for myself."

He can hear her hesitation down the line.

"I promise not to take any unnecessary risks," he adds.

"OK," she eventually says. "But please be careful, Martin. And call me as soon as you know anything."

"Of course."

Half an hour later he is standing in the basement of Villa Arcturus. Before him, a locked steel door with a warning sign:

DISTRICT HEATING. ENTRY ONLY FOR AUTHORIZED PERSONNEL.

Hill sticks the key Karin Irving gave him into the lock.

The door glides open without a sound.

Inside, everything is pitch-black. The smells he detected back in the basement are much stronger here. Damp, earth, metal.

The bedrock's breath.

He feels his anxiety rising. The last time he experienced this smell was in the Mountain King's lair.

He turns on his flashlight. Inside the door, he finds a large heating pipe and a grated metal footbridge. He follows it, sweeping his flashlight around him.

After around thirty feet, a cavity appears to his right. He shines the light down it and finds a much older spiral staircase that plunges straight into the darkness.

The staircase winds twenty-five to thirty feet down before it meets the ground.

Hill composes himself, then slowly starts following the staircase down into the depths. The frame rocks gently, making the old metal screech ominously.

After a minute or so he reaches the bottom of the stairwell.

The darkness is thicker here, the bedrock's breath more potent.

He shines the light around himself. The walls of the stairwell are still smooth, but beside him he finds an opening in the rock. It is maybe ten feet high and just as wide, supported by hefty wooden props.

It doesn't take him many steps to realize this must be one of the old mine tunnels. Hill can hear his mechanical heart valve clicking excitedly in his chest.

So the secret tunnels are no urban myth; the network of passages under Astroholm really does exist.

He lights up the walls, which are rawer and much more ruggedly hewn than just moments ago. The scent of bedrock is almost overwhelming.

Hill takes a few slow breaths to calm himself, performing a risk assessment as he does. Should he turn back and return to Villa Arcturus?

No one knows he is here, his car is outside the house, and everyone thinks he is busily working away, as instructed. His phone is still in the kitchen, to add to that impression.

Hill sweeps his flashlight down the tunnel again. He has visited similar places before. Knows the safest ways to pass through the underworld.

He should have brought a helmet and rubber boots with him, plus some way to raise the alarm should anything go wrong. Not to mention the fact that he is alone, which goes against every rule in the urban explorer's handbook.

To continue into the darkness doubtless entails certain risks. Even so, his passion for discovery wins out. Besides, he tells himself, he is here for Leo's sake.

He slowly sets off down the tunnel into the darkness.

He buttons up his jacket against the cold, pulls on the gloves he had in his pockets. Carefully moves forward while letting the light play across the walls.

In some places the ceiling is reinforced with beams that look like normal spruce trunks that have been coated in tar.

He touches one of them gingerly. Its surface feels almost petrified.

He can't help but think about the Astrofield Mine collapse of 1965. But that was far deeper and due to water ingress from the lake, he tells himself. This part of the mine appears to be relatively dry. Still, he decides to keep his eyes open for leaks or rubble on the ground, which are indicators of old collapses and subsidence.

After around a hundred yards he sees an opening in the wall that has been blocked off by a partially collapsed wall of planks. Through the fallen planks he glimpses another tunnel. That one is smaller, and it appears to be in worse condition. A few yards in lies a waist-high pile of fallen rubble, but the passage still appears to be accessible, at least as far as the flashlight extends. On one of the walls something is written in white, sprawling text.

Villa C, followed by an arrow pointing into the darkness.

Hill shivers with both cold and excitement.

So Villa Canopus is also connected to the mine tunnels. That would suggest that all the guesthouses are linked to one another and to the manor house—and perhaps even to Boulder Isle, just as he hoped.

The UFO story was all made up, the burial chamber likely a myth, but a secret tunnel network of this scope will make almost as

much of a splash—especially if it's linked to an underground laboratory, as he hopes.

In an ideal world he would have liked to explore all the passages,
to figure out how expansive the network really is. But he has limited
time and must focus on the task at hand. If the laboratory lies under
the manor house, as he believes it does, he must continue down the
passage that he is already walking.

Here and there he finds traces of the miners. Scrawls on the
walls, twisted metal details from long-since rusted tools, even the
plastic lid of an old thermos, a conspicuous blob of color among all
the black, grays, and browns.

To his relief he sees no more rubble, and no more aged props
either.

But as he continues, he does feel the humidity increasing.

A faint sound reaches him through the darkness. A sound that
worries him.

The sound of running water.

THE GLASS MAN

The gate to Boulder Isle has been locked for a long time. But now it suddenly stands open, and the island is once again part of his domain.

A prize for all that he has forgone; his restraint with Martin Hill.

At least that is how he sees it.

He hurries there. Hurries to once again seize possession of the place, only to find that it no longer is his.

Someone has been here. Has felled trees, cleared it, spruced it up.

His sacred place has been laid to waste, his treasures gone.

This makes him angry.

Furious.

He knows whose work this is. Can feel His presence hanging over the place like a gray fog.

He who is feared, all-powerful, ruthless.

He who time and again forces him to return from the eternal darkness. Forces him to endure pain and torment.

And who, for all his own sacrifices, punishes him in this way.

The Father.

HELLMAN

Hellman leads the convoy north. As always, he is the one in the driver's seat. By this point Eskil has learned his preference and obediently taken the passenger seat. It's where he now sits, fielding calls and handling radio communications.

Behind them drive another few unmarked cars, followed by four riot vans carrying heavily armed tactical officers, and, at the rear, the bespoke mobile command center.

"Shit, we should almost be playing 'Ride of the Valkyries,'" Eskil says with a smirk. "You know, like in *Apocalypse Now*. Walter Kurtz, remember? Korpi's fake ID."

Hellman doesn't respond. They are police officers on official business, not twenty-something rookies on their military service.

Still, at the mere mention of the piece the dramatic melody strikes up in his head. Again and again it plays, intensifying his lust for revenge, heralding the triumph to come.

The sweetness of retribution.

Their mission is to arrest Per Asker, ideally without anyone getting hurt.

But deep down inside he wants to see the man humiliated.

Crushed.

And he knows why.

Leo Asker.

Leo fucking Asker, who gives him no peace.

Who torments him even at home, in the security of his bed. Wakes him up in the middle of the night, horny and frustrated. Reminds him of his weakness, challenges his authority. He must get rid of her, chase her from his head, from his life.

By every means at his disposal.

His phone starts to ring. Her name appears on the hands-free display, almost as though she could tell he was thinking about her.

"It's Leo Asker," Eskil says, entirely unnecessarily. "What the fuck do you think she wants?"

Hellman hits the answer button.

"What do you want, Asker?" he says, without even a glance at Eskil.

"To try to stop you from making a huge mistake," she replies. "You're heading to the Farm with all your cavalry. But I have a lead on another suspect."

"Oh, have you now?" Hellman tries to keep his voice neutral, but it's impossible.

"Tord Korpi did a job for Gunnar Irving at Astroholm Manor just before he was murdered. A secret job that he got paid for in cash. I have credible information that—"

Hellman takes a deep breath.

"So you're telling me it was Gunnar Irving who murdered Korpi and then tried to frame your father? Is that what you're saying?"

"Not exactly . . ."

"Oh no, both Eskil and I heard you. You're claiming that a world-renowned business leader and multimillionaire murdered a black-market builder. Him and not your insane, violent, doomsday-prepper dad who was in possession of the victim's money and lives next door to where the body was found."

He and Eskil exchange smirks.

"All I'm saying is . . ."

To his satisfaction he hears her reining herself in.

". . . that you should hold off. Don't take any unnecessary risks. Per's dangerous when backed into a corner. Give me another day and I'll have enough evidence for you. You can get all the glory again, just like . . ."

She bites her tongue, but it's too late. The gist has already slipped out.

Has hit him straight in his sore point. She knows it, he knows it—fuck, even Eskil knows it.

Hellman clenches his jaw so hard he can feel his teeth creak.

"Now listen, Asker," he says, as calmly and collectedly as possible. "You're in no position to be asking me for a fucking thing. On multiple occasions I have expressly instructed you to stay away from this investigation. And now you call me and try to convince me to stand down a planned operation on your father. The police commissioner will be hearing about this, you can count on that. Your meddling will have consequences. Now, if you'll excuse me, I have a raid to conduct."

He ends the call abruptly and sits in silence for a few seconds, trying to regain his composure.

Eskil looks as though he wants to say something, but he doesn't know quite what.

"Fucking cunt!" he eventually splutters, which is a mild understatement.

"Hit the music," Hellman snarls. "I want Wagner at full fucking volume!"

Eskil does as he is told.

Hellman's fingers squeeze the wheel when the strings whirl to life through the speakers, and he hits the gas harder when the ominous horns strike up. Behind him the other cars also up their speed.

"Just like *Apocalypse Now*," Eskil whoops over the music.

Hellman doesn't reply.

The charge has begun, he thinks. The horsemen of destiny are on the move.

The hour of revenge and retribution is nigh.

ASKER

Hellman hangs up on her, which is pretty much what she expected. Still, Asker had to at least try to get him to come to his senses. Now that that option is blown, there is only one other way to put a stop to this madness.

Her mother picks up on the first ring.

"Isabel Lissander."

"I need your help," Asker says briskly.

"In what way?"

"I need the number for Per's satellite phone. The one he called you from when he asked for your help."

The line goes silent for a few seconds.

"May I ask why?"

"Because SWAT teams are on their way to the Farm. It could end in a bloodbath. I'm going to ask him to give himself up. Again."

Isabel clears her throat quietly but makes no reply.

"I need that number, Mom," she says, in as soft a tone as she can manage. "It's urgent."

The signals go through. Not the single, repeated tone one hears when calling a cellphone, but double rings, more metallic. After the fourth ring the line clicks.

"Isabel?" Per's voice says, almost a little surprised.

"No, it's me," she replies.

"Oh, my lost daughter." His tone flips to sarcastic. "So you've ganged up with your mother. Are you calling to ask me to give up?"

"I'm calling to ask you not to do anything stupid."

He chuckles. She hears a sound in the background. Perhaps a woman's voice?

"You're in no position to ask me for anything," he says sharply.

"That's almost exactly what Hellman told me just a minute ago, before he hung up on me. I was trying to convince him that I . . ."

she corrects herself, ". . . that *we* are close to finding who really killed Korpi and tried to frame you for the murder. Do you know of the company AlphaCent and the Irving family? Gunnar the Space Case?"

A brief silence.

"I'm listening," Per eventually says.

"Korpi was working on some kind of secret underground facility at their Astroholm estate. His car was found in the vicinity, abandoned but with the keys still in the ignition, as though someone wanted it to be stolen. Probably straight after the car was used to dump the body near the Farm so that you'd get the blame."

More silence.

"My team and I are working around the clock to tie up the case," she goes on. "I also have someone on the inside at Astroholm helping us, and I've had confirmation that someone in the Irving family met Korpi. All I'm asking for is a little more time."

Silence.

"Just a few days," she adds. She comes dangerously close to throwing in a *please*, but stops herself just in time.

The call ends with a click.

When she tries to call back, the satellite phone is no longer connected.

HILL

Water and old mines are not a good combination, that much he knows for sure. The water erodes walls and causes props to rot or rust. It makes the rock porous and unpredictable, leading to cave-ins.

Despite this, Hill moves closer to the rising sound.

He reaches a cave of around six hundred square feet in size. He sweeps his flashlight around, finds several gaping openings leading to other mine tunnels, presumably the ones that lead to the other guest villas.

The floor and walls are uneven, which suggests that the cave is natural and not excavated, unlike the tunnel he just came through. That's a good sign. Caves are significantly more structurally sound than old abandoned mine tunnels.

Through the middle of the cave runs a stream, maybe six feet wide.

It starts as a small, purling waterfall on one wall, then extends across the cave before disappearing through the floor on the other side.

In the glow of his flashlight the black water looks like liquid glass. Hill can't tell how deep it is.

He stops, tries to call to mind Bernhard's old map. He should be pretty close to the manor house by now.

He goes on probing the cave with his flashlight. The walls are dripping with humidity, and stalactites hang from the ceiling. Here and there he sees mottled fields of underground lichen that live their entire lives in darkness.

Hill's flashlight picks out a footbridge over the stream. It looks fragile, the damp having eaten away at both the metal and the wood. But on the other side he sees yet another passage, and he realizes that he must cross the water if he is to reach the manor house.

He takes a couple of tentative steps. The footbridge creaks faintly but shows no other sign of wanting to give way. Hill takes another few cautious steps.

When he is halfway across he hears a splash in the water below him. Something shiny and scaly flashes in the periphery of the light, but Hill doesn't get a chance to see what it is. What kind of creatures could live down here, in eternal darkness?

Does he even want to know?

He shudders, quickens his pace.

The passage on the other side is wider than the one he took earlier. It is probably one of the main tunnels that radiate from the original shaft, one that splits after the cave with the stream.

The sound of his footsteps suddenly changes, and when he shines his light on the floor of the tunnel he sees that it is covered in a layer of blast stone.

The air becomes dryer again, and the bedrock's breath has changed. Acquired another, more chemical note. Hill can also make out a faint sound. A muted bass note that grows in intensity with every step he takes.

He turns off the flashlight. The darkness before him has loosened to a kind of twilight. He keeps edging forward with cautious steps.

The tunnel veers to the right, then opens up into a cavernous man-made chamber, faintly lit by a reddish glow.

Most of the walls are lined with concrete, with only patches of bedrock peering out here and there.

In the middle of the chamber stands a construction, a rectangular concrete box that extends all the way to the ceiling. It is the size of a two-story house, but lacking in windows. On one side stands a large, horizontally inverted steel tank, on the other a large cabinet that appears to house some sort of technical equipment.

Hill can't help but gasp.

He has found the secret laboratory.

ASKER

Over the radio that Zafer has set up for her she hears that Hellman's gang have reached the designated command post, not far from the Farm. Before long they will start the deployment.

Once everything is ready, a negotiator will try to make contact with Per, presumably via the intercom. The very same intercom that Martin would use to get her out of there when they were kids.

She wonders how he is getting on at Astroholm. Has he found traces of the underground facility that Tord Korpi helped to build?

But if he has, shouldn't he have called her?

Restlessly she gets to her feet, thinking she should go get a cup of coffee. It is almost six o'clock, a wintry night has fallen outside, and she assumes that her other Lost Souls have already slipped off home for the night.

But out in the corridor the doors are all open, and to her surprise she hears a faint murmur of voices from their new briefing room.

Virgilsson pokes his head through the doorway.

"Good," he says. "I was just coming to fetch you."

Zafer, Rosen, and Attila are already waiting in the room.

"We have some updates on the deaths linked to the Irving family," says Virgilsson. "Take a seat!"

Asker sits down on one of the chairs.

Rosen quickly flicks through her papers, then stands up, walks over to the whiteboard, and picks up a pen. Her usual nervous energy has all but vanished.

"If we start with the head gardener."

She writes the year *1992* on the whiteboard, followed by the name *Björn Knudsen*.

"Knudsen had worked at Astroholm Manor for almost thirty years. He was found murdered in an area of woodland just over a mile from the estate—apparently the landowner had hired him to fell some trees. The cause of death was blunt force to the head. No evidence was found at the scene, nor could they find anyone who would have reason to wish Knudsen ill. The investigation was fairly ambitious: they interviewed people who lived around the scene of the murder, set up an anonymous line for tip-offs, even did a special report and reenactment on national TV to appeal for witnesses. But nothing ever came of it, and the case was eventually closed. Which brings us to the next death: the car crash in Miresjön Lake."

Virgilsson hands Rosen a piece of paper, and she writes the year *2001* on the board and beside it *Pontus Ursvik*.

"A black BMW flies off the road for some unknown reason on the night of January 6. It is the same night that a meteorite passes over the area, and people call the emergency services in their droves to report seeing a UFO."

Rosen glances at the piece of paper before going on.

"The car is driven by twenty-four-year old Viggo Irving, who has recently returned to the country after studying in the USA. He has had dinner with the rest of the Irving family at Astroholm Manor and is on his way back to Malmö, where he lives. With him in the car is twenty-eight-year-old Pontus Ursvik, who has worked in marketing at AlphaCent for two years. Ursvik is also Maud Irving's boyfriend."

There is a short pause while Rosen writes the name *Viggo Irving* diagonally under Ursvik's.

"The night is cold, and there are patches of ice on the road. The car tumbles down a slope, shatters through the ice on Miresjön Lake and sinks to the bottom. The emergency services find Viggo Irving in the water. By that point his body temperature is extremely low, and he is clinically dead. At the hospital doctors manage to revive him, but his injuries are so severe that he is never able to be questioned. The car is salvaged the very next day, and Pontus Ursvik's body is found in the back seat. The cause of death is drowning. The body also has a number of injuries to it, but the forensic examiner draws the conclusion that Ursvik must not have been wearing his seatbelt, and that those injuries were caused by him being thrown around in the car."

Rosen puts the lid back on the pen and gestures at Virgilsson to continue.

The little toad turns to Asker.

"Everything points to this being a tragic accident," he begins. "Except for one detail. It was Enok who noticed it."

"It was the middle of the night," Zafer says loudly. "The accident happened on a secluded stretch of road, and the car went through the ice. The area is mostly forestland, and there are no homes for miles around. Nor were any witnesses named in the report."

He adjusts his hearing aid, giving Asker time to see where he is going with this.

"So who raised the alarm?" she asks. "Who called for help fast enough that the emergency services could make it there in time to save Viggo's life?"

"Good question!" Zafer nods. The movement spreads to the rest of his colleagues.

"We've tried to access the report and the recording of the phone call," Virgilsson jumps in. "Unfortunately they have long since been removed. But someone must have reported it. Bearing in mind the fact that Pontus Ursvik's body was found in the back seat, one might deduce that there was a third person in the car. Someone who, like Viggo, was sitting in the passenger seat and who managed to get out of the car before it sank. Who then raised the alarm to the emergency services but left the scene before they could get there."

"That is of course just guesswork and nothing more," Zafer concludes. "Though rather good guesswork, if we may say so ourselves."

Rosen writes the words *third passenger?* beside Ursvik's name.

"There is also one other death that may have something to do with all of it."

She writes the year *1991* at the top of the board.

"Rickard Bure, seventeen years of age, was found beaten to death in a neighboring municipality around twenty miles from Astroholm. I found the case when I was looking for similarities between these deaths and other unsolved murders in the communities around Astroholm. Bure was found in a parking lot behind the local soccer club. Just like Björn Knudsen, the cause of death was blunt force trauma to the head, and, just like Knudsen, neither leads nor a motive were found. There was some speculation that it could have been a fight between youths that got out of hand, but they never found anything concrete. There is no clear link to either the Irving family or to Astroholm."

Rosen spins her pen between her fingers a few times.

"But," she says, "since Bure was found at the soccer club, with his sports bag beside him, I managed to find out what league he played in, and what teams he had recently played. Sports clubs are great—they save *everything*. Including old records of league matches and team lineups. Just two weeks before Bure's death, he played a team from Astroholm's area, for example. And the team captain was a fifteen-year-old by the name of . . ."

She turns to the whiteboard and begins to write.

"Viggo Irving," Asker mumbles.

"That's right," says Rosen, who then puts the lid back on her pen, more definitively this time.

Asker looks at the whiteboard.

"So we have three deaths in total," Virgilsson summarizes. "And Viggo Irving is the lowest common denominator we could find."

In just three hours, Asker adds inwardly.

"Good work," she says emphatically. "Really great work, everyone."

The Lost Souls nod, first at her, then at one another, as though agreeing with her conclusion.

"On the other hand, it's harder to link Viggo Irving to Tord Korpi," says Attila. "When Korpi died in 2006, Viggo was a care package. The same goes for 2019, when those urban adventurers, or whatever they're called, drowned in the lake. Either way, there do seem to be weird things going on out at Astroholm, and if Korpi somehow got wind of those, it could well have cost him a bullet in the neck."

Asker leans back in her seat. The information they have dug up is compelling, but it won't be enough to stop Hellman.

"Do we know anything more about the escape from the hospital? About the silver car that Per's accomplice used?" she asks.

Virgilsson shakes his head. "It looks like it's going to be a few days before my contact at the parking company can get the license number, I'm afraid. On that front we will come no further—at least not tonight."

The group's facial expressions reflect varying degrees of regret.

"OK," Asker says. "Thank you all. Really well done. Now go home and sleep in tomorrow, if you feel like it."

Her team get up and disappear one by one through the door.

Attila hangs around.

"I'll keep chasing my colleague for that old photo," he says. "Of Korpi and the unknown woman."

"Good. I'm pretty sure it's Karin Irving, but it would be good to have that confirmed."

"I'll keep at it," he agrees. "I'll let you know as soon as I have it."

He pauses for a second. "So what are you going to do now? With your dad and all?"

Asker shrugs.

"The only thing I can do. Drive up to the Farm."

HILL

With cautious steps he enters the cavernous chamber. Dotted around the walls are faint, red lights that allow him to move through the space with his flashlight off. The hum he heard earlier grows all the louder, and he suspects it is coming from a fan station at one side of the concrete structure.

Hill passes another old mining tunnel that has been refilled with large boulders. He wonders if it might have been Tord Korpi's idea to dump the boulders in some of the mine tunnels, instead of hauling them up to the surface when they excavated this place. One way of not revealing what was going on down below.

He walks along one wall of the concrete structure, then rounds the corner. So far he hasn't seen a door. The steel tank towers high above him. Large tubes link it to the structure, and a warning on one side reveals that it contains LN_2. Liquid nitrogen, a substance used to create extremely cold conditions.

Around the back of the structure he finds another mine tunnel, but this one is barred by a wrought-iron gate.

Inside the gate, on the rock wall, someone has painted an arrow with the letters *AM*. Hill's heart pounds a few extra beats. If AM stands for Astrofield Mine, then this passage could be the underground link between the mainland and Boulder Isle.

He feels the gate. It's unlocked.

Part of him wants nothing more than to explore the tunnel, but he realizes this is the wrong time for that kind of undertaking.

He turns back to the concrete structure, turns on the flashlight, and sweeps it over the windowless façade that stretches all the way up to the chamber ceiling.

When he lowers the flashlight again he discovers what appears to be an inscription at the very base of the concrete.

He steps closer. Someone has drawn in the concrete while it was still wet. Put their signature on the construction.

TK 2006

TK—that must stand for Tord Korpi.

He has found the proof that Korpi really was hired by the Irving family, just what Leo needed, and he should get out of there right now. But he still has one side of the concrete box to explore.

Curiosity gets the better of him, and he rounds the third corner of the structure.

His flashlight illuminates a small staircase and a steel door.

He tests the handle warily. The door is locked.

But Karin Irving's bunch of keys had two keys on it, and he has only used one. He has to at least give it a try.

ASKER

On the road north again. It feels like Asker has hardly done anything but drive in the past few days. Her entire journey is accompanied by the sounds of the police radio.

Hellman's gang have started to find their bearings up in the forest. The mobile command center is in place, scouts and snipers deployed. Next up will be the tactical teams, and then the helicopter.

So what is she going to do when she gets there? Try yet again to convince Hellman of her theory? Even though she is now certain that the Irving family is in some way implicated in Tord Korpi's death, she still has no watertight evidence that Tord Korpi was even at Astroholm Manor—only a note from Attila's notebook to state that he tailed Tord Korpi there, and Martin's word that Karin Irving confirmed having met him.

In other words, seen from Hellman's viewpoint:

A sixteen-year-old memo from a periodic alkie, and secondhand intel from a source with mental-health issues.

The photo Attila mentioned, of Korpi and Karin Irving, could perhaps make her information more stable—if it exists, that is. Or if Martin manages to find something to corroborate the fact that Korpi worked on the laboratory under the estate. But when it comes to him, so far, so silent.

In conclusion: she has nothing that can convince Hellman to stand down, and Per has disconnected his satellite phone.

So what does she think she can offer by being there?

The closest she can come to an answer to that question is that she can't just sit still. She has to at least be there.

See it with her own eyes.

Whatever it is that's coming.

HILL

Hill takes the other key on the ring and inserts it into the lock. Turns it with a click scarcely audible over the hum of the fans.

He presses the handle and opens the door a crack.

He is struck by a waft of cold air. The room inside is large, and only faintly lit. In the middle of the room stand what appear to be four large, white tanks that run from floor to ceiling, bearing the AlphaCent logo.

Beyond them a staircase leads upward.

A myriad of pipes and cables run in and out of the tanks, which have monitors on their fronts.

These must be the cryochambers that Nova was talking about.

Is it inside one of these that Gunnar plans to be frozen?

Hill can't resist the temptation to investigate. He walks over to the first chamber and touches its surface. It feels solid, dull. This is probably just a casing to insulate the vacuum flask inside. The pipes running in and out of the chamber must contain liquid nitrogen.

The thought of spending eternity in one of these containers, floating weightlessly just like that glass frog, is at once fascinating and deeply unpleasant.

Hill brushes against the monitor's screen. It immediately sparks to life, and a camera image appears on the display. It takes Hill a few seconds to realize the image depicts the inside of the tank.

It is empty, but beneath the image there is a name: *Gunnar Irving*.

Hill gulps. He guessed right: this is Gunnar's future resting place.

In this tank, frozen to minus three hundred degrees, his vitrified body will await resurrection.

Hill desperately wishes he had his phone to hand in spite of it all, so that he could photograph everything. In any case, it's high time he got out of here. Got back to ground level and contacted Leo.

He takes a few steps toward the door, but then stops.

There are three other cryochambers.

Who are they for? Are more family members going to be frozen in future? Or are they just reserves, in case one or two go wrong?

He listens carefully in the direction of the stairs, to try to hear if anyone's up there. But all is calm and still.

Hill walks over to the next tank and taps the monitor.

It comes to life, and the camera image of the inside of the tank appears. But instead of showing an empty container, a man's face is visible.

Hill jumps, and his heart valve starts to race.

The man's skin is white and granular, as though it were made of ice or crushed glass. His facial features are somewhat distorted.

Still, he has no difficulty recognizing the man inside the tank, even without the caption beneath.

It's Bernhard Irving.

Gunnar's father.

HELLMAN

The mobile command center is a repurposed trailer that has been fitted out with communications equipment and monitors. Hellman sits at the desk in the middle, alongside Eskil, the commander of the tactical unit, a radio operator, and an image technician.

"We have drone shots now," says the image technician, who then clatters away on a keyboard.

A bird's-eye view of the Farm appears on one of the big screens at the end of the unit: murky barracks and trailers clustered in the middle of a plot enclosed by a double barbed-wire fence.

Hellman turns to Eskil.

"Any news from the scouts?"

"No, nothing. Nothing on the thermal imaging cameras, either. Per Asker's lying low in his bunker."

"And the chopper?"

"Fueled and ready," the radio operator replies. "The pilot's awaiting orders."

"The power company?"

"They'll cut the power on our orders."

"Good." Hellman turns to the commander of the tactical unit. "Are the snipers in place?"

"Yes, we have the whole area covered. No living thing will move in there without us seeing it."

Hellman collects himself for a few seconds. Tries to resist an unprofessional smirk. They are ready. The forces are gathered. But before he can let them at it, one final task remains.

"Well, then," he says. "I suppose I'd better ring Per Asker's bell and kindly ask him to hand himself over. Anyone care to join me?"

ASKER

She has backed her car in between two thick spruce trees, where it won't be visible. Chosen a spot where she can keep an eye on the approach to the Farm while listening to the police radio. The mobile command center is less than a mile away, even closer as the crow flies. If she lowers her window, every now and then she can hear the hum of their drone.

By this point they are finalizing their preparations for the first act. At any moment now they will send out a negotiator to try to establish contact. Get Per to hand himself over voluntarily.

He's not going to do that, but for this kind of operation they still have to play it by the rule book.

Sure enough, a car does appear on the road, and she raises her binoculars.

A black reconnaissance vehicle with two people in it.

When the car passes, she manages to spot Hellman at the wheel. Clearly he plans to handle the negotiations himself.

Per knows their operation will start with someone ringing on that intercom to try to make contact—and he is an expert with explosives.

Which means that whoever sets their finger on that buzzer is risking their life.

Hellman is well aware of that, but still he is going there himself.

A brave move, she must admit.

Or maybe just stupid.

That remains to be seen.

HILL

Hill can barely breathe. Bernhard Irving hasn't been cremated or buried under the stone by the lake. He lies here in a tank, frozen to minus three hundred degrees. Vitrified; turned to glass.

On shaky legs Hill walks over to the next tank.

He takes a deep breath and taps the screen. Braces himself for what it is going to show.

Another glassy face appears. A young man who at first he doesn't recognize. Not until he reads the text beneath: *Elis Brorson, 2019.*

The hairs on the back of his neck scrape against his collar. Elis, the missing urban explorer who was presumed drowned.

He gulps, forces himself to walk to the fourth and final tank.

His hand is shaking when he touches the screen.

But the tank is empty, which comes as some relief.

The name at the bottom of the monitor nevertheless makes him flinch: *Viggo Irving, 2006.*

So Viggo also passed away and was frozen, five years after his car crash.

He has lain dead here in a freezer tank for the past sixteen years.

Something Nova Irving said pops into Hill's head.

Gunnar's been researching cryonics since the nineties.

Bernhard died in 1996. So was he Gunnar's first research specimen? That would make Viggo his second, and Elis his third.

But where is Viggo's body?

A sound makes Hill give a start. A door opens somewhere above him, and at the same time the lights in the ceiling spark to life.

Hill instinctively raises his hand to protect his eyes from the bright light.

"Hello? Who's there?" he hears Dr. Schiller's voice calling from up the steps.

Hill turns on his heel and races toward the exit.

HELLMAN

He and Eskil are standing in front of the intercom by the gate to the Farm. From a post some feet inside the double-barbed-wire fence a surveillance camera stares down at them.

Eskil fiddles nervously with his holster belt.

"How do we know Asker hasn't mined the intercom?" he asks.

"He hasn't," says Hellman.

"But how do we know for sure? Wouldn't it be better to bring in those mine guys from the military to take a look?"

Hellman shakes his head.

"Per Asker's a narcissist," he says. "He won't want to miss this opportunity to show us how fucking smart he is."

Eskil doesn't seem entirely convinced. "Are you sure about that?"

"Dead certain." Hellman immediately regrets his choice of words.

He steps forward, pauses for a moment with his finger by the button, and takes a deep breath. Then he presses it.

Nothing happens.

Hellman breathes a quiet sigh of relief; Eskil's is more audible.

A few seconds pass. Hellman presses the buzzer again.

"Maybe he doesn't want to talk," says Eskil.

Hellman shakes his head again.

"Per Asker loves the sound of his own voice. Just you wait."

The speaker crackles to life. Hellman holds up the police radio and locks the push-to-talk button, so that everyone tuned into the channel can hear.

"Detective Superintendent Hellman," says Per Asker's voice. "So nice of you to come for a visit. What can I do for you?"

"You can come out of your hole and walk toward the gate with your hands on your head," Hellman replies.

Per Asker gives a chuckle.

"You know, Jonas, you're funny. The last time we talked, you promised you'd keep me locked up for months. Why should I let you do that?"

"Because if you don't come out, then we're coming in to get you. There's no more to it than that."

"Do you like fireworks, Jonas?"

Hellman doesn't reply, merely glances up at the camera.

"Do you like fireworks?" Per Asker repeats. "If you do, I can promise you a real treat tonight."

"Is that a threat?" Hellman asks.

"All I'm saying is, if you try to enter the Farm by force, then there's going to be a real big bang. Maybe I should fire one off now, while you're standing by the gate?"

Hellman notices Eskil fidgeting anxiously.

"Is there anything I can say or do to get you to hand yourself over voluntarily?" Hellman asks.

"I think you know the answer to that question. And you probably also know that my daughter's right when she says she has the real murderer in her sights. But you don't care about that, do you, Jonas? You just can't stand the thought of her beating you yet again."

Hellman takes a deep breath. The man is trying to destabilize him. Making one last, pathetic attempt to fuck with him. He can't let himself be affected, especially not when all his colleagues are listening.

"Last warning, Per," he says, as calmly as he can. "Come out with your hands on your head and no one gets hurt."

Silence for a few seconds.

"Thanks for the offer, but I think I'll pass. Hope you like the fireworks."

A click signals that Per Asker has ended the call.

Hellman gives the camera one last look, then turns around and walks to the car with Eskil at his heels. He raises the police radio to his mouth.

"Well, there you have it, ladies and gentlemen. As you heard, Per Asker has no intention of giving himself up. Cut the power, deploy the helicopter, and prepare for entry."

HILL

Once he has sprinted halfway through the excavated chamber, an alarm starts to blare, telling him what he already knew.

He has been caught.

Hill tries to up his pace, but the blast stones on the ground make it difficult to find his footing. He looks over his shoulder. The red lights have been turned up brighter, revealing all that previously lay cloaked in shadow. On the wall of the concrete structure sits something that could be a dome security camera.

Fuck!

In his eagerness to explore the laboratory he hadn't even considered he might be being watched.

He races into the mine tunnel and rounds the corner. The sound of the alarm is immediately dampened, and the light disappears. Hill flicks on his flashlight and keeps running.

He hears no pursuers now. Perhaps they don't yet know where he went? Haven't had a chance to check the cameras. This gives him a small head start.

An opportunity to gather his thoughts.

Once he reaches the cave with the stream, he stops to catch his breath. He is low on oxygen and his pulse is thundering through his eardrums, and he must bend double with his hands on his knees just to stay on his feet. There is no way that he will be able to run all the way back to Villa Arcturus—especially not uphill.

He needs to conserve his energy. Use his head. But right now it's spinning from all his thoughts.

So Bernhard was frozen back in 1996. The tank containing his body must have been stored somewhere else for several years—perhaps up in the medical suite, or in the manor house's basement?

At some point in 2006 Tord Korpi is hired to build the secret underground laboratory. That same year, Viggo ends up in a freezer tank, and Korpi gets a bullet in his head.

He was going to help Viggo.

That's what Karin said about Tord Korpi.

But help him how? Why has Viggo's body disappeared, and what happened to poor Elis Brorson that meant that he, too, ended up in a freezer tank?

His break to think is over. Hill sets off again, at a slower pace this time. Carefully crosses the footbridge.

Still he doesn't hear any pursuers, only the purling water. But it no longer calms him—rather the reverse.

Dr. Schiller must have seen that it was him in the laboratory. He—or, more likely, Samuel—will go to Villa Arcturus and wait for him to show up in the basement. Find out whether he poses a threat to the project or to Gunnar, and deal with him accordingly.

Will he have time to make it back to the house and leave the estate before then?

He tries to do the math, estimating his own speed against theirs aboveground. The results don't come up in his favor.

He needs another plan.

A way of getting out of Astroholm without being discovered.

He reaches the half-boarded-up mine tunnel and stops. Then steps through the planks and shines his flashlight on the sprawling letters painted on the wall.

Villa C.

Hill nods to himself.

Not a bad idea at all.

THE GLASS MAN

The alarm signal rings out through the underground. He knows what it means.

There is an intruder in his dominion.

Someone who has uncovered its secrets, and who mustn't be allowed to get away.

He runs through the tunnels, stopping now and then to listen and take scents.

It doesn't take him long to realize who the intruder is. He can smell his familiar scent, hear his movements as he lurches on in the hope of escape. The sounds of his mechanical heart echoing through the darkness.

The Stranger's impudence knows no bounds.

This time no one can save him.

ASKER

She has heard every word of Per and Hellman's cockfight over the police radio. The rest has followed the expected script.

Hellman's gang have cut the power to the Farm, which is pointless, since Per has an underground tank with hundreds of gallons of diesel and no fewer than two emergency generators. But the measure is more symbolic than effective. A way for Hellman to flex his muscles.

Recently she heard the throb of a helicopter's rotors as it passed on its way to the loading area over by the command post.

Soon it will take off again.

Fly toward the Farm to drop one of the tactical teams inside the fence. And when it does, all hell will break loose.

The fireworks will begin, to quote Per.

But something about that description doesn't sit right.

Throughout her entire childhood, Per drummed it into Asker to use correct terminology. To distinguish a pistol from a revolver, a flag from a standard, detonation from deflagration.

Never before has she heard him describe explosions as fireworks. But perhaps he just wanted to mess around with Hellman. Speak a language that he understands.

The scar on her arm is itching wildly, and she needs to go to the bathroom.

She opens the car door and steps out into the darkness. Pulls down her pants and supports herself against a suitable tree trunk while she squats.

In the distance she hears the pulse of an approaching helicopter. It sounds like the clap of horses' hooves.

The sound turns to a roar when the helicopter sweeps past overhead, just above the treetops.

HILL

The tunnel to Villa Canopus is, as already noted, in poor condition. It has more wooden props, and here and there lie piles of rubble from small roof falls. In several places Hill must step around fallen blocks the size of soccer balls.

In addition, the ceiling is also getting gradually lower.

Normally Hill doesn't have a propensity for claustrophobia, but in this ever-contracting tunnel it is impossible not to imagine all the hundreds of tons of rock looming overhead, ready to fall at any minute.

If he can just make it to Villa Canopus, then he has a good chance of getting himself out of here, he keeps telling himself. If Maud is back from Malmö, he can ask her to smuggle him out in her car. Maud isn't one of the inner circle, and she probably doesn't know what is going on here—especially not the part that involves her brother's frozen body.

He stops to once again catch his breath. Turns off the flashlight and listens. All he hears is the drip of water and his own heavy breaths.

While gathering his strength, he tries to piece together the rest of the puzzle.

In 2001, Viggo dies in the icy waters of Miresjön Lake, only to be brought back to life.

His injuries are so severe that he requires a specialist's care—perhaps abroad, as so many have claimed. Or—which now seems more likely—he is cared for at Astroholm until his passing. According to the tank monitor he was frozen in 2006, the same year Tord Korpi was murdered.

One could of course imagine Gunnar wanting to freeze Viggo in the hope of curing him at some later date. Imagine his actions being motivated by fatherly love.

But then why was Tord Korpi murdered?

Did he try to help Karin put a stop to Gunnar's plans, and pay for it with his life?

The cryonics project is ultimately about giving Gunnar eternal life—on that point both he and Nova were clear.

By extension, every threat to the project is a direct threat to Gunnar himself.

The next piece of the puzzle relates to the dead urban explorer, Elis Brorson. Did he also drown, just like his partner? Or were the UFO couple partly right in their conviction that the urban explorers stumbled across something out on Boulder Isle? Only it wouldn't have been aliens they stumbled across, but something also connected to the cryonics project. Something that required that they both be eliminated.

Which brings Hill back to his own situation. He wonders what treatment Gunnar will think most suitable for him.

A bullet to the back of the head, a tragic drowning, or perhaps even worse: a place in one of the freezer tanks down in the laboratory, so that Gunnar and his gang can experiment on him.

The damp air has made him start to shiver. He flicks on the flashlight and starts walking again.

The tunnel's condition is increasingly poor, and he must zigzag between fallen rocks and debris. The short break he took has given him no energy to speak of, and his legs are starting to feel heavy.

He shines his flashlight up ahead, trying to figure out how far he has left.

But with his eyes off the ground, he trips on a stone and falls headlong.

His flashlight flies ahead of him, but it doesn't go out.

A sharp pain in his right knee makes him grimace.

He scrambles to his feet and inspects his leg.

A stone has slashed open his pants, leaving a gash on his kneecap. The fabric is already damp with blood.

He swears inwardly, but reminds himself that it could have been worse: he is on a break from his blood thinners, after all.

He walks over and reaches for the flashlight, which has landed by a small muddy puddle. On the edge of the puddle he sees a print that makes him freeze.

A footprint from an enormous boot, one whose tread reminds him of a tractor tire.

The same footprint that the giant, or creature, or whatever it was that chased him through the fog, left in the rose bed.

His unknown, abominable pursuer has been down in these very tunnels.

Perhaps is still here?

A sound makes Hill's heart skip a beat.

Heavy steps echoing through the darkness behind his back.

Coming all the closer.

HELLMAN

The atmosphere in the mobile command center is now electric.

"All tactical teams at the Farm, proceed," the tactical unit commander instructs his men through his headset. "Snipers have permission to shoot."

Two of the screens at the end of the center fill with camera galleries displaying footage from the bodycams of tactical officers on the move. On the biggest screen the drone camera remains. It films the police helicopter as it comes roaring over the treetops toward the Farm. The sight is both stirring and scary.

Its rotor blades are whipping the air, and tactical officers in black uniforms, helmets, and protective eyewear are hanging out of its open doors.

"The horsemen of destiny," Hellman mutters to himself.

The hour of revenge and retribution has finally struck. He can feel the adrenaline coursing through his body. It sharpens all his senses, making him feel strong, powerful, and alive.

He tries to draw out this moment.

In just a few minutes, all of this will be over. He will have won, to the Asker family's loss. Order will be restored.

The drone zooms out. On three sides of the enclosure, other officers dressed in black are moving toward the Farm. They stop to cut holes in the fence before continuing through.

The helicopter has reached its destination, and it hovers a few feet from the ground while the tactical officers leap out with their automatic weapons armed and ready.

As soon as they are out, the helicopter sweeps away, diving back over the treetops with a roar of its engine.

"Delta One, landing complete. Advancing toward the buildings," one of the team leaders confirms.

The radio continues to crackle with new status reports.

"Bravo One, we're through the fence and advancing," the next team updates.

"Alpha One, same thing."

"Charlie One, on the advance."

Hellman feels his pulse start to increase as he follows the action through drone images and bodycams.

This is the most delicate part of the entire operation.

He has over twenty heavily armed tactical officers inside the Farm, and at this very second they are crossing relatively exposed terrain.

"Snipers, any signs of movement from the buildings?" the tactical unit commander asks.

"No," a voice replies over the radio, echoed by several others.

The first team reaches the barracks, then the next, the third, and the fourth.

Hellman exhales. All that remains is to determine before they force entry whether Asker has mined the buildings.

"Bravo One, we have an unlocked door," one of the groups at the rear of the plot informs them. The voice sounds slightly surprised.

"Charlie One, us too."

Hellman frowns. Per Asker could have made one mistake. Forgotten to lock a door. But that he would forget to lock two doors is unlikely.

"Alpha One, we've also found an unlocked door," the third group states. "Movements detected inside. We're going in!"

"Wait!" says Hellman. "Don't go in, it could be a . . ."

A muffled explosion cuts him off. His belly lurches, and his blood runs cold.

ASKER

She stands on a hill among the trees, watching it all unfold through the binoculars: the helicopter; the disembarkation; the tactical teams breaching the fence and making their way to the barracks. Heading for the doors while preparing for entry.

She hears the cry over the radio, of Hellman trying to intervene to stop the amped-up tactical officers from getting ahead of themselves.

The muffled crack and blaze of light that follows makes her instinctively duck. For a brief moment, a millisecond that feels like an eternity, everything is still.

Then someone yells the words *"TAKE COVER!"* over the radio, and the spell is broken.

The sky explodes into a clattering rain of stars, screaming puffs of fire and smoke, and crackling cascades of color that illuminate the Farm and the forests around it. The police radio is flooded with cries and rounds of shots.

All of it mixes with the whirr of rockets, the crack of bangers, and the rumble of explosions, creating a maelstrom of sounds, a cacophony that ends only when Hellman's voice hollers over the radio.

"Hold your fire! Hold your fire, for god's sake! They're only fireworks! Just stupid fucking fireworks!"

HILL

Hill throws all caution to the wind and races, half stooping, through the confined tunnel, his flashlight held out in front of him. His heart valve is rattling, every breath a stab to his lungs, and the blood is flowing from his cut knee. The wound in his thigh has also come to life, protesting loudly at the intensity of his movements.

Behind him the heavy footsteps keep echoing through the darkness.

Hill tries to up his pace even more. He stumbles, crashes into walls, and even comes close to smacking his head against a low crossbar, but somehow he manages to stay on his feet.

The ground now consists mostly of blast stone again, and it has started to incline upward.

He must be close now, must be near Villa Canopus.

At least he hopes so.

His flashlight lights up something big and gray.

The tunnel has fallen in, forming a steep pile of boulders, gravel, and stone dust.

He is stuck, trapped like a rat deep underground.

The footsteps are coming all the closer, the sound mixing with the rap of his pounding heart.

Hill runs his flashlight over the rubble. There appears to be an opening right up by the ceiling.

Stones and gravel spatter around him as he starts climbing the wall of rubble as quickly as he can.

Just as he reaches the top, he turns and glances behind him.

A red glow appears in the darkness.

The sight makes his rib cage contract. An iron hand is squeezing his lungs, and he is frozen, just like in his nightmare. Through the darkness the creature with the red eyes comes racing straight toward him.

Hill forces one short breath into his lungs, then another.

His paralysis gives way, and he spins around and throws himself through to the other side of the rubble.

Somehow he manages to get his legs going and start running again.

Behind him he hears the creature attack the stone blocks.

The red glow is already visible on the ceiling, as though the creature knows exactly where to place his feet, climbing at an unreal pace.

Hill tries to keep his flashlight shining forward as he runs.

He stumbles again, and as he falls forward he throws out his hands to catch himself.

One hand hits something, and he grabs it instinctively to keep himself on his feet.

It's the banister of a spiral staircase, like the one by Villa Arcturus.

Hill grips the banister and starts running up.

Once he has reached the second spiral, he feels the staircase suddenly rock. He casts a quick glance down over the banister.

The creature with the red eyes is staring straight up at him from the base of the staircase. The sight makes Hill's tortured heart skip another few beats.

He forces his legs to move, pressing them up one step at a time, even though his whole body is a mass of pain and lactic acid.

The staircase has started to creak and sway wildly under the double weight of him and his enormous pursuer. For a brief moment Hill thinks the metal will snap; that the staircase will crumble to the bottom of the mine with both of them on it.

But then the flashlight finds a platform.

He has made it.

Hill staggers onto a footbridge similar to the one by Villa Arcturus. Long district heating pipes run beside him, and straight ahead stands a steel door with a handle.

Behind him the staircase groans under his pursuer's movements.

Hill drops the flashlight, throws himself at the door, and turns the thumb-turn lock while pushing down the handle.

The door opens and he falls straight into a laundry room. The room is dark, but the digital display on a washing machine gives him enough light to guide him.

Hill spins around and shuts the steel door, all while searching for something to barricade it with. His eyes land on a large, antique clothes wringer. He takes hold of one of its legs, and with a strength he never knew he possessed he manages to drag the machine across the floor.

No sooner has he gotten the wringer in place than his pursuer crashes into the steel door with a thud so hard the heavy machine rocks.

Hill puts his weight behind it and resists.

His pursuer rams the door again, harder this time.

The wringer moves a few inches, and now a crack appears between the door and the doorframe. Hill tries to get a better footing, but his feet simply slide on the smooth floor.

A third crash, and the crack in the door grows another few inches.

Through the gap he can hear the heavy breaths of his pursuer.

"Help!" he cries. "Maud!"

He throws all his weight behind the wringer while waiting for a fourth crash.

But none comes.

Instead he hears the sound of heavy footsteps, then the creak of the spiral staircase.

Hill thrusts the wringer back in front of the door, and this time positions it so that it blocks the handle and the door can no longer be opened.

Then he climbs the basement staircase on shaking legs.

"Hello?" he says into the house. "Maud? Elsa?"

No response.

Hill walks over to the windows, bowed. On the other side of the road, by Villa Arcturus, he sees headlights. He makes out movements in the light, sees lamps on in the windows. Samuel is waiting for him over there, and perhaps someone else. If his giantlike pursuer is working with them, then soon they will know where he is.

He should sneak out, weave through the forest. But the drone from the other night will surely be on the lookout for him.

Besides, he is completely drained, and his knee and thigh wounds are throbbing. He doubts he would even make it to the wall, let alone over it.

He needs to patch himself up, gather his strength, and come up with a plan, and ideally find a way to communicate with Leo.

But how? His cellphone is still over in Arcturus.

Might there be a landline somewhere in the house?

Staying low, Hill sneaks through the hallway and into the kitchen, but he sees no phone.

The room is rocking, and his legs have started to shake so much they can barely carry him. He sinks down with his back to the kitchen cabinets to stop himself from fainting.

Then a light sweeps across the living room, making him stiffen.

A car has just pulled up outside the front door.

THE GLASS MAN

His last human memory is of them driving in his car.

Maud, Pontus, and him.

The Father's words are still echoing through his head.

You can go now, Viggo.

Not Prince Pollux, but his normal, mortal name.

The final sign that nothing will ever go back to what it once was; that for now and evermore he shall remain banished, expelled, replaced.

Maud and Pontus are slightly tipsy and are chattering happily, with loud music playing on the radio. In the rearview mirror he sees Pontus gazing at Maud. Something in that gaze bothers him. He pulls over to one side and brakes suddenly.

"Need to pee," he mumbles, tearing open the door.

He stands between some tree trunks and relieves himself. Far below him glitter the black waters of Miresjön Lake, Boulder Isle's silhouette looming like a dark shadow. He has just regained control of his emotions when, without warning, Pontus comes and stands right beside him. Pulls out his penis and starts to pee, too. The stream is powerful, spouting every which way.

"I'm planning to propose to Maud," he says over his shoulder.

His eyes twinkle in the darkness, and there is something familiar about them. Familiar and frightening.

"I just spoke to Gunnar, and he gave me his permission."

Only when he hears the Father's name does he realize where he has seen that look before. That it has been haunting him all his life. Watching over him, judging him.

A thick branch is lying right beside his foot, and he picks it up.

Pontus goes on babbling as though they were old friends, boasting about the future that Gunnar has planned for him in the company.

But he isn't listening anymore. The hunger is tearing him apart, making his pulse pound loudly through his eardrums. It melds with the Father's voice.

You can go now, Viggo.

He swings the branch, aiming for the back of Pontus's head.

Before he knows it, he is sitting astride Pontus's chest, pressing his thumbs deep into his eyes. This time it won't be enough to watch him die. For Pontus's eyes are also the Father's. That very same ruthless, all-seeing gaze from which he cannot hide.

Whose fragile vitreous bodies he must crush to free himself.

Maud tugs and pulls at him, screams at him to stop, but he doesn't hear her.

Not until she grabs the branch from the ground and hits him over the head.

He falls to one side. The blow isn't hard enough to seriously hurt him, but when he gets up she has flung herself over Pontus's lifeless body.

She cries and sobs, screams that they have to save him.

Her tears glint like stars in the night sky.

He holds up his hands. They are covered in blood.

And suddenly it is as though he has awoken from a dream.

Realizes what he has done to her, she who never leaves his thoughts. His sister, his confidante.

He shoves her gently to one side, picks up Pontus, and places him in the back seat. Starts the car and drives as fast as he can toward the hospital.

Maud sobs loudly, urging him to hurry. From the back seat Pontus whimpers faintly, and it isn't too late.

Salvation is within reach.

But then the night turns to day.

A beam of light soars above the treetops, just like in the Father's story. It burns straight into his skull, lighting up his darkest recesses. Makes his heart stop in fear.

He raises his hand to shield his eyes, to escape the Father's all-seeing eye.

Hears Maud's scream, then feels them floating through the air.

The bang when the car slams into the water and his head hits the wheel.

After that he is consumed by the black depths.

Descends into the constant darkness from which no one returns.

He would like to have stayed there.

Should have been allowed to stay there.

HILL

Hill hears footsteps on the gravel outside, then the turn of a key in the front door to Villa Canopus. He presses his back against the kitchen cabinet. He has nowhere to hide, no way out.

The front door opens, and the lights are switched on. Then a dog barks.

"What is it, Orion?" asks Elsa's voice.

The dog barks again, and Hill exhales.

"It's just me, don't be afraid!" he says while getting up from the kitchen floor.

Elsa and Maud are standing in the hallway, still in their jackets. Both look surprised. The dog's eyes are locked on Hill, and he growls, baring his teeth.

"Sorry if I scared you," he says. "But I need a little help."

The dog yelps again, but Elsa shushes it.

"Quiet, Orion, it's only Martin. He's nice, you know that."

The dog stays silent, but he goes on glaring suspiciously at Hill.

Maud crosses the room and looks Hill over from top to toe. He realizes he must be a sight: he is soaked in sweat, his clothes are filthy and covered in rock dust, and one of his pant legs is ripped and bloodied.

"What in the world have you been up to now, Martin?" Maud asks. "Somehow you look even more beaten up than last time."

"It's a long story." He points at Elsa and signals protectively. "I took a tumble on a rock and cut my knee. I probably need patching up."

"Then you've come to the right place," says the girl. "Mom's the best at patching people up."

"My thoughts exactly," Hill replies.

"I'll take Orion out for a little walk," Elsa adds in an insinuating tone of voice. "So you can have your grown-up talk while I'm out."

Hill waits until she is out of earshot.

"I've found something," he then says quietly. "Something top secret. Gunnar and his henchmen are after me."

He points through the window at the lights in Villa Arcturus.

"Found what?" Maud's voice is skeptical, her face, too.

Hill steels himself.

"How involved are you in Gunnar's research projects?"

She gives a little shrug.

"Not at all. Gunnar's director of research, and he kept those kinds of things under wraps even when I was CEO. Now I have even less idea what he's working on."

"The cryonics project, do you know about that?"

"I know it's one of many fields that Gunnar's interested in, but no more than that. Now it's probably time that you told me what all this is about."

Hill takes a deep breath.

"One of Gunnar's projects involves experimenting on how to freeze people. Among others, he's had the bodies of your grandfather Bernhard and your brother Viggo frozen. But also that of a young man who disappeared a few years ago on Boulder Isle and was presumed drowned."

Maud's face goes pale.

"H-how do you know this?"

"It was actually your mother who tipped me off. The laboratory is down in the old mine tunnels under the estate. I got there through the district heating system, but Dr. Schiller caught me, so I didn't dare go back the same way. There was somebody chasing me through the tunnels, too. I fell and hurt myself, as you can see . . ."

"OK, hold up . . ." Maud says, holding her hands up as if trying to shield herself. "My brother isn't dead. Viggo has significant care needs and lives at a specialist facility . . ."

". . . abroad, where he can get the best possible care," Hill finishes her sentence. "That's what everyone says, but how sure can you be of that? When did you or your mother last visit Viggo?"

"We can't visit him," Maud replies. "He's too sick."

"Says who?"

"Gunnar." Her mouth purses to a tight line.

"The whole thing is Gunnar's idea," Hill says. "His plan is to freeze himself in the hope that in future his cancer will be curable.

And in his pursuit of eternal life he clearly doesn't seem to care about laws or ethics. Elis, the urban explorer lying in one of the freezer tanks down there, has a family that still hasn't been able to bury him. Gunnar's probably using his body for medical experiments. The same applies for Viggo and your grandfather. And I need to get out of here as quickly as possible, before they stop me from telling anyone else."

Maud shakes her head, still appears to be struggling to take in what he is saying.

"All of this sounds insane," she says. "I have no idea what you've seen, or think you've seen. But Astroholm is no prison camp, and if you want to get out of here, then of course I'll help you. But first we have to patch you up, before you lose any more blood."

She points at the wet leg of his pants.

"Let me fetch my first-aid kit."

She leaves Hill in the kitchen and disappears into another room. Now that the lights are on, Hill takes the opportunity to look around for a landline.

He finds one tucked away on a table by the banquette in the kitchen.

Picks up the handset and immediately gets a dial tone.

"Yes!" he mumbles to himself while dialing Leo's number.

ASKER

She has been watching the circus down on the Farm through her binocu-lars for a while now. Has seen frustrated officers turn the buildings and barracks inside out, while the helicopter flits around anxiously, sweeping its spotlight around the forest.

All of it is pointless. Per isn't there.

Was it her phone call that convinced him to leave? Made him sneak out through one of his escape tunnels, past Hellman's scouts? She would love to believe that.

But the truth is probably another story.

Cameras, intercom, lighting, sound, and movements—all the signs of life that Hellman's team picked up on—can be remotely controlled from anywhere in the world with an internet connection.

Per wanted them to think he was there.

Wanted her to call and yet again try to convince him to give in. Wanted to prove once and for all that he still has a hold over her. And she walked straight into his trap, just like everyone else.

That's why she isn't laughing out loud at Hellman's failure.

Every now and then she sees him through the binoculars. He and Eskil are trotting around the yard, talking by turns into their phones and their radios, trying to figure out what just happened. To take in the full extent of the ride that Per has taken them on.

Hundreds of thousands of kronor in public money, blown. Quite literally up in smoke, in a display as visually impressive yet pointless as the pyrotechnics that just lit up the forest.

However much she dislikes the whole thing, it is impossible not to admire Per.

He won the tussle, and he celebrated it exactly how he promised he would over the intercom. Rubbed his victory in their faces.

Hope you like the fireworks!

So where is her father now?

Nowhere. At least not where anyone can find him. But she has a feeling that she will be hearing from him again.

Soon.

Her phone starts to ring, and for a brief moment she thinks it is him. That Per couldn't resist the temptation to boast.

But the number calling her is on a landline.

"Hello?" she answers.

"Leo, it's Martin." He's speaking quietly, and his voice sounds tense and agitated. "I've found Tord Korpi's underground build. It's a laboratory, just like we thought, one where Gunnar Irving performs illegal experiments on dead people, including his own son. Korpi must have seen what the build was for, felt a pang of conscience, and then been silenced. And now they're after me. I don't dare use my cellphone; they're tracking it."

"Where are you now?" she jumps in.

"Still on the estate, in Villa Canopus, where Maud lives. She's going to help me get out of here."

"I'm by the Farm," she says. "I'll leave for Astroholm right away. I'll be there in an hour. Where shall we meet?"

"The UFO Café. It's . . ." A loud hum is heard on the line, and then the call cuts out.

"Hello?" she asks. "Martin?"

She calls the number again, but simply hears the beep of an engaged line.

Asker starts her car, but she makes it only a few hundred yards before her phone starts to buzz again. A text message—not from Martin, as she thought, but from Attila.

My colleague finally found the old reconnaissance photo of Korpi and the woman from Astroholm. It was taken in September 2006, and according to the memo their meeting lasted just under half an hour.

Asker pulls over at the side of the road and opens the image. It is taken from a distance through a hefty telescopic lens, and it shows two people sitting in a pickup truck. One of the vehicle's doors is a different color from the rest of the bodywork. It's Korpi's pickup, the same one she hid under when she was listening to his phone conversation.

I'll be there in around an hour. Just calm down . . .

She herself used a similar turn of phrase when she was just speaking to Martin.

As it happens, a similar tone of voice, too.

This whole time she has assumed that Korpi's conversation was work-related, but now that she thinks about it, she has her doubts.

Didn't it sound more personal? As though he was talking to someone he cared about? Sundin and Danielsson did think the woman Korpi met was his lover.

She zooms in on the cab. The two people inside are sitting face-to-face, to all appearances engaged in a serious discussion.

In the driving seat sits Tord Korpi. He looks almost exactly like Asker remembers him. Bearded, hard, and stony-faced.

When she sees the face of the woman in the passenger seat, Asker stiffens. She looks familiar, too: they met just days ago, at Villa Arcturus. Her face is emotional, one hand raised.

That isn't Karin Irving.

Asker throws her phone down onto the passenger seat, puts it into gear, and slams her foot on the gas.

HILL

"Hello!" he says down the line. "Hello, Leo?"

He presses the switch hook a few times, but the dial tone is gone. All the outgoing phone lines from the estate must have been cut. Perhaps they already know he has called Leo?

Maud comes back into the kitchen carrying her first-aid bag.

"Samuel's put out a warning over the app," she says, a troubled look on her face. "Apparently there are intruders on the grounds again. The main gate's closed until further notice, and everyone is advised to stay indoors for their own safety. Guards are patrolling the whole area."

"It's me they're after," says Hill. "The phone lines have just been cut. Check your cell, I'm sure you won't be able to call out of the estate either."

Maud pulls out her cellphone and taps her screen a few times.

"Hm," she mutters. "You're actually right."

She looks at him for a few seconds, then walks over to the window.

"There's a drone out," she says. "And a patrol car down the road."

"And Villa Arcturus?" he asks.

"The lights are still on, and it looks like someone's inside."

She draws the curtains, looks as though she is struggling to know what to believe.

"My friend Leo will meet me at the UFO Café," Hill says. "She's a police officer. All I need is a lift there."

Maud starts fiddling with her first-aid bag.

"We'll have to wait until the gate opens again; they won't let me out just like that either. But you don't need to worry. I'm Gunnar's daughter, after all; I don't even think Samuel would dare come here. And even if he does, I won't let him in, OK?"

"OK." Hill nods tensely.

"Good. Now, take a seat on the banquette and put your leg up so I can look at the wound."

Hill does as she says. He is safe here for now, he tells himself, and Leo is on her way to the UFO Café. He can let himself relax, recharge his batteries a little.

Maud pushes aside the kitchen table to reach him and cuts open the leg of his pants.

"Oh, that looks nasty. You'll need stitches. But I don't have any anesthetic here. Can you soldier through without?"

"Sure," says Hill.

She sits down at his side and cleans the wound, then prepares her needle and thread.

"Hold on."

She gets up, prepares something over at the kitchen counter, and returns with a whiskey glass.

"Old-fashioned anesthesia," she says. "Bottoms up!"

Hill knocks back the contents of the glass. The whiskey burns in his throat, makes him cough a few times.

"Are you ready?" Maud asks.

"Yes."

She inserts the needle at the edge of the wound. Hill groans.

"Just hold out," she says. Her fingers work skillfully with the needle and thread.

Hill shuts his eyes, leans back, and tries to take deep breaths.

After a minute or two the liquor starts to take the edge off the pain.

"You said you spoke to my mother," Maud says, without looking up.

"Mm."

"What did she say?"

"We talked about Tord Korpi. He worked here in 2006. Do you remember him?"

Maud pauses momentarily.

"Yes, though only vaguely." She tightens the sutures in a way that suggests that she has finished.

"Karin said that Tord Korpi promised to help her and Viggo. Does that sound familiar?"

She shakes her head.

"No, not at all."

She applies a dressing over the stitches.

"There, I'm done. Would you like another drink? I'm going to have a glass of wine."

"Thanks, I'm all right," he says. "And if you're going to be driving me, then maybe you should wait until . . ."

Maud doesn't listen. She walks over to the fridge, opens a bottle, and fills her glass to the brim. Then she sits down beside him on the banquette.

Her face is half-alarmed, half-skeptical.

"I get that this is a lot to take in," Hill says. "But what I'm saying is true. Gunnar is performing illegal experiments on dead people down in his laboratory. Including on your brother."

She downs half the wine.

"My brother isn't dead," she eventually says.

"I'm sorry," says Hill. "But it looks like he died in 2006."

Maud shakes her head.

"Viggo's alive," she says.

Hill chooses to stay silent. All of a sudden he feels faintly sick. Clearly the combination of whiskey and fading adrenaline wasn't a winning one.

"I agree it sounds completely craz . . ." he clears his throat, ". . . crazy," he continues. "Tord Korpi was a mining engineer. He made sure the lab was built in secret."

He gulps. His nausea is growing all the stronger, and he is starting to feel a little dizzy. His mouth is dry as dust.

"He and Karin were going to help Viggo. But Korpi . . ."

The sentence hangs in the air. He swallows, tries again.

"Korpi vanished . . ." His mouth doesn't quite want to obey, and his eyelids have started to feel heavy. His body sinks back onto the chair.

Maud gets up, then sighs heavily.

"Gunnar paid Tord for his silence," she says. "He'll do the same with you, Martin, there's no need to worry. Just do as he says."

Hill shakes his head, trying to dispel the fog that is cloaking his thoughts and blurring his vision.

"Kopri . . . Korpi . . ." Using every last ounce of focus that he has, Hill forces his lips to obey him, a few words at a time.

"Korpi's dead," he whispers. "Shot . . ."

His vision muddles even more, then fades to black.

He hears the front door opening. Then Samuel's rugged voice.

"Ah, there he is. Gunnar will be pleased."

ASKER

Asker speeds toward Astroholm as fast as she dares. Throws the car into tight curves, puts her foot down on the straight stretches. She is struggling to get her thoughts straight, knows only that Martin has told Maud Irving about his discoveries in Gunnar Irving's laboratory, believing her to be an ally. Sixteen years ago Tord Korpi did something similar. He trusted Maud, only to end up facedown in a shallow grave.

On top of that, Asker is the one who sent Martin straight into the lion's den, putting him in mortal danger.

She must find him, before it's too late.

Her phone starts to ring again, and Hellman's number appears on the car's display.

She has a good mind to ignore him, but taps the hands-free button anyway.

"Did you know?" Hellman doesn't even try to mask his anger.

"Did I know what?"

She heaves the car around another tight bend.

"That your father wasn't hiding at the Farm. That he was just toying with us?" Hellman's voice is bubbling with rage.

Asker sweeps past a Volvo with so little room to spare that an oncoming truck flashes its full beams at her.

"No, he led me on just as much as you," she says, which is at least almost the truth. "I warned you about Per, tried to explain that he thinks like a chess player: he's always multiple moves ahead. But you didn't fucking listen, since you were too thirsty for revenge—on him and on me."

She can almost hear Hellman gritting his teeth.

"If it makes you feel any better, I can tell you that Per genuinely didn't murder Tord Korpi. I'm on my way to arrest the real murderer instead. But I promise to call you if I need any help."

She hears Hellman inhale, but ends the call before he can get a word in edgewise. Then she presses the gas another half inch, until a warning message starts to flash on the console.

She must find Martin Hill.

HILL

He is asleep, and also not. His body may be dormant, but part of his brain is still awake. Perceives hands taking hold of him. Lifting him up and carrying him from Villa Canopus.

Outside, the driveway is full of bright lights that burn straight through his eyelids, into his brain. They light up every little recess in his head, including the nooks he would rather not see.

The Mountain King's horrific lair. His scent when he leaned over Hill and whispered that he would keep him down there in the shadows.

Then the creature from his childhood nightmares, the one with glowing red eyes that hunted him through the dark mine.

And then, finally, sixteen-year-old Leo and her insane father in the rowboat, the second before the bomb exploded. The bomb that was intended to kill her; the one that Hill might have prevented had he just stuck around and not left her.

The last memory is the most painful, even though it isn't actually his. But the relentless light won't allow him to shut it away.

Hill tries to block his eyes, but every link between brain and body appears to be broken.

The voices around him are at once hard and anxious.

One of them is crying.

Then he is lifted up and laid down on his back. In the trunk of a car. At least he thinks that is where he is.

For a brief moment his vision clears, and he sees the starry sky shining brightly above him. Recognizes the constellations.

Ursa Major.

Cassiopeia.

Leo.

"Double knot," he thinks he hears her whisper.

Then the trunk is closed, and the stars are snuffed out.

ASKER

She drives past the UFO Café, but as expected the parking lot is empty. The phone call came almost an hour ago, and Martin and Maud should have gotten here by now.

She drives on toward Astroholm, pulls up to the gates, and presses the buzzer.

"Hello," a voice answers through the intercom.

"Detective Inspector Asker, Police. Open the gate!"

"What's this regarding?"

"That information is way above your pay grade. Open the gate immediately and you won't be considered an accomplice."

She can hear the guard's hesitancy in the short pause that follows.

"I'm going to have to call my manager—" he begins.

"Do you have a family?" she interrupts. "Do you think they're going to like visiting you in prison? Do you think your wife will wait for you? That your friends will keep in touch? Keep holding me up and you'll have the answers to those questions sooner than you think."

The line goes silent for a few seconds.

Then the gates glide open. As soon as the gap between the two sides is big enough, Asker drives in. The guard has stepped out of his station and waves at her to stop, but she responds by hitting the gas and forcing him to jump aside.

A few minutes later she is outside Villa Arcturus. The villa is bathed in darkness, the front door unlocked.

"Hello?" she calls out in the doorway. "Martin!"

She steps inside, leaves the front door open and turns on the lights. The guard has probably already informed his manager that she is here, so she sees little reason to be discreet.

She looks around. It all looks like the last time she was here.

On a shelf in the kitchen lies Martin's cellphone. It has no signal. Nor does hers, she discovers when she checks.

She goes back to the living room. On the middle of the coffee table a new object catches her eye.

It is a glass jar containing a frog. The creature floats freely in some kind of liquid, so vibrant in color that for a moment she thinks it's still alive. She has seen similar jars in museums.

A preserved frog. She shakes off a shudder.

Hearing footsteps in the gravel outside, she turns toward the hallway.

"Hello?"

A girl is standing in the doorway. She is wearing dark glasses, with a black labrador on a lead.

"Hello!" says Asker. "You must be Elsa? My name's Leo, I'm a friend of Martin Hill's, and I'm looking for him and your mother."

"That makes two of us," says the girl. "Martin turned up at our house a while ago and said he was hurt. Mom was going to patch him up again, so I went out for a walk. When I got home they were gone. I heard a car driving off, so I thought maybe they'd driven here."

"How long ago was this?"

"Forty-five minutes, maybe. I tried calling her, but my phone isn't working."

"Nor mine; there seems to be something up with the signal." Asker tries to sound calming. "But I'm sure it'll be fixed soon."

The dog makes a strange sound, a mix between a growl and a yelp.

"Orion's worried," says Elsa. "Something's off tonight; I can feel it in the air. Like something terrible is about to happen."

Asker feels exactly the same, but she says nothing.

"Would you like a lift back home?" she asks instead.

"We'll walk. Orion doesn't like getting into strangers' cars. But thanks anyway."

Elsa turns and disappears into the darkness.

HILL

Hill wakes up slowly. It takes him several seconds to force his eyelids to open, and when he finally succeeds, he can make out hardly anything at all. His heart is pounding, but in spite of his attempts to sit up in the bed, his arms and legs refuse to comply.

Then his vision sharpens.

He finds himself in a small, windowless room with dimmed lighting. He has been here before, but he can't figure out when.

How the hell did he get here, and what happened to Maud?

He tries to get his brain to unravel it for him, but without success. His mouth tastes of metal and alcohol.

The whiskey. Maud must have put something in the whiskey. Sleeping pills, probably from one of the bottles in her bathroom cabinet. He remembers her saying something about Tord Korpi. But how involved is she in all this?

And how long can he have been out for?

With some effort he manages to sit up. Now he recognizes where he is. The walls, the cabinets, the graphite drawings of Boulder Isle on the walls—he is in the consulting room at the medical suite.

Beside him stands a device for monitoring pulse and blood pressure. Cables with small electrodes dangle from its front. Beyond the machine is a stand with an IV drip, and he spots a Band-Aid on one of his elbow creases. He must have been connected to these machines quite recently. So what have they pumped inside him?

Steps approach from out in the corridor, and then he hears someone pressing down the door handle.

Gunnar Irving is standing in the doorway, an apologetic look on his face.

"Dear Martin," he says. "How are you?"

Hill wets his lips.

"OK," he says warily.

"I must begin by apologizing for all this," Gunnar says. "Maud misunderstood her instructions. All I wanted was the chance to speak to you. I never asked her to . . ."

He gestures down at the bed and the medical apparatus, then tilts his head to one side in concern.

"I really am truly sorry. We've done our best to get you back on your feet, but do tell me what we can do to restore the trust between us?"

"Can I leave?" Hill asks.

"Of course." Gunnar holds his hands out to his sides. "But before you go, I should really like us to talk this through. You've seen things you weren't quite ready for, and you may have drawn some false conclusions. So, please, Martin—ask away! Any question you wish."

Gunnar pulls up a chair and sits down by the bed.

Hill tries to gauge how he should handle this situation.

Despite Gunnar's assurances and friendly manner, Hill will have to be extremely careful if he doesn't want to suffer the same fate as Tord Korpi.

But nor can he appear scared or submissive. Gunnar has viewed him as a confidant—and clearly he still does, or else they wouldn't be having this conversation.

"Maud," Hill says. "She called you before she gave me the sleeping pills."

"That's right."

"So how much does she know about what's going on?"

"Only precisely what she needs to know. I prefer to keep my inner circle as small as possible."

"But she still helps you?"

A self-satisfied look appears on Gunnar's face.

"Maud has always been very loyal. A good girl."

"Even though you banished her, Karin, and Viggo to Villa Canopus?"

"Naturally divorce is regrettable," Gunnar replies. "But I've always looked after my family."

"Even the more tainted parts of it?"

"Ah," Gunnar says with an impressed tone of voice. "You've dug deep into the family's darker secrets. What is it that you've discovered, Martin? Tell me!"

Hill gathers his thoughts one last time, steeling himself.

"Bernhard had a relationship with Karin's mother. He's her biological father. Which means you unwittingly married and had children with your own half sister. When you found out your shameful secret, you discarded your family and started a new, better one. More genetically apt."

"That was all Bernhard's fault," says Gunnar. "I simply did what had to be done to right his wrongs."

"In the same way that you concocted the UFO story to take control of the company."

Gunnar falls silent for a few seconds, as if in thought.

"You're onto something there, Martin. Yes, I was used to having to clean up after my father. Having to drag myself forward by my own bootstraps. That's how we Irvings survive—we look forward."

"So you disowned your family, stopped speaking to your father, and had him frozen after his death?"

Gunnar shakes his head.

"That's Karin's unfortunate understanding of it. Bernhard and I had our conflicts, but he willingly donated his body to science. All of it is meticulously documented. And, as regards my first family, the truth is that I provided for them. I gave them work and opportunities."

"At least until Nova was ready to take over."

"I assign my children's tasks based on their competence, talents, and ability to contribute," Gunnar says dryly. "Sometimes one must make difficult decisions; attend to the whole and not just the individual parts."

Hill observes him. The elderly man almost appears to be enjoying this conversation.

"Like when you decided to freeze Viggo's body, too?" Hill asks. "Was that his contribution? That you would get to experiment on him after death?"

"Dear Martin, I'm afraid you have the wrong end of the stick there, too," Gunnar chuckles. "Viggo was very gravely injured after his car accident. He was clinically dead for over an hour, but he survived because his body had been severely cooled. In short, the cold saved his life. He lay in a coma for several months. When they finally woke him, he was confused and unable to communicate. So we were forced to put him under again. The longer and deeper he slept, the better he felt during his short periods of waking."

"But he died in 2006, and instead of burying him you put him in a freezer tank, just like Bernhard," Hill adds. "Like that preserved frog that you gave me."

Gunnar's smile widens.

"As I said, you have the wrong end of the stick with Viggo. And the frog, for that matter. You see, Martin . . ." Gunnar lowers his voice. "Viggo isn't dead. He is very much alive and kicking. Viggo is my masterpiece. The original Glass Man."

ASKER

Once Elsa has left the house, Asker shuts the front door and returns to the living room. Again, the jar with the frog catches her eye. The animal looks as though it might twitch at any second and start to swim around. Try to find a way out of its glass prison.

Elsa said that both Martin and Maud Irving have vanished, which doesn't bode well.

A flash of light makes her look through the window.

A large, black Merc has pulled up outside, and two men step out of it. One is the security chief she crossed paths with the other day at the main gate. The other is short, round, and bald.

The men don't knock but rather walk straight in.

"Good evening," says the bald one. "You must be Leo Asker?"

His voice is nasal, and his dome bears a thin film of perspiration, in spite of the cold night air. Beneath his jacket she glimpses a doctor's coat.

"My name is Dr. Schiller. I hear you've already met Samuel."

He gestures over his shoulder at the security chief.

"I've come to collect Martin Hill," she says. "Where is he?"

The doctor gives a nervous smile.

"I'm afraid Martin Hill accidentally ingested a dose of sleeping pills. He is currently in our medical suite down in the manor house, where he is receiving treatment."

Asker casts a quick glance at Samuel. Like the previous time, he is watching her with an almost amused look on his face. His hands are crossed over his belt, and his jacket is open. She doesn't doubt for a second that he is wearing a gun beneath it.

"Great, then if you could show me to him," she says, "I'll take him off your hands right now."

"Unfortunately Associate Professor Hill is not in any condition to be moved," the doctor objects. "The best thing would be for him to spend the night in our medical suite for observation. Tomorrow I'm sure he will be feeling better. I'll ask him to contact you then."

He licks his lips, forces an apologetic grimace.

"I'm not leaving here without Martin Hill," Asker says. "Even if I have to kick down every door in this place."

Samuel takes half a step forward.

"You're not here in your capacity as a police officer," he says quietly. "Your reason for being here is entirely personal in nature, which I'm afraid gives you no authority. The best thing you can do is get in your car and leave."

"And if I don't?"

Asker raises her eyebrows.

"Then I'll help you," he says, lowering his brow an inch, which hardens his gaze even more.

"Now, let's calm down, shall we?" the doctor says hastily. "This is all just a misunderstanding. Associate Professor Hill is not in any kind of danger; of that I can assure you."

Asker and Samuel go on glaring at each other.

He is good at staring matches, and he doesn't appear to be bothered by her heterochrome eyes. Samuel is bigger and stronger than she is, and he definitely knows how to fight.

But that doesn't mean she is going to simply fold. Even big, strong men have their weak points.

The doctor licks his lips again. He seems much less keen on confrontation than the security chief.

"Would it help if you could speak to Professor Hill directly?" he suggests.

"I thought you said he was asleep?"

"No no no, he's awake, just a little groggy. Let me make a call."

He takes out his phone and steps through the open front door. She can hear the mumble of him speaking to someone. Evidently his phone has a signal.

Samuel is still standing opposite her.

"How's your father?" he asks. "I heard he's had a run-in with the law."

Asker doesn't break eye contact. She assumes he must have a source inside the police. Security personnel usually do.

Still, it doesn't feel like that explanation quite covers it. Samuel has been giving her strange looks ever since they first met. Smirking as though he knows who she is, as though he knows things about her—and apparently about her father, too.

The more she looks at him, the more convinced she becomes that not only would Samuel be capable of putting a bullet in Korpi's head, but she also wouldn't put it past him to come up with the idea of dumping the body outside the Farm, to lay the murder at her father's door. Could he have hurt Martin, too?

The thought makes her blood run cold.

The question is on the tip of her tongue, but before she can get it out, Dr. Schiller returns with his phone poised, interrupting their staring match.

"Here he is!" he says a little too loudly, his cellphone outstretched. "You're on loudspeaker now, Associate Professor Hill."

"Hello?" she hears Martin's voice say. "Leo?"

Asker's heart somersaults in relief.

"I'm here at Villa Arcturus," she says. "How are you?"

"I'm OK." His voice sounds sleepy. "Took something I shouldn't have. They want me to stay in overnight for observation. But I'll be in touch tomorrow."

"Are you sure? You sounded worried on the phone earlier."

"Yeah, definitely. I'm OK. I accidentally took some medicine, said some strange things. Sorry if I dragged you out here for no reason."

Asker glances at the doctor, who nods eagerly. Samuel goes on staring at her.

"I'd be happy to come get you if you want to leave now," she says.

"Thanks, Leo, I really appreciate it. But I'll stay at the medical suite tonight. My body's not in great shape. I have a headache, and my stomach's one big double knot."

"OK . . ." She drags out her response, feeling the gaze of both men on her. "We'll be in touch tomorrow then. Take care!"

Dr. Schiller ends the call and puts the phone away.

"There," he says, relieved. "So I take it this little misunderstanding has been cleared up, I hope?"

The doctor looks imploringly at Asker.

"Sure," she says.

"Wonderful! Samuel and I will escort you up to the main gate, to make sure you find your way out."

Dr. Schiller takes a step to one side, as if to let her pass.

Asker puts her hands in her jacket pockets and walks to the door between both men.

When she passes Samuel she thinks he almost looks a little disappointed.

HILL

"Thank you for that, Martin," says Gunnar, putting his phone away in his pocket. "Dr. Schiller and Samuel will see to it that your friend gets away. So you and I can iron things out in peace and quiet. Now, where were we?"

He clasps his chin thoughtfully.

"You were telling me about Viggo and his cryonic procedure."

Hill makes an effort to sound attentive, but all that he can think about is the phone call. Did Leo notice that he used their old distress code? Does she even remember they had one?

All he can do is hope, while going on feigning interest and compliance.

"Well, here's what happened." Gunnar's eyes regain the glint they had before the phone call interrupted them. "Viggo was in a bad way, with severe brain damage. But we realized that the longer and the deeper he slept, the better he would be when he woke up. Cryonics offers the deepest sleep anyone can imagine. So it was only natural that we should continue in that vein."

Hill is still trying to get his head around what Gunnar is telling him.

"So you froze Viggo to minus three hundred degrees. Beyond the point when all life ceases. You killed him."

"That's correct," Gunnar nods. "But, more importantly, we brought him back to life. Or reawakened him, as we prefer to call it. To full function."

Hill's head is starting to feel like a spinning centrifuge.

"Did you ask him?" he gets out. "Was Viggo involved in the decision to be frozen alive?"

"Of course! Viggo is well aware of his treatment, and he willingly participates in a range of different tests and therapies in his waking periods. In no way is he compelled to take part. Fact is, he is making great leaps forward."

Hill tries to still his churning thoughts.

"So that's why you lie about him," he says. "Claim that he's abroad. Because the experiments you're performing on him are both un-ethical and illegal."

Gunnar makes a nonchalant jerk of his head.

"Ethics and laws are changeable. In the not too distant future Viggo and his treatments will be viewed as a milestone for humanity. But not just yet. Viggo isn't ready for that kind of attention. He is very shy and easily disturbed. We prefer to keep him here at Astro-holm, in a secure environment. He spends a good deal of time on Boulder Isle."

The image of poor Elis's face in the cryochamber flashes in front of Hill's eyes.

Gunnar seems to notice.

"There is something else you want to ask, isn't there, Martin? Out with it!"

Hill doesn't know how forthright he dares be. At the same time, he has to say something.

"The two young men who drowned off Boulder Isle. I saw one of them in a freezer tank in the laboratory."

Gunnar makes a regretful gesture.

"A mere accident. They were trespassing on Boulder Isle and caught Viggo by surprise. He can be rather startling for those who don't know him."

The words call to mind the giant who chased Hill through the fog and later through the mine.

"So what happened?"

"Both young men fled, and they ended up in the water. We man-aged to retrieve one of them and get him to our facility here at Astro-holm, but alas his life couldn't be saved."

"But you never raised the alarm. Never called the police, or an ambulance."

Gunnar shakes his head.

"We didn't want to subject Viggo to that kind of scrutiny. After all, it wasn't his fault. Simply two intruders who tragically fell into the water, sank, and perished."

"And why did you freeze Elis? Deprive his family of a body to bury?"

Gunnar inhales through his teeth.

"That was my decision, and it was no easy one to make. Bernhard's body was frozen in the nineties. Back then our research was still in its infancy, and the freezing process damaged his tissues. Bernhard, sadly, will never be reawakened. But we did learn a great deal from that mistake, which we then applied to Viggo. Above all, it led us to study the biological processes in those frogs I mentioned previously. For us to be able to further develop those methods, we needed more test materials."

It takes all of Hill's brainpower not to show what he is really thinking.

"So you kept Elis's body for the sake of science," he says, trying to sound thoughtful. "Almost like the frog in the glass jar you gave me."

"Exactly," Gunnar nods. "As I said, sometimes you have to make difficult decisions. The young man was dead, his family had already mourned him, and this way he was able to make a great contribution to humanity."

Hill pauses for a few seconds. He wants to point out that Gunnar's tale contains so many instances of megalomania, serious crime, narcissism, and sheer ruthlessness that he has lost count of them all.

But he must keep in mind that he is in the hands of a sociopath. That the last person who got close to this secret was Tord Korpi, which means that he is in grave danger.

"So," says Gunnar. "What do you say now that you've seen the whole picture, Martin? Do you think we can move forward together?"

Hill gets up off the bed and slowly walks over to the cryotherapy machine that Dr. Schiller used to treat his wound.

He needs to buy himself some time, weigh his words carefully, and make it appear that, although he may have some reservations, he nevertheless agrees.

The kind of crapshoot that requires him to draw on every one of his social superpowers.

"Viggo's treatment is controversial," he says thoughtfully. "Not everyone will understand. A living man who was frozen and then reawakened. Returned from the dead, time and again. That will be hard for the general public to get their heads around."

He places his hand on the machine, sees Gunnar standing up out of the corner of his eye.

"At the same time, it's thanks to these kinds of sacrifices that medical research can progress. That it can offer new, more effective treatments to millions of people. Take my injury, for example."

The machine feels cool under his palm. He pats it a few times, as though drawing strength from it.

"History is full of similar examples. Brave people who dared to take the lead. Who took risks, sacrificing themselves for the good of humankind."

He turns and walks over to Gunnar.

"Just like the volcanic glass, you saw opportunity in the heart of disaster," he goes on solemnly. "Where before you created a glass knife, this time you have created a glass man. Your book should travel between those two points. Show how closely they are intertwined, almost fated. And that, finally, you are fulfilling your own destiny by having yourself frozen. An end that, at the same time, also marks a new beginning. That is how I envisage the narrative."

Hill meets Gunnar's gaze, assuming an expression that he hopes will appear both weighty and convincing. Gunnar observes him carefully. For a few seconds both stand in silence.

Then Gunnar nods in satisfaction and pats Hill on the shoulder.

"I knew you'd understand, dear Martin. You and I have a special connection, I've known it all along. I'm glad we've cleared the air."

He turns and opens the door.

"I'll ask you to wait here a few minutes. Nova and I need to confer on where to take things from here. Make a few decisions."

Gunnar disappears through the door. Hill hears the click of a lock, which means all that talk about him being free to go was of course just bullshit.

So what did Gunnar mean when he said he needed to make a few decisions?

About what?

Or perhaps, more accurately, about whom?

ASKER

She drives through the gate, taking the road that runs along the exterior of the wall. Waits before she slows down until she is so far from the main entrance that she no longer sees any lights.

My stomach's one big double knot.

If Martin said that, it must mean he is in danger. That he needs her help, and that all the rest was just for show.

She parks as close to the wall as she can, steps out, and takes stock of what is in her trunk. A warning triangle, a few yards of towrope, and a tire iron.

That's all she needs to make a simple but effective grappling hook—yet another skill that she has Prepper Per to thank for.

She climbs up onto the roof of the car. From there it's not so hard for her to get the hook in place over the top of the wall. She tests the rope by giving it a few tugs, trying to loosen up her injured shoulder.

This is going to hurt.

She grabs the rope as high up as she can, locks her feet around it, and starts to climb.

Her shoulder immediately protests, but she tries to breathe through the pain.

At the top of the wall she throws her leg over, then gives her shoulder a few seconds' rest while with her other hand she moves her makeshift grappling hook to the other side and unfurls the rope down the inside of the wall.

The moon and the stars peer out from between the clouds, giving her just enough light.

Everything looks calm on the other side of the wall. Just straight tree trunks and dark thickets, no trace of any cameras or alarms.

She adjusts her belt holster with her firearm before slowly inching down the other side. Sweat drips down her back, as much from the pain as the exertion.

Martin said that he was in the medical suite, and according to the nervous doctor, that is situated in the manor house.

But she doesn't want to run down there blind, without any information to speak of. Ideally what she wants is to get Martin out without having to confront Samuel, since she suspects an encounter like that will only end in violence.

Fortunately she knows who can help her.

She moves quietly between the trees, with soft, cautious steps.

When she reaches the road that runs through the estate, she stops and listens.

For a brief moment she thinks she hears the hum of a drone and slips in under a tree. But the sound disappears in the distance.

She crosses the road and works her way through the forest until she reaches the back of Villa Canopus.

Just as she is crossing the house's back lawn, the drone sound approaches again. Finding herself as far from the edge of the forest as she is from the shadows of the house, she makes a split-second decision. She sprints the last few yards to the house and presses herself up against the wall.

The drone comes humming over the treetops.

Asker resists the temptation to look up and show her pale face. All she can do is stand completely still and hope that the drone doesn't have a thermal imaging camera.

The drone stops, buzzing above her like an angry wasp. It hovers there for a few seconds, then the motor revs up again and the drone disappears in the direction of the guard station.

She exhales, looks around a few times and then slips along the wall of the house to the main entrance. Instead of using the heavy knocker, she taps gingerly on the door with her knuckles.

She hears the dog bark inside.

"Who is it?" Elsa asks.

She leans in closer to the door.

"It's Leo, Martin's friend. I need to ask you a few things."

The lock clicks and the girl opens up.

"Come in," she says. "Mom still hasn't turned up. I'm starting to get really worried."

Asker shuts the door behind her. Her original theory was that

Maud handed Martin over to Gunnar. That she betrayed him, just like she did Tord Korpi. But if so, where is she now? Would she really leave her daughter alone, without any explanation?

That doesn't sound entirely logical, which suggests the situation may be more complex than she first thought.

The big dog has positioned himself between her and the girl. He stares at her fixedly, as though trying to determine whether she poses a threat.

"Apparently Martin's down at the medical suite in the manor house," she says. "How do I get there?"

"There's an entrance in the east wing, but it's locked. You need a pass to get inside."

"Do you have one?"

The girl shakes her head.

"Grandma might, but she's gone, too. Something really weird is going on, isn't it?"

Asker nods, only to realize the girl can't see her.

"Yes, it is. I need to get hold of Martin; I think he may be in danger."

"He sounded scared when he was here," Elsa agrees. "And he was hurt, too."

"What exactly happened—do you remember?"

Elsa appears to think back.

"Martin was standing here in the kitchen when we got home. Said we shouldn't be afraid, that he didn't mean to scare us. Come to think of it, I don't actually know how he got inside."

"What do you mean?"

"Well, Mom unlocked the front door, I remember that clearly." She taps one of her ears. "Sound's kind of my thing, and I heard her turning the key. But Martin was already in the house when we got here. He said he was hurt, that he'd taken a tumble and needed some help, which didn't sound completely true. I figured it was probably a grown-up thing, so I went outside and left them to talk in peace."

"And that was all you heard?"

Elsa furrows her brow, as though trying to remember.

"Just before I shut the door, I heard Martin say something about mine tunnels and district heating."

"District heating?"

"Yeah. There's a door in the laundry that leads there. I'm good with doors, I know every one in the house. Would you like me to show you?"

HILL

As soon as Gunnar has left him, Hill stands up and looks around the consulting room. He checks the drawers, searching for any object that could be of use. For what, he isn't quite sure—to defend himself perhaps? Or escape?

But every drawer is locked, and he finds nothing to help him.

He thinks back to what Gunnar told him about Viggo. He must have been the one who chased him through the fog and the mine tunnels.

The same Viggo who is responsible for the deaths of both urban explorers and perhaps even more people. The head gardener, for example, or Maud's boyfriend Pontus Ursvik.

What would have happened to him had Viggo caught him?

His thoughts can get no further before the door opens and Gunnar is back, this time in the company of Nova. She is wearing the same black shell clothes and cap as the other day on Boulder Isle. Her jacket is open, and Hill glimpses the frog pendant that he noticed all the way back at AlphaCent's head office. Now he understands what it symbolizes.

But he also catches sight of something else. Nova is carrying a pistol in a shoulder holster.

"So, Martin, how about a little outing?"

She hands Hill a water bottle, and after a second's hesitation he swigs down the contents while trying to figure out what is going on.

"Nova and I have an idea," says Gunnar. "A way to bring you into our very innermost circle, once and for all."

He nods encouragingly at his daughter.

"We thought you should meet Viggo," she says. "Witness our advances with your own eyes. But that requires a little walk. Are you up to it, after this strange evening?"

Hill is pretty sure that there is only one correct answer to that question.

"Of course." He nods, trying not to betray his fear.

"Good. Put this jacket on and we'll get going."

Nova hands him a black jacket with AlphaCent's logo on the chest. They step out into the corridor and start heading toward the elevator. Mrs. Schiller peers out through a doorway but quickly pulls back when she sees them, as though she doesn't want to be seen. Or perhaps not implicated?

Hill glances back toward the exit. Nova is close on his tail, and even if he did manage to get past her, he would still be locked inside the manor.

His best chance right now is to play along.

They step inside the elevator, and Gunnar swipes a pass against the reader and presses the lowest button.

The elevator glides smoothly downward.

From this close it is clear that Gunnar is unwell. His skin appears stretched over his nose and forehead, his eyes are sunken, and his teeth look a size too big for his upper jaw, which means they must be dentures. But Gunnar's gaze and charisma are just as intense as before.

Hill sneaks another glance at Nova. Sees her adjust her holster, as though to make her weapon more easily accessible. A clear reminder that, although Hill did manage to talk his way out of the consulting room, he is still far from safe and dry.

The elevator stops and the doors open. The space outside is dark, with only a few faint red lights in the ceiling.

"It's for Viggo's sake," Gunnar explains. "His eyes are incredibly sensitive to white light. It's difficult for him; he can only go outside at night, and even then only with protective eyewear. A side effect of his treatment that we are working to resolve."

Hill thinks back to the red eyes he saw in the darkness.

Gunnar walks over to a heavy fire door and opens it with his pass.

On the other side there is a steel staircase. The air is cool, bordering on cold. Hill recognizes both the space and the scent. It is the staircase leading down to the cryogenics lab, where Dr. Schiller caught him not so long ago.

They go down the stairs and pass the cryochambers. The displays are all on standby, and Hill refrains from looking at the pod that contains Elis's body. He tries not to imagine the young man floating in there like a frog in a glass jar, reduced to a medical test subject.

Tries not to think that he himself might end up in an identical tank at any minute, if he doesn't play his cards extremely carefully.

They continue through the back door and out into the cavernous, excavated room.

Gunnar and Nova each light their own flashlights.

"We're going this way," says Gunnar, walking toward the tunnel with the wrought-iron gate and the letters *AM* on the wall. "Back to Boulder Isle. Only this time we'll be traveling under the water."

In any other situation Hill would have been over the moon. The underground passage that he has been searching for really exists.

But all he can think about now is how long it will take Leo to find him down here.

If she is even looking for him, that is.

ASKER

"It's the door on the right at the bottom of the steps," says Elsa. "I'll try calling Mom again in the meantime."

Elsa heads back in the direction of the living room with the dog at her heels. She moves freely, clearly knows the house's every nook and cranny.

Asker follows the staircase to enter a large basement room. Shelves line the walls, and in the middle there is a large island that houses two integrated washing machines and a tumble dryer.

An old-fashioned wringer is placed diagonally in front of the door that Elsa was referring to. It is wedged in place, blocking the door handle.

When Asker examines the wringer more closely, she finds a bloody handprint on one side. She guesses that it belongs to Martin, and that he is wounded, just like Elsa heard him say.

But why did he barricade the door to the district heating room?

She puts her good shoulder to the wringer and shoves it aside.

The door catches a little, and when she manages to get it open she realizes why. The metal on the other side is severely dented, as though someone has rammed the door with breathtaking force.

The district heating room turns out to be a passage with long pipes and cables. A light a few yards away catches her eye.

A flashlight, still lit.

She picks it up and examines it.

M. Hill is written in marker pen along one side.

Asker continues down the passage, where she finds an old spiral staircase that extends straight down into the darkness.

She stops to piece together what she has seen. Martin must have come to Villa Canopus this way. Wounded and with someone hard on his heels.

He dropped or threw down his flashlight, made it to the basement, and managed to barricade the door with the wringer. After that he went up into the house, found Elsa and Maud, and phoned her.

She shines Martin's flashlight down the spiral staircase.

It must lead to the underground lab that Martin told her about, the one that Tord Korpi built. But right now she isn't here to find proof of who killed Tord Korpi; she is here to find Martin.

A sound makes her jump. It sounded like a dog barking.

Asker turns out the flashlight and returns to the laundry.

"Elsa?" she calls out.

She makes for the basement staircase, moving her hand to her holster.

When she is halfway through the room, the basement door at the top of the staircase opens, and Samuel steps down onto the top step.

In his hands he is holding a gun with a silencer. He looks at the open district heating door, then at her.

Raises his weapon the very second their eyes meet.

Instinctively she leaps to one side.

Samuel's gun sputters to life. Asker feels the draft of the bullets as they pass mere inches overhead.

She tucks her head in, juts out her left elbow to break her fall. Does a somersault that sends a shock of pain running through her injured shoulder, and lands behind the island with the integrated washing machines.

She pulls in her legs, presses herself to the concrete floor.

Samuel's pistol sputters out more bullets. They hit the washing machines. Some are stopped by the motor block, while others pierce the sheet metal and emerge on the other side.

A ricochet whines right past her.

Asker makes herself as flat as she can while Samuel continues to shoot. She notes that he is moving his hit pattern, to narrow the space behind which she can hide.

He is on the front foot, and he also has the advantage of knowing exactly where she is, while from her hiding place she can't see him.

All she can do is take cover and make herself as small as possible while fumbling for her own weapon.

She must try to figure out exactly where he is.

A bullet cuts through the sheet metal mere inches away, ripping open a sharp, jagged hole that could just as easily be in her skull.

Then she hears the rattle of Samuel's pistol shooting on an empty magazine.

Against an amateur she would have taken this chance to get up and fire off a few rounds, but Samuel is far too professional.

He drops the magazine and has fed in another before the empty one even hits the ground. Had she stood up she would now be dead.

But at least she got a few seconds' respite from the shower of bullets.

Asker moves her head to get a glimpse of Samuel from between the washing machines. He is halfway down the staircase, that much she manages to establish. He's moving toward her to maintain the upper hand, just as he is trained to do.

He has reloaded now, resumes his fire while continuing to edge down the stairs. The next hit is closer, as though he has sneaked a glimpse of her too. Asker presses herself flat against the concrete floor. Yet another hit, so close that she gasps. This time the washing machine's motor block saves her.

From her new position she spots that the machines are standing on large rubber blocks. The space beneath them is around five inches, just enough for her to see the bottom step.

Yet another bullet punches through the machines, whistling close by her ear. Samuel is shooting right at her now. Within seconds he will have hit his target.

She presses herself to the ground and extends her arm into the narrow space beneath the washing machines.

Everyone shoots instinctively at the upper body, she hears Prepper Per's voice say. *But sometimes you have to take the targets you get.*

Samuel shoots again; it claps against the sheet metal and something sharp and hot nicks her diagonally above her eye.

Asker forces herself to keep her eyes open, even though she can feel the blood running down her forehead. Keeps her finger on the trigger while she waits.

Then one of Samuel's feet appears on the bottom step.

Asker fires off three shots in such quick succession that the bangs all melt into one in her ears. She sees one of the bullets rip open the black, well-polished leather of his shoes.

Samuel cries out in pain, and his foot buckles beneath him.

He squeezes the trigger to fire off another few bullets in her direction, but now without precision. He tries desperately to regain his balance.

But he can't stop himself from falling.

One of his knees hits the ground, and when it does Asker shoots again. The bullet strikes his other kneecap and sweeps that leg out from beneath him, sending him clattering to the floor.

His head hits the concrete a few yards from her, and she sees the pain and shock in his eyes, just before he catches sight of her.

She sees his expression change when he realizes that her pistol is pointed straight at his face through the narrow space under the machines. Realizes that he has lost control, and that only two options remain.

It could have all ended there.

But men like Samuel rarely give up; that's not how they are trained. Men like him refuse to believe they can ever be beaten—not by anyone, and especially not by a woman.

Which is why Samuel heaves his pistol hand toward her, in the certainty that he is faster than her. That he is still the most dangerous person in the room.

He is wrong.

She shoots him straight through the forehead.

Samuel jerks, then lies there with his eyes wide open, as though he still can't quite believe what just happened.

He almost looks surprised.

Asker scrambles to her feet, wipes the blood from her face with her jacket sleeve. Her pulse is thundering through her ears, and the adrenaline burns in her mouth. A pungent stench of gunpowder hangs in the room.

She fills her lungs with air, trying to compose herself. Out of habit she kicks Samuel's gun away when she passes his lifeless body.

Then she goes upstairs.

"Elsa," she calls. "Are you there?"

She hears a dog bark, finds her way to a closed door.

"It's Leo," she says. "Are you OK?"

She opens the door a crack. The girl is sitting in a corner behind the bed with her arms around Orion. She looks afraid.

The dog's bristle is raised, and his teeth are bared.

"Are you OK?" Asker repeats.

The girl nods. "Samuel scared us. He threatened to shoot Orion if I didn't make him quiet. Is he still here?"

Asker shakes her head, then remembers once again that the girl can't see her.

"You don't need to worry about Samuel, OK? You and Orion are safe here. Now, don't go anywhere and I'll try to find out what's happened to Martin and your mom."

"OK," Elsa says and nods. "Dr. Schiller might know. He and Samuel came in the same car, I heard them talking. The car is still outside."

Asker carefully parts the blinds. Elsa is right: the black Merc is still parked with its lights off in front of the house. Inside she sees the light of a phone screen.

"Is there a back door?" she asks.

She sneaks toward the car, keeping to an angle from which she won't be visible in the rearview mirror.

The doctor is in the front seat, speaking on the phone.

When he spots her, he starts to fumble with the ignition in terror. Asker smashes the side window with the barrel of her pistol, sending a cascade of glass all over him.

He squeals like a pig, stops only when she presses the gun to his sweat-shiny head.

"Martin Hill," she says doggedly. "Take me to him. Now!"

HILL

The tunnel they enter slopes downward. To begin with the ground is made of blast stone, just like in the other tunnels, but after a certain point it is superseded by a grated walkway.

The air is growing all the damper, rivulets of water trickling down the walls here and there. Hill looks down. The grated walkway must be on piles, because now he sees black water glinting beneath his feet.

Gunnar, who has taken the lead, keeps a fairly brisk pace. For a man of almost eighty who is terminally ill, his movements are smooth and lissome.

Hill, meanwhile, isn't in the best of shape, but whatever was in that drip at the medical suite is at least keeping him on his feet.

The tunnel continues to slope downward, widening all the while. The water extends outward on either side, the walkway is supplemented with railings, and after a while it feels like walking on a bridge.

The beams of the flashlight are sharpened by the damp air. They cut through the darkness like light sabers, making the water beneath them sparkle.

Gunnar stops and shines his light around him.

"Well, what do you think?"

Hill catches his breath.

"It's remarkable," he pants. "An underground lake."

Gunnar nods.

"It was formed by the same leak that caused the tragic collapse in the sixties. We're constantly pumping out water, or else the tunnel would be completely flooded by now. But such beauty is worth the effort, no?"

"Absolutely," Hill nods, and this time he truly means it. He wishes he could take some pictures, but his cellphone is still in Villa Arcturus. He thinks of Leo again.

He really needs her help to get himself out of this bind. But how will she find him all the way out on Boulder Isle?

He looks around cautiously over his shoulder, but Nova is blocking his escape route. Her jacket is unbuttoned, the butt of her pistol clearly visible.

"Shall we go on?" she asks.

Hill nods. He follows Gunnar's back as it leads him farther down into the darkness.

ASKER

She brings the Mercedes screeching to a halt outside the door to the medical suite. Jumps out of the car, opens the trunk, and pulls out Dr. Schiller. He is still scared out of his wits, and squeaks like a mouse when she shoves him toward the door.

"Open it!" she commands, waving her pistol at him.

He fiddles with a pass, trembling so much that he almost drops it. The door swings open, revealing an illuminated corridor.

"Move!" Asker orders with a jerk of her head. "Show me to Martin Hill."

The doctor's eyes flit around wildly, but he does as he is told. Everything is dead silent; there isn't a single sound to be heard in the corridor.

"Y-you should know I tried to stop him," Dr. Schiller says over his shoulder. "Samuel, I mean. I asked him to refrain from violence."

"Oh you did, did you? So you were just waiting to give him a lift back once he was done? Once he'd shot me in the head, like he did Tord Korpi."

The statement is mostly an educated guess, but the doctor's reaction tells Asker that she has hit the nail on the head. He stiffens, then raises his hand to his bald head, as though trying to shield himself.

"I kn-kn-know nothing about that," he stutters, but even with his back to her it is clear that he is lying. "My wife and I have been dragged into all of this against our will. We aren't violent people."

They are nearing a corner where the corridor winds to the right.

"Hello?" A voice says ahead of them. "Is there anybody there?"

An elderly woman steps around the corner. Gives a start when she sees Asker and the terrified doctor.

Asker raises her gun.

"Oh, God!" the woman says in terror.

The doctor holds up his hands between them.

"Please! This is my wife. She also knows nothing about . . . Gunnar's . . ." He is unable to finish the sentence.

Asker studies the woman. She is tall and elegant, with a genteel appearance.

"What has happened?" she asks her husband. "Where is Samuel?"

The doctor gives a gentle shake of his head, casting an anxious look at Asker.

"This woman would like to find Martin Hill. Would you be so kind as to help her?"

The woman stares at her husband, then at Asker, and then at her husband again.

"But Gunnar said . . ." She trails off, and her eyes fix on the gun.

"I don't care what Gunnar said," Asker hisses. "Take me to Martin."

Mrs. Schiller gulps a few times, then nods.

"Just this way," she whispers with a small gesture.

She shows them through to a consulting room, unlocking the door with a bunch of keys that she carries on her belt.

Asker shoves the doctor inside and then follows him. Dr. Schiller flicks some switches, and when the ceiling lights flicker on, they reveal a consulting room with an empty bed that appears to have recently been used.

The doctor turns to Asker with a confounded look.

"I don't understand . . ." he begins, before he catches sight of something over Asker's shoulder. His eyes widen, and the confusion turns to shock.

Asker spins around and raises her arm, but she can only make it halfway before she feels a blow to her right shoulder, followed by a searing pain. She reels backward while trying to raise the pistol, but her arm refuses to obey.

Mrs. Schiller comes straight for her. Her genteel look has vanished: her face is pale and dogged, her gaze hard, and in her hand she is holding a scalpel.

The blood pours from Asker's shoulder, where the woman just stabbed her.

"Get her!" Mrs. Schiller screams at her husband.

The doctor looks at a loss, but then he raises his hands and takes a wavering step toward Asker.

Asker kicks him in the crotch with full force. The doctor gurgles, grabs his crown jewels, and falls to the floor.

Mrs. Schiller lets out an indignant scream. She charges toward Asker and lunges at her again with the scalpel, this time aiming for her face. Asker jumps to one side, avoiding the sharp blade by mere inches. The woman charges again, brandishing the scalpel, but she trips on her husband and loses her balance.

Asker sees her chance and swings her reluctant right arm. Raps Mrs. Schiller straight on the bridge of her nose with the barrel of her gun. The blow is hard: Asker feels it all the way through her arm.

Mrs. Schiller's eyes roll back. Her knees give way, and she crumples down almost on top of her husband.

Asker kicks the scalpel out into the corridor and manages to point her weapon at the couple on the ground. The doctor is still clutching at his crotch, groaning quietly. His wife has a deep gash in her forehead and appears to have lost consciousness. Asker crouches down beside the man on the floor and takes his cellphone, then swipes his wife's bunch of keys.

"Look, Doctor," she says. "Your wife's wound needs dressing. Once you're done, you can polish up your witness statements. I think you'll need to."

She backs out of the room and locks the door on the Schillers.

The adrenaline is coursing through her body, which means she hardly feels the pain of the scalpel stab. At least not yet. But the blood is dripping down her right arm. She needs to find something to dress the wound with as soon as possible.

A pounding noise makes her stop dead. It sounds like someone is beating on one of the other doors beside her.

"Hello?" a woman's voice cries. "Hello, can anyone hear me?"

HILL

They have been crossing the underground lake for what must be ten minutes when they leave the grated walkway and once again have firm ground underfoot.

Hill has started to shiver from the cold and the damp in the air, but he barely feels it. The tunnel they have now entered must belong to Astrofield Mine, so they are probably somewhere under Boulder Isle.

So it was down here in the darkness that Artur Nilsson and his miners dug for Bernhard Irving's meteorite. Bored deeper and deeper in their futile attempts to prove a man's obsession, until the water brought everything crumbling down on top of them.

The mine tunnel inclines quite steeply upward, and soon Hill stops shivering and starts sweating instead.

"Would you like to catch your breath for a minute?" Gunnar asks.

Hill nods. He puts his hands on his knees and takes a few deep breaths.

"There's one thing I have to ask," he says.

"Of course."

"Karin."

Hill tries to calm his pulse enough to formulate his question without sounding all too breathless.

"Does she know about Viggo? That he's alive, that is—that he's part of a . . . controversial experiment?"

"Karin's not of sound mind," Gunnar snorts. "You've met her yourself. She was always a little delicate, and the shock of finding out that Bernhard was her father more or less made her snap. And then with Viggo's accident . . ."

"But does she know about the experiment itself? Is she OK with it?"

He knows the answer, or at least suspects it. Karin asked first Tord Korpi and now him to help Viggo.

"We don't burden Karin with that kind of information," Nova steps in. "All she knows is that Viggo is getting the best possible care, which is completely true. He's been making real strides. We're very proud of him."

"I see . . . and Maud, what happened to her after you collected me?"

Hill isn't entirely sure why he asks. Why he cares, for that matter, after she handed him over to Gunnar. Maybe because he thinks that she was the one he heard crying when he was being bundled into the car.

"Maud's resting up a little in the medical suite. She's had a rough night."

"So what about Elsa? Is she at home all alone?"

Gunnar looks at him searchingly.

"What could happen to her there? She's completely safe in Villa Canopus."

"Yes, but she's alone. Her mother's gone—won't she get worried? She's only thirteen."

"She'll be fine," Gunnar says with a snort. "Kids are resilient."

An irritated look has appeared on his face. He sizes Hill up, almost as though he has started to regret this entire outing.

"Shall we go on?" he says, turning around.

The tunnel continues to slope upward for a while, before it eventually levels out. They walk on at an even pace, and with every step Hill takes behind Gunnar Irving it is as though his loathing for him grows. The egomaniacal man only deigns to tolerate the people around him—even his own children and grandchildren—if he can make use of them somehow; if they cause him no inconvenience. He takes his own son's life, again and again, merely so that he might later lengthen his own.

And Hill's own life is now on a knife edge. All it would take is a sudden change of heart on Gunnar's part.

He decides to turn to the old man's favorite topic.

"So, you're planning to freeze yourself alive?" he asks. "Based on what you've learned about the process with Viggo—you aren't going to wait until you're dead?"

Gunnar stops again.

"Exactly, Martin. Viggo has granted me a great gift. Perhaps the greatest of all."

"Eternal life," Hill says.

Gunnar gives him a long look.

"I'm glad you understand, dear Martin. We don't have far to go now."

After five minutes they reach another excavated chamber. This one is smaller and visibly older than the room below Astroholm. The concrete has started to crumble, and on one side stand a few rusty old mine carts.

Gunnar walks over to the wrought-iron gate on one wall. He flicks a breaker, and an electric motor starts to hum.

A large elevator cage slowly descends on the other side of the bars, then stops with a clatter.

Gunnar opens the gate and gestures at the cage.

"After you."

They step inside. Hill has time to wonder how old the elevator must be and how risky it is to travel in it. But he concludes that that risk is probably negligible in comparison to the danger he already faces.

Gunnar closes the gate and presses a button, and the elevator slowly chugs upward.

"Out of the darkness," says Nova.

She exchanges a glance with Gunnar. Hill gulps and forces a smile.

The elevator stops with a bang that almost makes Hill's heart do the same.

"Here we are, Martin," says Gunnar.

His grin reminds Hill of a skull's.

ASKER

Asker stands outside the door where the pounding is coming from.

"Hello?" the voice inside asks again. "Is there anyone there? What's happening?"

Asker hesitates. Whoever is knocking is locked inside, which should in theory mean they are on the same team.

She unlocks the door and shines her flashlight on the woman inside.

Her face is red and puffy with tears, and she shades her face from the flashlight.

It's Maud Irving.

Asker raises her pistol as well as she can.

"Where's Martin?" she asks.

Maud raises her hands in terror.

"I don't know. Gunnar's taken him somewhere."

"Because you tricked him? Handed him over to Gunnar?"

Maud hesitates for a moment, then nods.

"I had no choice. Gunnar had my mother. She's locked up in here, too. Can I see her?"

Asker doesn't respond.

"I understand if you don't trust me, but I need to see my mom."

Maud looks both distraught and sincere, and Asker remembers what Martin told her about Karin's breakdown.

"I don't know where Martin is!" Maud says again, this time more emphatically. "But my mother is unwell; I have to see her. You can lock me back in here after that, if you must."

Asker thinks. She should go on looking for Martin.

But this house is huge, and tearing open every door will take a long time. Karin shared things with Martin—perhaps she will have more idea of where he might be?

Asker takes a few steps back, then signals at Maud with her pistol to follow her. Out in the corridor, she throws her the bunch of keys while keeping a safe distance.

Maud unlocks the next door along. On a bed in the room lies an elderly woman in restraints.

"Mom," Maud exclaims. "Mom!"

She turns on the lights in the room, sits down on the bed, and loosens the restraints. Then she starts examining her mother with practiced hands.

Karin Irving's eyelids flutter open.

"Mom!" Maud repeats.

This time Karin opens her eyes. For a few seconds she looks confused, but she quickly composes herself.

"Where am I?" she asks. "What's happened?"

"You're in the medical suite. I had to call Dad. He promised I'd get to take you away from here, but they sedated me and locked me in, too."

Karin sits up.

"And Viggo?"

"I don't know, Mom. But Elsa's alone in the house."

She looks at Asker entreatingly.

"Elsa's my daughter. She's visually impaired."

"Yes, I know, I met her a little while ago. She was OK, but she was worried about where you and Martin had gone," Asker says sharply. "What did they do to him?"

Maud looks down.

"Gunnar said he just needed to talk to Martin. He promised it would all be all right."

"Is that what he said about Tord Korpi?"

Karin flinches.

"Tord?" she says to her daughter. "Did you tell Gunnar about him?"

Maud goes on looking at the ground.

"I've seen a picture of you and Tord together," says Asker. "Do you know what happened to him after you snitched to Gunnar?"

Maud nods sadly.

"Martin told me Tord was dead just before they came to take him," she says. "I had no idea. Gunnar told me he'd pay Tord for his silence. The same with Martin. I couldn't have imagined Gunnar would . . ." She gulps.

"Samuel murdered him and dumped him in a shallow grave," Asker says brusquely. "Because Tord tried to help you. And Martin risks a similar fate if I don't find him. So I need to know where he is."

"I don't know, I promise," says Maud. "I saw them put him in the trunk and drive away, but I didn't see where to."

She bursts into floods of tears. Karin wraps her arms around her daughter, strokes her hair.

"Maud's only failing is wanting to please her father," she says, with an unexpectedly lucid voice. "Viggo's the same, and Nova. Gunnar has bewitched them, ever since they were little."

"And Viggo?" Asker asks. "He's here, isn't he? Down in that lab?"

"That's right," says Karin. "I've been trying to get him out of there for years. But Gunnar has always stopped me. Has had me pumped full of drugs, made me out to be insane. Which perhaps I am. Who wouldn't be, given everything that has happened?"

She shakes her head slowly. Then she turns to look at Asker.

"Viggo is unwell," she says. "He probably always has been. But whatever he has done, he's still my boy."

"The soccer player?" Asker asks. "Knudsen the head gardener, Maud's boyfriend?"

Karin nods sadly.

"Gunnar claims it's all my fault. That our mixing of genes was morbid. Viggo had a twin brother who was malformed and died at birth. Perhaps we should have known then that Viggo, too, had something wrong with him, something dark and violent. But it was Gunnar who nurtured that seed in him, of that I am sure. Viggo should have received treatment. But Gunnar covered it all up and had him sent away. He was afraid it would damage his and the company's reputation if the world found out what Viggo was capable of."

"And then the accident happened. Maud was in the car, with her boyfriend, wasn't she?"

Maud nods, lets out another sob.

"Viggo had just come back from the USA," Karin says quietly. "He thought Gunnar would welcome him home, finally let him back in. But Gunnar had no such plans. The darkness in Viggo took hold of him once again, and on the way home he attacked Pontus. In the end Maud managed to bring Viggo back to his senses. They put Pontus in the car and set off for the hospital, but then the meteorite came. The flash made Viggo lose control of the car, and he crashed into the lake."

Maud sits up straighter, wipes away the last of her tears on the back of her hand.

"I got out of the car and managed to run home and raise the alarm," she says, her voice thick with tears. "Gunnar told me I couldn't tell anyone I was in the car. We made out that Viggo and Pontus had just been in a normal accident."

"Perhaps it would have been better had it all ended with Viggo being allowed to die," says Karin. "But Gunnar wanted to resuscitate him at all costs. Back then I thought it was out of love; only later did I realize he wanted to play God. And once Gunnar managed to bring Viggo back to life that first time, nothing could stop him."

She shakes her head sadly.

"Gunnar tortures Viggo, treats him like a guinea pig. He stops his heart and starts it again, pumps him full of steroids, experiments with new medicines that haven't yet been approved. Viggo has done despicable things. But Gunnar—Gunnar's the monster."

HILL

Nova slides open the elevator gate, and they step into a large cellar full of old machine parts. At the other end is a steel door. Gunnar opens it and guides them up a stone staircase.

The staircase leads to a large, dark factory space containing a big machine. Gunnar stops and sweeps his flashlight around. A couple of pigeons take off in fright. They circle the rafters a few times, then slip out through an opening in the roof.

"Do you know where we are, Martin?" Gunnar asks.

"At Astrofield Mine," he says. "In the large building with the stone crusher."

"Exactly!"

"Is this where Viggo spends his nights?" Hill asks.

"When he's able to, yes. Viggo loves the observatory. I'm fairly sure he's up there now. Shall we take a look?"

Hill exhales silently, then nods.

Nick and Elis must have been here, too. Must have taken Viggo by surprise in the darkness. And now they are dead—just like the head gardener, Pontus Ursvik, and others in Viggo and Gunnar's circle. Dead, after brutal violence was wrought on them.

He shouldn't be here; shouldn't be with these dangerous people in this dangerous place.

But he has no choice but to go on playing along. It's his only chance to hold out long enough for Leo to find him. *If* she finds him.

Gunnar walks over to a door, opens it, and ushers them out into the yard between the buildings. Above them the mine's headframe towers toward the sky.

"Viggo," Gunnar calls out. "Viggo, are you there?"

As they near the tower, the ground crunches underfoot. Sharp, black obsidian, just like in Hill's dream. A shiver runs down his spine.

Gunnar gestures at them to stop.

Everything is silent. Not even a breath of wind. Hill can make out the sound of his heart valve bolting in his chest.

Then suddenly a faint glow appears at the top of the tower. The sound of heavy footsteps echoes between the buildings.

And all of a sudden he is standing there at the edge of the roof. The red-eyed monster from Hill's childhood, from his nightmares.

The creature who chased him through the fog and through the mine, one who still makes him freeze in terror.

Viggo Irving.

The murderer.

The Glass Man.

ASKER

At Karin's request, Maud dresses the scalpel wound to Asker's shoulder using equipment from the consulting room. Her hands move confidently as she cleans the wound and applies a few stitches, but she avoids eye contact, working in a single-minded silence, as if wanting to focus on the task at hand and no more. To shut out the rest of the world. Asker recognizes that behavior; she has used the very same tactic herself, thousands of times.

"I . . ." she begins. "I know what it's like to have a father who's . . ." she searches for the right word, ". . . insane," she eventually decides. "Mine tried to blow us both to pieces when I was sixteen. You might know his name—Per Asker. He was a friend of Tord Korpi's, and it was just off his land that Samuel dumped Tord's body."

Maud looks up in surprise.

"I hadn't had any contact with my dad since then," Asker goes on. "But when he called me a week ago and said he was going to be blamed for Tord's murder, I still dropped everything to help him. I can't explain why. It's like he managed to get inside my head. He's still manipulating me, and it's impossible for me to shake him."

Maud nods slowly.

"So what actually happened with Tord Korpi?"

The other woman takes a deep breath.

"Mom told me that Tord had found out about Gunnar's plans for Viggo when he was working on the lab. He promised to try to help her get Viggo out of there. So I had a few meetings with him. I liked Tord, he was friendly. Considerate, even. He talked about the Farm. Said we could take Viggo there, to begin with. That not even Gunnar would be able to get inside."

She looks away.

"But Gunnar suspected something. He called me down to the manor house. Talked about my future at AlphaCent, the importance of loyalty. Said he was going to step down as CEO and wanted me to take over . . ."

"So you told him about Korpi's plans?"

"I genuinely believed Tord would only get fired. That Gunnar would pay him for his silence. That's what he told me."

Maud gulps.

"Where do you think they've taken Martin?" Leo asks just as Maud puts down the needle.

"I know." Karin Irving appears in the doorway. "Follow me."

She leads them through the corridor, to a window that looks out over the rear side of the building. Switches out the light and points across the lake.

In the compact darkness of Boulder Isle, flecks of light appear now and then that must be flashlights.

"They've gone to see Viggo," Karin says. "It won't end well."

"How do I get there?" Asker asks.

"There's a boat down at the jetty," says Maud. "But I don't know where the key is. And then there's a walk through a forest. Besides, you've lost a fair bit of blood. You won't make it in time."

Asker has hardly given it any thought, but now that the adrenaline has started to fade, she notices how tired she is. Both of her shoulders are injured, and she's struggling to even hold up her gun. She can't get there alone in this state. She needs a new plan.

New resources. And she knows someone who has plenty of those. Someone who is up shit creek and could really do with a paddle.

Her phone still has no signal, but Dr. Schiller's does, just as she hoped. She dials the number, and he picks up after two rings.

"It's Leo," she says. "I have an idea that could help us both out. But you have to act, now."

HILL

They climb the steel staircase that winds around the outside of the tower. Gunnar first, followed by Hill and Nova. In just a few seconds he will come face-to-face with his worst nightmare.

Gunnar turns out his flashlight and signals at Hill to come closer. Hill braces himself. Takes the last few steps that finally lead him onto the roof.

Viggo Irving is still standing at the edge of the tower, just a few yards away.

He is huge—must be almost seven feet tall—and broad-shouldered. He has long hair and a beard, and on his brow he wears a visor with a circle of red lights around each eye. It makes him look like a cross between a forest troll and a cyberpunk monster.

Hill gulps convulsively. This is the creature that chased him through the fog and the mine. The one that almost had him in his clutches.

"Impressive, no?" says Gunnar, placing his hand on Hill's shoulder. "Viggo, this is my friend Martin."

Viggo raises his head.

"Martin Hill," he says with a dull, guttural voice. "The Stranger."

"No, Viggo, he's no stranger. Martin's going to write a book about me, and about you, too, as it happens. Martin, tell him what the title will be."

Hill gulps again.

"*The Glass Man*," he says.

Viggo raises his head even higher.

"*The Glass Man*?"

"Quite right. Martin is going to make us famous. Immortal."

Viggo stares fixedly at Hill. Then he starts to walk toward them. His steps are heavy, and they make the floor quake.

Out of the corner of his eye, Hill notices Nova cautiously inching her hand closer to her pistol holster. Suddenly it hits him that the weapon might not be there primarily for his sake, but for Viggo's.

Viggo stops in front of Hill. Towers up above him like a giant. He is standing so close that Hill can make out his scent.

Damp, earth, darkness.

His face is large and steroid-angular. The gaze from behind his visor appears to see straight through him.

"Viggo and I are going to change the world," Gunnar says. "With your help, Martin, of course. We just need to find the right strategy for telling our story. Viggo has been frozen three times. Each time we make new advances. Learn new things about the process. Refine our tools."

Hill can hold his peace no longer.

"You've sacrificed your own child," he says. "For . . . for . . ."

Gunnar pats Viggo on the shoulder.

"A small price to pay if the reward is eternal life—isn't that so, Viggo?"

The giant man nods slowly.

"We don't view it as a sacrifice," Gunnar goes on. Every one of his words is loaded with such arrogant self-satisfaction that Hill must clench his fists. "Viggo's a good boy. He knows he's special. That he has been specially chosen to help his father. To help science."

Viggo is still staring straight at Hill. Then suddenly he raises his hands and takes hold of his visor.

The movement appears to take both Gunnar and Nova by surprise.

Viggo lifts the visor and raises it up onto his head.

"Dear God," Hill gasps.

The skin around Viggo's eyes is scaly, and his eyes are completely black. No whites, no irises.

His pupils are vertical yellow notches. His eyelids are heavy, making every blink slow. It gives him an amphibious look.

Suddenly Hill is overwhelmed by a feeling. A conviction.

"The frog," he whispers, unable to hold it in. "Viggo's the glass frog."

THE GLASS MAN

He still doesn't quite know what happened under Villa Canopus. Martin Hill escaped him again. Or perhaps he chose to end the hunt?

The steel door was almost open—all it would have taken is one last nudge.

But then Martin called out her name, which made him stop short.

Made him think of that night in the forest, of his last human moments. The time he actually showed mercy. Tried to put things right, for her sake.

The memory confused him. Shook him.

So he returned to the darkness, searched for the comfort it usually gives him. But this time it was in vain.

His steps led him to Boulder Isle, to what was once his sacred place. The room he had filled with treasures he had found, things that had given him solace.

But not even there did he find peace.

And now here comes the Father, with her. The one who replaced them, his new heir. Nova, *the new*.

And between them walks Martin Hill.

A peace offering.

The Father has brought him Martin Hill as a gesture. To help him still his hunger. The thought pleases him.

So he steps forward, towers over Martin Hill.

The Stranger is wounded and afraid; he can see it, smell it.

Hear the mechanical click of his terror-stricken heart.

"Viggo and I are going to change the world," the Father says, and everything feels right again. Once again he is Prince Pollux. The chosen one.

His father hasn't renounced him, hasn't banished him.

Everything is as it should be.

The Father pats him on the shoulder, and the light touch reinforces his belief that Martin Hill truly is a gift.

That he will get to lead him down into the darkness, just as he did the others.

But then he is struck by an impulse, an overwhelming desire to look Martin Hill in the eye, with no filter.

Experience his journey unmediated.

So he raises his visor.

Sees the Stranger tremble under his gaze. Everything is just as he imagined it.

Until the moment Martin Hill opens his mouth and says those words. Not in meanness, or spite. Without jealousy or resentment.

But out of pity.

Viggo's the glass frog.

The realization cuts through him like an obsidian knife.

All this time he has known that Martin Hill was special, but not in what way.

Now he does.

Martin Hill's heart is different. It is capable of feeling compassion, even in a moment like this. Martin Hill fears him, but he also pities him.

And suddenly it is as though his vision clears. As though an extraterrestrial beam of light appears over the headframe, illuminating the darkness.

He can finally see clearly—can finally see the extent of what has been happening. Of what he has suspected all too long, but has not had the courage to accept.

That he isn't Prince Pollux, the immortal twin.

That he never will be that again.

That he is simply a frog in a jar.

A creature that exists solely for someone else to observe. So that they can tap on the glass, shock his poor little heart back to life.

Send him down into the abyss and then draw him back up, time and again, regardless of the toll that journey takes on him.

Within him something begins to swell. His hunger turns into something else.

A blazing orb of wrath that grows only stronger.

He clenches his fists.

"Viggo," the Father says in warning, taking him by the arm. "Calm yourself, now!"

His voice is hard, devoid of love and compassion. Perhaps it has always been this way. The Father loves only himself.

The orb within him continues to swell, moving through his chest and up toward his vocal cords.

He catches his breath, opens his mouth.

The Father grips his arm even tighter.

"Damn it, calm yourself, Viggo!" the Father hisses, just as he used to do when he and Maud were children. When they would disturb him in his VERY IMPORTANT work.

He turns to the Father, and the man's eyes are gray and cold.

Martin Hill's gaze is softer. Filled with sympathy. That pains him almost as much.

The Stranger and the Father stand before him.

They torment him with their gazes, giving him no peace.

He throws his head back. The rage and sorrow finally burst from his chest, turning into an abysmal roar.

He thrusts out his arms and does what he has so long hungered to do.

Grabs him, picks him up, and squeezes him as tightly as he can. Until the bones snap like shards of glass.

HILL

He stands as though frozen in concrete. Viggo flings his arms around Gunnar and pulls him up into a ferocious bear hug. Tips his head back and lets out a roar so powerful and so choked that Hill feels it through his entire body.

Gunnar tries to extricate himself, but Viggo simply hugs him tighter. Then he raises his father into the air and squeezes him with all his might, until Gunnar's body lets out a crack and the man stops struggling.

Viggo turns around and walks toward the edge of the tower, his father in his arms.

"Viggo!" Nova screams. "Stop, Viggo!"

Her pistol is out of her shoulder holster.

A shot fires, two. Nova is holding the pistol with both hands. She stands with her feet parted and panic in her eyes, firing shot after shot at her half brother's enormous back. Viggo keeps on walking.

Hill can see the bullets enter his flesh, sees the enormous man totter and then stop.

Viggo is only feet away from the edge of the tower, and his legs appear to be about to give way.

Nova shoots him again, and again. Screams at him to let Gunnar go.

Hill still can't bring himself to move.

With a seemingly inhuman effort, Viggo straightens his back. Hugs Gunnar even tighter and leaps straight into the air.

"Nooo!" Nova cries, only to be cut off by the heavy thud of bodies hitting the ground.

She races to the edge, stands there fumbling for her flashlight.

Hill's paralysis suddenly gives way.

On shaking legs he follows her.

Nova's flashlight lights up the bodies on the ground. They have landed in the black field of obsidian glass.

Gunnar is lying on his back, with Viggo's enormous body above him—crushed between his son's body and the sharp glass.

Even from all the way up, Hill can see his eyes staring blankly up into space. Up at the stars.

Nova sobs, presses the back of her hand to her mouth. Hill can't take his eyes off the dead men.

After a few seconds Nova collects herself.

"This is your fault," she hisses at Hill. "You made Viggo do this!"

Hill holds up his hands.

"Viggo was sick," he says. "He murdered several people, and Gunnar was well aware. Yet he kept Viggo here. His research was more important than either justice or Viggo's well-being—"

"My father was a great man," she interrupts. "A genius!"

"Gunnar was a monster," Hill replies. "He treated his children like possessions. You, too—even if you don't yet see that for yourself."

He gestures down at the ground.

"In other circumstances that could just as easily have been you."

"Shut your fucking mouth!" Nova screams.

In spite of the darkness, her face looks incandescent with rage.

"That was just an accident," she says, pointing at the ground. "Nothing else. Gunnar and Viggo fell. It's a family tragedy, but Alpha-Cent will survive. Provided you and I are agreed on that—OK?"

Hill says nothing. He could mention that Viggo must have ten bullets in his body, but he lets it go. The shock appears to have made Nova lose her grip.

She stares at him, and her eyes narrow.

"Or . . ." she says softly. "Or all three of you fell. Maybe it's better that way. Viggo pulled both of you down with him, and I tried to save you."

She nods, as though she is convincing herself of it.

"Yes, that's it. Simpler, cleaner." She raises her weapon at Hill. "Jump!"

"Wait!" he says, raising his hands again. "You haven't thought this through."

Nova simply shakes her head.

"Jump," she says again. "Either you do it, or I shoot."

Her eyes are wide and her red lips are retracted, reminding him of a predator.

"Jump. I'm not saying it again!"

Hill takes a cautious step toward the edge, while his brain desperately scrabbles for some way out of this. He looks down over the edge—first at the dead bodies, then at the floor on the level below him. But the angle is too narrow. Any jump is doomed to fail.

Out of the corner of his eye he sees Nova raise her gun even higher. He clenches his eyes shut, waiting for the bang.

Instead a faint hum starts to spread over the lake. A pulsing rumble that draws all the closer, building to a roar.

A floating white light is heading straight for the tower. It grows in brightness, dazzling them from the sky, like the spaceship in Gunnar's story, the flash of light that Hill thought he saw as a teen. He gasps.

Nova totters, raises her hand to shade her eyes. Hill seizes his chance.

He leaps at the gun and tries to tear it from her hands. But Nova is strong, and the long walk has depleted most of his strength.

The beam of light turns toward them, a spotlight that illuminates their tussle. A helicopter separates from the darkness to hover above them, its engine growling.

The rotor blades whip up dust from the roof's floor.

Nova tries to knee him in the crotch, but Hill manages to twist to one side. Her knee strikes his wound instead. He groans in pain, but still keeps hold of the gun.

Nova's face is right next to his. Her eyes are wide and her teeth are bared, as though she is preparing to bite him.

Hill realizes that his strength is about to give out, and he won't be able to keep up his resistance. He must do something—anything—to end this fight. What would Leo do in the same situation?

Hill tips back his head, closes his eyes, and lurches forward face-first. His forehead hits Nova right over her mouth, with such force that his eyes see black.

He feels something crack, feels a tooth cut his forehead.

They both stagger backward, away from each other. Hill loses his grip on the gun, his legs buckle, and he collapses down onto the concrete.

Nova, however, manages to stay on her feet.

"This is the police," a voice rings out over a megaphone. "Drop the weapon and lie down on the ground!"

Hill cautiously lifts his head.

Nova is standing in the spotlight with the pistol in her hand, blood running from her mouth.

A red dot from a laser sight flutters over her chest.

Hill holds his breath.

The laser dot continues to flutter over Nova.

"Drop your weapon!"

Nova stares blankly into the air.

For a brief moment time stands still.

Then Nova appears to come to her senses. She drops the pistol, falls to her knees, and lies down on her belly.

The helicopter comes closer. Stops a few feet over the top of the tower with its engine rumbling and its rotor blades whipping, while dark shadows leap out.

Some of them immediately throw themselves over Nova.

Hands take hold of Hill. A flashlight dazzles him.

"Are you OK?" someone asks.

"Yes!" Hill manages to respond.

"He's OK!" the same voice yells.

The helicopter rises and glides off over the lake with a rumble.

The flashlight in Hill's face is turned off, and he is lifted to his feet. More shadows surround him.

"We have to stop meeting like this, Martin," says a familiar voice.

Leo is standing before him. She has a dressing on her forehead and is wearing an oversized police jacket. Her smile twinkles in the semidarkness.

Hill is about to throw his arms around her, but since they are surrounded by grave-looking police officers he abstains.

"I'm sure you remember Detective Superintendent Jonas Hellman," says Leo, pointing at the man beside her.

"Jonas is leading the investigation into the murder of Tord Korpi, and he's a little behind. It would be good if you could bring him up to date as quickly as possible."

Hellman gives Leo a dark look, which she completely ignores.

Hill simply smiles, mute.

He can't take his eyes off her.

Doesn't even try.

TWO DAYS LATER

ASKER

The small briefing room at the end of the corridor on level minus one is so silent you could hear a pin drop. Before her, on the fold-out chairs, sit the Lost Souls.

"So, to build on what was said at the press conference: Maud and Karin Irving have given their version of events. Nova has acquired herself a full battery of lawyers, but she'll have a hard time talking herself out of the attempted murder of Martin Hill. Not to mention the illegal and unethical research her company has been conducting. Legally speaking, poor Viggo Irving was murdered several times over."

"Martin Hill seems nice," Rosen adds. "He came across well at the press conference."

Asker suppresses a little smile. "Yes, he did well."

"And the rest of them?" Attila asks.

"The Schillers have made certain admissions. The doctor is particularly talkative. It may be possible to link Samuel, the security chief, to the murder of Tord Korpi. Perhaps not well enough to convict him in a court of law, but then again that won't be necessary . . ."

". . . since someone put a well-deserved bullet in his head," Attila summarizes with a grim smile.

"Something like that." Asker nods. "However, all of that should be enough to shut down any suspicions against Per. And, as you already know, Sweden has such a fantastic system that fleeing detention—or even prison for that matter—isn't a punishable offense. So Per walks free."

"And us, then?" Zafer asks. "What do we get out of all this?"

"A good question," Asker replies. "Above all the satisfaction that it took you less than twenty-four hours to crack a case that Serious Crime couldn't get their heads around in a week."

Her four colleagues fidget in disgruntlement.

"Without you this crime would never have been solved, and even though Hellman and Serious Crime yet again took most of the glory, there are already whispers around this building about who was really behind the job."

The four of them look slightly less disgruntled.

"Besides, I've brought you all a savory quiche," she concludes. "A *smörgåstårta*, as a personal thanks for the help."

"What kind?" Virgilsson asks.

"Salmon and prawn. It's in the kitchen. And it goes without saying that you can take home any leftovers."

The Lost Souls exchange glances, then nod cheerily before getting to their feet and disappearing in the direction of the food.

Asker turns out the lights in the briefing room and follows them.

Her body is aching, but she has been able to lower her dose of painkillers, at least.

Pain is just weakness leaving the body, Prepper Per used to say.

Bullshit, like so much else.

As she steps into the corridor, her phone rings. Martin's name appears on the display.

"How's the hero feeling?" she says.

"I'm OK. I've found a good psychiatrist."

She can't quite tell if he is joking, so she changes the subject.

"And the book—or books?"

He gives a dry laugh.

"Right now I'd rather not think about the Irving family, Astroholm, or Boulder Isle ever again for as long as I live."

"And the flash of light you saw as a teenager—did you ever find out what it was?"

Another tired laugh.

"No, I guess some questions will remain unanswered. But that's OK."

"The press conference went well, at least," she says. "You and Hellman are a real match made in heaven."

"Yeah, he's a pro."

The sentence hangs in the air.

"But?" she asks.

"But I don't think he likes me."

"No? But you're so nice."

"I know, right? People usually love me," he says jokingly. "But apparently not Hellman. I get the impression it might have something to do with you. Whenever I mention your name, he gets a strange look in his eyes and changes the subject."

Asker smirks, but doesn't respond.

"And Samuel?" Martin asks, with a graver tone of voice. "Will there be any repercussions because you . . . because he's . . . ?"

"An internal investigation is underway. Just like with the Mountain King. It's standard procedure, so I'm not concerned."

"And how do you feel?"

"Fine," she says quickly.

She understands that he means well. In the past few weeks she has killed two people, and she *should* feel something. But she isn't sure that she does. Perhaps it has something to do with the fact that both the Mountain King and Samuel were murderers—they were evil. That, or Per has stripped her of any empathy. Either way, she doesn't want to talk about it. In some way Martin seems to understand.

"Thanks for everything, Leo," he says. "You saved me yet again."

His soft voice makes something move in her chest. She likes that feeling, unusual as it feels. Perhaps there is hope for her yet?

"It's me who has you to thank," she says. "Without you there'd still be a manhunt on for Per. You helped me get him exonerated for murder."

"Uh, yeah." He clears his throat. "Honestly, I have kind of mixed feelings about that part of it. Has he contacted you?"

"No."

"Good. If he does, I want you to tell me, OK?"

"OK," she says.

She wants to say more. In just three weeks she has not only found Martin again; she has also come close to losing him twice.

But she can't find the words.

Virgilsson is walking toward her with a file in his hand, and he appears to want her attention.

"Look, Martin, I have to go. Work calls. But we'll speak soon?"

"Of course. I thought I might go away for a week or two. Lie on a beach and recover a little. But we'll be in touch when I'm back."

"Good idea," she says, a little too breezily. She comes dangerously close to asking if Sofie will be going with him but manages to contain herself.

"Have a good trip, and we'll be in touch," she says instead.

"Bye, Leo."

She hangs up reluctantly.

"So, Chief," says Virgilsson. "We located the car in the end. A silver Toyota Camry. It belongs to a Helén Trolle, forty-two years of age, registered address around fifty miles away in Tyringe. No criminal record—the only thing exciting about her is that she's worked for the armed forces and been active in a number of forums for armchair generals, or other people with an overenthusiastic interest in the military. Here's the photo on her driving license."

He hands Asker the photo.

The woman in the photo has short hair and an alert gaze.

Asker immediately recognizes her: she is the new receptionist at Lissander and Partners. Per must have planted her there to keep an eye on Isabel, to be ready should she choose to reveal his tax affairs. Or simply for the satisfaction of having a secret informant at his ex-wife's workplace.

So how do Per and Helén Trolle know each other? That question she would love an answer to.

She opens her office door.

On her desk lies a package that wasn't there around half an hour before.

Brown wrapping paper, a string with a bow.

Leonore Asker written on the front, in a handwriting that makes her freeze midstep.

Prepper Per's.

She should back out of the room. Call the bomb squad, find out how the fuck he managed to get a package into the heart of police HQ. Let her brain run amok over the contents.

Instead she walks over to the desk and sits down.

Per wants to scare her. Wants her to understand that he can reach her at any time. That he still has a hold over her.

She looks at Helén Trolle's photo again. The same sheet of paper lists the woman's home address, as well as the address of a cottage that she owns a few hours north, near Växjö. Asker starts her computer and loads an online map. Types in the address to the cottage and pulls a satellite photo. Her phone begins to buzz. The number is hidden, but she knows who it is.

"Did you get my package?" her father asks. His voice makes her scar immediately twitch to life.

"What package?" she answers dryly.

"So you haven't dared open it," he notes confidently. "Afraid it might contain something nasty?"

Her scar roils under her skin, tries to tempt her into rolling up her shirtsleeve.

"What do you want, Per?" She cuts him off.

"Fact is, I just wanted to give you a little token of my appreciation. A thanks for the help. Is that so strange?"

"Is there anything else?"

His voice hardens. "Only that I want you to know I'll be keeping an eye on you going forward, dear daughter. In case our paths cross again. After all, you've proven to be a good resource. And, as you know, resources need to be managed."

The scar is making her skin boil.

She moves her hand to the computer mouse and zooms in as far as she can on the satellite image. Helén Trolle's cottage is a red dwelling with white trim in the middle of a spruce forest, far from any neighbor.

In the garden stand two outbuildings, and on the very edge of the forest she spots something that could be the entrance to an underground storehouse.

Or perhaps a bunker. The perfect place to lie low.

"And I have my eye on you, Per," she says. "In more ways than you might think."

She ends the call before he has a chance to reply.

The next second she gets a knock on her door. It's Virgilsson.

He has changed into his sweater vest with the piano keys and treble clefs.

"Choir practice starts in ten minutes," he says cheerily. "See you there. It'll be exciting to see which voice range suits you best. See to it that your vocal cords are properly warmed up."

He disappears around the corner while humming.

Asker lets out a sigh.

She gets up, picks up the package from Per, and weighs it in her hands for a few seconds before dropping it into the trash.

Only now does she notice that her scar has stopped itching.

Resilience, she thinks.

And then she walks to the door.

ACKNOWLEDGMENTS

Many people are involved in making a book, and all deserve thanks: my ever-supportive Anette, my diplomatic agent Federico, my patient Swedish publisher Ebba, my indefatigable editor Caroline, my dynamic project manager Eva, my skillful Excel brother Göran, and the rest of the team at Bokförlaget Forum.

In addition I would like to thank Gunilla Leining for the superb Swedish reading that you may have just listened to, and of course everyone who has read or listened to this book. It's thanks to you that I have the best job in the world.

As with *The Mountain King*, I would like to extend particular thanks to Calle Bergendorf, author of the book *Skåne's Forgotten Spaces*, who also runs the urban explorer site *Tillträde Förbjudet* (No Trespassing). Both resources contain wonderful images of abandoned places, from which I have drawn many ideas for the settings in this book.